Mrs. Julian Marshall

The Life and Letters of Mary Wollstonecraft Shelley

Vol. II

Mrs. Julian Marshall

The Life and Letters of Mary Wollstonecraft Shelley
Vol. II

ISBN/EAN: 9783337016715

Printed in Europe, USA, Canada, Australia, Japan

Cover: Foto ©Raphael Reischuk / pixelio.de

More available books at **www.hansebooks.com**

E. J. TRELAWNY.

From a portrait after Severn.

in the possession of Sir Percy F. Shelley Bart.

THE LIFE & LETTERS

OF

Mary Wollstonecraft Shelley

BY

Mrs. JULIAN MARSHALL

WITH PORTRAITS AND FACSIMILE

IN TWO VOLUMES
VOL. II

LONDON
RICHARD BENTLEY & SON
Publishers in Ordinary to Her Majesty the Queen
1889

CONTENTS

CHAPTER XVII

JULY–SEPTEMBER 1822

CHAPTER XVIII

SEPTEMBER 1822–JULY 1823

CHAPTER XIX

JULY 1823–DECEMBER 1824

CHAPTER XX

JANUARY 1825–JULY 1827

CHAPTER XXI

JULY 1827–AUGUST 1830

CHAPTER XXII

AUGUST 1830–OCTOBER 1831

CHAPTER XXIII

OCTOBER 1831–OCTOBER 1839

CHAPTER XVII

JULY–SEPTEMBER 1822

THEY set off at once, death in their hearts, yet clinging outwardly to any semblance of a hope. They crossed to Lerici, they posted to Pisa; they went first to Casa Lanfranchi. Byron was there; he could tell them nothing. It was midnight, but to rest or wait was impossible; they posted on to Leghorn. They went about inquiring for Trelawny or Roberts. Not finding the right inn they were forced to wait till next morning before prosecuting their search. They found Roberts; he only knew the *Ariel* had sailed on Monday; there had been a storm, and no more had been heard of her. Still they did not utterly despair. Contrary winds might have driven the boat to Corsica or elsewhere, and information was perhaps withheld.

"So remorselessly," says Trelawny, "are the quarantine
laws enforced in Italy that, when at sea, if you render assistance to a vessel in distress, or rescue a drowning stranger, on
returning to port you are condemned to a long and rigorous
quarantine of fourteen or more days. The consequence is,
should one vessel see another in peril, or even run it down by
accident, she hastens on her course, and by general accord not
a word is said or reported on the subject."

Trelawny accompanied the forlorn women
back to Casa Magni, whence, for the next seven
or eight days, he patrolled the coast with the
coastguards, stimulating them to keep a good
look-out by the promise of a reward. On Thursday, the 18th, he left for Leghorn, and on the next
day a letter came to him from Captain Roberts
with the intelligence that the bodies of Shelley
and Williams had been washed ashore. The
letter was received and opened by Clare Clairmont. To communicate its contents to Mary or
Jane was more than she could do : in her distress
she wrote to Leigh Hunt for help or counsel.

Friday Evening, 19*th July* 1822.

MY DEAR SIR—Mr. Trelawny went for Livorno last night.
There came this afternoon a letter to him from Captain
Roberts—he had left orders with Mary that she might open it ;
I did not allow her to see it. He writes there is no hope, but
they are lost, and their bodies found three miles from Via
Reggio. This letter is dated 15th July, and says he had
heard this news 14th July. Outside the letter he has added,
"I am now on my way to Via Reggio, to ascertain the facts or
no facts contained in my letter." This then implies that he
doubts, and as I also doubt the report, because we had a

letter from the captain of the port at Via Reggio, 15th July, later than when Mr. Roberts writes, to say nothing had been found, for this reason I have not shown his letter either to Mary or Mrs. Williams.   How can I, even if it were true?

I pray you to answer this by return of my messenger.   I assure you I cannot break it to them, nor is my spirit, weakened as it is from constant suffering, capable of giving them consolation, or protecting them from the first burst of their despair. I entreat you to give me some counsel, or to arrange some method by which they may know it.   I know not what further to add, except that their case is desperate in every respect, and death would be the greatest kindness to us all.—Ever your sincere friend,   CLARE.

This letter can hardly have been despatched before Trelawny arrived.   He had seen the mangled, half-devoured corpses, and had identified them at once.   It remained for him now to pronounce sentence of doom, as it were, on the survivors.   This is his story, as he tells it—

I mounted my horse and rode to the Gulf of Spezzia, put up my horse, and walked until I caught sight of the lone house on the sea-shore in which Shelley and Williams had dwelt, and where their widows still lived.   Hitherto in my frequent visits—in the absence of direct evidence to the contrary—I had buoyed up their spirits by maintaining that it was not impossible but that the friends still lived; now I had to extinguish the last hope of these forlorn women.   I had ridden fast to prevent any ruder messenger from bursting in upon them.   As I stood on the threshold of their house, the bearer or rather confirmer of news which would rack every fibre of their quivering frames to the uttermost, I paused, and, looking at the sea, my memory reverted to our joyous parting only a few days before.   The two families then had all been in the verandah, overhanging a sea so clear and calm that every star was reflected on the water as if it had been a mirror ; the young mothers singing some merry tune with the accompaniment of a guitar. Shelley's shrill laugh—I heard it still— rang in my ears, with Williams' friendly hail, the general *buona notte* of all the joyous party, and the earnest entreaty to me to return as soon as possible, and not to forget the commissions they had severally given me. I was in a small boat beneath them, slowly rowing myself on board the *Bolivar*, at anchor in the bay, loath to part from what I verily believed to have been at that time the most united and happiest set of human beings in the whole world. And now by the blow of an idle puff of wind the scene was changed. Such is human happiness.

My reverie was broken by a shriek from the nurse Caterina as, crossing the hall, she saw me in the doorway. After asking her a few questions I went up the stairs, and unannounced entered the room. I neither spoke nor did they question me. Mrs. Shelley's large gray eyes were fixed on my face. I turned away. Unable to bear this horrid silence, with a convulsive effort she exclaimed—

"Is there no hope?"

I did not answer, but left the room, and sent the servant with the children to them. The next day I prevailed on them to return with me to Pisa. The misery of that night and the journey of the next day, and of many days and nights that followed, I can neither describe nor forget.

There is no journal or contemporary record of the next three or four weeks; only from a few scattered hints in letters can any idea be gleaned of this dark time, when the first realisation of incredible misfortune was being lived out in detail. Leigh Hunt was almost broken-hearted.

"Dearest Mary," he wrote from Casa Lanfranchi on the 20th July, "I trust you will have set out on your return from that dismal place before you receive this. You will also have

seen Trelawny. God bless you, and enable us all to be a support for one another. Let us do our best if it is only for that
purpose. It is easier for me to say that I will do it than for
you : but whatever happens, this I can safely say, that I belong
to those whom Shelley loves, and that all which it is possible
to me to do for them now and for ever is theirs. I will
grieve with them, endure with them, and, if it be necessary,
work for them, while I have life.—Your most affectionate
friend,   LEIGH HUNT.

Marianne sends you a thousand loves, and longs with
myself to try whether we can say or do one thing that can
enable you and Mrs. Williams to bear up a little better. But
we rely on your great strength of mind.

Mary bore up in a way that surprised those
who knew how ill she had been, how weak she
still was, and how much she had previously been
suffering in her spirits. It was a strange, tense,
unnatural endurance. Except to Miss Curran at
Rome, she wrote to no one for some time, not
even to her father. This, which would naturally
have been her first communication, may well have
appeared harder to make than any other. Godwin's relations with Shelley had of late been
strained, to say the least,—and then, Mary could
not but remember his letters to her after Williams'
death, and the privilege he had claimed "as a
father and a philosopher" of rebuking, nay, of
contemptuously deprecating her then excess of
grief. How was she to write now in such a tone
as to avert an answer of that sort? how write at
all? She did accomplish it at last, but before her

letter arrived Godwin had heard of the catastrophe through Miss Kent, sister of Mrs. Leigh Hunt. His fatherly feeling of anxiety for his daughter was aroused, and after waiting two days for direct news, he wrote to her as follows—

GODWIN TO MARY.

No. 195 STRAND, *6th August* 1822.

DEAR MARY—I heard only two days ago the most afflicting intelligence to you, and in some measure to all of us, that can be imagined—the death of Shelley on the 8th ultimo. I have had no direct information; the news only comes in a letter from Leigh Hunt to Miss Kent, and, therefore, were it not for the consideration of the writer, I should be authorised to disbelieve it. That you should be so overcome as not to be able to write is perhaps but too natural; but that Jane could not write one line I could never have believed; and the behaviour of the lady at Pisa towards us on the occasion is peculiarly cruel.

Leigh Hunt says you bear up under the shock better than could have been imagined; but appearances are not to be relied on. It would have been a great relief to me to have had a few lines from yourself. In a case like this, one lets one's imagination loose among the possibilities of things, and one is apt to rest upon what is most distressing and intolerable. I learned the news on Sunday. I was in hope to have had my doubts and fears removed by a letter from yourself on Monday. I again entertained the same hope to-day, and am again disappointed. I shall hang in hope and fear on every post, knowing that you cannot neglect me for ever.

All that I expressed to you about silence and not writing to you again is now put an end to in the most melancholy way. I looked on you as one of the daughters of prosperity, elevated in rank and fortune, and I thought it was criminal to intrude on you for ever the sorrows of an unfortunate old man and a

beggar. You are now fallen to my own level; you are surrounded with adversity and with difficulty; and I no longer
hold it sacrilege to trouble you with my adversities. We shall
now truly sympathise with each other; and whatever misfortune or ruin falls upon me, I shall not now scruple to lay it
fully before you.

This sorrowful event is, perhaps, calculated to draw us nearer
to each other. I am the father of a family, but without
children; I and my wife are falling fast into infirmity and
helplessness; and in addition to all our other calamities, we
seem destined to be left without connections and without aid.
Perhaps now we and you shall mutually derive consolation
from each other.

Poor Jane is, I am afraid, left still more helpless than you
are. Common misfortune, I hope, will incite between you
the most friendly feelings.

Shelley lived, I know, in constant anticipation of the uncertainty of his life, though not in this way, and was anxious
in that event to make the most effectual provision for you. I
am impatient to hear in what way that has been done; and
perhaps you will make me your lawyer in England if any steps
are necessary. I am desirous to call on Longdill, but I should
call with more effect if I had authority and instructions from
you. Mamma desires me to say how truly and deeply she
sympathises in your affliction, and I trust you know enough
of her to feel that this is the language of her heart.

I suppose you will hardly stay in Italy. In that case we
shall be near to, and support each other.—Ever and ever
affectionately yours,　　　　　　　WILLIAM GODWIN.

I have received your letter dated (it has no date) since
writing the above; it was detained for some hours by being
directed to the care of Monro, for which I cannot account.
William wrote to you on the 14th of June, and I on the 23d
of July. I will call on Peacock and Hogg as you desire.
Perhaps Williams' letter, and perhaps others, have been kept
from you. Let us now be open and unreserved in all things.

This letter was doubtless intended to be kind
and sympathetic, even in the persistent promi-
nence given to the business aspect of recent events.
Yet it was comical in its solemnity. For when
had Godwin held it sacrilege to trouble his
daughter with his adversities, or shown the
slightest scruple in laying before her any misfortune or ruin that may have fallen on him ? and
what new prospect was afforded her in the future
by his promise of doing so now?   No; this
privilege of a father and a philosopher had never
been neglected by him.

Well indeed might he feel anxious as to what
provision had been made for his daughter by her
husband.   In these matters he had long ceased to
have a conscience, yet it was impossible he should
be unaware that the utmost his son-in-law had
been able to effect, and that at the expense of
enormous sacrifices on the part of himself and his
heirs, and of all the credit he possessed with publishers and the one or two friends who were .not
also dependents, had been to pay his, Godwin's,
perpetual debts, and to keep him, as long as he
could be kept, afloat.

Small opportunity had Shelley's "dear"[1]
friends allowed him as yet to make provision for
his family in case of sudden misfortune!

Godwin, however, was really anxious about

---

[1] Leigh Hunt used often to say that he was the dearest friend Shelley
had ; I believe he was the most costly.—*Trelawny's Recollections.*

Mary, and his anxiety was perhaps increased by his letter; for in three days he wrote again, with out alluding to money.

GODWIN TO MARY.

9th August 1822.

MY DEAR MARY—I am inexpressibly anxious to hear from you, and your present situation renders the reciprocation of letters and answers—implying an interval of a month between each letter I receive from you to the next—intolerable.

My poor girl, what do you mean to do with yourself? You surely do not mean to stay in Italy? How glad I should be to be near you, and to endeavour by new expedients each day to endeavour to make up your loss. But you are the best judge. If Italy is a country to which in these few years you are naturalised, and if England is become dull and odious to you, then stay!

I should think, however, that now that you have lost your closest friend, your mind would naturally turn homeward, and to your earliest friend. Is it not so? Surely we might be a great support to each other under the trials to which we are reserved. What signify a few outward adversities if we find a friend at home?

One thing I would earnestly recommend in our future intercourse, is perfect frankness. I think you are of a frank nature, I am sure I am so. We have now no battle to fight,—no contention to maintain,—that is over now.

Above all, let me entreat you to keep up your courage. You have many duties to perform; you must now be the father as well as the mother; and I trust you have energy of character enough to enable you to perform your duties honourably and well.—Ever and ever most affectionately yours,

W. GODWIN.

The stunning nature of the blow she had endured, the uncertainty and complication of her affairs, and the absence of any one preponderating motive, made it impossible for Mary to settle at once on any scheme for the future. Her first idea was to return to England without delay, so as to avoid any possible risk to her boy from the Italian climate. Her one wish was to possess herself, before leaving, of the portrait of Shelley begun at Rome by Miss Curran, and laid aside in an unfinished state as a failure. In the absence of any other likeness it would be precious, and it might perhaps be improved. It was on this subject that she had written to Miss Curran in the quite early days of her misfortune ; no answer had come, and she wrote again, now to request " that favour now nearer my heart than any other thing —the picture of my Shelley."

"We leave Italy soon," she continued, "so I am particularly anxious to obtain this treasure, which I am sure you will give me as soon as possible. I have no other likeness of him, and in so utter desolation, how invaluable to me is your picture. Will you not send it? Will you not answer me without delay? Your former kindness bids me hope every-thing."

She was awakening to life again ; in other words, to pain : with keen anguish, like that of returning circulation to a limb which has been frozen and numb, her feelings, her forces, her intellect, began to respond to outward calls upon them, with a sensation, at times, of even morbid activity. It was a kind of relief, now, to write to Mrs. Gisborne that letter which contains the most graphic and connected of all accounts of the past tragedy.

MRS. SHELLEY TO MRS. GISBORNE.

15th August 1822.

I said in a letter to Peacock, my dear Mrs. Gisborne, that I would send you some account of the last miserable months of my disastrous life. From day to day I have put this off, but I will now endeavour to fulfil my design. The scene of my existence is closed, and though there be no pleasure in retracing the scenes that have preceded the event which has crushed my hopes, yet there seems to be a necessity in doing so, and I obey the impulse that urges me. I wrote to you either at the end of May or the beginning of June. I described to you the place we were living in—our desolate house, the beauty yet strangeness of the scenery, and the delight Shelley took in all this. He never was in better health or spirits than during this time. I was not well in body or mind. My nerves were wound up to the utmost irritation, and the sense of misfortune hung over my spirits. No words can tell you how I hated our house and the country about it. Shelley reproached me for this—his health was good, and the place was quite after his own heart. What could I answer? That the people were wild and hateful, that though the country was beautiful yet I liked a more *countrified* place, that there was great difficulty in living, that all our Tuscans would leave us, and that the very jargon of these *Genovesi* was disgusting. This was all I had to say, but no words could describe my feelings; the beauty of the woods made me weep and shudder; so vehement was my feeling of dislike that I used to rejoice when the winds and waves permitted me to go out in the boat, so that I was not obliged to take my usual walk among the shaded paths, alleys of vine festooned trees—all that before I doated on, and that now weighed on me. My only moments of peace were on board that unhappy boat when, lying down with my head on his knee, I shut my eyes and felt the wind and our swift motion alone. My ill health might account for much of this. Bathing in the sea somewhat relieved me, but on the 8th of June (I think it was) I was threatened with a miscarriage, and after a week of great ill health, on Sunday, the 16th, this took place at 8 in the morning. I was so ill that for seven hours I lay nearly lifeless—kept from fainting by brandy, vinegar, and eau-de-Cologne, etc. At length ice was brought to our solitude; it came before the doctor, so Clare and Jane were afraid of using it, but Shelley overruled them, and by an unsparing application of it I was restored. They all thought, and so did I at one time, that I was about to die, I hardly wished that I had,—my own Shelley could never have lived without me; the sense of eternal misfortune would have pressed too heavily upon him, and what would have become of my poor babe? My convalescence was slow, and during it a strange occurrence happened to retard it. But first I must describe our house to you. The floor on which we lived was thus—

5	7		3
6	2		4
	1		

1 is a terrace that went the whole length of our house and was precipitous to the sea; 2, the large dining-hall; 3, a private staircase; 4, my bedroom; 5, Mrs. Williams' bedroom; 6, Shelley's; and 7, the entrance from the great staircase. Now to return. As I said, Shelley was at first in

perfect health, but having over-fatigued himself one day, and
then the fright my illness gave him, caused a return of nervous
sensations and visions as bad as in his worst times. I think
it was the Saturday after my illness, while yet unable to walk,
I was confined to my bed—in the middle of the night I was
awoke by hearing him scream and come rushing into my
room; I was sure that he was asleep, and tried to waken him
by calling on him, but he continued to scream, which inspired
me with such a panic that I jumped out of bed and ran across
the hall to Mrs. Williams' room, where I fell through weakness,
though I was so frightened that I got up again immediately.
She let me in, and Williams went to Shelley, who had been
wakened by my getting out of bed—he said that he had not
been asleep, and that it was a vision that he saw that had
frightened him.   But as he declared that he had not screamed,
it was certainly a dream, and no waking vision.   What had
frightened him was this.   He dreamt that, lying as he did in
bed, Edward and Jane came in to him; they were in the most
horrible condition; their bodies lacerated, their bones starting
through their skin, their faces pale yet stained with blood;
they could hardly walk, but Edward was the weakest, and
Jane was supporting him.   Edward said, "Get up, Shelley,
the sea is flooding the house, and it is all coming down."
Shelley got up, he thought, and went to his window that looked
on the terrace and the sea, and thought he saw the sea rushing
in.   Suddenly his vision changed, and he saw the figure of
himself strangling me; that had made him rush into my room,
yet, fearful of frightening me, he dared not approach the bed,
when my jumping out awoke him, or, as he phrased it, caused
his vision to vanish.   All this was frightful enough, and
talking it over the next morning, he told me that he had had
many visions lately; he had seen the figure of himself, which
met him as he walked on the terrace and said to him, "How
long do you mean to be content?" no very terrific words, and
certainly not prophetic of what has occurred.   But Shelley had
often seen these figures when ill; but the strangest thing is
that Mrs. Williams saw him.   Now Jane, though a woman of

sensibility, has not much imagination, and is not in the slightest degree nervous, neither in dreams nor otherwise. She was standing one day, the day before I was taken ill, at a window that looked on the terrace, with Trelawny. It was day. She saw, as she thought, Shelley pass by the window, as he often was then, without a coat or jacket; he passed again. Now, as he passed both times the same way, and as from the side towards which he went each time there was no way to get back except past the window again (except over a wall 20 feet from the ground), she was struck at her seeing him pass twice thus, and looked out and seeing him no more, she cried, "Good God, can Shelley have leapt from the wall? Where can he be gone?" "Shelley," said Trelawny, "no Shelley has passed. What do you mean?" Trelawny says that she trembled exceedingly when she heard this, and it proved, indeed, that Shelley had never been on the terrace, and was far off at the time she saw him. Well, we thought no more of these things, and I slowly got better. Having heard from Hunt that he had sailed from Genoa, on Monday, 1st July, Shelley, Edward, and Captain Roberts (the gentleman who built our boat) departed in our boat for Leghorn to receive him. I was then just better, had begun to crawl from my bedroom to the terrace, but bad spirits succeeded to ill health, and this departure of Shelley's seemed to add insufferably to my misery. I could not endure that he should go. I called him back two or three times, and told him that if I did not see him soon I would go to Pisa with the child. I cried bitterly when he went away. They went, and Jane, Clare, and I remained alone with the children. I could not walk out, and though I gradually gathered strength, it was slowly, and my ill spirits increased. In my letters to him I entreated him to return; "the feeling that some misfortune would happen," I said, "haunted me." I feared for the child, for the idea of danger connected with him never struck me. When Jane and Clare took their evening walk, I used to patrol the terrace, oppressed with wretchedness, yet gazing on the most beautiful scene in the world. This Gulf of Spezzia is

subdivided into many small bays, of which ours was far the
most beautiful. The two horns of the bay (so to express
myself) were wood-covered promontories, crowned with castles;
at the foot of these, on the farthest, was Lerici, on the nearest
San Terenzo; Lerici being above a mile by land from us, and
San Terenzo about a hundred or two yards. Trees covered
the hills that enclosed this bay, and their beautiful groups
were picturesquely contrasted with the rocks, the castle, and
the town. The sea lay far extended in front, while to the
west we saw the promontory and islands, which formed one of
the extreme boundaries of the Gulf. To see the sun set
upon this scene, the stars shine, and the moon rise, was a
sight of wondrous beauty, but to me it added only to my
wretchedness. I repeated to myself all that another would
have said to console me, and told myself the tale of love,
peace, and competence which I enjoyed; but I answered
myself by tears—Did not my William die, and did I hold my
Percy by a firmer tenure? Yet I thought when he, when
my Shelley, returns, I shall be happy; he will comfort me, if
my boy be ill he will restore him, and encourage me. I had
a letter or two from Shelley, mentioning the difficulties he had
in establishing the Hunts, and that he was unable to fix the
time of his return. Thus a week passed. On Monday, 8th,
Jane had a letter from Edward, dated Saturday; he said that
he waited at Leghorn for Shelley, who was at Pisa; that
Shelley's return was certain; "but," he continued, "if he
should not come by Monday, I will come in a felucca, and you
may expect me Tuesday evening at farthest. This was Monday, the fatal Monday, but with us it was stormy all day, and
we did not at all suppose that they could put to sea. At 12 at
night we had a thunderstorm; Tuesday it rained all day, and
was calm—wept on their graves. On Wednesday the wind
was fair from Leghorn, and in the evening several feluccas
arrived thence; one brought word that they had sailed on
Monday, but we did not believe them. Thursday was another
day of fair wind, and when 12 at night came, and we did
not see the tall sails of the little boat double the promontory

before us, we began to fear, not the truth, but some illness—
some disagreeable news for their detention. Jane got so
uneasy that she determined to proceed the next day to
Leghorn in a boat, to see what was the matter. Friday came,
and with it a heavy sea and bad wind. Jane, however,
resolved to be rowed to Leghorn (since no boat could sail),
and busied herself in preparations. I wished her to wait for
letters, since Friday was letter day. She would not; but the
sea detained her; the swell rose so that no boat could venture
out. At 12 at noon our letters came; there was one from
Hunt to Shelley; it said, "Pray write to tell us how you got
home, for they say that you had bad weather after you sailed
Monday, and we are anxious." The paper fell from me. I
trembled all over. Jane read it. "Then it is all over," she
said. "No, my dear Jane," I cried, "it is not all over, but
this suspense is dreadful. Come with me, we will go to
Leghorn; we will post to be swift, and learn our fate." We
crossed to Lerici, despair in our hearts; they raised our
spirits there by telling us that no accident had been heard of,
and that it must have been known, etc., but still our fear was
great, and without resting we posted to Pisa. It must have
been fearful to see us—two poor, wild, aghast creatures
driving (like Matilda) towards the sea, to learn if we were to
be for ever doomed to misery. I knew that Hunt was at
Pisa, at Lord Byron's house, but I thought that Lord Byron
was at Leghorn. I settled that we should drive to Casa
Lanfranchi, that I should get out, and ask the fearful question
of Hunt, "Do you know anything of Shelley?" On entering
Pisa, the idea of seeing Hunt for the first time for four years,
under such circumstances, and asking him such a question,
was so terrific to me, that it was with difficulty that I
prevented myself from going into convulsions. My struggles
were dreadful. They knocked at the door, and some one
called out, *chi è?* It was the Guiccioli's maid. Lord
Byron was in Pisa. Hunt was in bed; so I was to see Lord
Byron instead of him. This was a great relief to me. I
staggered upstairs; the Guiccioli came to meet me, smiling,

while I could hardly say, "Where is he—Sapete alcuna cosa di Shelley?" They knew nothing; he had left Pisa on Sunday; on Monday he had sailed; there had been bad weather Monday afternoon. More they knew not. Both Lord Byron and the lady have told me since, that on that terrific evening I looked more like a ghost than a woman—light seemed to emanate from my features; my face was very white; I looked like marble. Alas! I had risen almost from a bed of sickness for this journey; I had travelled all day; it was now 12 at night, and we, refusing to rest, proceeded to Leghorn—not in despair—no, for then we must have died; but with sufficient hope to keep up the agitation of the spirits, which was all my life. It was past 2 in the morning when we arrived. They took us to the wrong inn; neither Trelawny nor Captain Roberts were there, nor did we exactly know where they were, so we were obliged to wait until daylight: we threw ourselves drest on our beds, and slept a little, but at 6 o'clock we went to one or two inns, to ask for one or the other of these gentlemen. We found Roberts at the "Globe." He came down to us with a face that seemed to tell us that the worst was true, and here we learned all that occurred during the week they had been absent from us, and under what circumstances they had departed on their return.

Shelley had passed most of the time at Pisa, arranging the affairs of the Hunts, and screwing Lord Byron's mind to the sticking place about the journal. He had found this a difficult task at first, but at length he had succeeded to his heart's content with both points. Mrs. Mason said that she saw him in better health and spirits than she had ever known him, when he took leave of her, Sunday, July 7, his face burnt by the sun, and his heart light, that he had succeeded in rendering the Hunts tolerably comfortable. Edward had remained at Leghorn. On Monday, July 8, during the morning, they were employed in buying many things, eatables, etc., for our solitude. There had been a thunderstorm early, but about noon the weather was fine, and the wind right fair for Lerici. They

were impatient to be gone.   Roberts said, "Stay until to-
morrow, to see if the weather is settled;" and Shelley might
have stayed, but Edward was in so great an anxiety to reach
home, saying they would get there in seven hours with that
wind, that they sailed; Shelley being in one of those extravagant fits of good spirits, in which you have sometimes seen him.
Roberts went out to the end of the mole, and watched them
out of sight; they sailed at 1, and went off at the rate of about
seven knots.   About 3, Roberts, who was still on the mole,
saw wind coming from the Gulf, or rather what the Italians
call a *temporale*.   Anxious to know how the boat would weather
the storm, he got leave to go up the tower, and, with the glass,
discovered them about ten miles out at sea, off Via Reggio;
they were taking in their topsails.   "The haze of the storm," he
said, "hid them from me, and I saw them no more.   When
the storm cleared, I looked again, fancying that I should see
them on their return to us, but there was no boat on the sea."

This, then, was all we knew, yet we did not despair;
they might have been driven over to Corsica, and not
knowing the coast, have gone God knows where.   Reports
favoured this belief; it was even said that they had been
seen in the Gulf.   We resolved to return with all possible
speed; we sent a courier to go from tower to tower, along
the coast, to know if anything had been seen or found,
and at 9 A.M. we quitted Leghorn, stopped but one moment
at Pisa, and proceeded towards Lerici.   When at two miles
from Via Reggio, we rode down to that town to know if
they knew anything.   Here our calamity first began to break
on us; a little boat and a water cask had been found five
miles off—they had manufactured a *piccolissima lancia* of thin
planks stitched by a shoemaker, just to let them run on shore
without wetting themselves, as our boat drew four feet of water.
The description of that found tallied with this, but then this
boat was very cumbersome, and in bad weather they might
have been easily led to throw it overboard,—the cask frightened
me most,—but the same reason might in some sort be given
for that.   I must tell you that Jane and I were not alone.

Trelawny accompanied us back to our home. We journeyed on and reached the Magra about half-past 10 P.M. I cannot describe to you what I felt in the first moment when, fording this river, I felt the water splash about our wheels. I was suffocated — I gasped for breath — I thought I should have gone into convulsions, and I struggled violently that Jane might not perceive it. Looking down the river I saw the two great lights burning at the *foce;* a voice from within me seemed to cry aloud, "That is his grave." After passing the river I gradually recovered. Arriving at Lerici we were obliged to cross our little bay in a boat. San Terenzo was illuminated for a festa. What a scene! The waving sea, the sirocco wind, the lights of the town towards which we rowed, and our own desolate hearts, that coloured all with a shroud. We landed. Nothing had been heard of them. This was Saturday, July 13, and thus we waited until Thursday July 18, thrown about by hope and fear. We sent messengers along the coast towards Genoa and to Via Reggio; nothing had been found more than the *Lancetta;* reports were brought us; we hoped; and yet to tell you all the agony we endured during those twelve days, would be to make you conceive a universe of pain—each moment intolerable, and giving place to one still worse. The people of the country, too, added to one's discomfort; they are like wild savages; on festas, the men and women and children in different bands—the sexes always separate—pass the whole night in dancing on the sands close to our door; running into the sea, then back again, and screaming all the time one perpetual air, the most detestable in the world; then the sirocco perpetually blew, and the sea for ever moaned their dirge. On Thursday, 18th, Trelawny left us to go to Leghorn, to see what was doing or what could be done. On Friday I was very ill; but as evening came on, I said to Jane, "If anything had been found on the coast, Trelawny would have returned to let us know. He has not returned, so I hope." About 7 o'clock P.M. he did return; all was over, all was quiet now; they had been found washed on shore. Well, all this was to be endured.

Well, what more have I to say? The next day we returned
to Pisa, and here we are still. Days pass away, one after
another, and we live thus; we are all together; we shall
quit Italy together. Jane must proceed to London. If
letters do not alter my views, I shall remain in Paris.
Thus we live, seeing the Hunts now and then. Poor
Hunt has suffered terribly, as you may guess. Lord Byron
is very kind to me, and comes with the Guiccioli to see me
often. To-day, this day, the sun shining in the sky, they
are gone to the desolate sea-coast to perform the last offices
to their earthly remains, Hunt, Lord Byron, and Trelawny.
The quarantine laws would not permit us to remove them
sooner, and now only on condition that we burn them to
ashes. That I do not dislike. His rest shall be at Rome
beside my child, where one day I also shall join them.
Adonais is not Keats', it is his own elegy; he bids you
there go to Rome. I have seen the spot where he now lies,
—the sticks that mark the spot where the sands cover him;
he shall not be there, it is too near Via Reggio. They are
now about this fearful office, and I live!

One more circumstance I will mention. As I said, he took
leave of Mrs. Mason in high spirits on Sunday. "Never," said
she, "did I see him look happier than the last glance I had of
his countenance." On Monday he was lost. On Monday
night she dreamt that she was somewhere, she knew not where,
and he came, looking very pale and fearfully melancholy. She
said to him, "You look ill; you are tired; sit down and eat."
"No," he replied, "I shall never eat more; I have not a
soldo left in the world." "Nonsense," said she, "this is no inn,
you need not pay." "Perhaps," he answered, "it is the worse for
that." Then she awoke; and, going to sleep again, she dreamt
that my Percy was dead; and she awoke crying bitterly—so
bitterly, and felt so miserable—that she said to herself, "Why,
if the little boy should die, I should not feel it in this manner."
She was so struck with these dreams, that she mentioned them
to her servant the next day, saying she hoped all was well with us.

Well, here is my story—the last story I shall have to tell.

All that might have been bright in my life is now despoiled.
I shall live to improve myself, to take care of my child, and
render myself worthy to join him.   Soon my weary pilgrimage
will begin.   I rest now, but soon I must leave Italy, and then
there is an end of all but despair.   Adieu! I hope you are
well and happy.   I have an idea· that while he was at Pisa,
he received a letter from you that I have never seen ; so
not knowing where to direct, I shall send this letter to
Peacock.   I shall send it open ; he may be glad to read it. —
Yours ever truly,   MARY W. S.

PISA, 15*th August* 1822.

I shall probably write soon again.   I have left out a material
circumstance.   A fishing-boat saw them go down.   It was
about 4 in the afternoon.   They saw the boy at mast-head,
when baffling winds struck the sails.   They had looked away
a moment, and, looking again, the boat was gone.   This is
their story, but there is little doubt that these men might have
saved them, at least Edward, who could swim.   They could
not, they said, get near her ; but three-quarters of an hour
after passed over the spot where they had seen her.   They
protested no wreck of her was visible ; but Roberts, going on
board their boat, found several spars belonging to her : perhaps
they let them perish to obtain these.   Trelawny thinks he can
get her up, since another fisherman thinks that he has found
the spot where she lies, having drifted near shore.   Trelawny
does this to know, perhaps, the cause of her wreck ; but I care
little about it.

All readers know Trelawny's graphic account
of the burning of the bodies of Shelley and
Williams.   Subsequent to this ceremony a painful episode took place between Mary and Leigh
Hunt.   Hunt had witnessed the obsequies (from
Lord Byron's carriage), and to him was given
by Trelawny the heart of Shelley, which in the

flames had remained unconsumed.   This precious
relic he refused to give up to her who was its
rightful owner, saying that, to induce him to part
with it, her claim must be maintained by "strong
and conclusive arguments."   It was difficult to
advance arguments strong enough if the nature of
the case was not in itself convincing.   He showed
no disposition to yield, and Mary was desperate.
Where logic, justice, and good feeling failed, a
woman's tact, however, succeeded.   Mrs. Williams
"wrote to Hunt, and represented to him how
grievous it was that Shelley's remains should become a source of dissension between his dearest
friends.   She obtained her purpose.   Hunt said
she had brought forward the only argument that
could have induced him to yield."

Under the influence of a like feeling Mary
seems to have borne Hunt no grudge for what
must, at least, have appeared to her as an act of
most gratuitous selfishness.

But Mary Shelley and Jane Williams had, both
of them, to face facts and think of the future.
Hardest of all, it became evident that, for the
present, they must part.   Their affection for each
other, warm in happier times, had developed by
force of circumstances into a mutual need; so
much nearer, in their sorrow, were they to each
other than either could be to any one else.   But
Jane had friends in England, and she required to

enlist the interest of Edward's relations in behalf of his orphan children.

Meanwhile, if Mary had for the moment any outward tie or responsibility, it was towards the Leigh Hunts, thus expatriated at the request and desire of others, with a very uncertain prospect of permanent result or benefit. Byron, having helped to start the *Liberal* with contributions of his own, and thus fulfilled a portion of his bond, might give them the slip at any moment. Shelley, although little disposed toward the "coalition," had promised assistance, and any such promise from him would have been sure to mean, in practice, more, and not less, than it said. Mary had his MSS.; she knew his intentions; she was, as far as any mortal could be, his fitting literary representative. She had little to call her elsewhere. The Hunts were friendly and affectionate and full of pity for her; they were also poor and dependent. All tended to one result; she and they must for the present join forces, so saving expense; and she was to give all the help she could to the *Liberal.* Lord Byron was going to Genoa. Mary and the Hunts agreed to take a house together there for several months or a year.

Once more she wrote from Pisa to her friend.

MARY SHELLEY TO MRS. GISBORNE.

PISA, 10*th September* 1822.

And so here I am! I continue to exist—to see one day succeed the other; to dread night, but more to dread morning, and hail another cheerless day. My Boy, too, is alas! no consolation. When I think how he loved him, the plans he had for his education, his sweet and childish voice strikes me to the heart. Why should he live in this world of pain and anguish? At times I feel an energy within me to combat with my destiny; but again I sink. I have but one hope for which I live, to render myself worthy to join him,—and such a feeling sustains one during moments of enthusiasm, but darkness and misery soon overwhelm the mind when all near objects bring agony alone with them. People used to call me lucky in my star; you see now how true such a prophecy is! I was fortunate in having fearlessly placed my destiny in the hands of one who, a superior being among men, a bright "planetary" spirit enshrined in an earthly temple, raised me to the height of happiness. So far am I now happy, that I would not change my situation as his widow with that of the most prosperous woman in the world; and surely the time will at length come when I shall be at peace, and my brain and heart no longer be alive with unutterable anguish. I can conceive of but one circumstance that could afford me the semblance of content, that is the being permitted to live where I am now, in the same house, in the same state, occupied alone with my child, in collecting his manuscripts, writing his life, and thus to go easily to my grave. But this must not be! Even if circumstances did not compel me to return to England, I would not stay another summer in Italy with my child. I will at least do my best to render him well and happy, and the idea that my circumstances may at all injure him is the fiercest pang my mind endures.

I wrote you a long letter containing a slight sketch of my sufferings. I sent it directed to Peacock, at the India House, because accident led me to fancy that you were no longer in London. I said in that, that on that day (15th August) they had gone to perform the last offices for him; however, I erred in this, for on that day those of Edward were alone fulfilled, and they returned on the 16th to celebrate Shelley's. I will say nothing of the ceremony, since Trelawny has written an

account of it, to be printed in the forthcoming journal. I will
only say that all, except his heart (which was inconsumable),
was burnt, and that two days ago I went to Leghorn and beheld
the small box that contained his earthly dross; those smiles,
that form—Great God ! no, he is not there, he is with me, about
me—life of my life, and soul of my soul ; if his divine spirit
did not penetrate mine I could not survive to weep thus.

I will mention the friends I have here, that you may form
an idea of our situation. Mrs. Williams, Clare, and I live all
together ; we have one purse, and, joined in misery, we are
for the present joined in life. She, poor girl, withers like a
lily ; she lives for her children, but it is a living death. Lord
Byron has been very kind ; the Guiccioli restrains him. She,
being an Italian, is capable of being jealous of a living corpse,
such as I. Of Hunt I will speak when I see you. But the
friend to whom we are eternally indebted is Trelawny. I
have, of course, mentioned him to you as one who wishes to
be considered eccentric, but who was noble and generous at
bottom. I always thought so, even when no fact proved it,
and Shelley agreed with me, as he always did, or rather I with
him. We heard people speak against him on account of his
vagaries ; we said to one another, "Still we like him—we
believe him to be good." Once, even, when a whim of his
led him to treat me with something like impertinence, I forgave
him, and I have now been well rewarded. In my outline of
events you will see how, unasked, he returned with Jane and
me from Leghorn to Lerici ; how he stayed with us poor
miserable creatures[1] five days there, endeavouring to keep
up our spirits ; how he left us on Thursday, and, finding our
misfortune confirmed, then without rest returned on Friday to
us, and again without rest returned to Pisa on Saturday.
These were no common services. Since that he has gone
through, by himself, all the annoyances of dancing attendance

---

[1] Mrs. Shelley's letter says twelve days, but this is an error, due, no
doubt, to her distress of mind. She gives the date of Trelawny's return to
Leghorn as the 25th of July ; it should have been the 18th.

on Consuls and Governors for permission to fulfil the last duties
to those gone, and attending the ceremony himself; all the
disagreeable part, and all the fatigue, fell on him. As Hunt
said, "He worked with the meanest and felt with the best."
He is generous to a distressing degree. But after all these
benefits to us, what I most thank him for is this. When on
that night of agony, that Friday night, he returned to announce
that hope was dead for us; when he had told me that his
earthly frame being found, his spirit was no longer to be my
guide, protector, and companion in this dark world, he did not
attempt to console me—that would have been too cruelly useless,—but he launched forth into, as it were, an overflowing
and eloquent praise of my divine Shelley, till I was almost
happy that thus I was unhappy, to be fed by the praise of
him, and to dwell on the eulogy that his loss thus drew from
his friend. Of my friends I have only Mrs. Mason to mention; her coldness has stung me; yet she felt his loss keenly,
and would be very glad to serve me; but it is not cold offers
of service one wants; one's wounded spirit demands a number
of nameless slight but dear attentions that are a balm, and
wanting these, one feels a bitterness which is a painful addition
to one's other sufferings.

God knows what will become of me! My life is now very
monotonous as to outward events, yet how diversified by
internal feeling! How often in the intensity of grief does one
instant seem to fill and embrace the universe! As to the
rest, the mechanical spending of my time: of course I have
a great deal to do preparing for my journey. I make no
visits, except one once in about ten days to Mrs. Mason. I
have not seen Hunt these nine days. Trelawny resides chiefly
at Leghorn, since he is captain of Lord Byron's vessel, the
Bolivar; he comes to see us about once a week, and Lord
Byron visits me about twice a week, accompanied by the
Guiccioli; but seeing people is an annoyance which I am
happy to be spared. Solitude is my only help and resource;
accustomed, even when he was with me, to spend much of my
time alone, I can at those moments forget myself, until some

idea, which I think I would communicate to him, occurs, and then the yawning and dark gulph again displays itself, unshaded by the rainbow which the imagination had formed. Despair, energy, love, desponding and excessive affliction are like clouds driven across my mind, one by one, until tears blot the scene, and weariness of spirit consigns me to temporary repose.

I shudder with horror when I look back on what I have suffered, and when I think of the wild and miserable thoughts that have possessed me I say to myself, " Is it true that I ever felt thus ? " and then I weep in pity of myself ; yet each day adds to the stock of sorrow, and death is the only end. I would study, and I hope I shall. I would write, and when I am settled I may. But were it not for the steady hope I entertain of joining him, what a mockery would be this world ! without that hope I could not study or write, for fame and usefulness (except as regards my child) are nullities to me. Yet I shall be happy if anything I ever produce may exalt and soften sorrow, as the writings of the divinities of our race have mine. But how can I aspire to that ?

The world will surely one day feel what it has lost when this bright child of song deserted her. Is not *Adonais* his own elegy ? and there does he truly depict the universal woe which should overspread all good minds since he has ceased to be their fellow-labourer in this worldly scene. How lovely does he paint death to be, and with what heartfelt sorrow does one repeat that line——

> But I am chained to Time, and cannot thence depart.

How long do you think I shall live ? as long as my mother ? Then eleven long years must intervene. I am now on the eve of completing my five and twentieth year ; how drearily young for one so lost as I. How young in years for one who lives ages each day in sorrow. Think you that these moments are counted in my life as in other people's ? Oh no ! The day before the sea closed over mine own Shelley he said to Marianne, " If I die to-morrow I have lived to be older than my father ; I am ninety years of age." Thus, also, may I say.

The eight years I passed with him was spun out beyond the usual length of a man's life, and what I have suffered since will write years on my brow and intrench them in my heart. Surely I am not long for this world; most sure should I be were it not for my boy, but God grant that I may live to make his early years happy.

Well, adieu! I have no events to write about, and can, therefore, only scrawl about my feelings; this letter, indeed, is only the sequel of my last. In that I closed the history of all events that can interest me; that letter I wish you to send my Father, the present one it is best not.

I suppose I shall see you in England some of these days, but I shall write to you again before I quit this place. Be as happy as you can, and hope for better things in the next world; by firm hope you may attain your wishes. Again, adieu!—Affectionately yours,   M. S.

Do not write to me again here, or at all, until I write to you.

Within a day or two after this letter was written, Mary, with Jane Williams and their children, quitted Pisa; Clare only remaining behind.

From a letter—a very indignant one—of Mrs. Mason's, it may be inferred that appeals for a little assistance had been made on Clare's behalf to Byron, who did not respond. He had been, unwittingly, contributing to her support during the last few weeks of Shelley's life; Shelley having undertaken to get some translations (from Goethe) made for Byron, and giving the work secretly to Clare. The truth now came out, and she found more difficulty than heretofore in getting paid. Dependent for the future on her own exertions, she was going, according to her former resolution, to Vienna, where Charles Clairmont was now established. Mary's departure left her dreadfully solitary, and within a few hours she despatched one of her characteristic epistles, touched with that motley of bitter cynicism and grotesque, racy, humour which developed in her later letters.

Half-past 2, Wednesday Morning.

MY DEAR MARY—You have only been gone a few hours. I have been inexpressibly low-spirited. · I hope dear Jane will be with you when this arrives. Nothing new has happened— what should? To me there seems nothing under the sun, except the old tale of misery, misery !

. . . .

Thursday.

I am to begin my journey to Vienna on Monday. Mrs. Mason will make me go, and the consequence is that it will be double as much, as I am to go alone. Imagine all the lonely inns, the weary long miles, if I do. Observe, whatever befalls in life, the heaviest part, the very dregs of the misfortune fall on me.

> Alone, alone, all, all alone,
> Upon a wide, wide sea,
> And Christ would take no mercy
> Upon my soul in agony.

But I believe my Minerva [1] is right, for I might wait to all eternity for a party. You may remember what Lord Byron said about paying for the translation ; now he has mumbled and grumbled and demurred, and does not know whether it is worth it, and will only give forty crowns, so that I shall not be overstocked when I arrive at Vienna, unless, indeed, God shall spread a table for me in the wilderness. I mean to chew rhubarb the whole way, as the only diversion I can think of at all suited to my present state of feeling, and if I

---

[1] Mrs. Mason.

should write you scolding letters, you will excuse them, knowing that, with the Psalmist, "Out of the bitterness of my mouth have I spoken."

Kiss the dear little Percy for me, and if Jane is with you, tell her how much I have thought of her, and that her image will always float across my mind, shining in my dark history like a ray of light across a cave. Kiss her children also with all a grandmother's love. Accept my best wishes for your happiness. Dio ti da, Maria, ventura.—Your affectionate　　　CLARE.

Mary answered this letter from Genoa.

FROM MARY TO CLARE.

GENOA, 15*th September* 1822.

MY DEAR CLARE—I do not wonder that you were and are melancholy, or that the excess of that feeling should oppress you. Great God! what have we gone through, what variety of care and misery, all close now in blackest night. And I, am I not melancholy? here in this busy hateful Genoa, where nothing speaks to me of him, except the sea, which is his murderer. Well, I shall have his books and manuscripts, and in those I shall live, and from the study of these I do expect some instants of content. In solitude my imagination and ever-moving thoughts may afford me some seconds of exaltation that may render me both happier here and more worthy of him hereafter.

Such as I felt walking up a mountain by myself at sunrise during my journey, when the rocks looked black about me, and a white mist concealed all but them. I thought then, that, thinking of him and exciting my mind, my days might pass in a kind of peace; but these thoughts are so fleeting; and then I expect unhappiness alone from all the worldly part of my life—from my intercourse with human beings. I know that will bring nothing but unhappiness to me, if, indeed, I except Trelawny, who appears so truly generous and kind.

But I will not talk of myself, you have enough to annoy and make you miserable, and in nothing can I assist you. But I do hope that you will find Germany better suited to you in every way than Italy, and that you will make friends, and, more than all, become really attached to some one there.

I wish, when I was in Pisa, that you had said that you thought you should be short of money, and I would have left you more; but you seemed to think 150 francesconi plenty. I would not go on with Goethe except with a fixed price per sheet, to be paid regularly, and that price not less than five guineas. Make this understood fully through Hunt before you go, and then I will take care that you get the money; but if you do not *fix* it, then I cannot manage so well. You are going to Vienna—how anxiously do I hope to find peace; I do not hope to find it here. Genoa has a bad atmosphere for me, I fear, and nothing but the horror of being a burthen to my family prevents my accompanying Jane. If I had any fixed income I would go at least to Paris, and I shall go the moment I have one. Adieu, my dear Clare; write to me often, as I shall to you.—Affectionately yours,

Mary W. S.

I cannot get your German dictionary now, since I must have packed it in my great case of books, but I will send it by the first opportunity.

Jane and her children were the next to depart, and for a short time Mary Shelley and her boy were alone. Besides taking a house for the Hunts and herself, she had the responsibility of finding one for Lord Byron. People never scrupled to make her of use; but any object, any duty to fulfil, was good for her in her solitary misery, and she devoted some of her vacant time to sending an account of her plans to Mrs. Gisborne.

MARY SHELLEY TO MRS. GISBORNE.

GENOA, 17*th September* 1822.

. . . I am here alone in Genoa ; quite, quite alone ! J. has
left me to proceed to England, and, except my sleeping child,
I am alone.   Since you do not communicate with my Father,
you will perhaps be surprised, after my last letter, that I do
not come to England.   I have written to him a long account
of the arguments of all my friends to dissuade me from that
miserable journey ; Jane will detail them to you ; and, therefore, I merely say now that, having no business there, I am
determined not to spend that money which will support me
nearly a year here, in a journey, the sole end of which appears
to me the necessity I should be under, when arrived in
London, of being a burthen to my Father.   When my crowns
are gone, if Sir Timothy refuses, I hope to be able to support
myself by my writings and mine own Shelley's MSS.   At
least during many long months I shall have peace as to money
affairs, and one evil the less is much to one whose existence
is suffering alone.   Lord Byron has a house here, and will
arrive soon.   I have taken a house for the Hunts and myself
outside one of the gates.   It is large and neat, with a *podere*
attached ; we shall pay about eighty crowns between us, so I
hope that I shall find tranquillity from care this winter, though
that may be the last of my life so free, yet I do not hope it,
though I say so; hope is a word that belongs not to my
situation.   He — my own beloved, the exalted and divine
Shelley—has left me alone in this miserable world ; this earth,
canopied by the eternal starry heaven—where he is—where,
oh, my God ! yes, where I shall one day be.

Clare is no longer with me.   Jane quitted me this morning
at 4.   After she left me I again went to rest, and thought
of Pugnano, its halls, its cypresses, the perfume of its mountains, and the gaiety of our life beneath their shadow.   Then
I dozed awhile, and in my dream saw dear Edward most
visibly ; he came, he said, to pass a few hours with us, but
could not stay long.   Then I woke, and the day began.   I

went out, took Hunt's house; but as I walked I felt that which is with me the sign of unutterable grief. I am not given to tears, and though my most miserable fate has often turned my eyes to fountains, yet oftener I suffer agonies unassuaged by tears. But during these last sufferings I have felt an oppression at my heart I never felt before. It is not a palpitation, but a *stringimento* which is quite convulsive, and, did I not struggle greatly, would cause violent hysterics. Looking on the sea, or hearing its roar, his dirge, it comes upon me; but these are corporeal sufferings I can get over, but that which is insurmountable is the constant feeling of despair that shadows me: I seem to walk on a narrow path with fathomless precipices all around me. Yet where can I fall? I have already fallen, and all that comes of bad or good is a mere mockery.

Those about me have no idea of what I suffer; none are sufficiently interested in me to observe that, though my lips smile, my eyes are blank, or to notice the desolate look that I cast up towards the sky. Pardon, dear friend, this selfishness in writing thus. There are moments when the heart must *sfogare* or be suffocated, and such a moment is this—when quite alone, my babe sleeping, and dear Jane having just left me, it is with difficulty I prevent myself from flying from mental misery by bodily exertion, when to run into that vast grave (the sea) until I sink to rest, would be a pleasure to me, and instead of this I write, and as I write I say, Oh God, have pity on me. At least I will have pity on you. Goodnight, I will finish this when people are about me, and I am in a more cheerful mood. Good-night. I will go look at the stars. They are eternal, so is he, so am I.

You have not written to me since my misfortune. I understand this; you first waited for a letter from me, and that letter told you not to write. But answer this as soon as you receive it; talk to me of yourselves, and also of my English affairs. I am afraid that they will not go on very well in my absence, but it would cost more to set them right than they are worth. I will, however, let you know what I think my friends ought to do, that when you talk to Peacock he may learn what I wish. A claim should be made on the part of Shelley's executors for a maintenance for my child and myself from Sir Timothy. Lord Byron is ready to do this or any other service for me that his office of executor demands from him ; but I do not wish it to be done separately by him, and I want to hear from England before I ask him to write to Whitton on the subject. Secondly, Ollier must be asked for all MSS., and some plan be reflected on for the best manner of republishing Shelley's works, as well as the writings he has left. Who will allow money to Ianthe and Charles ?

As for you, my dear friends, I do not see what you can do for me, except to send me the originals or copies of Shelley's most interesting letters to you. I hope soon to get into my house, where writing, copying Shelley's MSS., walking, and being of some use in the education of Marianne's children will be my occupations. Where is that letter in verse Shelley once wrote to you ? Let me have a copy of it. Is not Peacock very lukewarm and insensible in this affair ? Tell me what Hogg says and does, and my Father also, if you have an opportunity of knowing. Here is a long letter all about myself, but though I cannot write, I like to hear of others. Adieu, dear friends.—Your sincerely attached,

MARY W. SHELLEY.

The fragment that follows is from Mrs. Williams' first letter, written from Geneva, where she and Edward had lived in such felicity, and where they had made friends with Medwin, Roberts, and Trelawny : a happy, light-hearted time on which it was torture to look back.

JANE WILLIAMS TO MARY SHELLEY.

GENEVA, *September* 1822.

I only arrived this day, my dearest Mary, and find your letter, the only friend who welcomes me. I will not detail all the misery I have suffered, let it be added to the heap that must be piled up; and when the measure is brimful, it needs must overflow; and then, peace! What have been my feelings to-day? I have gazed on that lake, still and ever the same, rolling on in its course, as if this gap in creation had never been made. I have passed that place where our little boat used to land, but where is the hand stretched out to meet mine, where the glad voice, the sweet smile, the beloved form? Oh! Mary, is my heart human that I endure scenes like this, and live? My arrival at the inn here has been one of the most painful trials I have yet undergone. The landlady, who came to the door, did not recognise me immediately, and when she did, our mutual tears prevented both interrogation and answer for some minutes. I then bore my sorrowful burden up these stairs he had formerly passed in all the pride of youth, hope, and love. When will these heartrending scenes be finished? Never! for, when they cease, memory will furnish others.

. . . .

God bless you, dearest girl; take care of yourself. Remember me to the Hunts.—Ever yours,   JANE.

Not long after this Byron arrived at Genoa with his train, and the Hunts with their tribe.

"All that were now left of our Pisan circle," writes Trelawny, "established themselves at Albaro,—Byron, Leigh Hunt, and Mrs. Shelley. The fine spirit that had animated and held us together was gone. Left to our own devices, we degenerated apace."

CHAPTER XVIII

SEPTEMBER 1822–JULY 1823

AN eminent contemporary writer, speaking of Trelawny's writings, has remarked : "So long as he dwells on Shelley, he is, like the visitants to the *Witch of Atlas*, 'imparadised.'" This was true, in fact not as to the writings, but the natures, of all who had friendly or intimate relations with Shelley. His personality was like a clear, deep lake, wherein the sky and the surrounding objects were reflected. Now and again a breeze, or even a storm, might sweep across the "watery glass," playing strange, grotesque pranks with the distorted reflections. But in general those who surrounded it saw themselves, and saw each other, not as they were, but as they appeared,—transfigured, idealised, glorified, by the impalpable, fluid, medium. And like a tree that overhangs the water's edge, whose branches dip and play in the clear ripples, nodding and beckoning to their own living likeness there, so Mary had grown up by the side of this, her own image in him,—herself

indeed, but "imparadised" in the immortal un-
reality of the magic mirror.

Now the eternal frost had fallen : black ice and
dreary snow had extinguished that reflection for
ever, and the solitary tree was left to weather all
storms in a wintry world, where no magic mirror
was to be hers any more.

Mary Shelley's diary, now she was alone,
altered its character. In her husband's lifetime it
had been a record of the passing facts of every
day ; almost as concise in statement as that of her
father. Now and then, in travelling, she would
stereotype an impression of beautiful scenery by an
elaborate description ; sometimes, but very rarely,
she had indulged (as at Pisa) on reflections on
people or things in general.

The case was now exactly reversed. Alone
with her child, with no one else to live for ; having
no companion-mind with which to exchange ideas,
and having never known what it was to be without
one before, her diary became her familiar,—or
rather her shadow, for it took its sombre colouring
from her and could give nothing back. The
thoughts too monotonously sad, too harrowing in
their eloquent self-pity to be communicated to
other people, but which filled her heart, the more
that heart was thrown back on itself, found here an
outlet, inadequate enough, but still the only one
they had. In thus recording her emotions for her

own benefit, she had little idea that these melancholy self-communings would ever be gathered up
and published for the satisfaction of the " reading
world"; a world that loves nothing so well as
personal details, and would rather have the object
of its interest misrepresented than not represented
at all.   Outwardly uneventful as Mrs. Shelley's
subsequent life was, its few occurrences are, as a
rule, not even alluded to in her journal.   Such
things for the most part lost their intrinsic importance to her when Shelley disappeared ; it was
only in the world of abstractions that she felt or
could imagine his companionship.   Her journal,
in reality, records her first essay in living alone.
It was, to an almost incredible degree, a beginning.

Her existence, from its outset, had been offered
up at the shrine of one man.   To animate his
solitude, to foster his genius, to help—as far as
possible—his labours, to companion him in a
world that did not understand him,—this had
been her life-work, which lay now as a dream
behind her, while she awakened to find herself
alone with the solitude, the work, the cold un-
friendly world, and without Shelley.

Could any woman be as lonely ? All who share
an abnormal lot must needs be isolated when cut
adrift from the other life which has been their
raison d'être ; and Mary had begun so early, that
she had grown, as it were, to this state of double

solitude. She had not been unconscious of the
slight hold they had on actualities.

"Mary," observed Shelley one day at Pisa, when Trelawny
was present, "Trelawny has found out Byron already. How
stupid we were; how long it took us!"

"That," she observed, "is because he lives with the living
and we with the dead."

And as a fact, Shelley lived with the immortals;
finite things were outside his world; in his contemporaries it was what he would have considered
their immortal side that he cared for. There are
conjurors who can be tied by no knot from which
they cannot escape, and so the limitations of
practical convention, those "ideas and feelings
which are but for a day," had no power to hold
Shelley.

And Mary knew no world but his. Now,
young,—only twenty-five,—yet with the past experience of eight years of chequered married life,
and of a simultaneous intellectual development
almost perilously rapid, she stood, an utter novice,
on the threshold of ordinary existence.

Journal, October 2.—On the 8th of July I finished my
journal. This is a curious coincidence. The date still
remains—the fatal 8th—a monument to show that all ended
then. And I begin again? Oh, never! But several motives
induce me, when the day has gone down, and all is silent
around me, steeped in sleep, to pen, as occasion wills, my reflections and feelings. First, I have no friend. For eight
years I communicated, with unlimited freedom, with one whose
genius, far transcending mine, awakened and guided my

thoughts. I conversed with him, rectified my errors of judgment; obtained new lights from him; and my mind was satisfied. Now I am alone—oh, how alone! The stars may behold my tears, and the wind drink my sighs, but my thoughts are a sealed treasure which I can confide to none. But can I express all I feel? Can I give words to thoughts and feelings that, as a tempest, hurry me along? Is this the sand that the ever-flowing sea of thought would impress indelibly? Alas! I am alone. No eye answers mine; my voice can with none assume its natural modulation. What a change! O my beloved Shelley! how often during those happy days—happy, though chequered—I thought how superiorly gifted I had been in being united to one to whom I could unveil myself, and who could understand me! Well, then, now I am reduced to these white pages, which I am to blot with dark imagery. As I write, let me think what he would have said if, speaking thus to him, he could have answered me. Yes, my own heart, I would fain know what to think of my desolate state; what you think I ought to do, what to think. I guess you would answer thus: " Seek to know your own heart, and, learning what it best loves, try to enjoy that." Well, I cast my eyes around, and, looking forward to the bounded prospect in view, I ask myself what pleases me there. My child ;—so many feelings arise when I think of him, that I turn aside to think no more. Those I most loved are gone for ever; those who held the second rank are absent; and among those near me as yet, I trust to the disinterested kindness of one alone. Beneath all this, my imagination never flags. Literary labours, the improvement of my mind, and the enlargement of my ideas, are the only occupations that elevate me from my lethargy : all events seem to lead me to that one point, and the courses of destiny having dragged me to that single resting-place, have left me. Father, mother, friend, husband, children—all made, as it were, the team which conducted me here, and now all, except you, my poor boy (and you are necessary to the continuance of my life), all are gone, and I am left to fulfil my task. So be it.

October 5.—Well, they are come;[1] and it is all as I said.
I awoke as from sleep, and thought how I had vegetated these
last days; for feeling leaves little trace on the memory if it be,
like mine, unvaried. I have felt for, and with myself alone, and
I awake now to take a part in life. As far as others are concerned, my sensations have been most painful. I must work
hard amidst the vexations that I perceive are preparing for me,
to preserve my peace and tranquillity of mind. I must preserve some, if I am to live; for, since I bear at the bottom of
my heart a fathomless well of bitter waters, the workings of
which my philosophy is ever at work to repress, what will be
my fate if the petty vexations of life are added to this sense of
eternal and infinite misery?

Oh, my child! what is your fate to be? You alone reach
me; you are the only chain that links me to time; but for you,
I should be free. And yet I cannot be destined to live long.
Well, I shall commence my task, commemorate the virtues of
the only creature worth loving or living for, and then, may be,
I may join him. Moonshine may be united to her planet, and
wander no more, a sad reflection of all she loved on earth.

October 7.—I have received my desk to-day, and have
been reading my letters to mine own Shelley during his
absences at Marlow. What a scene to recur to! My William,
Clara, Allegra, are all talked of. They lived then, they
breathed this air, and their voices struck on my sense; their
feet trod the earth beside me, and their hands were warm with
blood and life when clasped in mine, where are they all? This
is too great an agony to be written about. I may express my
despair, but my thoughts can find no words.

.   .   .   .

I would endeavour to consider myself a faint continuation
of his being, and, as far as possible, the revelation to the earth
of what he was, yet, to become this, I must change much, and,
above all, I must acquire that knowledge and drink at those
fountains of wisdom and virtue from which he quenched his

---

[1] The Hunts.

thirst. Hitherto I have done nothing; yet I have not been discontented with myself. I speak of the period of my residence here. For, although unoccupied by those studies which I have marked out for myself, my mind has been so active that its activity, and not its indolence, has made me neglectful. But now the society of others causes this perpetual working of my ideas somewhat to pause; and I must take advantage of this to turn my mind towards its immediate duties, and to determine with firmness to commence the life I have planned. You will be with me in all my studies, dearest love! your voice will no longer applaud me, but in spirit you will visit and encourage me: I know you will. What were I, if I did not believe that you still exist? It is not with you as with another, I believe that we all live hereafter; but you, my only one, were a spirit caged, an elemental being, enshrined in a frail image, now shattered. Do they not all with one voice assert the same? Trelawny, Hunt, and many others. And so at last you quitted this painful prison, and you are free, my Shelley; while I, your poor chosen one, am left to live as I may.

What a strange life mine has been! Love, youth, fear, and fearlessness led me early from the regular routine of life, and I united myself to this being, who, not one of *us*, though like to us, was pursued by numberless miseries and annoyances, in all of which I shared. And then I was the mother of beautiful children, but these stayed not by me. Still he was there; and though, in truth, after my William's death this world seemed only a quicksand, sinking beneath my feet, yet beside me was this bank of refuge—so tempest-worn and frail, that methought its very weakness was strength, and, since Nature had written destruction on its brow, so the Power that rules human affairs had determined, in spite of Nature, that it should endure. But that is gone. His voice can no longer be heard; the earth no longer receives the shadow of his form; annihilation has come over the earthly appearance of the most gentle creature that ever yet breathed this air; and I am still here— still thinking, existing, all but hoping. Well, I close my book. To-morrow I must begin this new life of mine.

October 19.—How painful all change becomes to one, who, entirely and despotically engrossed by [his] own feelings leads, as it were, an *internal* life, quite different from the outward and apparent one! Whilst my life continues its monotonous course within sterile banks, an under-current disturbs the smooth face of the waters, distorts all objects reflected in it, and the mind is no longer a mirror in which outward events may reflect themselves, but becomes itself the painter and creator. If this perpetual activity has power to vary with endless change the everyday occurrences of a most monotonous life, it appears to be animated with the spirit of tempest and hurricane when any real occurrence diversifies the scene. Thus, to-night, a few bars of a known air seemed to be as a wind to rouse from its depths every deep-seated emotion of my mind. I would have given worlds to have sat, my eyes closed, and listened to them for years. The restraint I was under caused these feelings to vary with rapidity; but the words of the conversation, uninteresting as they might be, seemed all to convey two senses to me, and, touching a chord within me, to form a music of which the speaker was little aware. I do not think that any person's voice has the same power of awakening melancholy in me as Albé's. I have been accustomed, when hearing it, to listen and to speak little; another voice, not mine, ever replied—a voice whose strings are broken. When Albé ceases to speak, I expect to hear *that other* voice, and when I hear another instead, it jars strangely with every association. I have seen so little of Albé since our residence in Switzerland, and, having seen him there every day, his voice—a peculiar one—is engraved on my memory with other sounds and objects from which it can never disunite itself. I have heard Hunt in company and in conversation with many, when my own one was not there. Trelawny, perhaps, is associated in my mind with Edward more than with Shelley. Even our older friends, Peacock and Hogg, might talk together, or with others, and their voices suggest no change to me. But, since incapacity and timidity always prevented my mingling in the nightly conversations of Diodati, they were, as it were, entirely *tête-à-tête* between my Shelley and Albé ; and thus, as I have said, when Albé speaks and Shelley does not answer, it is as thunder without rain,—the form of the sun without light or heat,—as any familiar object might be shorn of its best attributes ; and I listen with an unspeakable melancholy that yet is not all pain.

The above explains that which would otherwise be an enigma—why Albé, by his mere presence and voice, has the power of exciting such deep and shifting emotions within me. For my feelings have no analogy either with my opinion of him, or the subject of his conversation.   With another I might talk, and not for the moment think of Shelley—at least not think of him with the same vividness as if I were alone ; but, when in company with Albé, I can never cease for a second to have Shelley in my heart and brain with a clearness that mocks reality—interfering even by its force with the functions of life —until, if tears do not relieve me, the hysterical feeling, analogous to that which the murmur of the sea gives me, presses painfully upon me.

Well, for the first time for about a month, I have been in company with Albé for two hours, and, coming home, I write this, so necessary is it for me to express in words the force of my feelings.   Shelley, beloved !   I look at the stars and at all nature, and it speaks to me of you in the clearest accents. Why cannot you answer me, my own one ?   Is the instrument so utterly destroyed ?   I would endure ages of pain to hear one tone of your voice strike on my ear ! ·

For nearly a year—not a happy one—Mary lived with the Hunts. A bruised and bleeding heart exposed to the cuffs and blows of everyday life, a nervous temperament—too recently strained to its utmost pitch of endurance—liable to constant, unavoidable irritation, a nature sensitive and reserved, accustomed to much seclusion and much

independence, thrown into the midst of a large,
noisy, and disorderly family, — these conditions
could hardly result in happiness. Leigh Hunt
was nervous, delicate, overworked, and variable in
mood : his wife an invalid, condemned by the
doctors on her arrival in Italy, now expecting her
confinement in the ensuing summer, an event
which she was told would be, for good or evil, the
crisis of her fate. Six children they had already
had, who were allowed—on principle—to do exactly as they chose, "until such time as they were
of an age to be reasoned with."

The opening for activity and usefulness would,
at another time, have been beneficial to Mary, and,
to some extent, was so now ; but it was too early,
the change from her former state was too violent ;
she was not fit yet for such severe bracing. She
met her trials bravely ; but it was another case
where buoyancy of spirits was indispensable to real
success, and buoyancy of spirits she had not, nor
was likely to acquire in her present surroundings.

There was another person to whom these surroundings were even more supremely distasteful
than to her, and this was Byron. Small sympathy
had he for domestic life or sentiment even in their
best aspects, and this virtuous, slipshod, cockney
Bohemianism had no attraction for him whatever.
The poor man must have suffered many things
while the Hunts were in possession of his *pian*

terreno at Pisa ; he was rid of them now, but the very sight of them was too much for him.

LORD BYRON TO MRS. SHELLEY.

6th October 1822.

The sofa—which I regret is *not* of your furniture—it was purchased by me at Pisa since you left it.

It is convenient for my room, though of little value (about 12 pauls), and I offered to send another (now sent) in its stead. I preferred retaining the purchased furniture, but always intended that you should have as good or better in its place. I have a particular dislike to anything of Shelley's being within the same walls with Mrs. Hunt's children. They are dirtier and more mischievous than Yahoos. What they can't destroy with their filth they will with their fingers. I presume you received ninety and odd crowns from the wreck of the *Don Juan*, and also the price of the boat purchased by Captain R., if not, you will have *both*. Hunt has these in hand.

With regard to any difficulties about money, I can only repeat that I will be your banker till this state of things is cleared up, and you can see what is to be done ; so there is little to hinder you on that score. I was confined for four days to my bed at Lerici. Poor Hunt, with his six little black-guards, are coming slowly up ; as usual he turned back once —was there ever such a *kraal* out of the Hottentot country before ?   N. B.

Among those of their former acquaintance who now surrounded Mary, the one who by his presence ministered most to the needs of her fainting moral nature was Trelawny. Leigh Hunt, when not disagreeing from her, was affectionate, nay, gushing, and he had truly loved Shelley, but he was a feeble, facetious, feckless creature,—a hypochondriac,—

unable to do much to help himself, still less another. Byron was by no means ill-disposed, especially just now, but he was egotistic and indolent, and too capricious,—as the event proved,— to be depended on.

Trelawny's fresh vigorous personality, his bright originality and rugged independence, and his unbounded admiration for Shelley, made him wonderfully reviving to Mary; he had the effect on her of a gust of fresh air in a close crowded room. He was unconventional and outspoken, and by no means always complimentary, but he had a just appreciation of Mary's real mental and moral superiority to the people around her, and a frank liking for herself. Their friendship was to extend over many years, during which Mary had ample opportunity of repaying the debt of obligation she always felt she owed him for his kindness to her and Mrs. Williams at the time of their great misery.

The letters which follow were among the earliest of a long and varied correspondence.

MARY SHELLEY TO TRELAWNY.

November 1822.

MY DEAR TRELAWNY—I called on you yesterday, but was too late for you. I was much pained to see you out of spirits the other night. I can in no way make you better, I fear, but I should be glad to see you. Will you dine with me Monday after your ride? If Hunt rides, as he threatens, with Lord

Byron, he will also dine late and make one of our party.
Remember, you will also do Hunt good by this, who pines in
this solitude.   You say that I know so little of the world that
I am afraid I may be mistaken in imagining that you have a
friendship for me, especially after what you said of Jane the
other night ; but besides the many other causes I have to
esteem you, I can never remember without the liveliest gratitude all you said that night of agony when you returned to
Lerici.   Your praises of my lost Shelley were the only balm
I could endure, and he always joined with me in liking you
from the first moment we saw you.   Adieu.—Your attached
friend,   M. W. S.

Have you got my books on shore from the *Bolivar?*   If
you have, pray let me have them, for many are odd volumes,
and I wish to see if they are too much destroyed to rank with
those I have.

TRELAWNY TO MRS. SHELLEY.

November 1822.

DEAR MARY—I will gladly dine on Monday with you.
As to melancholy, I refer you to the good Antonio in Shylock.
" Alas ! I know now why I am so sad.   It is time, I think."
You are not so learned in human dealings as Iago, but you
cannot so sadly err as to doubt the extent or truth of my
friendship.   As to gain esteem, I do not think it a word
applicable to such a lawless character.   Ruled by impulse, not
by reason, I am satisfied you should like me upon my own
terms—impulse.   As to gratitude for uttering my thoughts of
him I so loved and admired, it was a tribute that all who knew
him have paid to his memory.   " But weeping never could
restore the dead," and if it could, hope would prevent our
tears.   You may remember I always in preference selected as
my companion Edward, not Jane, and that I always dissented
from your general voice of her being perfection.   I am still of
the same opinion ; nothing more.   But I have and ever shall
feel deeply interested, and would do much to serve her, and

if thinking on those trifles which diminish her lustre in my eyes makes me flag, Edward's memory and my perfect friendship for him is sufficient excitement to spur me on to anything. It is impossible to dislike Jane; but to have an unqualified liking, such as I had for Edward, no—no—no! Talking of gratitude, I really am and ought to be so to you, for bearing on, untired, with my spleen, humours, and violence; it is a proof of real liking, particularly as you are not of the sect who profess or practise meekness, humility, and patience in common.   T.

Mary had not as yet been successful in getting possession of the half-finished portrait of Shelley. Her letters had followed Miss Curran to Paris, whence, in October, a reply at last arrived.

"I am sorry," Miss Curran wrote, "I am not at Rome to execute your melancholy commission. I mean to return in spring, but it may be then too late. I am sure Mr. Brunelli would be happy to oblige you or me, but you may have left Pisa before this, so I know not what to propose. Your picture and Clare's I left with him to give you when you should be at Rome, as I expected, before you returned to England. The one you now write for I thought was not to be inquired for; it was so ill done, and I was on the point of burning it with others before I left Italy. I luckily saved it just as the fire was scorching, and it is packed up with my other pictures at Rome; and I have not yet decided where they can be sent to, as there are serious difficulties in the way I had not adverted to. I am very sorry indeed, dear Mary, but you shall have it as soon as I possibly can." . . .

This was the early history of that portrait, which was recovered a year or two later, and which has passed, and passes still, for Shelley's likeness, and which, bad or good, is the only authentic one in existence.

Mary now began to feel it a matter of duty as well as of expediency to resume literary work, but she found it hard at first.

"I am quite well, but very nervous," she wrote to Mrs. Gisborne; "my excessive nervousness (how new a disorder for me—my illness in the summer is the foundation of it) is the cause I do not write."

She made a beginning with an article for the *Liberal*. Shelley's *Defence of Poetry* was, also, to be published in the forthcoming number, and the MS. of this had to be got from England. She had reason to believe, too, that Ollier, the publisher, had in his keeping other MSS. of Shelley's, and she was restlessly desirous to get possession of all these, feeling convinced that among them there was nothing perfect, nothing ready for publication exactly as it stood. In her over-anxiety she wrote to several people on this subject, thereby incurring the censure of her father, whom she had also consulted about her literary plans. His criticisms on his daughter's style were not unsound; she had not been trained in a school of terseness, and, like many young authors, she was apt to err on the side of length, and not to see that she did so.

GODWIN TO MARY.

No. 195 STRAND, 15*th November* 1822.

MY DEAR MARY—I have devoted the last two days to the seeing everybody an interview with whom would best enable me to write you a satisfactory letter. Yesterday I saw Hogg and Mrs. Williams, and to-day Peacock and Hanson junior. From Hogg I had, among other things, to learn Mrs. Williams' address, for, owing to your neglect, she had been a fortnight in London before I knew of her arrival. She appeared to be in better health and better spirits than I expected; she did not drop one tear; occasionally she smiled. She is a picturesque little woman, and, as far as I could judge from one interview, I like her.

Peacock has got Ollier's promise to deliver all Shelley's manuscripts, and as earnest, he has received *Peter Bell* and *A Curse on L.E.*, which he holds at your disposal. By the way, you should never give one commission but to one person; you commissioned me to recover these manuscripts from Ollier, you commissioned Peacock, and, I believe, Mrs. Gisborne. This puts us all in an awkward situation. I heard of Peacock's applying just in time to prevent me from looking like a fool. Peacock says he cannot make up a parcel for you till he has been a second time to Marlow on the question, which cannot be till about Christmas. He appears to me, not lukewarm, but assiduous. Mrs. Williams told me she should write to you by this day's post. She had been inquiring in vain for Miss Curran's address—you should have referred her to me for it, but you referred her to me for nothing. This, by the way, is another instance of your giving one commission to more than one person. You gave the commission about Miss Curran to Mrs. Williams and to me. I received your letter, inclosing one to Miss Curran, 21st October, which I immediately forwarded to her by a safe hand, through her brother. You have probably heard from her by this time; she is in Paris. . . . I have a plan upon the house of Longman respecting *Castruccio*, but that depends upon coincidences, and I must have patience.

You ask my opinion of your literary plans. If you expect any price, you must think of something new: *Manfred* is a subject that nobody interests himself about; the interest, therefore, must be made, and no bookseller understands anything about that contingency. A book about Italy as it is, written with any talent, would be sure to sell; but I am afraid you know very little about the present race of Italians.

As to my own affairs, nothing is determined. I expected something material to have happened this week, but as yet I have heard nothing. If the subscription fills, I shall perhaps be safe; if not, I shall be driven to sea on a plank.

Perhaps it may be of some use to you if I give you my opinion of *Castruccio*. I think there are parts of high genius, and that your two females are exceedingly interesting; but I am not satisfied. *Frankenstein* was a fine thing; it was compressed, muscular, and firm; nothing relaxed and weak; no proud flesh. *Castruccio* is a work of more genius; but it appears, in reading, that the first rule you prescribed to yourself was, I will let it be long. It contains the quantity of four volumes of *Waverley*. No hard blow was ever hit with a woolsack! Mamma desires me to remember her to you in the kindest manner, and to say that she feels a deep interest in everything that concerns you. She means to take the earliest opportunity to see Mrs. Williams, both as she feels an earnest sympathy in her calamity, and as she will be likely to learn a hundred particulars respecting the dispositions and prospects of yourself and Jane, which she might in vain desire to learn in any other quarter. You asked Mamma for some present, a remembrance of your mother. She has reserved for you a ring of hers, with Fanny Blood's hair set round with pearls.

You will, of course, rely on it that I will send you the letters you ask for by Peacock's parcel. Miss Curran's address is Hotel de Dusseldorf Rue Petits St. Augustin, à Paris. —Believe me, ever your most affectionate Father,

WILLIAM GODWIN.

My last letter was dated 11th October.

Journal, November 10.—I have made my first probation in writing, and it has done me much good, and I get more calm; the stream begins to take to its new channel, insomuch as to make me fear change. But people must know little of me who think that, abstractedly, I am content with my present mode of life. Activity of spirit is my sphere. But we cannot be active of mind without an object; and I have none. I am allowed to have some talent—that is sufficient, methinks, to cause my irreparable misery; for, if one has genius, what a delight it is to be associated with a superior! Mine own Shelley! the sun knows of none to be likened to you—brave, wise, noble-hearted, full of learning, tolerance, and love. Love! what a word for me to write! yet, my miserable heart, permit me yet to love,—to see him in beauty, to feel him in beauty, to be interpenetrated by the sense of his excellence; and thus to love singly, eternally, ardently, and not fruitlessly; for I am still his—still the chosen one of that blessed spirit—still vowed to him for ever and ever!

November 11.—It is better to grieve than not to grieve. Grief at least tells me that I was not always what I am now. I was once selected for happiness; let the memory of that abide by me. You pass by an old ruined house in a desolate lane, and heed it not. But if you hear that that house is haunted by a wild and beautiful spirit, it acquires an interest and beauty of its own.

I shall be glad to be more alone again; one ought to see no one, or many; and, confined to one society, I shall lose all energy except that which I possess from my own resources; and I must be alone for those to be put in activity.

A cold heart! Have I a cold heart? God knows! But none need envy the icy region this heart encircles; and at least the tears are hot which the emotions of this cold heart forces me to shed. A cold heart! yes, it would be cold enough if all were as I wished it—cold, or burning in the flame for whose sake I forgive this, and would forgive every other imputation—that flame in which your heart, beloved, lay unconsumed. My heart is very full to-night.

I shall write his life, and thus occupy myself in the only

manner from which I can derive consolation. That will be a task that may convey some balm. What though I weep? All is better than inaction and—not forgetfulness—that never is—but an inactivity of remembrance.

And you, my own boy! I am about to begin a task which, if you live, will be an invaluable treasure to you in after times. I must collect my materials, and then, in the commemoration of the divine virtues of your Father, I shall fulfil the only act of pleasure there remains for me, and be ready to follow you, if you leave me, my task being fulfilled. I have lived; rapture, exultation, content—all the varied changes of enjoyment—have been mine. It is all gone; but still, the airy paintings of what it has gone through float by, and distance shall not dim them. If I were alone, I had already begun what I had determined to do; but I must have patience, and for those events my memory is brass, my thoughts a never-tired engraver. France—Poverty—A few days of solitude, and some uneasiness—A tranquil residence in a beautiful spot—Switzerland—Bath—Marlow—Milan—the Baths of Lucca—Este—Venice—Rome—Naples—Rome and misery—Leghorn—Florence—Pisa—Solitude—The Williams'—The Baths—Pisa: these are the heads of chapters, and each containing a tale romantic beyond romance.

I no longer enjoy, but I love. Death cannot deprive me of that living spark which feeds on all given it, and which is now triumphant in sorrow. I love, and shall enjoy happiness again. I do not doubt that; but when?

These fragments of journal give the course of her inward reflections; her letters sometimes supply the clue to her outward life, *au jour le jour*.

MARY SHELLEY TO CLARE CLAIRMONT.

20th December 1822.

MY DEAR CLARE—I have delayed writing to you so long for two reasons. First, I have every day expected to hear

from you ; and secondly, I wished to hear something decisive
from England to communicate to you. But I have waited in
vain for both things. You do not write, and I begin to despair
of ever hearing from you again. A few words will tell you all
that has been done in England. When I wrote to you last, I
think that I told you that Lord Byron had written to Hanson,
bidding him call upon Whitton. Hanson wrote to Whitton
desiring an interview, which Whitton declined, requesting
Hanson to make his application by letter, which Hanson has
done, and I know no more. This does not look like an abso-
lute refusal, but Sir Timothy is so capricious that we cannot
trust to appearances.

And now the chapter about myself is finished, for what can
I say of my present life? The weather is bitterly cold with a
sharp wind, very unlike dear, *carissima* Pisa ; but soft airs and
balmy gales are not the attributes of Genoa, which place I
daily and duly join Marianne in detesting. There is but one
fireplace in the house, and although people have been for a
month putting up a stove in my room, it smokes too much to
permit of its being lighted. So I am obliged to pass the
greater part of my time in Hunt's sitting-room, which is, as
you may guess, the annihilation of study, and even of pleasure
to a great degree. For, after all, Hunt does not like me : it
is both our faults, and I do not blame him, but so it is. I
rise at 9, breakfast, work, read, and if I can at all endure
the cold, copy my Shelley's MSS. in my own room, and if
possible walk before dinner. After that I work, read Greek,
etc., till 10, when Hunt and Marianne go to bed. Then I
am alone. Then the stream of thought, which has struggled
against its *argine* all through the busy day, makes a *piena*, and
sorrow and memory and imagination, despair, and hope in
despair, are the winds and currents that impel it. I am alone,
and myself ; and then I begin to say, as I ever feel, " How I
hate life ! What a mockery it is to rise, to walk, to feed, and
then go to rest, and in all this a statue might do my part. One
thing alone may or can awake me, and that is study ; the rest
is all nothing." And so it is ! I am silent and serious.

Absorbed in my own thoughts, what am I then in this world if my spirit live not to learn and become better? That is the whole of my destiny; I look to nothing else. For I dare not look to my little darling other than as—not the sword of Damocles, that is a wrong simile, or to a wrecked seaman's plank—true, he stands, and only he, between me and the sea of eternity; but I long for that plunge! No, I fear for him pain, disappointment,—all, all fear.

You see how it is, it is near 11, and my good friends repose. This is the hour when I can think, unobtruded upon, and these thoughts, *malgré moi*, will stain this paper. But then, my dear Clare, I have nothing else except my nothingless self to talk about. You have doubtless heard from Jane, and I have heard from no one else. I see no one. The Guiccioli and Lord Byron once a month. Trelawny seldom, and he is on the eve of his departure for Leghorn. . . .

Marianne suffers during this dreadfully cold weather, but less than I should have supposed. The children are all well. So also is my Percy, poor little darling: they all scold him because he speaks loud *à l'Italien*. People love to, nay, they seem to exist on, finding fault with others, but I have no right to complain, and this unlucky stove is the sole source of all my *dispiacere ;* if I had that, I should not tease any one, or any one me, or my only one; but after all, these are trifles. I have sent for another *ingeniere*, and I hope, before many days are elapsed, to retire as before to my hole.

I have again delayed finishing this letter, waiting for letters from England, that I might not send you one so barren of all intelligence. But I have had none. And nothing new has happened except Trelawny's departure for Leghorn, so that our days are more monotonous than ever. The weather is drearily cold, and an eternal north-east whistles through every crevice. Percy, however, is far better in this cold than in summer; he is warmly clothed, and gets on.

Adieu. Pray write. My love to Charles; I am ashamed

that I do not write to him, but I have only an old story to repeat, and this letter tells that.—Affectionately yours,

MARY SHELLEY.

Journal, December 31.—So this year comes to an end. Shelley, beloved! the year has a new name from any thou knewest. When spring arrives leaves you never saw will shadow the ground, and flowers you never beheld will star it; the grass will be of another growth, and the birds sing a new song—the aged earth dates with a new number.

Sometimes I thought that fortune had relented towards us; that your health would have improved, and that fame and joy would have been yours, for, when well, you extracted from Nature alone an endless delight. The various threads of our existence seemed to be drawing to one point, and there to assume a cheerful hue.

Again, I think that your gentle spirit was too much wounded by the sharpness of this world; that your disease was incurable, and that in a happy time you became the partaker of cloudless days, ceaseless hours, and infinite love. Thy name is added to the list which makes the earth bold in her age and proud of what has been. Time, with unwearied but slow feet, guides her to the goal that thou hast reached, and I, her unhappy child, am advanced still nearer the hour when my earthly dress shall repose near thine, beneath the tomb of Cestius.

It must have been at about this time that Mary wrote the sad, retrospective poem entitled " The Choice."

THE CHOICE.

My Choice!—My Choice, alas! was had and gone
With the red gleam of last autumnal sun;
Lost in that deep wherein he bathed his head,
My choice, my life, my hope together fled :—

A wanderer here, no more I seek a home,
The sky a vault, and Italy a tomb.
Yet as some days a pilgrim I remain,
Linked to my orphan child by love's strong chain ;
And, since I have a faith that I must earn,
By suffering and by patience, a return
Of that companionship and love, which first
Upon my young life's cloud like sunlight burst,
And now has left me, dark, as when its beams,
Quenched in the might of dreadful ocean streams,
Leave that one cloud, a gloomy speck on high,
Beside one star in the else darkened sky ;—
Since I must live, how would I pass the day,
How meet with fewest tears the morning's ray,
How sleep with calmest dreams, how find delights,
As fireflies gleam through interlunar nights ?

First let me call on thee !   Lost as thou art,
Thy name aye fills my sense, thy love my heart.
Oh, gentle Spirit ! thou hast often sung,
How fallen on evil days thy heart was wrung ;
Now fierce remorse and unreplying death
Waken a chord within my heart, whose breath,
Thrilling and keen, in accents audible
A tale of unrequited love doth tell.
It was not anger,—while thy earthly dress
Encompassed still thy soul's rare loveliness,
All anger was atoned by many a kind
Caress or tear, that spoke the softened mind.—
It speaks of cold neglect, averted eyes,
That blindly crushed thy soul's fond sacrifice :—
My heart was all thine own,—but yet a shell
Closed in its core, which seemed impenetrable,
Till sharp-toothed misery tore the husk in twain,
Which gaping lies, nor may unite again.
Forgive me ! let thy love descend in dew
Of soft repentance and regret most true ;—

In a strange guise thou dost descend, or how
Could love soothe fell remorse,—as it does now?—
By this remorse and love, and by the years
Through which we shared our common hopes and fears,
By all our best companionship, I dare
Call on thy sacred name without a fear;—
And thus I pray to thee, my friend, my Heart!
That in thy new abode, thou'lt bear a part
In soothing thy poor Mary's lonely pain,
As link by link she weaves her heavy chain!—
And thou, strange star! ascendant at my birth,
Which rained, they said, kind influence on the earth,
So from great parents sprung, I dared to boast
Fortune my friend, till set, thy beams were lost!
And thou, Inscrutable, by whose decree
Has burst this hideous storm of misery!
Here let me cling, here to the solitudes,
These myrtle-shaded streams and chestnut woods;
Tear me not hence—here let me live and die,
In my adopted land—my country—Italy.

A happy Mother first I saw this sun,
Beneath this sky my race of joy was run.
First my sweet girl, whose face resembled *his*,
Slept on bleak Lido, near Venetian seas.
Yet still my eldest-born, my loveliest, dearest,
Clung to my side, most joyful then when nearest.
An English home had given this angel birth,
Near those royal towers, where the grass-clad earth
Is shadowed o'er by England's loftiest trees:
Then our companion o'er the swift-passed seas,
He dwelt beside the Alps, or gently slept,
Rocked by the waves, o'er which our vessel swept,
Beside his father, nurst upon my breast,
While Leman's waters shook with fierce unrest.
His fairest limbs had bathed in Serchio's stream;
His eyes had watched Italian lightnings gleam;

His childish voice had, with its loudest call,
The echoes waked of Este's castle wall ;
Had paced Pompeii's Roman market-place ;
Had gazed with infant wonder on the grace
Of stone-wrought deities, and pictured saints,
In Rome's high palaces—there were no taints
Of ruin on his cheek—all shadowless
Grim death approached—the boy met his caress,
And while his glowing limbs with life's warmth shone,
Around those limbs his icy arms were thrown.
His spoils were strewed beneath the soil of Rome,
Whose flowers now star the dark earth near his tomb :
Its airs and plants received the mortal part,
His spirit beats within his mother's heart.
Infant immortal ! chosen for the sky !
No grief upon thy brow's young purity
Entrenched sad lines, or blotted with its might
The sunshine of thy smile's celestial light ;—
The image shattered, the bright spirit fled,
Thou shin'st the evening star among the dead.
And thou, his playmate, whose deep lucid eyes,
Were a reflection of these bluest skies ;
Child of our hearts, divided in ill hour,
We could not watch the bud's expanding flower,
Now thou art gone, one guileless victim more,
To the black death that rules this sunny shore.

Companion of my griefs ! thy sinking frame
Had often drooped, and then erect again
With shows of health had mocked forebodings dark ;—
Watching the changes of that quivering spark,
I feared and hoped, and dared to trust at length,
Thy very weakness was my tower of strength.
Methought thou wert a spirit from the sky,
Which struggled with its chains, but could not die,
And that destruction had no power to win
From out those limbs the soul that burnt within.

Tell me, ye ancient walls, and weed-grown towers,
Ye Roman airs and brightly painted flowers,
Does not his spirit visit that recess
Which built of love enshrines his earthly dress ?—
No more ! no more !—what though that form be fled,
My trembling hand shall never write thee—dead—
Thou liv'st in Nature, Love, my Memory,
With deathless faith for aye adoring thee,
The wife of Time no more, I wed Eternity.

'Tis thus the Past—on which my spirit leans,
Makes dearest to my soul Italian scenes.
In Tuscan fields the winds in odours steeped
From flowers and cypresses, when skies have wept,
Shall, like the notes of music once most dear,
Which brings the unstrung voice upon my ear
Of one beloved, to memory display
Past scenes, past hopes, past joys, in long array.
Pugnano's trees, beneath whose shade he stood,
The pools reflecting Pisa's old pine wood,
The fireflies beams, the aziola's cry
All breathe his spirit which can never die.
Such memories have linked these hills and caves,
These woodland paths, and streams, and knelling waves
Past to each sad pulsation of my breast,
And made their melancholy arms the haven of my rest.

Here will I live, within a little dell,
Which but a month ago I saw full well :—
A dream then pictured forth the solitude
Deep in the shelter of a lovely wood ;
A voice then whispered a strange prophecy,
My dearest, widowed friend, that thou and I
Should there together pass the weary day,
As we before have done in Spezia's bay,
As though long hours we watched the sails that neared
O'er the far sea, their vessel ne'er appeared ;

One pang of agony, one dying gleam
Of hope led us along, beside the ocean stream,
But keen-eyed fear, the while all hope departs,
Stabbed with a million stings our heart of hearts.
The sad revolving year has not allayed
The poison of these bleeding wounds, or made
The anguish less of that corroding thought
Which has with grief each single moment fraught.
Edward, thy voice was hushed—thy noble heart
With aspiration heaves no more—a part
Of heaven-resumèd past thou art become,
Thy spirit waits with his in our far home.

Trelawny had departed for Leghorn and his favourite Maremma, *en route* for Rome, where, by his untiring zeal for the fit interment of Shelley's ashes, he once more earned Mary's undying gratitude. The ashes, which had been temporarily consigned to the care of Mr. Freeborn, British Consul at Rome, had, before Trelawny arrived, been buried in the Protestant cemetery : the grave was amidst a cluster of others. In a niche—formed by two buttresses—in the old Roman wall, immediately under an ancient pyramid, said to be the tomb of Caius Cestius, Trelawny (having purchased the recess) built two tombs. In one of these the box containing Shelley's ashes was deposited, and all was covered over with solid stone. The details of the transaction, which extended over several months, are supplied in his letters.

TRELAWNY TO MARY SHELLEY.

PIOMBINO, 7*th* and 11*th January* 1823.

Thus far into the bowels of the land
Have we marched on without impediment.

DEAR MARY SHELLEY—Pardon my tardiness in writing, which from day to day I have postponed, having no other cause to plead than idleness. On my arrival at Leghorn I called on Grant, and was much grieved to find our fears well founded, to wit, that nothing definitely had been done. Grant had not heard from his correspondent at Rome after his first statement of the difficulties; the same letter that was enclosed me and read by you he (Grant) had written, but not received a reply. I then requested Grant to write and say that I would be at Rome in a month or five weeks, and if I found the impediments insurmountable, I would resume possession of the ashes, if on the contrary, to personally fulfil your wishes, and in the meantime to deposit them secure from molestation, so that, without Grant writes to me, I shall say nothing more till I am at Rome, which will be early in February. In the meantime Roberts and myself are sailing along the coast, shooting, and visiting the numerous islands in our track. We have been here some days, living at the miserable hut of a cattle dealer on the marshes, near this wretched town, well situated for sporting. To-morrow we cross over to Elba, thence to Corsica, and so return along the Maremma, up the Tiber in the boat, to Rome. . . .

. . . I like this Maremma, it is lonely and desolate, thinly populated, particularly after Genoa, where human brutes are so abundant that the air is dense with their garlic breath, and it is impossible to fly the nuisance. Here there is solitude enough: there are less of the human form here in midday than at Genoa midnight; besides, this vagabond life has restored my health. Next year I will get a tent, and spend my winter in these marshes. . . .

. . . Dear Mary, of all those that I know of, or you have

told me of, as connected with you, there is not one now living
has so tender a friendship for you as I have.   I have the far
greater claims on you, and I shall consider it as a breach of
friendship should you employ any one else in services that I
can execute.

> My purse, my person, my extremest means
> Lye all unlocked to your occasion.

I hope you know my heart so well as to make all professions
needless.   To serve you will ever be the greatest pleasure I
can experience, and nothing could interrupt the almost un-
mingled pleasure I have received from our first meeting but
you concealing your difficulties or wishes from me.   With
kindest remembrances to my good friends the Hunts, to whom
I am sincerely attached, and love and salaam to Lord Byron,
I am your very sincere   EDWARD TRELAWNY.

"Indeed, I do believe, my dear Trelawny," wrote Mary in
reply, on the 30th of January 1823, "that you are the best
friend I have, and most truly would I rather apply to you in
any difficulty than to any one else, for I know your heart, and
rely on it.   At present I am very well off, having still a
considerable residue of the money I brought with me from
Pisa, and besides, I have received £33 from the *Liberal.*
Part of this I have been obliged to send to Clare.   You will
be sorry to hear that the last account she has sent of herself
is that she has been seriously ill.   The cold of Vienna
has doubtless contributed to this,—as it is even a dangerous
aggravation of her old complaint.   I wait anxiously to hear
from her.   I sent her fifteen napoleons, and shall send more if
necessary and if I can.   Lord B. continues kind : he has
made frequent offers of money.   I do not want it, as you see."

Journal, February 2nd.—On the 21st of January those
rites were fulfilled.   Shelley ! my own beloved ! you rest
beneath the blue sky of Rome ; in that, at least, I am
satisfied.

What matters it that they cannot find the grave of my

William? That spot is sanctified by the presence of his pure earthly vesture, and that is sufficient—at least, it must be. I am too truly miserable to dwell on what at another time might have made me unhappy. He is beneath the tomb of Cestius. I see the spot.

February 3.—A storm has come across me; a slight circumstance has disturbed the deceitful calm of which I boasted. I thought I heard my Shelley call me—not my Shelley in heaven, but my Shelley, my companion in my daily tasks. I was reading; I heard a voice say, "Mary!" "It is Shelley," I thought; the revulsion was of agony. Never more. . . .

Mrs. Shelley's affairs now assumed an aspect which made her foresee the ultimate advisability, if not necessity, of returning to England. Sir Timothy Shelley had declined giving any answer to the application made to him for an allowance for his son's widow and child; and Lord Byron, as Shelley's executor, had written to him directly for a decisive answer, which he obtained.

SIR TIMOTHY SHELLEY TO LORD BYRON.

FIELD PLACE, *6th February* 1823.

MY LORD—I have received your Lordship's letter, and my solicitor, Mr. Whitton, has this day shown me copies of certificates of the marriage of Mrs. Shelley and of the baptism of her little boy, and also, a short abstract of my son's will, as the same have been handed to him by Mr. Hanson.

The mind of my son was withdrawn from me and my immediate family by unworthy and interested individuals, when he was about nineteen, and after a while he was led into a new society and forsook his first associates.

In this new society he forgot every feeling of duty and respect to me and to Lady Shelley.

Mrs. Shelley was, I have been told, the intimate friend of my son in the lifetime of his first wife, and to the time of her death, and in no small degree, as I suspect, estranged my son's mind from his family, and all his first duties in life; with that impression on my mind, I cannot agree with your Lordship that, though my son was unfortunate, Mrs. Shelley is innocent; on the contrary, I think that her conduct was the very reverse of what it ought to have been, and I must, therefore, decline all interference in matters in which Mrs. Shelley is interested. As to the child, I am inclined to afford the means of a suitable protection and care of him in this country, if he shall be placed with a person I shall approve; but your Lordship will allow me to say that the means I can furnish will be limited, as I have important duties to perform towards others, which I cannot forget.

I have thus plainly told your Lordship my determination, in the hope that I may be spared from all further correspondence on a subject so distressing to me and my family.

With respect to the will and certificates, I have no observation to make. I have left them with Mr. Whitton, and if anything is necessary to be done with them on my part, he will, I am sure, do it.—I have the honour, my Lord, to be your Lordship's most obedient humble servant,   T. SHELLEY.

Granting the point of view from which it was written, this letter, though hard, was not unnatural. The author of *Adonais* was, to Sir Timothy, a common reprobate, a prodigal who, having gone into a far country, would have devoured his father's living—could he have got it—with harlots; but who had come there to well-deserved grief, and for whose widow even husks were too good. To any possible colouring or modification of this view he had resolutely shut his eyes and ears. No modification of his conclusions was, therefore, to be looked for.

But neither could it be expected that his point of view should be intelligible to Mary. Nor did it commend itself to Godwin. It would have been as little for his daughter's interest as for her happiness to surrender the custody of her child.

MARY SHELLEY TO LORD BYRON.

MY DEAR LORD BYRON—. . . It appears to me that the mode in which Sir Timothy Shelley expresses himself about my child plainly shows by what mean principles he would be actuated. He does not offer him an asylum in his own house, but a beggarly provision under the care of a stranger.

Setting aside that, I would not part with him. Something is due to me. I should not live ten days separated from him. If it were necessary for me to die for his benefit the sacrifice would be easy; but his delicate frame requires all a mother's solicitude; nor shall he be deprived of my anxious love and assiduous attention to his happiness while I have it in my power to bestow it on him; not to mention that his future respect for his excellent Father and his moral wellbeing greatly depend upon his being away from the immediate influence of his relations.

This, perhaps, you will think nonsense, and it is inconceivably painful to me to discuss a point which appears to me as clear as noonday; besides I lose all—all honourable station and name—when I admit that I am not a fitting person to take charge of my infant. The insult is keen; the pretence of heaping it upon me too gross; the advantage to them, if the will came to be contested, would be too immense.

As a matter of feeling, I would never consent to it. I am said to have a cold heart; there are feelings, however, so strongly implanted in my nature that, to root them out, life will go with it.—Most truly yours,   MARY SHELLEY.

GODWIN TO MRS. SHELLEY,

STRAND, 14*th February* 1823.

MY DEAR MARY—I have this moment received a copy of
Sir Timothy Shelley's letter to Lord Byron, dated 6th February, and which, therefore, you will have seen long before this
reaches you. You will easily imagine how anxious I am to
hear from you, and to know the state of your feelings under
this, which seems like the last, blow of fate.

I need not, of course, attempt to assist your judgment
upon the proposition of taking the child from you. I am
sure your feelings would never allow you to entertain such a
proposition.

. . . .

I requested you to let Lord Byron's letter to Sir Timothy
Shelley pass through my hands, and you did so ; but to my
great mortification, it reached me sealed with his Lordship's
arms, so that I remained wholly ignorant of its contents.
If you could send me a copy, I should be then much better
acquainted with your present situation.

Your novel is now fully printed and ready for publication,
I have taken great liberties with it, and I fear your *amour
propre* will be proportionately shocked. I need not tell you
that all the merit of the book is exclusively your own.
Beatrice is the jewel of the book ; not but that I greatly
admire Euthanasia, and I think the characters of Pepi, Binda,
and the witch decisive efforts of original genius. I am promised a character of the work in the *Morning Chronicle* and
the *Herald*, and was in hopes to have sent you the one or the
other by this time. I also sent a copy of the book to the
Examiner for the same purpose.

Tuesday, 18*th February.*

Do not, I entreat you, be cast down about your worldly
circumstances. You certainly contain within yourself the
means of your subsistence. Your talents are truly extraordinary.
Frankenstein is universally known, and though it can never be

a book for vulgar reading, is everywhere respected. It is the most wonderful work to have been written at twenty years of age that I ever heard of. You are now five and twenty, and, most fortunately, you have pursued a course of reading, and cultivated your mind, in a manner the most admirably adapted to make you a great and successful author. If you cannot be independent, who should be?

Your talents, as far as I can at present discern, are turned for the writing of fictitious adventures.

If it shall ever happen to you to be placed in sudden and urgent want of a small sum, I entreat you to let me know immediately; we must see what I can do. We must help one another.—Your affectionate Father, WILLIAM GODWIN.

Mary felt the truth of what her father said, but, wounded and embittered as she was, she had little heart for framing plans.

Journal, February 24.—Evils throng around me, my beloved, and I have indeed lost all in losing thee. Were it not for my child, this would be rather a soothing reflection, and, if starvation were my fate, I should fulfil that fate without a sigh. But our child demands all my care now that you have left us. I must be all to him : the Father, death has deprived him of; the relations, the bad world permits him not to have. What is yet in store for me? Am I to close the eyes of our boy, and then join you?

The last weeks have been spent in quiet. Study could not give repose to, but somewhat regulated, my thoughts. I said: "I lead an innocent life, and it may become a useful one. I have talent, I will improve that talent; and if, while meditating on the wisdom of ages, and storing my mind with all that has been recorded of it, any new light bursts upon me, or any discovery occurs that may be useful to my fellows, then the balm of utility may be added to innocence.

What is it that moves up and down in my soul, and makes

me feel as if my intellect could master all but my fate? I
fear it is only youthful ardour—the yet untamed spirit which,
wholly withdrawn from the hopes, and almost from the affections of life, indulges itself in the only walk free to it, and,
mental exertion being all my thought except regret, would
make me place my hopes in that. I am indeed become a
recluse in thought and act; and my mind, turned heavenward,
would, but for my only tie, lose all commune with what is
around me. If I be proud, yet it is with humility that I am
so. I am not vain. My heart shakes with its suppressed
emotions, and I flag beneath the thoughts that oppress me.

Each day, as I have taken my solitary walk, I have felt
myself exalted with the idea of occupation, improvement,
knowledge, and peace. Looking back to my life as a delicious
dream, I steeled myself as well as I could against such severe
regrets as should overthrow my calmness. Once or twice,
pausing in my walk, I have exclaimed in despair, "Is it even
so?" yet, for the most part resigned, I was occupied by reflection—on those ideas you, my beloved, planted in my
mind—and meditated on our nature, our source, and our
destination. To-day, melancholy would invade me, and I
thought the peace I enjoyed was transient. Then that letter
came to place its seal on my prognostications. Yet it was
not the refusal, or the insult heaped upon me, that stung me
to tears. It was their bitter words about our Boy. Why, I
live only to keep him from their hands. How dared they
dream that I held him not far more precious than all, save
the hope of again seeing you, my lost one. But for his smiles,
where should I now be?

Stars that shine unclouded, ye cannot tell me what will be
—yet I can tell you a part. I may have misgivings, weaknesses, and momentary lapses into unworthy despondency,
but—save in devotion towards my Boy—fortune has emptied
her quiver, and to all her future shafts I oppose courage, hope-
lessness of aught on this side, with a firm trust in what is beyond the grave.

Visit me in my dreams to-night, my beloved Shelley! kind,

loving, excellent as thou wert! and the event of this day shall be forgotten.

March 19.—As I have until now recurred to this book to discharge into it the overflowings of a mind too full of the bitterest waters of life, so will I to-night, now that I am calm, put down some of my milder reveries; that, when I turn it over, I may not only find a record of the most painful thoughts that ever filled a human heart even to distraction.

I am beginning seriously to educate myself; and in another place I have marked the scope of this somewhat tardy education, intellectually considered. In a moral point of view, this education is of some years' standing, and it only now takes the form of seeking its food in books. I have long accustomed myself to the study of my own heart, and have sought and found in its recesses that which cannot embody itself in words—hardly in feelings. I have found strength in the conception of its faculties; much native force in the understanding of them; and what appears to me not a contemptible penetration in the subtle divisions of good and evil. But I have found less strength of self-support, of resistance to what is vulgarly called temptation; yet I think also that I have found true humility (for surely no one can be less presumptuous than I), an ardent love for the immutable laws of right, much native goodness of emotion, and purity of thought.

Enough, if every day I gain a profounder knowledge of my defects, and a more certain method of turning them to a good direction.

Study has become to me more necessary than the air I breathe. In the questioning and searching turn it gives to my thoughts, I find some relief to wild reverie; in the self-satisfaction I feel in commanding myself, I find present solace; in the hope that thence arises, that I may become more worthy of my Shelley, I find a consolation that even makes me less wretched than in my most wretched moments.

March 30.—I have now finished part of the *Odyssey*. I mark this. I cannot write. Day after day I suffer the most

tremendous agitation.   I cannot write, or read, or think.
Whether it be the anxiety for letters that shakes a frame not
so strong as hitherto—whether it be my annoyances here—
whether it be my regrets, my sorrow, and despair, or all these
—I know not; but I am a wreck.

A letter from Trelawny gladdened her heart.
It said—

I must confess I am to blame in not having sooner written,
particularly as I have received two letters from you here.
Nothing particular has happened to me since our parting but
a desperate assault of Maremma fever, which had nearly
reunited me to my friends, or, as Iago says, removed me.
On my arrival here, my first object was to see the grave of
the noble Shelley, and I was most indignant at finding him
confusedly mingled in a heap with five or six common vaga-
bonds.   I instantly set about removing this gross neglect,
and selecting the only interesting spot.   I enclosed it apart
from all possibility of sacrilegious intrusion, and removed his
ashes to it, placed a stone over it, am now planting it, and
have ordered a granite to be prepared for myself, which I
shall place in this beautiful recess (of which the enclosed is a
drawing I took), for when I am dead, I have none to do me
this service, so shall at least give one instance in my life of
proficiency.

In reply Mary wrote informing him of her
change of plan, and begging for all minute details
about the tomb, which she was not likely, now, to
see.   Trelawny was expecting soon to rejoin
Byron at Genoa, but he wrote at once.

TRELAWNY TO MRS. SHELLEY.

ROME, *27th April* 1823.

DEAR MARY—I should have sooner replied to your last,
but that I concluded you must have seen Roberts, who is or

ought to be at Genoa. He will tell you that the ashes
are buried in the new enclosed Protestant burying-ground,
which is protected by a wall and gates from every possible
molestation, and that the ashes are so placed apart,
and yet in the centre and most conspicuous spot of the
burying-ground. I have just planted six young cypresses and
four laurels, in front of the recess you see by the drawing is
formed by two projecting parts of the old ruin. My own
stone, a plain slab till I can decide on some fitting inscription, is placed on the left hand. I have likewise dug my
grave, so that, when I die, there is only to lift up my coverlet
and roll me into it. You may lie on the other side, if you
like. It is a lovely spot. The only inscription on Shelley's
stone, besides the *Cor cordium* of Hunt, are the lines I have
added from Shakespeare—

> Nothing of him that doth fade,
> But doth suffer a sea-change
> Into something rich and strange.

This quotation, by its double meaning, alludes both to the
manner of his death and his genius, and I think the element
on which his soul took wing, and the subtle essence of his
being mingled, may still retain him in some other shape.
The waters may keep the dead, as the earth may, and fire
and air. His passionate fondness might have been from
some secret sympathy in their natures. Thence the fascination which so forcibly attracted him, without fear or caution,
to trust an element almost all others hold in superstitious
dread, and venture as cautiously on as they would in a lair of
lions. I have just compiled an epitaph for Keats and sent it
to Severn, who likes it much better than the one he had
designed. He had already designed a lyre with only two of
the strings strung, as indicating the unaccomplished maturity
and ripening of his genius. He had intended a long inscription about his death having been caused by the *neglect* of his
countrymen, and that, as a mark of his displeasure, he said—
'thus and then. What I wished to substitute is simply
thus—

Here lies the spoils
of a
Young English Poet,
" Whose master-hand is cold, whose silver lyre unstrung,"
And by whose desire is inscribed,
That his name was writ in water.

The line quoted, you remember, is in Shelley, *Adonais*, and the last Keats desired might be engraved on his tomb. Ask Hunt if he thinks it will do, and to think of something to put on my ante-dated grave. I am very anxious to hear how Marianne is getting on, and Hunt. You never mention a word of them or the *Liberal*.

I have been delayed here longer than I had intended, from want of money, having lent and given it away thoughtlessly. However, old Dunn has sent me a supply, so I shall go on to Florence on Monday. I will assuredly see you before you go, and, if my exchequer is not exhausted, go part of the way with you. However, I will write further on this topic at Florence. Do not go to England, to encounter poverty and bitter retrospections. Stay in Italy. I will most gladly share my income with you, and if, under the same circumstances, you would do the same by me, why then you will not hesitate to accept it. I know of nothing would give me half so much pleasure. As you say, in a few years we shall both be better off. Commend me to Marianne and Hunt, and believe me, yours affectionately,   E. TRELAWNY.

Poste Restante a Gènes.

.   .   .   .

You need not tell me that all your thoughts are concentrated on the memory of your loss, for I have observed it, with great regret and some astonishment. You tell me nothing in your letters of how the *Liberal* is getting on. Why do you not send me a number? How many have come out? Does Hunt stay at Genoa the summer, and what does Lord Byron determine on? I am told the *Bolivar* is lent to some one, and at sea. Where is Jane? and is Mrs. Hunt likely to

recover?   I shall certainly go on to Switzerland if I can raise
the wind.

.   .   .   .

MARY SHELLEY TO TRELAWNY.

10th May 1823.

MY DEAR TRELAWNY—You appear to have fulfilled my entire
wish in all you have done at Rome.   Do you remember the
day you made that quotation from Shakespeare in our living
room at Pisa?   Mine own Shelley was delighted with it, and
thus it has for me a pleasing association.   Some time hence
I may visit the spot which, of all others, I desire most to see.

.   .   .   .

It is not on my own account, my excellent friend, that I
go to England.   I believe that my child's interests will be
best consulted by my return to that country. . . .

Desiring solitude and my books only, together with the
consciousness that I have one or two friends who, although
absent, still think of me with affection, England of course
holds out no inviting prospect to me.   But I am sure to be
rewarded in doing or suffering for my little darling, so I am
resigned to this last act, which seems to snap the sole link
which bound the present to the past, and to tear aside the
veil which I have endeavoured to draw over the desolations
of my situation.   Your kindness I shall treasure up to comfort
me in future ill.   I shall repeat to myself, I have such a friend,
and endeavour to deserve it.

Do you go to Greece?   Lord Byron continues in the same
mind.   The G—— is an obstacle, and certainly her situation
is rather a difficult one.   But he does not seem disposed to
make a mountain of her resistance, and he is far more able to
take a decided than a petty step in contradiction to the wishes
of those about him.   If you do go, it may hasten your return
hither.   I remain until Mrs. Hunt's confinement is over; had
it not been for that, the fear of a hot journey would have
caused me to go in this month,—but my desire to be useful
to her, and my anxiety concerning the event of so momentous

a crisis has induced me to stay. You may think with what awe and terror I look forward to the decisive moment, but I hope for the best. She is as well, perhaps better, than we could in any way expect.

I had no opportunity to send you a second No. of the *Liberal;* we only received it a short time ago, and then you were on the wing: the third number has come out, and we had a copy by post. It has little in it we expected, but it is an amusing number, and L. B. is better pleased with it than any other. . . .

I trust that I shall see you soon, and then I shall hear all your news. I shall see you—but it will be for so short a time —I fear even that you will not go to Switzerland; but these things I must not dwell upon,—partings and separations, when there is no circumstance to lessen any pang. I must brace my mind, not enervate it, for I know I shall have much to endure.

I asked Hunt's opinion about your epitaph for Keats; he said that the line from *Adonais,* though beautiful in itself, might be applied to any poet, in whatever circumstances or whatever age, that died; and that to be in accord with the two-stringed lyre, you ought to select one that alluded to his youth and immature genius. A line to this effect you might find in *Adonais.*

Among the fragments of my lost Shelley, I found the following poetical commentary on the words of Keats,—not that I recommend it for the epitaph, but it may please you to see it.

> Here lieth one, whose name was writ in water,
> But, ere the breath that could erase it blew,
> Death, in remorse for that fell slaughter,
> Death, the immortalising winter, flew
> Athwart the stream, and time's mouthless torrent grew
> A scroll of crystal, emblazoning the name
> Of Adonais.

I have not heard from Jane lately; she was well when she last wrote, but annoyed by various circumstances, and impatient of her lengthened stay in England. How earnestly do I hope that Edward's brother will soon arrive, and show himself worthy of his affinity to the noble and unequalled creature she has lost, by protecting one to whom protection is so necessary, and shielding her from some of the ills to which she is exposed.

Adieu, my dear Trelawny. Continue to think kindly of me, and trust in my unalterable friendship.

MARY SHELLEY.

Albaro, 10th May.

On his journey to Genoa, Trelawny stayed a night at Lerici, and paid a last visit to the Villa Magni. There, "sleeping still on the mud floor," its mast and oars broken, was Shelley's little skiff, the " Boat on the Serchio."

He mounted the "stairs, or rather ladder," into the dining-room.

As I surveyed its splotchy walls, broken floor, cracked ceiling, and poverty-struck appearance, while I noted the loneliness of the situation, and remembered the fury of the waves that in blowing weather lashed its walls, I did not marvel at Mrs. Shelley's and Mrs. Williams' groans on first entering it; nor that it had required all Ned Williams' persuasive powers to induce them to stop there.

But these things were all far away in the past.

> As music and splendour
> Survive not the lamp and the lute,
>   The heart's echoes render
> No song when the spirit is mute.
>
>   No song but sad dirges,
> Like the wind through a ruined cell,
>   Or the mournful surges
> That ring the dead seaman's knell.

At Genoa he found the " Pilgrim " in a state of
supreme indecision.   He had left him discontented when he departed in December.   The
new magazine was not a success.   Byron had
expected that other literary and journalistic advantages, leading to fame and power, would
accrue to him from the coalition with Leigh
Hunt and Shelley, but in this he was disappointed,
and he was left to bear the responsibility of the
partnership alone.

"The death of Shelley and the failure of the *Liberal* irritated Byron," writes Trelawny; "the cuckoo-note, 'I told
you so,' sung by his friends, and the loud crowing of enemies,
by no means allayed his ill humour.   In this frame of mind
he was continually planning how to extricate himself.   His
plea for hoarding was that he might have a good round
tangible sum of current coin to aid him in any emergency. . . .

"He exhausted himself in planning, projecting, beginning,
wishing, intending, postponing, regretting, and doing nothing :
the unready are fertile in excuses, and his were inexhaustible."

Since that time he had been flattered and persuaded into joining the Greek Committee, formed
in London to aid the Greeks in their war of independence.   Byron's name and great popularity
would be a tower of strength to them.   Their
proposals came to him at a right moment, when
he was dissatisfied with himself and his position.
He hesitated for months before committing himself, and finally summoned Trelawny, in peremp-
tory terms, to come to him and go with him.

15th June 1823.

My dear T.—You must have heard that I am going to Greece. Why do you not come to me? I want your aid and am extremely anxious to see you. . . . They all say I can be of use in Greece. I do not know how, nor do they; but, at all events, let us go.—Yours, etc., truly,   N. Byron.

And, always ready for adventure, the " Pirate " came. Before his arrival Mary's journey had been decided on. Mrs. Hunt's confinement was over : she and the infant had both done well, and she was now in a fair way to live, in tolerable health, for many years longer. Want of funds was now the chief obstacle in Mary's way, but Byron was no longer ready, as he had been, with offers of help. Changeable as the wind, and utterly unable to put himself in another person's place, he, without absolutely declining to fulfil his promises, made so many words about it, and treated the matter as so great a favour on his own part, that Mary at last declined his assistance, although it obliged her to take advantage of Trelawny's often-repeated offers of help, which she would not rather have accepted, as he was poor, while Byron was rich. The whole story unfolds itself in the three ensuing letters.

MARY SHELLEY TO JANE WILLIAMS.

ALBARO, NEAR GENOA, *July* 1823.

I write to you in preference to my Father, because you, to a great degree, understand the person I have to deal with, and in communicating what I say concerning him, you can, *viva voce*, add such comments as will render my relation more intelligible.

The day after Marianne's confinement, the 9th June, seeing all went on so prosperously, I told Lord Byron that I was ready to go, and he promised to provide means. When I talked of going post, it was because he said that I should go so, at the same time declaring that he would regulate all himself. I waited in vain for these arrangements. But, not to make a long story, since I hope soon to be able to relate the details—he chose to transact our negotiation through Hunt, and gave such an air of unwillingness and sense of the obligation he conferred, as at last provoked Hunt to say that there was no obligation, since he owed me £1000.

> Glad of a quarrel, straight I clap the door !

Still keeping up an appearance of amity with Hunt, he has written notes and letters so full of contempt against me and my lost Shelley that I could stand it no longer, and have refused to receive his still proffered aid for my journey. This, of course, delays me. I can muster about £30 of my own. I do not know whether this is barely sufficient, but as the delicate constitution of my child may oblige me to rest several times on the journey, I cannot persuade myself to commence my journey with what is barely necessary. I have written, therefore, to Trelawny for the sum requisite, and must wait till I hear from him. I see you, my poor girl, sigh over these mischances, but never mind, I do not feel them. My life is a shifting scene, and my business is to play the part allotted for each day well, and, not liking to think of to-morrow, I never think of it at all, except in an intellectual way ; and as to money difficulties, why, having nothing, I can lose nothing. Thus, as far as regards what are called worldly concerns, I am perfectly tranquil, and as free or freer from care as if my signature should be able to draw £1000 from some banker. The extravagance and anger of Lord Byron's letters also relieve me from all pain that his dereliction might occasion

me, and that his conscience twinges him is too visible from
his impatient kicks and unmannerly curvets.   You would
laugh at his last letter to Hunt, when he says concerning his
connection with Shelley "that he let himself down to the level
of the democrats."

In the meantime Hunt is all kindness, consideration, and
friendship—all feeling of alienation towards me has disappeared
even to its last dregs.   He perfectly approves of what I have
done.   So I am still in Italy, and I doubt not but that its sun
and vivifying geniality relieve me from those biting cares which
would be mine in England, I fear, if I were destitute there.
But I feel above the mark of Fortune, and my heart too much
wounded to feel these pricks, on all occasions that do not
regard its affections, *s'arma di se, e d'intero diamante.*   Thus
am I changed; too late, alas! for what ought to have been,
but not too late, I trust, to enable me, more than before, to
be some stay and consolation to my own dear Jane.

Mary.

Trelawny to Mrs. Shelley.

Saturday.

Dear Mary—Will you tell me what sum you want, as I
am settling my affairs?   You must from time to time let me
know your wants, that I may do my best to relieve them.
You are sure of me, so let us use no more words about it.   I
have been racking my memory to remember some person in
England that would be of service to you for my sake, but my
rich friends and relations are without hearts, and it is useless
to introduce you to the unfortunate; it would but augment
your repinings at the injustice of Fortune.   My knight-errant
heart has led me many a weary journey foolishly seeking the
unfortunate, the miserable, and the outcast; and when found,
I have only made myself as one of them without redressing
their grievances, so I pray you avoid, as you value your peace
of mind, the wretched.   I shall see you, I hope, to-day.—
Yours very faithfully,   E. Trelawny.

Mary Shelley to Jane Williams.

Albaro, 23d *July* 1823.

Dearest Jane—I have at length fixed with the *vetturino*. I depart on the 25th, my best girl. I leave Italy; I return to the dreariest reality after having dreamt away a year in this blessed and beloved country.

Lord Byron, Trelawny, and Pierino Gamba sailed for Greece on the 17th inst. I did not see the former. His unconquerable avarice prevented his supplying me with money, and a remnant of shame caused him to avoid me. But I have a world of things to tell you on that score when I see you. If he were mean, Trelawny more than balanced the moral account. His whole conduct during his last stay here has impressed us all with an affectionate regard, and a perfect faith in the unalterable goodness of his heart. They sailed together; Lord Byron with £10,000, Trelawny with £50, and Lord Byron cowering before his eye for reasons you shall hear soon. The Guiccioli is gone to Bologna—*e poi cosa farà ? Chi lo sa? Cosa vuoi che lo dico ?* . . .

I travel without a servant. I rest first at Lyons; but do you write to me at Paris, Hotel Nelson. It will be a friend to await me. Alas! I have need of consolation. Hunt's kindness is now as active and warm as it was dormant before; but just as I find a companion in him I leave him. I leave him in all his difficulties, with his head throbbing with overwrought thoughts, and his frame sometimes sinking under his anxieties. Poor Marianne has found good medicine, *facendo un bimbo*, and then nursing it, but she, with her female providence, is more bent by care than Hunt. How much I wished, and wish, to settle near them at Florence; but I must submit with courage, and patience may at last come and give opiate to my irritable feelings.

Both Hunt and Trelawny say that Percy is much improved since Maria left me. He is affectionately attached to Sylvan, and very fond of *Bimbo nuovo*. He kisses him by the hour, and tells me, *Come il Signore Enrico ha comprato un Baby nuovo—forse ti darà il Baby vecchio*, as he gives away an old toy on the appearance of a new one.

I will not write longer. In conversation, nay, almost in thought, I can, at this most painful moment, force my excited feelings to laugh at themselves, and my spirits, raised by emotion, to seem as if they were light, but the natural current and real hue overflows me and penetrates me when I write, and it would be painful to you, and overthrow all my hopes of retaining my fortitude, if I were to write one word that truly translated the agitation I suffer into language.

I will write again from Lyons, where I suppose I shall be on the 3d of August. Dear Jane, can I render you happier than you are? The idea of that might console me, at least you will see one that truly loves you, and who is for ever your affectionately attached   MARY SHELLEY.

If there is any talk of my accommodations, pray tell Mrs. Gisborne that I cannot sleep on any but a *hard* bed. I care not how hard, so that it be a mattress.

And now Mary's life in Italy was at an end. Her resolution of returning to England had been welcomed by her father in the letter which follows, and it was to his house, and not to Mrs. Gisborne's that she finally decided to go on first arriving.

GODWIN TO MARY.

No. 195 STRAND, *6th May* 1823.

It certainly is, my dear Mary, with great pleasure that I anticipate that we shall once again meet. It is a long, long time now since you have spent one night under my roof. You are grown a woman, have been a wife, a mother, a widow. You have realised talents which I but faintly and doubtfully anticipated. I am grown an old man, and want a child of my own to smile on and console me.   I shall then feel less alone than I do at present.

What William will be, I know not; he has sufficient understanding and quickness for the ordinary concerns of life, and something more; and, at any rate, he is no smiler, no consoler.

When you first set your foot in London, of course I and Mamma expect that it will be in this house.   But the house is smaller, one floor less, than the house in Skinner Street. It will do well enough for you to make shift with for a few days, but it would not do for a permanent residence. But I hope we shall at least have you near us, within a call.   How different from your being on the shores of the Mediterranean!

Your novel has sold five hundred copies—half the impression.

Peacock sent your box by the *Berbice*, Captain Wayth. I saw him a fortnight ago, and he said that he had not yet received the bill of lading himself, but he should be sure to have it in time, and would send it.   I ought to have written to you sooner.   Your letter reached me on the 18th ult., but I have been unusually surrounded with perplexities.—Your affectionate Father,   WILLIAM GODWIN.

On the 25th of July she left Genoa, Hunt accompanying her for the first twenty miles.   If one thought more than any other sustained her in her unprotected loneliness, it was that of being reunited in England to her sister in misfortune, Jane Williams, to whom her heart turned with a singular tenderness, and to whom on her journey she addressed one more letter, full of grateful affection and of a touching humility, new in her character.

MARY SHELLEY TO JANE WILLIAMS.

ST. JEAN DE LA MAURIENNE,
30th July 1823.

MY BEST JANE—I wrote to you from Genoa the day before
I quitted it, but I afterwards lost the letter. I asked the
Hunts to look for it, and send it if found, but ten to one you
will never receive it. It contained nothing, however, but
what I can tell you in five minutes if I see you. It told you
of the departure of Lord Byron and Trelawny for Greece, the
former escaping with all his crowns, and the other disbursing
until he had hardly £10 left. It went to my heart to borrow
the sum from him necessary to make up my journey, but he
behaved with so much quiet generosity that one was almost
glad to put him to that proof, and witness the excellence
of his heart. In this and in another trial he acquitted
himself so well that he gained all our hearts, while the other
—but more when we meet.

I left Genoa Thursday, 25th. Hunt and Thornton accompanied me the first twenty miles. This was much, you will
say, for Hunt. But, thank heaven, we are now the best
friends in the world. He set his heart on my quitting Italy
with as comfortable feelings as possible, and he did so much
that notwithstanding all the [bitterness] that such an event,
joined to parting with a dear friend, occasioned me, yet I have
borne up with better spirits than I could in any way have
hoped. It is a delightful thing, my dear Jane, to be able to
express one's affection upon an old and tried friend like
Hunt, and one so passionately attached to my Shelley as he
was, and is. It is pleasant also to feel myself loved by one
who loves me. You know somewhat of what I suffered
during the winter, during his alienation from me. He was
displeased with me for many just reasons, but he found me
willing to expiate, as far as I could, the evil I had done, so
his heart was again warmed ; and if, my dear friend, when I
return, you find me more amiable and more willing to suffer

with patience than I was, it is to him that I owe this benefit, and you may judge if I ought not to be grateful to him. I am even so to Lord Byron, who was the cause that I stayed at Genoa, and thus secured one who, I am sure, can never change.

The illness of one of our horses detains me here an afternoon, so I write, and shall put the letter in the post at Chambéry. I have come without a servant or companion; but Percy is perfectly good, and no trouble to me at all. We are both well; a little tired or so. Will you tell my Father that you have heard from me, and that I am so far on my journey. I expect to be at Lyons in three days, and will write to him from that place. If there be any talk of my accommodations, pray put in a word for a *hard* bed, for else I am sure I cannot sleep.

So I have left Italy, and alone with my child I am travelling to England. What a dream I have had! and is it over? Oh no! for I do nothing but dream; realities seem to have lost all power over me,—I mean, as it were, mere tangible realities,—for, where the affections are concerned, calamity has only awakened greater sensitiveness.

I fear things do not go on well with you, my dearest girl! you are not in your mother's house, and you cannot have settled your affairs in India,—mine too! Why, I arrive poor to nothingness, and my hopes are small, except from my own exertions; and living in England is dear. My thoughts will all bend towards Italy; but even if Sir Timothy Shelley should do anything, he will not, I am sure, permit me to go abroad. At any rate we shall be together a while. We will talk of our lost ones, and think of realising my dreams; who knows? Adieu, I shall soon see you, and you will find how truly I am your affectionate   MARY SHELLEY.

With the following fragment, the last of her Italian journal, this chapter may fitly close.

Journal, May 31.—The lanes are filled with fire-flies;

they dart between the trunks of the trees, and people the land with earth-stars. I walked among them to-night, and descended towards the sea. I passed by the ruined church, and stood on the platform that overlooks the beach. The black rocks were stretched out among the blue waters, which dashed with no impetuous motion against them. The dark boats, with their white sails, glided gently over its surface, and the star-enlightened promontories closed in the bay : below, amid the crags, I heard the monotonous but harmonious voices of the fishermen.

How beautiful these shores, and this sea ! Such is the scene—such the waves within which my beloved vanished from mortality.

The time is drawing near when I must quit this country. It is true that, in the situation I now am, Italy is but the corpse of the enchantress that she was. Besides, if I had stayed here, the state of things would have been different. The idea of our child's advantage alone enables me to keep fixed in my resolution to return to England. It is best for him—and I go.

Four years ago we lost our darling William ; four years ago, in excessive agony, I called for death to free me from all I felt that I should suffer here. I continue to live, and *thou* art gone. I leave Italy and the few that still remain to me. That I regret less ; for our intercourse is so much chequered with all of dross that this earth so delights to blend with kindness and sympathy, that I long for solitude, with the exercise of such affections as still remain to me. Away, I shall be conscious that these friends love me, and none can then gainsay the pure attachment which chiefly clings to them because they knew and loved you—because I knew them when with you, and I cannot think of them without feeling your spirit beside me.

I cannot grieve for you, beloved Shelley ; I grieve for thy friends—for the world—for thy child—most for myself, enthroned in thy love, growing wiser and better beneath thy gentle influence, taught by you the highest philosophy—your

pupil, friend, lover, wife, mother of your children! The glory
of the dream is gone. I am a cloud from which the light of
sunset has passed. Give me patience in the present struggle.
Meum cordium cor! Good-night!

> I would give all that I am to be as now thou art,
> But I am chained to time, and cannot thence depart.

CHAPTER XIX

JULY 1823–DECEMBER 1824

MARY's journey extended over a month, one week of which was passed in Paris and Versailles, for the sake of seeing the Horace Smiths and other old acquaintances now living there. Her letters to the Hunts, describing the incidents and impressions of her journey, were as lively and cheerful as she could make them. A few extracts follow here.

To LEIGH HUNT.

ASTI, 26<i>th July</i>.

. . . .

Percy is very good and does not in the least *annoy* me. In the state of mind I am now in, the motion and change is delightful to me: my thoughts run with the coach and wind, and double, and jerk, and are up and down, and forward, and most often backward, till the labyrinth of Crete is a joke in comparison to my intricate wanderings. They now lead me to you, Hunt. You rose early, wrote, walked, dined, whistled, sang and punned most outrageously, the worst puns in the world. My best Polly, you, full of your chicks and of your new darling, yet sometimes called " Henry " to see a beautiful new effect of light on the mountains. . . . Dear girl, I have a great affection for you, believe that, and don't talk or think

sorrowfully, unless you have the toothache, and then don't
think, but talk infinite nonsense mixed with infinite sense, and
Hunt will listen, as I used.   Thorny, you have not been cross
yet.   Oh, my dear Johnny (don't be angry, Polly, with this
nonsense), do not let your impatient nature ever overcome you,
or you may suffer as I have done—which God forbid !   Be
true to yourself, and talk much to your Father, who will teach
you as he has taught me.   It is the idea of his lessons of
wisdom that makes me feel the affection I do for him.   I
profit by them, so do you : may you never feel the remorse of
having neglected them when his voice and look are gone, and
he can no longer talk to you ; that remorse is a terrible
feeling, and it requires a faith and a philosophy immense not
to be destroyed by the stinging monster.

28th July.

. . . I was too late for the post yesterday at Turin, and
too early this morning, so as I determined to put this letter in
the post myself, I bring it with me to Susa, and now open it
to tell you how delighted I am with my morning's ride—the
scenery is so divine.   The high, dark Alps, just on this
southern side tipt with snow, close in a plain ; the meadows
are full of clover and flowers, and the woods of ash, elm, and
beech descend and spread, and lose themselves in the fields ;
stately trees, in clumps or singly, arise on each side, and
wherever you look you see some spot where you dream of
building a home and living for ever.   The exquisite beauty of
nature, and the cloudless sky of this summer day soothe me,
and make this 28th so full of recollections that it is almost
pleasurable.   Wherever the spirit of beauty dwells, *he* must
be ; the rustling of the trees is full of him ; the waving of
the tall grass, the moving shadows of the vast hills, the blue
air that penetrates their ravines and rests upon their heights.
I feel him near me when I see that which he best loved.
Alas ! nine years ago he took to a home in his heart this
weak being, whom he has now left for more congenial spirits
and happier regions.   She lives only in the hope that she
may become one day as one of them.

Absolutely, my dear Hunt, I will pass some three summer months in this divine spot, you shall all be with me. There are no gentlemen's seats at Palazzi, so we will take a cottage, which we will paint and refit, just as this country here is, in which I now write, clean and plain. We will have no servants, only we will give out all the needlework. Marianne shall make puddings and pies, to make up for the vegetables and meat which I shall boil and spoil. Thorny shall sweep the rooms, Mary make the beds, Johnny clean the kettles and pans, and then we will pop him into the many streams hereabouts, and so clean him. Swinny, being so quick, shall be our Mercury, Percy our gardener, Sylvan and Percy Florence our weeders, and Vincent our plaything; and then, to raise us above the vulgar, we will do all our work, keeping time to Hunt's symphonies; we will perform our sweepings and dustings to the March in *Alceste*, we will prepare our meats to the tune of the *Laughing Trio*, and when we are tired we will lie on our turf sofas, while all our voices shall join in chorus in *Notte e giorno faticar*. You see my paper is quite out, so I must say, for the last time, Adieu! God bless you. MARY W. S.

Tuesday, 5th August.

I have your letter, and your excuses, and all. I thank you most sincerely for it : at the same time I do entreat you to take care of yourself with regard to writing; although your letters are worth infinite pleasure to me, yet that pleasure cannot be worth pain to you ; and remember, if you must write, the good, hackneyed maxim of *multum in parvo*, and, when your temples throb, distil the essence of three pages into three lines, and my "fictitious adventure"[1] will enable me to open them out and fill up intervals. Not but what three pages are best, but "you can understand me." And now let me tell you that I fear you do not rise early, since you doubt my *ore mattutine*. Be it known to you, then, that on the journey I always rise *before* 3 o'clock, that I *never* once made the *vetturino* wait, and, moreover, that there was no discontent

---

[1] See Godwin's letter, page 96.

in our jogging on on either side, so that I half expect to be a
Santa with him.   He indeed got a little out of his element
when he got into France,—his good humour did not leave
him, but his self-possession.   He could not speak French,
and he walked about as if treading on eggs.

When at Paris I will tell you more what I think of the
French.   They still seem miracles of quietness in comparison
with Marianne's noisy friends.   And the women's dresses
afford the drollest contrast with those in fashion when I first
set foot in Paris in 1814.   Then their waists were between
their shoulders, and, as Hogg observed, they were rather
curtains than gowns ; their hair, too, dragged to the top of
the head, and then lifted to its height, appeared as if each
female wished to be a Tower of Babel in herself.   Now their
waists are long (not so long, however, as the Genoese), and
their hair flat at the top, with quantities of curls on the temples.
I remember, in 1814, a Frenchman's pathetic horror at Clare's
and my appearance in the streets of Paris in " Oldenburgh "
(as they were called) hats ; now they all wear machines of
that shape, and a high bonnet would of course be as far out of
the right road as if the earth were to take a flying leap to
another system.

After you receive this letter, you must direct to me at
my Father's (pray put William Godwin, Esq., since the want of
that etiquette annoys him.   I remember Shelley's unspeakable
astonishment when the author of *Political Justice* asked him, half
reproachfully, why he addressed him *Mr.* Godwin), 195 Strand.

On the 25th of August Mary met her father
once more.   At his house in the Strand she
spent her first ten days in England.   Consideration for others, and the old habit of repressing all
show of feeling before Godwin helped to steel her
nerves and heart to bear the stings and aches of
this strange, mournful reunion.

And now again, too, she saw her friend Jane. But fondly as Mary ever clung to her, she must have been sensible of the difference between them. Mrs. Williams' situation was forlorn indeed; in some respects even more so than Mrs. Shelley's. But, though she had grieved bitterly, as well she might, for Edward's loss, her nature was not *impressible*, and the catastrophe which had fallen upon her had left her unaltered. Jane was unhappy, but she was not inconsolable; her grief was becoming to her, and lent her a certain interest which enhanced her attractions. And to men in general she was very attractive. Godwin himself was somewhat fascinated by the "picturesque little woman" who had called on him on her first arrival; who "did not drop one tear" and occasionally smiled. As for Hogg, he lost his heart to her at once.

All this Mary must have seen. But Jane was an attaching creature, and Mary loved her as the greater nature loves the lesser; she lavished on her a wealth of pent-up tenderness, content to get what crumbs she could in return. For herself a curious surprise was in store, which entertained, if it did not cheer her.

Just at the time of its author's return to England, *Frankenstein*, in a dramatised form, was having a considerable "run" at the English Opera House.

Mrs. Shelley to Leigh Hunt.

9th September 1823.

My dear Hunt—Bessy promised me to relieve you from any inquietude you might suffer from not hearing from me, so I indulged myself with not writing to you until I was quietly settled in lodgings of my own. Want of time is not my excuse; I had plenty, but, until I saw all quiet around me, I had not the spirit to write a line. I thought of you all—how much? and often longed to write, yet would not till I called myself free to turn southward; to imagine you all, to put myself in the midst of you, would have destroyed all my philosophy. But now I do so. I am in little neat lodgings, my boy in bed, I quiet, and I will now talk to you, tell you what I have seen and heard, and with as little repining as I can, try (by making the best of what I have, the certainty of your friendship and kindness) to rest half content that I am not in the "Paradise of Exiles." Well, first I will tell you, journalwise, the history of my sixteen days in London.

I arrived Monday, the 25th of August. My Father and William came for me to the wharf. I had an excellent passage of eleven hours and a half, a glassy sea, and a contrary wind. The smoke of our fire was wafted right aft, and streamed out behind us; but wind was of little consequence; the tide was with us, and though the engine gave a "short uneasy motion" to the vessel, the water was so smooth that no one on board was sick, and Persino played about the deck in high glee. I had a very kind reception in the Strand, and all was done that could be done to make me comfortable. I exerted myself to keep up my spirits. The house, though rather dismal, is infinitely better than the Skinner Street one. I resolved not to think of certain things, to take all as a matter of course, and thus contrive to keep myself out of the gulf of melancholy, on the edge of which I was and am continually peeping.

But lo and behold! I found myself famous. *Frankenstein*

had prodigious success as a drama, and was about to be repeated, for the twenty-third night, at the English Opera House.
The play-bill amused me extremely, for, in the list of *dramatis
personæ*, came "——, by Mr. T. Cooke." This nameless
mode of naming the unnameable is rather good.

On Friday, 29th August, Jane, my Father, William, and I
went to the theatre to see it. Wallack looked very well as
Frankenstein. He is at the beginning full of hope and expectation. At the end of the first act the stage represents a
room with a staircase leading to Frankenstein's workshop ; he
goes to it, and you see his light at a small window, through
which a frightened servant peeps, who runs off in terror when
Frankenstein exclaims "It lives!" Presently Frankenstein
himself rushes in horror and trepidation from the room, and,
while still expressing his agony and terror, "——" throws
down the door of the laboratory, leaps the staircase, and
presents his unearthly and monstrous person on the stage.
The story is not well managed, but Cooke played ——'s part
extremely well ; his seeking, as it were, for support ; his
trying to grasp at the sounds he heard ; all, indeed, he
does was well imagined and executed. I was much amused,
and it appeared to excite a breathless eagerness in the
audience. It was a third piece, a scanty pit filled at half-
price, and all stayed till it was over. They continue to play it
even now.

On Saturday, 30th August, I went with Jane to the
Gisbornes. I know not why, but seeing them seemed more
than anything else to remind me of Italy. Evening came on
drearily, the rain splashed on the pavement, nor star nor moon
deigned to appear. I looked upward to seek an image of
Italy, but a blotted sky told me only of my change. I tried
to collect my thoughts, and then, again, dared not think, for
I am a ruin where owls and bats live only, and I lost my last
singing bird when I left Albaro. It was my birthday, and it
pleased me to tell the people so ; to recollect and feel that
time flies, and what is to arrive is nearer, and my home not so
far off as it was a year ago. This same evening, on my return

to the Strand, I saw Lamb, who was very entertaining and amiable, though a little deaf. One of the first questions he asked me was, whether they made puns in Italy : I said, " Yes, now Hunt is there." He said that Burney made a pun in Otaheite, the first that was ever made in that country. At first the natives could not make out what he meant, but all at once they discovered the *pun*, and danced round him in transports of joy. . . .

. . . On the strength of the drama, my Father had published for my benefit a new edition of *Frankenstein*, for he despaired utterly of my doing anything with Sir Timothy Shelley. I wrote to him, however, to tell him of my arrival, and on the following Wednesday had a note from Whitton, where he invited me, if I wished for an explanation of Sir T. Shelley's intentions concerning my boy, to call on him. I went with my Father. Whitton was very polite, though long-winded : his great wish seemed to be to prevent my applying again to Sir T. Shelley, whom he represented as old, infirm, and irritable. However, he advanced me £100 for my immediate expenses, told me that he could not speak positively until he had seen Sir T. Shelley, but that he doubted not but that I should receive the same annually for my child, and, with a little time and patience, I should get an allowance for myself. This, you see, relieved me from a load of anxieties.

Having secured neat cheap lodgings, we removed hither last night. Such, dear Hunt, is the outline of your poor exile's history. After two days of rain, the weather has been *uncommonly* fine, *cioè*, without rain, and cloudless, I believe, though I trusted to other eyes for that fact, since the white-washed sky is anything but blue to any but the perceptions of the natives themselves. It is so cold, however, that the fire I am now sitting by is not the first that has been lighted, for my Father had one two days ago. The wind is east and piercing, but I comfort myself with the hope that softer gales are now fanning your *not* throbbing temples, that the climate of Florence will prove kindly to you, and that your health and spirits will return to you. Why am I not there ? This is quite a foreign country to me, the names of the places sound strangely, the voices of the people are new and grating, the vulgar English they speak particularly displeasing. But for my Father, I should be with you next spring, but his heart and soul are set on my stay, and in this world it always seems one's duty to sacrifice one's own desires, and that claim ever appears the strongest which claims such a sacrifice.

.   .   .   .

It is difficult to imagine *Frankenstein* on the stage; it must, at least, lose very much in dramatic representation. Like its modern successor, *Dr. Jekyll and Mr. Hyde,*—that remarkable story which bears a certain affinity to *Frankenstein,*—its subtle allegorical significance would be overweighted, if not lost, by the effect of the grosser and more material incidents which are all that could be *played,* and which, as described, must have bordered on the ludicrous. Still the charm of life imparted by a human impersonation to any portion, even, of one's own idea, is singularly powerful; and so Mary felt it. She would have liked to repeat the experience. Her situation, looked at in the face, was unenviable. She was unprovided for, young, delicate, and with a child dependent on her. Her rich connections would have nothing to do with her, and her boy did not possess in their eyes the importance which would have attached to him had he been heir to the baronetcy. She had talent, and it had been cultivated, but with her sorely-

tried health and spirits, the prospect of self-support by the compulsory production of imaginative
work must, at the time, have seemed unpromising
enough.

Two sheet-anchors of hope she had, and by
these she lived. They were, her child—so friendless but for her—and the thought of Shelley's
fame. The collecting and editing of his MSS.,
this was her work ; no one else should do it. It
seemed as though her brief life with him had had
for its purpose to educate her for this one object.

Those who now, in naming Shelley, feel they
name a part of everything beautiful, ethereal, and
spiritual—that his words are so inextricably inter-
woven with certain phases of love and beauty as
to be indistinguishable from the very thing itself
—may well find it hard to realise how little he
was known at the time when he died.

With other poets their work is the blossom
and fruit of their lives, but Shelley's poetry re-
sembles rather the perfume of the flower, that
subtle quality pertaining to the bloom which can
be neither described, nor pourtrayed, nor trans-
mitted ; an essence of immortality.

Not many months after this the news of
Byron's early death struck a kind of remorseful
grief into the hearts of his countrymen. A letter
of Miss Welsh's (Mrs. Carlyle) gives an idea of
the general feeling—

"I was told it," she says, "in a room full of people. Had I heard that the sun and moon had fallen out of their spheres it could not have conveyed to me the feeling of a more awful blank than did the simple words, 'Byron is dead.'"

How many, it may be asked, were conscious of any blank when the news reached them that Shelley had been "accidentally drowned"? Their numbers might be counted by tens.

The sale, in every instance, of Mr. Shelley's works has been very confined,

was his publishers' report to his widow. One newspaper dismissed his memory by the passing remark, "He will now find out whether there is a Hell or not."

The small number of those who recognised his genius did not even include all his personal friends.

"Mine is a life of failures;" so he summed it up to Trelawny and Edward Williams. "Peacock says my poetry is composed of day-dreams and nightmares, and Leigh Hunt does not think it good enough for the *Examiner.* Jefferson Hogg says all poetry is inverted sense, and consequently nonsense. . . .

"I wrote, and the critics denounced me as a mischievous visionary, and my friends said that I had mistaken my vocation, that my poetry was mere rhapsody of words. . . ."

Leigh Hunt, indeed, thought his own poetry more than equal to Shelley's or Byron's. Byron knew Shelley's power well enough, but cared little for the subjects of his sympathy. Trelawny was more appreciative, but his admiration for the poetry was quite secondary to his enthusiasm for the man. In Hogg's case, affection for the man may be said to have *excused* the poetry. All this Mary knew, but she knew too—what she was soon to find out by experience—that among his immediate associates he had created too warm an interest for him to escape posthumous discussion and criticism. And he had been familiar with some of those regarding whom the world's curiosity was insatiable, concerning whom any shred of information, true or false, was eagerly snapped up. His name would inevitably figure in anecdotes and gossip. His fame was Mary's to guard. During the years she lived at Albaro she had been employed in collecting and transcribing his scattered MSS., and at the end of this year, 1823, the volume of Posthumous Poems came out.

One would imagine that publishers would have bid against each other for the possession of such a treasure. Far from it. Among the little band of " true believers " three came forward to guarantee the expenses of publication. They were, the poet Thomas Lovell Beddoes, Procter, and T. F. Kelsall.

The appearance of this book was a melancholy satisfaction to Mary, though, as will soon be seen, she was not long allowed to enjoy it.

MRS. SHELLEY TO MRS. HUNT.

LONDON, *27th November* 1823.

MY DEAREST POLLY—Are you not a naughty girl? How could you copy a letter to that "agreeable, unaffected woman, Mrs. Shelley," without saying a word from yourself to your loving . . . . ? My dear Polly, a line from you forms a better picture for me of what you are about than—alas! I was going to say three pages, but I check myself—the rare one page of Hunt. Do not think that I forget you—even Percy does not, and he often tells me to bid the Signor Enrico and you to get in a carriage and then into a boat, and to come to *questo paese* with *Baby nuovo*, Henry, Swinburne, *e tutti*. But that will not be, nor shall I see you at Mariano; this is a dreary exile for me. During a long month of cloud and fog, how often have I sighed for my beloved Italy, and more than ever this day when I have come to a conclusion with Sir Timothy Shelley as to my affairs, and I find the miserable pittance I am to have. Nearly sufficient in Italy, here it will not go half-way. It is £100 per annum. Nor is this all, for I foresee a thousand troubles; yet, in truth, as far as regards mere money matters and worldly prospects, I keep up my philosophy with excellent success. Others wonder at this, but I do not, nor is there any philosophy in it. After having witnessed the mortal agonies of my two darling children, after that journey from and to Lerici, I feel all these as pictures and trifles as long as I am kept out of contact with the unholy. I was upset to-day by being obliged to see Whitton, and the prospect of seeing others of his tribe. I can earn a sufficiency, I doubt not. In Italy I should be content: here I will not bemoan. Indeed I never do, and Mrs. Godwin makes *large eyes* at the quiet way in which I take it all. It is England alone that annoys me, yet sometimes I get among friends and almost forget its fogs. I go to Shacklewell rarely, and sometimes see the Novellos elsewhere. He is my especial favourite, and his music always transports me to the seventh heaven. . . . I see the Lambs rather often, she ever amiable, and

Lamb witty and delightful. I must tell you one thing and make Hunt laugh. Lamb's new house at Islington is close to the New River, and George Dyer, after having paid them a visit, on going away at 12 at noonday, walked deliberately into the water, taking it for the high road. "But," as he said afterwards to Procter, "I soon found that I was in the water, sir." So Miss Lamb and the servant had to fish him out. . . . I must tell Hunt also a good saying of Lamb's,—talking of some one, he said, "Now some men who are very veracious are called matter-of-fact men, but such a one I should call a matter-of-lie man."

I have seen also Procter, with his "beautifully formed head" (it is beautifully formed), several times, and I like him. He is an enthusiastic admirer of Shelley, and most zealous in bringing out the volume of his poems; this alone would please me; and he is, moreover, gentle and gentlemanly, and apparently endued with a true poetic feeling. Besides, he is an invalid, and some time ago I told you, in a letter, that I have always a sneaking (for sneaking read open) kindness for men of literary and particularly poetic habits, who have delicate health. I cannot help revering the mind delicately attuned that shatters the material frame, and whose thoughts are strong enough to throw down and dilapidate the walls of sense and dikes of flesh that the unimaginative contrive to keep in such good repair. . . .

After all, I spend a great deal of my time in solitude. I have been hitherto too fully occupied in preparing Shelley's MSS. It is now complete, and the poetry alone will make a large volume. Will you tell Hunt that he need not send any of the MSS. that he has (except the Essay on Devils, and some lines addressed to himself on his arrival in Italy, if he should choose them to be inserted), as I have recopied all the rest? We should be very glad, however, of his notice as quickly as possible, as we wish the book to be out in a month at furthest, and that will not be possible unless he sends it immediately. It would break my heart if the book should appear without it.[1] When he does send a packet over (let it

---

[1] So it happened, however.

be directed to his brother), will he also be so good as to send me a copy of my "Choice," beginning after the line

> Entrenched sad lines, or blotted with its might?

Perhaps, dear Marianne, you would have the kindness to copy them for me, and send them soon. I have another favour to ask of you. Miss Curran has a portrait of Shelley, in many things very like, and she has so much talent that I entertain great hopes that she will be able to make a good one; for this purpose I wish her to have all the aids possible, and among the rest a profile from you.[1] If you could not cut another, perhaps you would send her one already cut, and if you sent it with a note requesting her to return it when she had done with it, I will engage that it will be most faithfully returned. At present I am not quite sure where she is, but if she should be there, and you can find her and send her this, I need not tell you how you would oblige me.

I heard from Bessy that Hunt is writing something for the *Examiner* for me. I *conjecture* that this may be concerning *Valperga*. I shall be glad, indeed, when that comes, or in lieu of it, anything else. John Hunt begins to despair.

．　　．　　．　　．　　．　　．

And now, dear Polly, I think I have done with gossip and business : with words of affection and kindness I should never have done. I am inexpressibly anxious about you all. Percy has had a similar though shorter attack to that at Albaro, but he is now recovered. I have a cold in my head, occasioned, I suppose, by the weather. Ah, Polly! if all the beauties of England were to have only the mirror that Richard III desires, a very short time would be spent at the looking-glass!

What of Florence and the gallery? I saw the Elgin marbles to-day; to-morrow I am to go to the Museum to look over the prints : that will be a great treat. The Theseus is a divinity, but how very few statues they have! Kiss the children. Ask Thornton for his forgotten and promised P.S., give my love to

---

[1] Mrs. Hunt, an amateur sculptress of talent, was also skilful in cutting out profiles in cardboard. From some of these, notably from one of Lord Byron, successful likenesses were made.

Hunt, and believe me, my dear Marianne, the exiled, but ever, most affectionately yours,   Mary W. Shelley.

Journal, January 18 (1824).—I have now been nearly four months in England, and if I am to judge of the future by the past and the present, I have small delight in looking forward. I even regret those days and weeks of intense melancholy that composed my life at Genoa. Yes, solitary and unbeloved as I was there, I enjoyed a more pleasurable state of being than I do here. I was still in Italy, and my heart and imagination were both gratified by that circumstance. I awoke with the light and beheld the theatre of nature from my window; the trees spread their green beauty before me, the resplendent sky was above me, the mountains were invested with enchanting colours. I had even begun to contemplate painlessly the blue expanse of the tranquil sea, speckled by the snow-white sails, gazed upon by the unclouded stars. There was morning and its balmy air, noon and its exhilarating heat, evening and its wondrous sunset, night and its starry pageant. Then, my studies; my drawing, which soothed me; my Greek, which I studied with greater complacency as I stole every now and then a look on the scene near me; my metaphysics, that strengthened and elevated my mind. Then my solitary walks and my reveries; they were magnificent, deep, pathetic, wild, and exalted. I sounded the depths of my own nature; I appealed to the nature around me to corroborate the testimony that my own heart bore to its purity. I thought of *him* with hope; my grief was active, striving, expectant. I was worth something then in the catalogue of beings. I could have written something, been something. Now I am exiled from these beloved scenes; its language is becoming a stranger to mine ears; my child is forgetting it. I am imprisoned in a dreary town; I see neither fields, nor hills, nor trees, nor sky; the exhilaration of enwrapt contemplation is no more felt by me; aspirations agonising, yet grand, from which the soul reposed in peace, have ceased to ascend from the quenched altar of my mind. Writing has become a task; my studies irksome; my life dreary. In this prison it is only in human intercourse that I can pretend to find consolation; and woe, woe, and triple woe to whoever seeks pleasure in human intercourse when that pleasure is not founded on deep and intense affection; as for the rest—

> The bubble floats before,
> The shadow stalks behind.

My Father's situation, his cares and debts, prevent my enjoying his society.

I love Jane better than any other human being, but I am pressed upon by the knowledge that she but slightly returns this affection. I love her, and my purest pleasure is derived from that source—a capacious basin, and but a rill flows into it. I love some one or two more, " with a degree of love," but I see them seldom. I am excited while with them, but the reaction of this feeling is dreadfully painful, but while in London I cannot forego this excitement. I know some clever men, in whose conversation I delight, but this is rare, like angels' visits. Alas! having lived day by day with one of the wisest, best, and most affectionate of spirits, how void, bare, and drear is the scene of life!

Oh, Shelley, dear, lamented, beloved! help me, raise me, support me; let me not feel ever thus fallen and degraded! my imagination is dead, my genius lost, my energies sleep. Why am I not beneath that weed-grown tower? Seeing Coleridge last night reminded me forcibly of past times; his beautiful descriptions reminded me of Shelley's conversations. Such was the intercourse I once daily enjoyed, added to supreme and active goodness, sympathy, and affection, and a wild, picturesque mode of living that suited my active spirit and satisfied its craving for novelty of impression.

I will go into the country and philosophise; some gleams of past entrancement may visit me there.

Lonely, poor, and dull as she was, these first months were a dreadful trial. She was writing,

or trying to write, another novel, *The Last Man*,
but it hung heavy ; it did not satisfy her.   Shrinking from company, yet recoiling still more from the
monotony of her own thoughts, she was possessed
by the restless wish to write a drama, perhaps with
the idea that out of dramatic creations she might
(Frankenstein-like) manufacture for herself companions more living than the characters of a novel.
It may have been fortunate for her that she did
not persevere in the attempt.   Her special gifts
were hardly of a dramatic order, and she had not the
necessary experience for a successful playwright.
She consulted her father, however, sending him
at the same time some specimens of her work, and
got some sound advice from him in return.

Godwin to Mary.

No. 195 Strand, *27th February* 1824.

My dear Mary—Your appeal to me is a painful one, and
the account you give of your spirits and tone of mind is more
painful.   Your appeal to me is painful, because I by no means
regard myself as an infallible judge, and have been myself an
unsuccessful adventurer in the same field toward which, in this
instance, you have turned your regards.   As to what you say
of your spirits and tone of mind, your plans, and your views,
would not that much more profitably and agreeably be made
the subject of a conversation between us ?   You are aware
that such a conversation must be begun by you.   So begun,
it would be quite a different thing than begun by me.   In the
former case I should be called in as a friend and adviser, from
whom some advantage was hoped for ; in the latter I should
be an intruder, forcing in free speeches and unwelcome truths,
and should appear as if I wanted to dictate to you and direct

you, who are well capable of directing yourself. You have able critics within your command—Mr. Procter and Mr. Lamb. You have, however, one advantage in me; I feel a deeper interest in you than they do, and would not mislead you for the world.

As to the specimens you have sent me, it is easy for me to give my opinion. There is one good scene—Manfred and the Two Strangers in the Cottage; and one that has some slight hints in it—the scene where Manfred attempts to stab the Duke. The rest are neither good nor bad; they might be endured, in the character of cement, to fasten good things together, but no more. Am I right? Perhaps not. I state things as they appear to my organs. Thus far, therefore, you afford an example, to be added to Barry Cornwall, how much easier it is to write a detached dramatic scene than to write a tragedy.

Is it not strange that so many people admire and relish Shakespeare, and that nobody writes or even attempts to write like him? To read your specimens, I should suppose that you had read no tragedies but such as have been written since the date of your birth. Your personages are mere abstractions— the lines and points of a mathematical diagram—and not men and women. If A crosses B, and C falls upon D, who can weep for that? Your talent is something like mine—it cannot unfold itself without elbow-room. As Gray sings, "Give ample room and verge enough the characters of hell to trace." I can do tolerably well if you will allow me to explain as much as I like—if, in the margin of what my personage says, I am permitted to set down and anatomise all that he feels. Dramatic dialogue, in reference to any talent I possess, is the devil. To write nothing more than the very words spoken by the character is a course that withers all the powers of my soul. Even Shakespeare, the greatest dramatist that ever existed, often gives us riddles to guess and enigmas to puzzle over. Many of his best characters and situations require a volume of commentary to make them perspicuous. And why is this? Because the law of his composition confines him to set down barely words that are to be delivered.

For myself, I am almost glad that you have not (if you
have not) a dramatic talent. How many mortifications and
heart-aches would that entail on you. Managers are to be
consulted; players to be humoured; the best pieces that were
ever written negatived, and returned on the author's hands
If these are all got over, then you have to encounter the
caprice of a noisy, insolent, and vulgar-minded audience,
whose senseless *non fiat* shall turn the labour of a year in a
moment into nothing.

> Full little knowest thou, that hast not tried,
> What hell it is——
> To fret thy soul with crosses and with cares,
> To eat thy heart through comfortless despairs;
> To fawn, to crouch, to wait, to ride, to run,
> To spend, to give, to want, to be undone.

It is laziness, my dear Mary, that makes you wish to be a
dramatist. It seems in prospect a short labour to write a play,
and a long one to write a work consisting of volumes; and as
much may be gained by the one as by the other. But as
there is no royal road to geometry, so there is no idle and
self-indulgent activity that leads to literary eminence.

As to the idea that you have no literary talent, for God's
sake, do not give way to such diseased imaginations. You
have, fortunately, ascertained that at a very early period.
What would you have done if you had passed through my
ordeal? I did not venture to face the public till I was seven
and twenty, and for ten years after that period could not contrive to write anything that anybody would read; yet even I
have not wholly miscarried.

Much of this was shrewd, and undeniable, but
the *wish* to write for the stage continued to haunt
Mary, and recurred two years later when she saw
Kean play *Othello*. To the end of her life she
expressed regret that she had not tried her hand
at a tragedy.

Meanwhile, besides her own novel, she was at no loss for literary jobs and literary occupation; her friends took care of that. Her pen and her powers were for ever at their service, and they never showed any scruple in working the willing horse. Her disinterested integrity made her an invaluable representative in business transactions. The affairs of the *Examiner* newspaper, edited in England by Leigh Hunt's brother John, were in an unsatisfactory condition; and there was much disagreement between the two brothers as to both pecuniary and literary arrangements. Mary had to act as arbiter between the two, softening the harsh and ungracious expressions which, in his annoyance, were used by John; looking after Leigh Hunt's interests, and doing all she could to make clear to him the complicated details of the concern. In this she was aided by Vincent Novello, the eminent musician, and intimate friend of the Hunts, to whom she had had a letter of introduction on arriving in Italy. The Novellos had a large, old-fashioned house on Shacklewell Green; they were the very soul of hospitality and kindness, and the centre of a large circle of literary and artistic friends, they had made Shelley's acquaintance in the days when the Leigh Hunts lived at the Vale of Health in Hampstead, and they now welcomed his widow, as well as Mrs. Williams, doing all in their power to shed a little cheerfulness over these two broken and melancholy lives.

" Very, very fair both ladies were," writes Mrs. Cowden Clarke, then Mary Victoria Novello, who in her charming *Recollections of Writers* has given us a pretty sketch of Mary Shelley as she then appeared to a "damsel approaching towards the age of 'sweet sixteen,' privileged to consider herself one of the grown-up people."

"Always observant as a child," she writes, " I had now become a greater observer than ever ; and large and varied was the pleasure I derived from my observation of the interesting men and women around me at this time of my life. Certainly Mary Wollstonecraft Godwin Shelley was the central figure of attraction then to my young-girl sight ; and I looked upon her with ceaseless admiration,—for her personal graces, as well as for her literary distinction.

"The daughter of William Godwin and Mary Wollstonecraft Godwin, the wife of Shelley, the authoress of *Frankenstein*, had for me a concentration of charm and interest that perpetually excited and engrossed me while she continued a visitor at my parents' house."

Elsewhere she describes

. . . " Her well-shaped, golden-haired head, almost always a little bent and drooping ; her marble-white shoulders and arms statuesquely visible in the perfectly plain black velvet dress, which the customs of that time allowed to be cut low, and which her own taste adopted (for neither she nor her sister-in-sorrow ever wore the conventional 'widow's weeds' and 'widow's cap') ; her thoughtful, earnest eyes ; her short upper lip and intellectually curved mouth, with a certain close-compressed and decisive expression while she listened, and a relaxation into fuller redness and mobility when speaking ; her exquisitely formed, white, dimpled, small hands, with rosy palms, and plumply commencing fingers, that tapered into tips as slender and delicate as those in a Vandyke portrait."

And though it was not in the power of these kind genial people to change Mary's destiny, or even to modify very sensibly the tenour of her inner life and thought, still their friendship was a solace to her; she was grateful for it, and did her utmost to respond with cheerfulness to their kindly efforts on her behalf. To Leigh Hunt (from whom depression, when it passed into querulousness, met with almost as little quarter as it did from Godwin) she wrote—

I am not always in spirits, but if my friends say that I am good, contrive to fancy that I am so, and so continue to love yours most truly,   MARY SHELLEY.

The news of Lord Byron's death in Greece, which in May of this year created so profound a sensation in England, fell on Mary's heart as a fresh calamity. She had small reason, personally, to esteem or regret him. Circumstances had made her only too painfully familiar with his worst side, and she might well have borne him more than one serious grudge. But he was associated in her mind with Shelley, and with early, happy days, and now he, like Shelley, was dead and gone, and his faults faded into distance, while all that was great and might have been noble in him—the hero that should have been rather than the man that was—survived, and stood

out in greater clearness and beauty, surrounded
by the tearful halo of memory. The tidings
reached her at a time of unusual—it afterwards
seemed of prophetic—dejection.

Journal, May 14. — This, then, is my English life;
and thus I am to drag on existence; confined in my small
room, friendless. Each day I string me to the task. I
endeavour to read and write, my ideas stagnate and my
understanding refuses to follow the words I read; day after
day passes while torrents fall from the dark clouds, and my
mind is as gloomy as this odious sky. Without human friends
I must attach myself to natural objects; but though I talk of
the country, what difference shall I find in this miserable
climate. Italy, dear Italy, murderess of those I love and of all
my happiness, one word of your soft language coming unawares
upon me, has made me shed bitter tears. When shall I hear
it again spoken, when see your skies, your trees, your streams?
The imprisonment attendant on a succession of rainy days has
quite overcome me. God knows I strive to be content, but
in vain. Amidst all the depressing circumstances that weigh
on me, none sinks deeper than the failure of my intellectual
powers; nothing I write pleases me. Whether I am just in
this, or whether the want of Shelley's (oh, my loved Shelley,
it is some alleviation only to write your name!) encouragement
I can hardly tell, but it seems to me as if the lovely and
sublime objects of nature had been my best inspirers, and, wanting them, I am lost. Although so utterly miserable at Genoa,
yet what reveries were mine as I looked on the aspect of the
ravine, the sunny deep and its boats, the promontories clothed
in purple light, the starry heavens, the fireflies, the uprising
of spring. Then I could think, and my imagination could
invent and combine, and self became absorbed in the grandeur
of the universe I created. Now my mind is a blank, a gulf
filled with formless mist.

The Last Man! Yes, I may well describe that solitary being's feelings : I feel myself as the last relic of a beloved race, my companions extinct before me.

And thus has the accumulating sorrow of days and weeks been forced to find a voice, because the word *lucena* met my eyes, and the idea of lost Italy sprang in my mind. What graceful lamps those are, though of base construction and vulgar use ; I thought of bringing one with me ; I am glad I did not. I will go back only to have a *lucena*.

If I told people so they would think me mad, and yet not madder than they seem to be now, when I say that the blue skies and verdure-clad earth of that dear land are necessary to my existence.

If there be a kind spirit attendant on me in compensation for these miserable days, let me only dream to-night that I am in Italy ! Mine own Shelley, what a horror you had (fully sympathised in by me) of returning to this miserable country ! To be here without you is to be doubly exiled, to be away from Italy is to lose you twice. Dearest, why is my spirit thus losing all energy ? Indeed, indeed, I must go back, or your poor utterly lost Mary will never dare think herself worthy to visit you beyond the grave.

May 15.—This then was the coming event that cast its shadow on my last night's miserable thoughts. Byron had become one of the people of the grave—that miserable conclave to which the beings I best loved belong. I knew him in the bright days of youth, when neither care nor fear had visited me—before death had made me feel my mortality, and the earth was the scene of my hopes. Can I forget our evening visits to Diodati ? our excursions on the lake, when he sang the Tyrolese Hymn, and his voice was harmonised with winds and waves. Can I forget his attentions and consolations to me during my deepest misery ?—Never.

Beauty sat on his countenance and power beamed from his eye. His faults being, for the most part, weaknesses, induced one readily to pardon them.

Albé—the dear, capricious, fascinating Albé—has left this

desert world! God grant I may die young! A new race is springing about me. At the age of twenty-six I am in the condition of an aged person. All my old friends are gone, I have no wish to form new. I cling to the few remaining ; but they slide away, and my heart fails when I think by how few ties I hold to the world. "Life is the desert and the solitude—how populous the grave"—and that region—to the dearer and best beloved beings which it has torn from me, now adds that resplendent spirit whose departure leaves the dull earth dark as midnight.

June 18.—What a divine night it is! I have just returned from Kentish Town ; a calm twilight pervades the clear sky ; the lamp-like moon is hung out in heaven, and the bright west retains the dye of sunset. If such weather would continue, I should write again ; the lamp of thought is again illumined in my heart, and the fire descends from heaven that kindles it. Such, my loved Shelley, now ten years ago, at this season, did we first meet, and these were the very scenes—that churchyard, with its sacred tomb, was the spot where first love shone in your dear eyes. The stars of heaven are now your country, and your spirit drinks beauty and wisdom in those spheres, and I, beloved, shall one day join you. Nature speaks to me of you. In towns and society I do not feel your presence ; but there you are with me, my own, my unalienable!

I feel my powers again, and this is, of itself, happiness ; the eclipse of winter is passing from my mind. I shall again feel the enthusiastic glow of composition, again, as I pour forth my soul upon paper, feel the winged ideas arise, and enjoy the delight of expressing them. Study and occupation will be a pleasure, and not a task, and this I shall owe to sight and companionship of trees and meadows, flowers and sunshine.

England, I charge thee, dress thyself in smiles for my sake! I will celebrate thee, O England! and cast a glory on thy name, if thou wilt for me remove thy veil of clouds, and let me contemplate the country of my Shelley and feel in communion with him!

I have been gay in company before, but the inspiriting

sentiment of the heart's peace I have not felt before to-night ;
and yet, my own, never was I so entirely yours. In sorrow and
grief I wish sometimes (how vainly !) for earthly consolation.
At a period of pleasing excitement I cling to your memory
alone, and you alone receive the overflowing of my heart.

Beloved Shelley, good-night. One pang will seize me
when I think, but I will only think, that thou art where I shall
be, and conclude with my usual prayer,—from the depth of
my soul I make it,—May I die young !

Trelawny to Mrs. Shelley.

Missolonghi, *30th April* 1824.

My dear Mary—My brain is already dizzy with business
and writing. I am transformed from the listless being you
knew me to one of all energy and fire. Not content with the
Camp, I must needs be a great diplomatist, I am again, dear
Mary, in my *element*, and playing no *second* part in Greece.
If I live, the outcast Reginald will cut his name out on the
Grecian hills, or set on its plains. I have had the merit of
discovering and bringing out a noble fellow, a gallant *soldier*,
and a man of most wonderful mind, with as little bigotry as
Shelley, and nearly as much imagination ; he is a glorious
being. I have lived with him—he calls me brother—wants
to connect me with his family. We have been inseparable
now for eight months—fought side by side. But I am sick at
heart with losing my friend,[1]—for still I call him so, you know,
with all his weakness, you know I loved him. I cannot live
with men for years without feeling—it is weak, it is want of
judgment, of philosophy,—but this is my weakness. Dear Mary,
if you love me,—*write*—write—write, for my heart yearns after
you. I certainly must have you and Jane out. I am serious.

This is the place after my own heart, and I am certain
of our good cause triumphing. Believe nothing you hear ;
Gamba will tell you everything about me — about Lord
Byron, but he knows nothing of Greece—nothing ; nor does

---

[1] Lord Byron.

it appear any one else does by what I see published. Colonel
Stanhope is here; he is a good fellow, and does much good.
The loan is achieved, and that sets the business at rest, but it
is badly done—the Commissioners are bad. A word as to
your wooden god, Mavrocordato. He is a miserable Jew, and
I hope, ere long, to see his head removed from his worthless
and heartless body. He is a mere shuffling soldier, an aristocratic brute—wants Kings and Congresses; a poor, weak,
shuffling, intriguing, cowardly fellow; so no more about him.
Dear Mary, dear Jane, I am serious, turn you thoughts this
way. No more a nameless being, I am now a Greek Chieftain,
willing and able to shelter and protect you; and thus I will
continue, or follow our friends to wander over some other
planet, for I have nearly exhausted this.—Your attached

TRELAWNY.

Care of John Hunt, Esq., *Examiner* Office,
     Catherine Street, London.

Tell me of Clare, do write me of her! This is written with
the other in desperate haste. I have received a letter from
you, one from Jane, and none from Hunt.

This letter reached Mary at about the same
time as the fatal news. Trelawny also sent her
his narrative of the facts (now so well known to
every one) of Byron's death. It had been intended for Hobhouse, but the writer changed his
mind and entrusted it to Mrs. Shelley instead,
adding, "Hunt may pick something at it if he
please."

Trelawny had been Byron's friend, and clearly
as he saw the Pilgrim's faults and deficiencies,
there would seem no doubt that he genuinely
admired him, in spite of all. But his mercurial,
impulsive temperament, ever in extremes, was

liable to the most sudden revulsions of feeling, and
retrospect hardened his feeling as much as it
softened Mary Shelley's towards the great man
who was gone.   Only four months later he was
writing again, from Livadia—

I have much to say to you, Mary, both as regards myself
and the part I am enacting here.   I would give much that I
could, as in times dead, look in on you in the evening of every
day and consult with you on its occurrences, as I used to do
in Italy.   It is curious, but, considering our characters, natural
enough, that Byron and I took the diametrically opposite
roads in Greece—I in Eastern, he in Western.   He took part
with, and became the paltry tool of the weak, imbecile,
cowardly being calling himself Prince Mavrocordato.   Five
months he dozed away.   By the gods! the lies that are said
in his praise urge one to speak the truth.   It is well for his
name, and better for Greece, that he is dead.   With the aid
of his name, his fame, his talents, and his fortune, he might
have been a tower of strength to Greece, instead of which the
little he did was in favour of the aristocrats, to destroy the
republic, and smooth the road for a foreign King.   But he is
dead, and I now feel my face burn with shame that so weak
and ignoble a soul could so long have influenced me.   It is a
degrading reflection, and ever will be.   I wish he had lived a
little longer, that he might have witnessed how I would have
soared above him here, how I would have triumphed over
his mean spirit.   I would do much to see and talk to you, but
as I am now too much irritated to disclose the real state of
things, I will not mislead you by false statements.

With this fine flourish was enclosed a "Description of the Cavern Fortress of Mount
Parnassus," which he was commanding (and of
which a full account is given in his *Recollections*),
and then followed a P.S. to this effect—

DEAR MARY—Will you make an article of this, as Leigh
Hunt calls it, and request his brother to publish it in the
Examiner, which will very much oblige me.

FROM MARY SHELLEY TO TRELAWNY.

28th July 1824.

So, dear Trelawny, you remember still poor Mary Shelley;
thank you for your remembrance, and a thousand times for
your kind letter.   It is delightful to feel that absence does not
diminish your affection, excellent, warm-hearted friend, remnant
of our happy days, of my vagabond life in beloved Italy, our
companion in prosperity, our comforter in sorrow.   You will
not wonder that the late loss of Lord Byron makes me cling
with greater zeal to those dear friends who remain to me.   He
could hardly be called a friend, but, connected with him in a
thousand ways, admiring his talents, and (with all his faults)
feeling affection for him, it went to my heart when, the other
day, the hearse that contained his lifeless form—a form of
beauty which in life I often delighted to behold—passed my
windows going up Highgate Hill on his last journey to the last
seat of his ancestors.   Your account of his last moments was
infinitely interesting to me.   Going about a fortnight ago to
the house where his remains lay, I found there Fletcher and
Lega—Lega looking a most preposterous rogue,—Fletcher I
expect to call on me when he returns from Nottingham.
From a few words he imprudently let fall, it would seem that
his Lord spoke of Clare in his last moments, and of his wish to
do something for her, at a time when his mind, vacillating between consciousness and delirium, would not permit him to do
anything.   Did Fletcher mention this to you?   It seems that
this doughty Leporello speaks of his Lord to strangers with the
highest respect; more than he did a year ago,—the best, the
most generous, the most wronged of peers,—the notion of his
leading an irregular life,—quite a false one.   Lady B. sent for
Fletcher; he found her in a fit of passionate grief, but perfectly
implacable, and as much resolved never to have united herself

again to him as she was when she first signed their separation.
Mrs. Claremont (the governess) was with her.

His death, as you may guess, made a great sensation here,
which was not diminished by the destruction of his Memoirs,
which he wrote and gave to Moore, and which were burned by
Mrs. Leigh and Hobhouse. There was not much in them, I
know, for I read them some years ago at Venice, but the
world fancied it was to have a confession of the hidden feelings
of one concerning whom they were always passionately curious.
Moore was by no means pleased : he is now writing a life of
him himself, but it is conjectured that, notwithstanding he had
the MS. so long in his possession, he never found time to
read it. I breakfasted with him about a week ago, and he is
anxious to get materials for his work. I showed him your
letter on the subject of Lord Byron's death, and he wishes very
much to obtain from you any anecdote or account you would
like to send. If you know anything that ought to be known,
or feel inclined to detail anything that you may remember
worthy of record concerning him, perhaps you will communicate with Moore. You have often said that you wished to
keep up our friend's name in the world, and if you still entertain the same feeling, no way is more obvious than to assist
Moore, who asked me to make this request. You can write
to him through me or addressed to Longmans. . . .

Here then we are, Jane and I, in Kentish Town. . . . We
live near each other now, and, seeing each other almost daily,
for ever dwell on one subject. . . . The country about here is
really pretty ; lawny uplands, wooded parks, green lanes, and
gentle hills form agreeable and varying combinations. If we
had orange sunsets, cloudless noons, fireflies, large halls, etc.
etc., I should not find the scenery amiss, and yet I can attach
myself to nothing here ; neither among the people, though
some are good and clever, nor to the places, though they be
pretty. Jane is my chosen companion and only friend. I
am under a cloud, and cannot form near acquaintances among
that class whose manners and modes of life are agreeable to

me, and I think myself fortunate in having one or two pleasing
acquaintances among literary people, whose society I enjoy
without dreaming of friendship.   My child is in excellent
health ; a fine, tall, handsome boy.

And then for money and the rest of those necessary annoyances, the means of getting at the necessaries of life ; Jane's
affairs are yet unsettled. . . . . . .

My prospects are somewhat brighter than they were.   I
have little doubt but that in the course of a few months I shall
have an independent income of £300 or £400 per annum
during Sir Timothy's life, and that with small sacrifice on my
part.   After his death Shelley's will secures me an income
more than sufficient for my simple habits.

One of my first wishes in obtaining the independence I
mention, will be to assist in freeing Clare from her present
painful mode of life.   She is now at Moscow ; sufficiently uncomfortable, poor girl, unless some change has taken place : I
think it probable that she will soon return to England.   Her
spirits will have been improved by the information I sent her
that his family consider Shelley's will valid, and that she may
rely upon receiving the legacy. . . .

But Mary's hopes of better fortune were again
and again deferred, and she now found that any
concession on the part of her husband's family
must be purchased by the suppression of his later
poems.   She was too poor to do other than
submit.

MARY SHELLEY TO LEIGH HUNT.

KENTISH TOWN, 22d *August* 1824.

. . . A negotiation has begun between Sir Timothy Shelley
and myself, by which, on sacrificing a small part of my future
expectations on the will, I shall ensure myself a sufficiency for
the present, and not only that, but be able, I hope, to relieve

Clare from her disagreeable situation at Moscow.   I have been
obliged, however, as an indispensable preliminary, to suppress
the posthumous poems.   More than 300 copies had been sold,
so this is the less provoking, and I have been obliged to promise not to bring dear Shelley's name before the public again
during Sir Timothy's life.   There is no great harm in this,
since he is above seventy; and, from choice, I should not
think of writing memoirs now, and the materials for a volume
of more works are so scant that I doubted before whether I
could publish it.   Such is the folly of the world, and so do
things seem different from what they are; since, from Whitton's
account, Sir Timothy writhes under the fame of his incomparable son, as if it were the most grievous injury done to him;
and so, perhaps, after all it will prove.

All this was pending when I wrote last, but until I was certain I did not think it worth while to mention it.   The affair is
arranged by Peacock, who, though I seldom see him, seems
anxious to do me all these kind of services in the best manner
that he can.

It is long since I saw your brother, nor had he any news
for me.   I lead a most quiet life, and see hardly any one.
The Gliddons are gone to Hastings for a few weeks.   Hogg is
on Circuit.   Now that he is rich he is so very queer, so un-
amiable, and so strange, that I look forward to his return
without any desire of shortening the term of absence.

Poor Pierino is now in London, *Non fosse male questo paese*,
he says, *se vi vedesse mai il sole.*   He is full of Greece, to which
he is going, and gave us an account of our good friend, Trelawny, which was that he was not at all changed.   Trelawny
has made a hero of the Greek chief, Ulysses, and declares that
there is a great cavern in Attica which he and Ulysses have
provisioned for seven years, and to which, if the cause fails, he
and this chieftain are to retire; but if the cause is triumphant,
he is to build a city in the Negropont, colonise it, and Jane
and I are to go out to be queens and chieftainesses of the island.
When he first came to Athens he took to a Turkish life, bought
twelve or fifteen women, *brutti mostri*, Pierino says, one a

Moor, of all things, and there he lay on his sofa, smoking, these gentle creatures about him, till he got heartily sick of idleness, shut them up in his harem, and joined and combated with Ulysses. . . .

.   .   .   .

One of my principal reasons for writing just now is that I have just heard Miss Curran's address (64 Via Sistina, Roma), and I am anxious that Marianne should (if she will be so very good) send one of the profiles already cut to her, of Shelley, since I think that, by the help of that, Miss Curran will be able to correct her portrait of Shelley, and make for us what we so much desire—a good likeness. I am convinced that Miss Curran will return the profile immediately that she has done with it, so that you will not sacrifice it, though you may be the means of our obtaining a good likeness.

Journal, September 3.—With what hopes did I come to England? I pictured little of what was pleasurable, the feeling I had could not be called hope; it was expectation. Yet at that time, now a year ago, what should I have said if a prophet had told me that, after the whole revolution of the year, I should be as poor in all estimable treasures as when I arrived.

I have only seen two persons from whom I have hoped or wished for friendly feeling. One, a poet, who sought me first, whose voice, laden with sentiment, passed as Shelley's, and who read with the same deep feeling as he; whose gentle manners were pleasing, and who seemed to a degree pleased; who once or twice listened to my sad plaints, and bent his dark blue eyes upon me. Association, gratitude, esteem, made me take interest in his long, though rare, visits.

The other was kind; sought me, was pleased with me. I could talk to him; that was much. He was attached to another, so that I felt at my ease with him. They have disappeared from my horizon. Jane alone remains; if she loved me as well as I do her it would be much; she is all gentleness, and she is my only consolation, yet she does not console me.

I have just completed my twenty-seventh year ; at such a time hope and youth are still in their prime, and the pains I feel, therefore, are ever alive and vivid within me. What shall I do? Nothing. I study, that passes the time. I write; at times that pleases me, though double sorrow comes when I feel that Shelley no longer reads and approves of what I write ; besides, I have no great faith in my success. Composition is delightful; but if you do not expect the sympathy of your fellow-creatures in what you write, the pleasure of writing is of short duration.

I have my lovely Boy, without him I could not live. I have Jane ; in her society I forget time ; but the idea of it does not cheer me in my griefful moods. It is strange that the religious feeling that exalted my emotions in happiness, deserts me in my misery. I have little enjoyment, no hope. I have given myself ten years more of life. God grant that they may not be augmented. I should be glad that they were curtailed. Loveless beings surround me; they talk of my personal attractions, of my talents, my manners.

The wisest and best have loved me. The beautiful, and glorious, and noble, have looked on me with the divine expression of love, till death, the reaper, carried to his overstocked barns my lamented harvest.

But now I am not loved! Never, oh, never more shall I love. Synonymous to such words are, never more shall I be happy, never more feel life sit triumphant in my frame. I am a wreck. By what do the fragments cling together? Why do they not part, to be borne away by the tide to the boundless ocean, where those are whom day and night I pray that I may rejoin.

I shall be happier, perhaps, in Italy ; yet, when I sometimes think that she is the murderess, I tremble for my boy. We shall see ; if no change comes, I shall be unable to support the burthen of time, and no change, if it hurt not his dear head, can be for the worse.

In the month of July Mary had received an-

other request for literary help; this time from
Medwin, who wanted her aid in eking out and
correcting his notes of conversations with Lord
Byron, shortly to be published.

"You must have been, as I was, very much affected with
poor Lord Byron's death," he wrote to Mary. "All parties
seem now writing in his favour, and the papers are full of his
praise. . . .

"How do you think I have been employing myself? With
writing; and the subject I have chosen has been Memoirs of
Lord Byron. Every one here has been disappointed in the
extreme by the destruction of his private biography, and have
urged me to give the world the little I know of him. I wish
I was better qualified for the task. When I was at Pisa I·
made very copious notes of his conversations, for private reference only, and was surprised to find on reading them (which I
have never done till his death, and hearing that his life had
been burnt) that they contained so many anecdotes of his life.
During many nights that we sat up together he was very con-
fidential, and entered into his history and opinions on most
subjects, and from them I have compiled a volume which is, I
am told, highly entertaining. Shelley I have made a very pro-
minent feature in the work, and I think you will be pleased
with that part, at least, of the Memoir, and all the favourable
sentiments of Lord Byron concerning him. But I shall certainly not publish the work till you have seen it, and would
give the world to consult you in person about the whole; you
might be of the greatest possible use to me, and prevent many
errors from creeping in. I have been told it cannot fail of
having the greatest success, and have been offered £500 for it
—a large and tempting sum—in consequence of what has been
said in its praise by Grattan. . . .

"Before deciding finally on the publication there are many
things to be thought of. Lady Byron will not be pleased with
my account of the marriage and separation; in fact, I shall be

assailed on all sides. Now, my dear friend, what do you advise? Let me have your full opinion, for I mean to be guided by it. I hear to-day that Moore is manufacturing five or six volumes out of the *burnt materials*, for which Longman advanced £2000, and is to pay £2000 more; *they* will be in a great rage. If I publish, promptitude is everything, so that I know you will answer this soon."

The idea of entertaining the world, however, highly, at whatever price, with "tit-bits" from the private life and after-dinner talk of her late intimate friends, almost before those friends were cold in their graves, did not find favour with Mrs. Shelley. As an excuse for declining to have any hand in this work, she gave her own desire to avoid publicity or notice. In a later letter Medwin assured her that her name was not even mentioned in the book. He frankly owned that most of his knowledge of Byron had been derived from her and Shelley, but added, by way of excuse—

They tell me it is highly interesting, and there is at this moment a longing after and impatience to know something about the most extraordinary man of the age that must give my book a considerable success.

What Mary felt about this publication can be gathered from her allusion to it in the following letter—

MRS. SHELLEY TO MRS. HUNT.

KENTISH TOWN, 10*th October* 1824.

. . . I write to you on the most dismal of all days, a rainy Sunday, when dreary church-going faces look still more drearily from under dripping umbrellas, and the poor plebeian dame looks reproachfully at her splashed white stockings,—not her gown,—that has been warily held high up, and the to-be-concealed petticoat has borne all the ill-usage of the mud. Dismal though it is, dismal though I am, I do not wish to write a discontented letter, but in a few words to describe things as they are with me. A weekly visit to the Strand, a monthly visit to Shacklewell (when we are sure to be caught in the rain) forms my catalogue of visits. I have no visitors; if it were not for Jane I should be quite alone. The eternal rain imprisons one in one's little room, and one's spirits flag without one exhilarating circumstance. In some things, however, I am better off than last year, for I do not doubt but that in the course of a few months I shall have an independence; and I no longer balance, as I did last winter, between Italy and England. My Father wished me to stay, and, old as he is, and wishing as one does to be of some use somewhere, I thought that I would make the trial, and stay if I could. But the joke has become too serious. I look forward to the coming winter with horror, but it *shall be* the last. I have not yet made up my mind to the where in Italy. I shall, if possible, immediately on arriving, push on to Rome. Then we shall see. I read, study, and write; sometimes that takes me out of myself; but to live for no one, to be necessary to none, to know that "Where is now my hope? for my hope, who shall see it? They shall go down to the base of the pit, when our rest together is in the dust." But change of scene and the sun of Italy will restore my energy; the very thought of it smooths my brow. Perhaps I shall seek the heats of Naples, if they do not hurt my darling Percy. And now, what news? . . .

.   .   .   .

Hazlitt is abroad; he will be in Italy in the winter; he wrote an article in the *Edinburgh Review* on the volume of poems I published. I do not know whether he meant it to be favourable or not; I do not like it at all; but when I saw him I could not be angry. I never was so shocked in my life, he has become so thin, his hair scattered, his cheek-bones projecting; but for his voice and smile I should not have known him; his smile brought tears into my eyes, it was like a sunbeam illuminating the most melancholy of ruins, lightning that assured you in a dark night of the identity of a friend's ruined and deserted abode. . . .

Have you, my Polly, sent a profile to Miss Curran in Rome? Now pray do, and pray write; do, my dear girl. Next year by this time I shall, perhaps, be on my way to you; it will go hard but that I contrive to spend a week (that is, if you wish) at Florence, on my way to the Eternal City. God send that this prove not an airy castle; but I own that I put faith in my having money before that; and I know that I could not, if I would, endure the torture of my English life longer than is absolutely necessary. By the bye, I heard that you are keeping your promise to Trelawny, and that in due time he will be blessed with a namesake. How is *Occhi Turchini*, Thornton the reformed, Johnny the—what Johnny? the good boy? Mary the merry, Irving the sober, Percy the martyr, and dear Sylvan the good?

Percy is quite well; tell his friend he goes to school and learns to read and write, being very handy with his hands, perhaps having a pure anticipated cognition of the art of painting in his tiny fingers. Mrs. Williams' little girl, who calls herself Dina, is his wife. Poor Clare, at Moscow! at least she will be independent one day, and if I am so soon, her situation will be quickly ameliorated.

Have you heard of Medwin's book? Notes of conversations which he had with Lord Byron (when tipsy); every one is to be in it; every one will be angry. He wanted me to have a hand in it, but I declined. Years ago, when a man died, the worms ate him; now a new set of worms feed on the carcase of the scandal he leaves behind him, and grow fat upon the world's love of tittle-tattle. I will not be numbered among them. Have you received the volume of poems? Give my love to "Very," and so, dear, very patient, Adieu.—
Yours affectionately,   MARY SHELLEY.

Journal, October 26.—Time rolls on, and what does it bring? What can I do? How change my destiny? Months change their names, years their cyphers. My brow is sadly trenched, the blossom of youth faded. My mind gathers wrinkles. What will become of me?

How long it is since an emotion of joy filled my once exulting heart, or beamed from my once bright eyes. I am young still, though age creeps on apace; but I may not love any but the dead. I think that an emotion of joy would destroy me, so strange would it be to my withered heart. Shelley had said—

> Lift not the painted veil which men call life.

Mine is not painted; dark and enshadowed, it curtains out all happiness, all hope. Tears fill my eyes; well may I weep, solitary girl! The dead know you not; the living heed you not. You sit in your lone room, and the howling wind, gloomy prognostic of winter, gives not forth so despairing a tone as the unheard sighs your ill-fated heart breathes.

I was loved once! still let me cling to the memory; but to live for oneself alone, to read, and communicate your reflections to none; to write, and be cheered by none; to weep, and in no bosom; no more on thy bosom, my Shelley, to spend my tears—this is misery!

Such is the Alpha and Omega of my tale. I can speak to none. Writing this is useless; it does not even soothe me; on the contrary, it irritates me by showing the pitiful expedient to which I am reduced.

I have been a year in England, and, ungentle England, for what have I to thank you? For disappointment, melancholy, and tears; for unkindness, a bleeding heart, and despairing thoughts. I wish, England, to associate but one idea with thee—immeasurable distance and insurmountable barriers, so that I never, never might breathe thine air more.

Beloved Italy! you are my country, my hope, my heaven!

December 3.—I endeavour to rouse my fortitude and calm my mind by high and philosophic thoughts, and my studies aid this endeavour. I have pondered for hours on Cicero's description of that power of virtue in the human mind which render's man's frail being superior to fortune.

"Eadem ratio habet in re quiddam amplum at que magnificum ad imperandum magis quam ad parendum accommodatum; omnia humana non tolerabilia solum sed etiam levia ducens; altum quiddam et excelsum, nihil temens, nemini cedens, semper invictum."

What should I fear? To whom cede? By whom be conquered?

Little truly have I to fear. One only misfortune can touch me. That must be the last, for I should sink under it. At the age of seven and twenty, in the busy metropolis of native England, I find myself alone. The struggle is hard that can give rise to misanthropy in one, like me, attached to my fellow-creatures. Yet now, did not the memory of those matchless lost ones redeem their race, I should learn to hate men, who are strong only to oppress, moral only to insult. Oh ye winged hours that fly fast, that, having first destroyed my happiness, now bear my swift-departing youth with you, bring patience, wisdom, and content! I will not stoop to the world, or become like those who compose it, and be actuated by mean pursuits and petty ends. I will endeavour to remain unconquered by hard and bitter fortune; yet the tears that start in my eyes show pangs she inflicts upon me.

So much for philosophising. Shall I ever be a philosopher?

CHAPTER XX

AT the beginning of 1825 Mrs. Shelley's worldly affairs were looking somewhat more hopeful. The following extract is from a letter to Miss Curran, dated 2d January—

. . . I have now better prospects than I had, or rather, a better reality, for my prospects are sufficiently misty. I receive now £200 a year from my Father-in-law, but this in so strange and embarrassed a manner that, as yet, I hardly know what to make of it. I do not believe, however, that he would object to my going abroad, as I daresay he considers that the first step towards kingdom come, whither, doubtless, he prays that an interloper like me may speedily be removed. I talk, therefore, of going next autumn, and shall be grateful to any power, divine or human, that assists me to leave this desert country. Mine I cannot call it; it is too unkind to me.

What you say of my Shelley's picture is beyond words interesting to me. How good you are! Send it, I pray you, for perhaps I cannot come, and, at least, it would be a blessing to receive it a few months earlier. I am afraid you can do nothing about the cameo. As you say, it were worth nothing, unless like; but I fancied that it might be accomplished under your directions. Would it be asking too much to lend me the copy you took of my darling William's portrait, since

mine is somewhat injured? But from both together I could
get a nice copy made.

You may imagine that I see few people, so far from the
centre of bustling London ; but, in truth, I found that even
in town, poor, undinner-giving as I was, I could not dream of
society. It was a great confinement for Percy, and I could
not write in the midst of smoke, noise, and streets. I live
here very quietly, going once a week to the Strand. My chief
dependence for society is on Mrs. Williams, who lives at no
great distance. As to theatres, etc., how can a "lone woman"
think of such things? No ; the pleasures and luxuries of life
await me in divine Italy ; but here, privation, solitude, and
desertion are my portion. What a change for me ! But I
must not think of that. I contrive to live on as I am ; but
to recur to the past and compare it with the present is to
deluge me in grief and tears.

My Boy is well; a fine tall fellow, and as good as I can
possibly expect ; he is improved in looks since he came here.
Clare is in Moscow still, not very pleasantly situated ; but she
is in a situation, and being now well in health, waits with more
patience for better times. The Godwins go on as usual. My
Father, though harassed, is in good health, and is employed in
the second volume of the *Commonwealth*.

The weather here is astonishingly mild, but the rain continual ; half England is under water, and the damage done at
seaports from storms incalculable. In Rome, doubtless, it
has been different. Rome, dear name ! I cannot tell why,
but to me there is something enchanting in that spot. I have
another friend there, the Countess Guiccioli, now unhappy
and mournful from the death of Lord Byron. Poor girl ! I
sincerely pity her, for she truly loved him, and I cannot think
that she can endure an Italian after him. You have there
also a Mr. Taaffe, a countryman of yours, who translates
Dante, and rides fine horses that perpetually throw him. He
knew us all very well.

The English have had many a dose of scandal. First poor
dear Lord Byron, from whom, now gone, many a poor devil

of an author is now fearless of punishment, then Mr. Fauntleroy, then Miss Foote ; these are now dying away.   The fame
of Mr. Fauntleroy, indeed, has not survived him ; that of
Lord Byron bursts forth every now and then afresh ; whilst
Miss Foote smokes most dismally still.   Then we have had
our quantum of fires and misery, and the poor exiled Italians
and Spaniards have added famine to the list of evils.   A
subscription, highly honourable to the poor and middle classes
who subscribed their mite, has relieved them.

Will you write soon ?   How much delight I anticipate this
spring on the arrival of the picture !   In all thankfulness,
faithfully yours,   MARY W. SHELLEY.

The increase of allowance, from £100 to £200,
had not been actually granted at the beginning of
the year, but it appeared so probable an event
that, thanks partly to the good offices of Mr.
Peacock, Sir Timothy's lawyers agreed, while the
matter was pending, to advance Mrs. Shelley the
extra £100 on their own responsibility.   The
concession was not so great as it looks, for all
money allowed to her was only advanced subject
to an agreement that every penny was to be repaid, with interest, to Sir Timothy's executors
at the time when, according to Percy Bysshe
Shelley's will, she should come into the property ;
and every cheque was endorsed by her to this
effect.   But her immediate anxieties were in some
measure relieved by this addition to her income.
Not, indeed, that it set her free from pressing
money cares, for the ensuing letter to Leigh Hunt
incidentally shows that her father was a perpetual

drain on her resources, that there was every probability of her having to support him partly—at
times entirely—in the future, and that she was
endeavouring, with Peacock's help, to raise a large
sum, on loan, to meet these possible emergencies.

The main subject of the letter is an article of
Hunt's about Shelley, the proof of which had
been sent to Mary to read. It contained, in an
extended form, the substance of that biographical
notice, originally intended for a preface to the
volume of Posthumous Poems.

Mrs. Shelley to Leigh Hunt.

8th April 1825.

My dear Hunt—I have just finished reading your article
upon Shelley. It is with great diffidence that I write to thank
you for it, because perceiving plainly that you think that I
have forfeited all claim on your affection, you may deem my
thanks an impertinent intrusion. But from my heart I thank
you. You may imagine that it has moved me deeply. Of
course this very article shows how entirely you have cast me
out from any corner in your affections. And from various
causes—none dishonourable to me—I cannot help wishing
that I could have received your goodwill and kindness, which
I prize, and have ever prized ; but you have a feeling, I had
almost said a prejudice, against me, which makes you construe
foreign matter into detraction against me (I allude to the, to
me, deeply afflicting idea you got upon some vague expression
communicated to you by your brother), and insensible to any
circumstances that might be pleaded for me. But I will not
dwell on this. The sun shines, and I am striving so hard for
a continuation of the gleams of pleasure that visit my intolerable state of regret for the loss of beloved companionship

during cloudless days, that I will dash away the springing tears and make one or two necessary observations on your article.

I have often heard our Shelley relate the story of stabbing an upper boy with a fork, but never as you relate it. He always described it, in my hearing, as being an almost involuntary act, done on the spur of anguish, and that he made the stab as the boy was going out of the room. Shelley did not allow Harriet half his income. She received £200 a year. Mr. Westbrook had always made his daughter an allowance, even while she lived with Shelley, which of course was continued to her after their separation. I think if I were near you, I could readily persuade you to omit all allusion to Clare. After the death of Lord Byron, in the thick of memoirs, scandal, and turning up of old stories, she has never been alluded to, at least in any work I have seen. You mention (having been obliged to return your MS. to Bowring, I quote from memory) an article in *Blackwood*, but I hardly think that this is of date subsequent to our miserable loss. In fact, poor Clare has been buried in entire oblivion, and to bring her from this, even for the sake of defending her, would, I am sure, pain her greatly, and do her mischief. Would you permit this part to be erased? I have, without waiting to ask your leave, requested Messrs. Bowring to leave out your mention that the remains of dearest Edward were brought to England. Jane still possesses this treasure, and has once or twice been asked by his mother-in-law about it,—once an urn was sent. Consequently she is very anxious that her secret should be kept, and has allowed it to be believed that the ashes were deposited with Shelley's at Rome. Such, my dear Hunt, are all the alterations I have to suggest, and I lose no time in communicating them to you. They are too trivial for me to apologise for the liberty, and I hope that you will agree with me in what I say about Clare—Allegra no more—she at present absent and forgotten. On Sir Timothy's death she will come in for a legacy which may enable her to enter into society,—perhaps to marry, if she wishes it, if the past be forgotten.

I forget whether such things are recorded by "Galignani," or, if recorded, whether you would have noticed it. My Father's complicated annoyances, brought to their height by the failure of a very promising speculation and the loss of an impossible-to-be-lost law-suit, have ended in a bankruptcy, the various acts of which drama are now in progress; that over, nothing will be left to him but his pen and me. He is so full of his *Commonwealth* that in the midst of every anxiety he writes every day now, and in a month or two will have completed the second volume, and I am employed in raising money necessary for my maintenance, and in which he must participate. This will drain me pretty dry for the present, but (as the old women say) if I live, I shall have more than enough for him and me, and recur, at least to some part of my ancient style of life, and feel of some value to others. Do not, however, mistake my phraseology; I shall not live with my Father, but return to Italy and economise, the moment God and Mr. Whitton will permit. My Percy is quite well, and has exchanged his constant winter occupation of drawing for playing in the fields (which are now useful as well as ornamental), flying kites, gardening, etc. I bask in the sun on the grass reading Virgil, that is, my beloved *Georgics* and Lord Shaftesbury's *Characteristics*. I begin to live again, and as the maids of Greece sang joyous hymns on the revival of Adonis, does my spirit lift itself in delightful thanksgiving on the awakening of nature.

Lamb is superannuated—do you understand? as Madame says. He has left the India House on two-thirds of his income, and become a gentleman at large—a delightful consummation. What a strange taste it is that confines him to a view of the New River, with houses opposite, in Islington! I saw the Novellos the other day. Mary and her new babe are well; he, Vincent all over, fat and flourishing moreover, and she dolorous that it should be her fate to add more than her share to the population of the world. How are all yours —Henry and the rest? Percy still remembers him, though occupied by new friendships and the feelings incident to his state of matrimony, having taken for better and worse to wife Mrs. Williams' little girl.

I suppose you will receive with these letters Bessy's new book, which she has done very well indeed, and forms with the other a delightful prize for plant and flower worshippers, those favourites of God, which enjoy beauty unequalled and the tranquil pleasures of growth and life, bestowing incalculable pleasure, and never giving or receiving pain. Have you seen Hazlitt's notes of his travels? He is going over the same road that I have travelled twice. He surprised me by calling the road from Susa to Turin dull; there, where the Alps sink into low mountains and romantic hills, topped by ruined castles, watered by brawling streams, clothed by magnificent walnut trees; there, where I wrote to you in a fit of enchantment, exalted by the splendid scene; but I remembered, first, that he travelled in winter, when snow covers all; and, besides, he went from what I approached, and looked at the plain of Lombardy with the back of the diligence between him and the loveliest scene in nature; so much can *relation* alter circumstances.

Clare is still, I believe, at Moscow. When I return to Italy I shall endeavour to enable her to go thither also. I shall not come without my Jane, who is now necessary to my existence almost. She has recourse to the cultivation of her mind, and amiable and dear as she ever was, she is in every way improved and become more valuable.

Trelawny is in the cave with Ulysses, not in Polypheme's cave, but in a vast cavern of Parnassus; inaccessible and healthy and safe, but cut off from the rest of the world. Trelawny has attached himself to the part of Ulysses, a savage chieftain, without any plan but personal independence and opposition to the Government. Trelawny calls him a hero. Ulysses speaks a word or two of French; Trelawny, no Greek! Pierino has returned to Greece.

Horace Smith has returned with his diminished family (little Horace is dead). He already finds London too expensive, and they are about to migrate to Tunbridge Wells. He is very kind to me.

I long to hear from you, and I am more tenderly attached to you and yours than you imagine; love me a little, and make Marianne love me, as truly I think she does. Am I mistaken, Polly?—Your affectionate and obliged,

MARY W. SHELLEY.

Outwardly, this year was uneventful. Mary was busily working at her novel, *The Last Man*. The occupation was good for her, and perhaps it was no bad thing that Necessity should stand at her elbow to stimulate her to exertion when her interest and energy flagged. For, in spite of her utmost efforts to the contrary, her heart and spirit were often faint at the prospect of an arduous and lonely life. And when, in early autumn, Shelley's portrait was at last sent to her by Miss Curran, the sight of it brought back the sense of what she had lost, and revived in all its irrecoverable bitterness that past happy time, than to remember which in misery there is no greater sorrow.

Journal, September 17 (1825).—Thy picture is come, my only one! Thine those speaking eyes, that animated look; unlike aught earthly wert thou ever, and art now!

If thou hadst still lived, how different had been my life and feelings!

Thou art near to guard and save me, angelic one! Thy divine glance will be my protection and defence. I was not worthy of thee, and thou hast left me; yet that dear look assures me that thou wert mine, and recalls and narrates to my backward-looking mind a long tale of love and happiness.

My head aches. My heart—my hapless heart—is deluged in bitterness. Great God! if there be any pity for human suffering, tell me what I am to do. I strive to study, I strive to write, but I cannot live without loving and being loved, without sympathy ; if this is denied to me I must die.   Would that the hour were come !

On the same day when Mary penned these melancholy lines, Trelawny was writing to her from Cephalonia.

He had been treacherously shot by an inmate of his mountain fortress, an Englishman newly arrived, whom he had welcomed as a guest.   The true instigator of the crime was one Fenton, a Scotchman, who in the guise of a volunteer had ostensibly served under Trelawny for a twelve-month past, and who by his capability and apparent zeal had so won his confidence as to be entrusted with secret missions.   He was, in fact, an emissary of the Greek Government, foisted on Trelawny at Missolonghi to act as a spy on Odysseus, the insurgent Greek chieftain.

Through his machinations Odysseus was betrayed and murdered, and Trelawny narrowly escaped death.

TRELAWNY TO MRS. SHELLEY.

CEPHALONIA, 17th September 1825.

DEAR MARY—I have just escaped from Greece and landed here, in the hopes of patching up my broken frame and shattered constitution.   Two musket balls, fired at the distance of two paces, struck me and passed through my framework, which damn'd near finished me ; but 'tis a long story, and my writing arm is rendered unfit for service, and I am yet unpractised with the left.   But a friend of mine here, a Major

Bacon, is on his way to England, and will enlighten you as to me. I shall be confined here some time. Write to me then at this place. I need rest and quiet, for I am shook to the foundation. Love to Jane and Clare, and believe me still your devoted friend, EDWARD TRELAWNY.

It would seem that this letter was many months in reaching Mary, for in February 1826 she was writing to him in these terms—

I hear at last that Mr. Hodges has letters for me, and that prevents a thousand things I was about to say concerning the pain your very long silence had occasioned me. Consider, dear friend, that your last was in April, so that nearly a year has gone by, and not only did I not hear *from* you, but until the arrival of Mr. Hodges, many months had elapsed since I had heard of you.

Sometimes I flattered myself that the foundations of my little habitation would have been shaken by a "ship Shelley ahoy" that even Jane, distant a mile, would have heard. That dear hope lost, I feared a thousand things.

Hamilton Browne's illness, the death of many English, the return of every other from Greece, filled me with gloomy apprehensions.

But you live,—what kind of life your letters will, I trust, inform me,—what possible kind of life in a cavern surrounded by precipices,—inaccessible ! All this will satisfy your craving imagination. The friendship you have for Odysseus, does that satisfy your warm heart ? . . . I gather from your last letter and other intelligence that you think of marrying the daugther of your favourite chief, and thus will renounce England and even the English for ever. And yet,—no ! you love some of us, I am sure, too much to forget us, even if you neglect us for a while ; but truly, I long for your letters, which will tell all. And remember, dear friend, it is about yourself I am anxious. Of Greece I read in the papers. I see many informants, but I can learn your actions, hopes, and, above all valuable to me, the continuation of your affection for me, from your letters only.

.   .   .   .

27th February.

I now close my letter—I have not yet received yours.

Last night Jane and I went with Gamba and my Father to see Kean in *Othello*. This play, as you may guess, reminded us of you. Do you remember, when delivering the killing news, you awoke Jane, as Othello awakens Desdemona from her sleep on the sofa? Kean, abominably supported, acted divinely; put as he is on his mettle by recent events and a full house and applause, which he deserved, his farewell is the most pathetic piece of acting to be imagined. Yet, my dear friend, I wish we had seen it represented as was talked of at Pisa. Iago would never have found a better representative than that strange and wondrous creature whom one regrets daily more,—for who here can equal him? Adieu, dear Trelawny, take care of yourself, and come and visit us as soon as you can escape from the sorceries of Ulysses.—In all truth, yours affectionately,   M. W. S.

At Pisa, 1822, Lord Byron talked vehemently of our getting up a play in his great hall at the Lanfranchi; it was to be *Othello*. He cast the characters thus: Byron, Iago; Trelawny, Othello; Williams, Cassio; Medwin, Roderigo; Mrs. Shelley, Desdemona; Mrs. Williams, Emilia. "Who is to be our audience?" I asked. "All Pisa," he rejoined. He recited a great portion of his part with great gusto; it exactly suited him,—he looked it, too.

All this time Miss Clairmont was pursuing her vocation as a governess in Russia, and many interesting glimpses into Russian family and social life are afforded by her letters to Mrs. Shelley and Mrs. Williams. She was a voluminous letter-writer, and in these characteristic epistles she unconsciously paints, as no other hand could have done, a vivid portrait of herself. We can see her, with all her vivacity, versatility, and resource, her great cleverness,— never at a loss for a word, an excuse, or a good story,—her indefatigable energy, her shifting moods and wild caprices, the bewildering activity of her restless brain, and the astonishing facility with which she transferred to paper all her passing impressions. In narration, in description, in panegyric, and in complaint she is equally fluent. Unimpeachably correct as her conduct always was after her one miserable adventure, she had, from first to last, an innate affinity for anything in the shape of social gossip and scandal ; her really generous impulses were combined with the worldliest of worldly wisdom, and the whole tinctured with the highest of high-flown sentiment.

Fill in the few details wanting, the flat, sleek, black hair,— eyes so black that the pupil was hardly to be distinguished from the iris (eyes which seemed unmistakably to indicate an admixture of Portuguese, if not of African, blood in her descent),—a complexion which may in girlhood have been olive, but in later life was sallow,— features not beautiful, and depending on expression for any charm they might have,—and she stands before the reader, the unmanageable,

amusing, runaway schoolgirl; a stumbling-block
first, then a bugbear, to Byron; a curse, which
he persistently treated as a blessing, to Shelley;
a thorn in the side of Mary and of every one who
ever was responsible for her; yet liked by her
acquaintance, admired in society, commiserated
by her early friends, and regarded with well-
deserved affection and gratitude by many of her
pupils and *protégés*.

CLARE TO JANE.

Moscow, *27th October* 1825.

MY DEAREST JANE—It is now so long since I heard from you
that I begin to think you have quite forgotten me. I wrote twice
to you during the summer; both letters went by private hand,
and to neither of which have I received your answer. I enclosed also a letter or letters for Trelawny, and I hope very
much you have received them. Whenever some time elapses
without hearing from England, then I begin to grow miserable
with fear. In a letter I received from Mary in the autumn,
she mentions the approaching return of the Hunts from Italy,
and I console myself with believing that you are both so much
taken up with them that you have delayed from day to day to
write to me. Be that as it may, I have never been in greater
need of your letters than for these last two months, for I have
been truly wretched. To convince you that I am not given
to fret for trifles, I will tell you how they have been passed.
I spent a very quiet time, if not a very agreeable one, until
the 12th of August; then a French newspaper fell into my
hands, in which it mentioned that Trelawny had been danger-
ously wounded in a duel on the 13th of June. You who
have known the misery of anxiety for the safety and wellbeing of those dear to us may imagine what I suffered. At
last a letter from Mary came, under date of 26th of July, not

mentioning a word of this, and I allowed myself to hope that
it was not true, because certainly she would have heard of it
by the time she wrote. Then, a week after, another newspaper
mentioned his being recovered. This was scarcely passed
when our two children fell ill; one got better, but the other,
my pupil, a little girl of six years and a half old, died. I was
truly wretched at her loss, and our whole house was a scene
of sorrow and confusion, that can only happen in a savage
country, where a disciplined temper is utterly unknown. We
came to town, and directly the little boy fell sick again of a
putrid fever, from which he was in imminent danger for some
time. At last after nights and days of breathless anxiety he
did recover. By the death of the little girl, I became of little
or no use in the house, and the thought of again entering a
new house, and having to learn new dispositions, was quite
abhorrent to me. Nothing is so cruel as to change from
house to house and be perpetually surrounded by strangers;
one feels so forlorn, so utterly alone, that I could not have
the courage to begin the career over again; so I settled to
remain in the same house, to continue the boy's English, and
to give lessons out-of-doors. I do not know whether my plan
will succeed yet, but, at any rate, I am bent upon trying it.
It is not very agreeable to walk about in the snow and in a
cold of twenty, sometimes thirty degrees; but anything is
better than being a governess in the common run of Moscow
houses. But you have not yet heard my greatest sorrow, and
which I think might well have been spared. I had one
Englishwoman here, to whom I was attached—a woman of the
most generous heart, and whom misfortune, perhaps imprudence, had driven to Russia. She thought with me that
nothing can equal the misery of our situation, and accordingly
she went last spring to Odessa, hoping to find some means of
establishing a boarding-house in order to have a home. If
it succeeded, she was to have sent for me; but, however,
she wrote to me that, after well considering everything, she
found such a plan would not succeed, and that I might expect
her shortly in Moscow, to resume her old manner of life. I

expected her arrival daily, and began to grow uneasy, and at length some one wrote to another acquaintance of hers here that she had destroyed herself. I, who knew her thoughts, have no doubt the horror of entering again as governess made her resolve upon this as the only means to escape it. You see, dearest Jane, whether these last two months have been fruitful in woes. I cannot tell you what a consolation it would have been to have received a letter from you whilst I have been suffering under such extreme melancholy. The only amelioration in my present situation is that I can withdraw to my room and be much more alone than I could formerly, and this solitude is so friendly to my nature that it has been my only comfort. I have heard all about the change in my mother's situation, and am truly glad of it. I am sure she will be much better off than she was before. As for Mary, her affairs seem inexplicable. Nothing can ever persuade me that a will can dispose of estates which the maker of it never possessed. Do clear up this mystery to me. What a strange way of thinking must that be which can rely on such a hope! Yet my brother, my mother, and Mary never cease telling me that one day I shall be free, and the state of doubt, the contradiction between their assertions and my intimate persuasion of the contrary, that awakens in my mind, is very painful. You are almost quite silent upon the subject, but I wish, my dear Jane, that you would answer me the following questions. Has any professional man ever been consulted on the subject? What is Hogg's opinion? Why in this particular case should the law be set aside, which says that no man can dispose of what he has never possessed? Do have the goodness to ask these questions very clearly and to give me the answers, which no one has ever done yet. They simply tell me, " Whitton has come forward," " Whitton thinks the will valid," etc. etc., all of which cannot prove to me that it is so. I know you will excuse my giving you so much trouble, but really when you consider the painful uncertainty which hangs on my mind, you will think it very natural that I should wish to know the reasons of what is asserted to

me. To say the truth, I daily grow more indifferent about
the issue of the affair. The time is past when independence would have been an object of my desires, and I am now
old enough to know that misery is the universal malady of the
human race, and that there is no escaping from it, except by
a philosophic indifference to all external circumstances, and
by a disciplined mind completely absorbed in intellectual
subjects. I fashion my life accordingly to this, and I often
enjoy moments of serenest calm, which I owe to this way of
thinking. Do not mistake and think that I am indifferent to
seeing you again; so far from this, I dream of this as one
dreams of Paradise after death, as a thing of another world,
and not to be obtained here. It would be too much happiness for me to venture to hope it. I endeavour often to
imagine the circle in which you live, but it is impossible, and
I think it would be equally difficult for you to picture to
yourself my mode of life. I often think what in the world
Mary or Jane would do in the dull routine I tread; no talk
of public affairs, no talk of books, no subject do I ever hear
of except cards, eating, and the different manner of managing
slaves. Now and then some heroic young man devotes himself like a second Marcus Curtius to the public good, and, in
order to give the good ladies of Moscow something new to
talk of, rouses them from their lethargic gossipings by getting
himself shot in a duel; or some governess disputes with the
mother of her pupils, and what they both said goes over the
town. Mary mentioned in her last that she thought it very
likely you might both go to Paris. I hope you may be there,
for I am sure you would find the mode of life more cheerful
than London. As I have told you so many of my sorrows, I
must tell you the only good piece of news I have to communicate. I have lately made acquaintance with a German gentleman, who is a great resource to me. In such a country as
Russia, where nothing but ignorant people are to be met, a
cultivated mind is the greatest treasure. His society recalls
our former circle, for he is well versed in ancient and

modern literature, and has the same noble, enlarged way of
thinking.   You may imagine how delighted he was to find me
so different from everything around him, and capable of understanding what has been so long sealed up in his mind as treasures too precious to be wasted on the coarse Russian soil.   I
talk to you thus freely about him, because I know you will not
believe that I am in love, or that I have any other feeling
than a most sincere and steady friendship for him.   What
you felt for Shelley I feel for him.   I feel it also my duty to
tell you I have a real friend, because, in case of sickness or
death happening to me, you would at least feel the consolation
of knowing that I had not died in the hands of strangers.   I
talk to him very often of you and Mary, until his desire to see
you becomes quite a passion.   He is, like all Germans, very
sentimental, a very sweet temper, and uncommonly generous.
His attachment to me is extreme, but I have taken the very
greatest care to explain to him that I cannot return it in the
same degree.   This does not make him unhappy, and therefore our friendship is of the utmost importance to both.   I
hope, my dear Jane, that you will one day see him, and that
both you and Mary may find such an agreeable friend in him
as I have had.   I must now turn from this subject to speak
of Trelawny, which comes naturally into my mind with the
idea of friendship ; you cannot think how uneasy I am at not
hearing from him.   I am not afraid of his friendship growing
cold for me, for I am sure he is unchangeable on that point,
but I am afraid for his happiness and safety.   Is it true that
his friend Ulysses is dead ? and if so, do pray write to him and
prevail upon him to return.   I should be at ease if I were to
know him near you and Mary.   Do think if you can do anything
to draw him to you, my dearest Jane.   It would render me the
happiest of human beings to know him in the hands of two
such friends.   If this could be, how hard I should work to gain
a little independence here, and return perhaps in ten years and
live with you.   As yet I have done nothing, notwithstanding
my utmost exertions, towards such a plan, but I am turning
over every possible means in my brain for devising some

scheme to get money, and perhaps I may. That is my reason
for staying in Russia, because there is no country so favourable to foreigners. Pray, my dear Jane, do write to me the
moment you receive this, and answer very particularly
the questions I have asked you. I have filled this whole
letter, do you the same in your answer, and tell me every
particular about Percy, Neddy, and Dina ; they little guess how
warm a friend they have in this distant land, who thinks perpetually of them, and wishes for nothing so much as to see
them and to play with them. Give my love to Mary. I will
write soon again to her. In the meantime do some of you
pray write. These horrid long winters, and the sky, which is
from month to month of the darkest dun colour, need some
news from you to render life supportable. Kiss all the dear
children for me, and tell me everything about them.—Ever
your affectionate friend,   CLARE.

Pray beg Mary to tell my mother that I wrote to her on or
about the 22d of August ; has she had this letter ? and do tell
me in yours what you know of her. I have just received your
letter of the 3d of September, for which I thank you most
cordially. Thank heaven, you are all well ! What you say
of Trelawny distresses me, as it seems to me that you are un-
willing to say what you have heard, as it is of a disagreeable
nature. You could do me a great benefit if you could make
yourself mistress of the Logier's system of teaching music, and
communicate it to me in its smallest details. I am sure it
would take here. Do, pray, make serious inquiries of some one
who has been taught by him. If any one would undertake to
write me a very circumstantial account of his method, I would
cheerfully pay them. It might be the means of my making a
small independence here, and then I could join you soon in
Italy without fear for the future. Do think seriously of this,
my dear Jane, and do not take it into your head that it is an
idle project, for it would be of the greatest use to me. As to
your admirer, I think he is mad, and his society, which would
otherwise be a relief, must now be a burthen. You are very

right in saying you only find solace in mental occupation ; it is
the only thing that saves me from such a depression of spirits
taking hold of me when I have an instant to reflect upon the past
that I am ready for any rash act ; but I am occupied from 6 in
the morning until 10 at night, and then am so worn out I have
no time for thinking.   Once more farewell.   My address is—
Chez Monsieur Lenhold, Marchand de Musique, a Moscow.

The Last Man, Mrs. Shelley's third novel, was
published early in 1826.   It differed widely from
its predecessors.   *Frankenstein* was an allegorical
romance ; *Valperga* a historical novel, Italian, of
the fifteenth century ; the plot of the one depends
for its interest chiefly on incident, that of the other
on the development of character, but both have a
definite purpose in the inculcation of certain moral
or philosophical truths.   The story of *The Last
Man* is purely romantic and imaginary, probabili-
ties and possibilities being entirely discarded.   Its
supposed events take place in the twenty-first
century of our era, when a devouring plague de-
populates by degrees the whole world, until the
narrator remains, to his own belief, the only sur-
viving soul.   At the book's conclusion he is left,
in a little boat, coasting around the shores of the
sea-washed countries of the Mediterranean, with
the forlorn hope of finding a companion solitary.
He writes the history of his fate and that of his
race on the leaves of trees,—supposed to be discovered and deciphered long afterwards in the
Sibyl's Cave at Baiae,—the world having been (as

we must infer) repeopled by that time. It is not difficult to understand the kind of fascination this curious, mournful fancy had for Mary in her solitude. Much other matter is, of course, inter-woven with the leading idea. The characteristics of the hero, Adrian, his benevolence of heart, his winning aspect, his passion of justice and self-devotion, and his fervent faith in the possibilities of human nature and the future of the human race, are unmistakably sketched from Shelley, and the portrait was at once recognised by Shelley's earliest friend, the value of whose appreciation was, if anything, enhanced by the fact of the great unlikeness between his temperament and Shelley's.

T. J. Hogg to Mrs. Shelley.

York, 22d *March* 1826.

My dear Mary—As I am about to send a frank to dearest Jane, I enclose a note to you to thank you for the pleasure you have given me. I read your *Last Man* with an intense interest and not without tears. I began it at Stamford yesterday morn-ing as soon as it was light; I read on all day, even during the short time that was allowed us for dinner, and, if I had not finished it before it was dark, I verily believe that I should have bought a candle and held it in my hand in the mail. I think that it is a decided improvement, and that the character of Adrian is most happy and most just.—I am, dear Mary, yours ever faithfully, T. J. Hogg.

The appearance of Mary's novel had for its practical consequence the stoppage of her supplies. The book was published anonymously, as " by the

author of *Frankenstein*," but Mrs. Shelley's name
found its way into some newspaper notices, and
this misdemeanour (for which she was not responsible) was promptly punished by the suspension of
her allowance.   Peacock's good offices were again
in request, to try and avert this misfortune, but it
was not at once that he prevailed.   He impressed
on Whitton (the solicitor) that the name did not
appear in the title-page, and that its being brought
forward at all was the fault of the publisher and
quite contrary to the wishes of the writer, who,
solitary and despondent, could not be reasonably
condemned for employing her time according to
her tastes and talents, with a view to bettering her
condition.   This Whitton acknowledged, but said,
" the name was the matter; it annoyed Sir
Timothy."   He would promise nothing, and
Peacock could only assure Mary that he felt little
doubt of her getting the money at last, though she
might be punished by a short delay.

It may be assumed that this turned out so.
Late in the year, however, another turn was given
to Mary's affairs by the death of Shelley's eldest
boy.

Journal, September 1826.—Charles Shelley died during
this month.   Percy is now Shelley's only son.

Mary's son being now direct heir to the estates,
and her own prospects being materially improved
by this fact, she at once thought of others whom

Shelley had meant to benefit by his will, and who, she was resolved, should not be losers by his early death, if she lived to carry out for him his unwritten intentions. She did not think, when she wrote to Leigh Hunt the letter which follows, that nearly twenty years more would elapse before the will could take effect.

MARY SHELLEY TO LEIGH HUNT.

5 BARTHOLOMEW PLACE, KENTISH TOWN,
30th October 1826.

MY DEAR HUNT—Is it, or is it not, right that these few lines should be addressed to you now? Yet if the subject be one that you may judge better to have been deferred, set my *delay* down to the account of over-zeal in writing to relieve you from a part of the care which I know is just now oppressing you; too happy I shall be if you permit any act of mine to have that effect.

I told you long ago that our dear Shelley intended on rewriting his will to have left you a legacy. I think the sum mentioned was £2000. I trust that hereafter you will not refuse to consider me your debtor for this sum merely because I shall be bound to pay it you by the laws of honour instead of a legal obligation. You would, of course, have been better pleased to have received it immediately from dear Shelley's bequest; but as it is well known that he intended to make such an one, it is in fact the same thing, and so I hope by you to be considered; besides, your kind heart will receive pleasure from the knowledge that you are bestowing on me the greatest pleasure I am capable of receiving. This is no resolution of to-day, but formed from the moment I knew my situation to be such as it is. I did not mention it, because it seemed almost like an empty vaunt to talk and resolve on things so far off. But futurity approaches, and a feeling haunts me as if this futurity were not far distant. I have spoken vaguely to you on this subject before, but now, you having had a recent disappointment, I have thought it as well to inform you in express terms of the meaning I attached to my expressions.   I have as yet made no will, but in the meantime, if I should chance to die, this present writing may serve as a legal document to prove that I give and bequeath to you the sum of £2000 sterling.   But I hope we shall both live, I to acknowledge dear Shelley's intentions, you to honour me so far as to permit me to be their executor.

I have mentioned this subject to no one, and do not intend ; an act is not aided by words, especially an act unfulfilled, nor does this letter, methinks, require any answer, at least not till after the death of Sir Timothy Shelley, when perhaps this explanation would have come with better grace ; but I trust to your kindness to put my writing now to a good motive.—I am, my dear Hunt, yours affectionately and obliged,

MARY WOLLSTONECRAFT SHELLEY.

It was admitted by the Shelley family that, Percy being now the heir, some sort of settlement should be made for his mother, yet for some months longer nothing was done or arranged. Apparently Mary wrote to Trelawny in low spirits, and to judge from his reply, her letter found him in little better plight than herself.

TRELAWNY TO MRS. SHELLEY.

ZANTE, 16*th December* 1826.

DEAR MARY—I received your letter the other day, and nothing gives me greater pleasure than to hear from you, for however assured we are of a friend's durability of affection, it is soothing to be occasionally reassured of it.   I sympathise in your distresses.   I have mine, too, on the same score—a bountiful will and confined means are a curse, and often have I execrated my fortunes so ill corresponding with my wishes.   But

who can control his fate? Old age and poverty is a frightful
prospect; it makes the heart sick to contemplate, even in the
mind's eye the reality would wring a generous nature till the
heart burst. Poverty is the vampyre which lives on human
blood, and haunts its victims to destruction. Hell can fable
no torment exceeding it, and all the other calamities of human
life—wars, pestilence, fire—cannot compete with it. It is the
climax of human ill. You may be certain that I could not
write thus on what I did not feel. I am glad you say
you have better hopes; when things are at the worst, they say,
there is hope. So do I hope. Lord Cochrane and his naval
expedition having so long and unaccountably been kept back,
delayed me here from month to month till the winter has de-
finitively set in, and I am in no state for a winter's voyage;
my body is no longer weatherproof. But I must as soon as
possible get to England, though my residence there will be
transitory. I shall then most probably hurry on to Italy.

The frigate from America is at last arrived in Greece, but
whether Cochrane is on board of her I know not. With the
loss of my friend Odysseus, my enthusiasm has somewhat
abated; besides that I could no longer act with the prospect
of doing service, and toiling in vain is heartless work. But
have I not done so all my life? The affairs of Greece are so
bad that little can be done to make them worse. If Cochrane
comes, and is supported with means sufficient, there is still
room for hope. I am in too melancholy a mood to say more
than that, whatever becomes of me.—I am always your true
and affectionate   E. TRELAWNY.

Mary answered him at once, doing and saying,
to console him, all that friendship could.

KENTISH TOWN, 4*th March* 1827.
[Direct me at W. Godwin, Esq., 44 Gower Place, Gower
Street, London.]

MY DEAR TRELAWNY—Your long silence had instilled into
me the delusive hope that I should hear you sooner than from

you. I have been silly enough sometimes to start at a knock,
—at length your letter is come. [By] that indeed I entertain more reasonable hopes of seeing you. You will come—
Ah, indeed you must; if you are ever the kind-hearted being
you were—you must come to be consoled by my sympathy,
exhilarated by my encouragements, and made happy by my
friendship. You are not happy! Alas! who is that has a
noble and generous nature? It is not only, my noble-hearted
friend, that your will is bountiful and your means small,—
were you richer you would still be tormented by ingratitude,
caprice, and change. Yet I say Amen to all your anathema
against poverty, it is beyond measure a torment and despair.
I am poor, having once been richer; I live among the needy,
and see only poverty around. I happen, as has always been
my fate, to have formed intimate friendships with those who
are great of soul, generous, and incapable of valuing money
except for the good it may do—and these very people are all
even poorer than myself, is it not hard? But turning to you
who are dearest to me, who of all beings are most liberal, it
makes me truly unhappy to find that you are hard pressed:
do not talk of old age and poverty, both the one and the other
are in truth far from you,—for the one it will be a miracle if
you live to grow old,—this would appear a strange compliment
if addressed to another, but you and I have too much of the
pure spirit of fire in our souls to wish to live till the flickering
beam waxes dim;—think then of the few present years only.
I have no doubt you will do your fortunes great good by
coming to this country. A too long absence destroys the interest that friends take, if they are only friends in the common
acceptation of the word; and your relations ought to be reminded of you. The great fault to us in this country is its
expensiveness, and the dreadful ills attendant here on poverty;
elsewhere, though poor, you may live—here you are actually
driven from life, and though a few might pity, none would
help you were you absolutely starving. You say you shall
stay here but a short time and then go to Italy—alas!
alas!

It is impossible in a letter to communicate the exact state of one's feelings and affairs here—but there is a change at hand —I cannot guess whether for good or bad as far as regards me. This winter, whose extreme severity has carried off many old people, confined Sir Tim. for ten weeks by the gout— but he is recovered. All that time a settlement for me was delayed, although it was acknowledged that Percy now being the heir, one ought to be made ; at length after much parading, they have notified to me that I shall receive a magnificent £250 a year, to be increased next year to £300. But then I am not permitted to leave this cloudy nook. My desire to get away is unchanged, and I used to look forward to your return as a period when I might contrive—but I fear there is no hope for me during Sir T.'s life. He and his family are now at Brighton. John Shelley, dear S.'s brother, is about to marry, and talks of calling upon me. I am often led to reflect in life how people situated in a certain manner with regard to me might make my life less drear than it is—but it is always the case that the people that might—won't, and it is a very great mistake to fancy that they will. Such thoughts make me anxious to draw tighter the cords of sympathy and friendship which are so much more real than those of the world's forming in the way of relationship or connection.

From the ends of the world we were brought together to be friends till death ; separated as we are, this tie still subsists. I do not wonder that you are out of heart concerning Greece ; the mismanagement here is not less than the misgovernment there, the discord the same, save that here ink is spilt instead of blood. Lord Cochrane alone can assist them—but without vessels or money how can he acquire sufficient power ? at any rate except as the Captain of a vessel I do not see what good you can do them. But the mischief is this,—that while some cold, unimpressive natures can go to a new country, reside among a few friends, enter into the interests of an intimate and live as a brother among them for a time, and then depart, leaving small trace, retaining none,—as if they had ascended from a bath, they change their garments and pass on ;

—while others of subtler nature receive into their very essences a part of those with whom they associate, and after a while they become enchained, either for better or worse, and during a series of years they bear the marks of change and attachment. These natures indeed are the purest and best, and of such are you, dear friend; having you once, I ever have you; losing you once, I have lost you for ever; a riddle this, but true. And so life passes, year is added to year, the word youth is becoming obsolete, while years bring me no change for the better. Yet I said, change is at hand—I know it, though as yet I do not feel it—you will come, in the spring you will come and add fresh delight for me to the happy change from winter to summer. I cannot tell what else material is to change, but I feel sure the year will end differently from its beginning. Jane is quite well, we talk continually of you, and expect you anxiously. Her fortunes have been more shifting than mine, and they are about to conclude,—differently from mine,—but I leave her to say what she thinks best concerning herself, though probably she will defer the explanation until your arrival. She is my joy and consolation. I could never have survived my exile here but for her. Her amiable temper, cheerfulness, and never ceasing sympathy are all so much necessary value for one wounded and lost as I.

Come, dear friend, again I read your melancholy sentences and I say, come! let us try if we can work out good from ill; if I may not be able to throw a ray of sunshine on your path, at least I will lead you as best I may through the gloom. Believe me that all that belongs to you must be dear to me, and that I shall never forget all I owe to you.

Do you remember those pretty lines of Burns?—

> A monarch may forget his crown
> That on his head an hour hath been,
> A bridegroom may forget his bride
> Who was his wedded wife yest'reen,
> A mother may forget her child
> That smiles so sweetly on her knee,
> But I'll remember thee, dear friend,
> And all that thou hast done for me.

Such feelings are not the growth of the moment. They must have lived for years—have flourished in smiles, and retained their freshness watered by tears; to feel them one must have sailed much of life's voyage together—have undergone the same perils, and sympathised in the same fears and griefs; such is our situation; and the heartfelt and deep-rooted sentiments fill my eyes with tears as I think of you, dear friend, we shall meet soon. Adieu, M. S.

. . . I cannot close this letter without saying a word about dear Hunt—yet that must be melancholy. To feed nine children is no small thing. His health has borne up pretty well hitherto, though his spirits sink. What is it in the soil of this green earth that is so ill adapted to the best of its sons? He speaks often of you with affection.

To Edward Trelawny, Esq.,
    To the care of Samuel Barff, Esq.,
        Zante, The Ionian Isles.

Seal—Judgment of Paris.
    Endorsed—Received 10th April 1827.

Change was indeed at hand, though not of a kind that Mary could have anticipated. The only event in prospect likely to affect her much was a step shortly to be taken by Mrs. Williams. That intended step, vaguely foreshadowed in Jane's correspondence, aroused the liveliest curiosity in Clare Clairmont, as was natural.

Miss Clairmont to Mrs. Williams.

My dearest Jane—If I have not written to you before, it is owing to low spirits. I have not been able to take the pen, because it would have been dipped in too black a melancholy. I am tired of being in trouble, particularly as it goes on augmenting every day. I have had a hard struggle with myself

lately to get over the temptation I had to lay down the
burthen at once, and be free as spirits are, and leave this
horrid world behind me.   In order to let you understand
what now oppresses me, I must tell you my history since I
came to Moscow.   I came here quite unknown.   I was at
first ill treated on that account, but I soon acquired a great
reputation, because all my pupils made much more progress
in whatever they undertook than those of other people.   I
had few acquaintances among the English; to these I had
never mentioned a single circumstance of myself or fortunes,
but took care, on the contrary, to appear content and happy,
as if I had never known or seen any other society all my days.
I sent you a letter by Miss F., because I knew your name
would excite no suspicions; but it seems my mother got hold
of Miss F., sought her out, and has thereby done me a most
incalculable mischief.   Miss F. came back full of my story
here, and though she is very friendly to me, yet others who
are not so have already done me injury.   The Professor at
the University here is a man of a good deal of talent, and was
in close connection with Lockhart, the son-in-law of Sir
Walter Scott, and all that party; he has a great deal of
friendship for me, because, as he says, very truly, I am the
only person here besides himself who knows how to speak
English.   He professes the most rigid principles, and is come
to that age when it is useless to endeavour to change them.
I, however, took care not to get upon the subject of principles, and so he was of infinite use to me both by counselling
and by protecting me with the weight of his high approbation.
You may imagine this man's horror when he heard who I
was; that the charming Miss Clairmont, the model of good
sense, accomplishments, and good taste, was brought, issued
from the very den of freethinkers.   I see that he is in a complete puzzle on my account; he cannot explain to himself
how I can be so extremely delightful, and yet so detestable.
The inveteracy of his objections is shaken.   This, however,
has not hindered him from doing me serious mischief.   I was
to have undertaken this winter the education of an only

daughter, the child of a very rich family where the Professor reigns despotic, because he always settles every little dispute with some unintelligible quotation or reference to a Latin or Greek author. I am extremely interested in the child, he used to say, and no one can give her the education she ought to have but Miss Clairmont. The father and the mother have been running after me these years to persuade me to enter when the child should be old enough. I consented, when now, all is broken off, because the scruples of my professor do not allow of it. God knows, he says, what Godwinish principles she might not instil. You may, therefore, think how teased I have been ; more so from the uncertainty of my position, as I do not know how far this may extend. If this is only the beginning, what may be the end? I am not angry with this man, he only acts according to his conscience ; nor am I surprised. I shall never cease feeling and thinking that if I had my choice, I had rather a thousand times have a child of mine resigned to an early grave, and lost for ever to me, than have it brought up in principles I abhor. If you ask me what I shall do, I can only answer you as did the Princess Mentimiletto, when buried under the ruins of her villa by an earthquake, "I await my fate in silence." In the meantime, while the page of fate is unrolling, I feel a secret agitation which consumes me, the more so for being repressed. I am fallen again into a bad state· of health, but this is habitual to me upon the recurrence of winter. What torments me the most is the restraint I am under of always appearing gay in society, which I am obliged to do to avoid their odious curiosity. Farewell awhile dismay and terror, and let us turn to love and happiness. Never was astonishment greater than mine on receiving your letter. I had somehow imagined to myself that you never would love again, and you may say what you like, dearest Jane, you won't drive that out of my head. "Blue Bag" may be a friend to you, but he never can be a lover. A happy attachment that has seen its end leaves a void that nothing can fill up ; therefore I counsel the timorous and the prudent to take the greatest

care always to have an unhappy attachment, because with it
you can veer about like a weathercock to every point of life.
What would I not give to have an unhappy passion, for then
one has full permission and a perfect excuse to fall into a
happy one; one has something to expect, but a *happy passion*,
like death, has *finis* written in such large characters in its face
there is no hoping for any possibility of a change. You will
allow me to talk upon this subject, for I am unhappily the
victim of a *happy passion*. I had one; like all things perfect
in its kind, it was fleeting, and mine only lasted ten minutes,
but these ten minutes have discomposed the rest of my life.
The passion, God knows for what cause, from no faults of
mine, however, disappeared, leaving no trace whatever behind
it except my heart wasted and ruined as if it had been
scorched by a thousand lightnings. You will therefore, I
hope, excuse my not following the advice you give me in your
last letter, of falling in love, and you will readily believe me
when I tell you that I am not in love, as you suspected, with
my German friend Hermann. He went away last spring for
five years to the country. I have a great friendship for him,
because he has the most ardent love of all that is good and
beautiful of any one I know. I feel interested for his happiness and welfare, but he is not the being who could make
life feel less a burthen to me than it does. It would, however, seem that you are a little happier than you were, therefore I congratulate you on this change of life. I am delighted
that you have some one to watch over you and guard you
from the storms of life. Do pray tell me Blue Bag's name,
(for what is a man without a name?), or else I shall get into the
habit of thinking of him as Blue Bag, and never be able to
divest myself of this disagreeable association all my life. You
say Trelawny is coming home, but you have said so so long,
I begin to doubt it. If he does come, how happy you will be
to see him. Happy girl! you have a great many happinesses.
I have written to him many times, but he never answers my
letters; I suppose he does not wish to keep up the correspondence, and so I have left off. If he comes home I am

sure he will fall ill, because the change of climate is most pernicious to the health. The first winter I passed in Russia I
thought I should have died, but then a good deal was caused
by extreme anxiety. So take care of Trelawny, and do not
let him get his feet wet. You ask me to tell you every particular of my way of life. For these last six months I have
been tormented to death; I am shut up with five hateful
children; they keep me in a fever from morning till night.
If they fall into their father's or mother's way, and are trouble-
some, they are whipped; but the instant they are with me,
which is pretty nearly all the day, they give way to all their
violence and love of mischief, because they are not afraid of
my mild disposition. They go on just like people in a
public-house, abusing one another with the most horrid names
and fighting; if I separate them, then they roll on the ground,
shrieking that I have broken their arm, or pretend to fall into
convulsions, and I am such a fool I am frightened. In short,
I never saw the evil spirit so plainly developed. What is
worse, I cannot seriously be angry with them, for I do not
know how they can be otherwise with the education they receive. Everything is a crime; they may neither jump, nor
run, nor laugh. It is now two months they have never been
out of the house, and the only thing they are indulged in is
in eating, drinking, and sleeping, so that I look upon their
defects as proceeding entirely from the pernicious lives they
lead. This is a pretty just picture of all Russian children,
because the Russians are as yet totally ignorant of anything
like real education. You may, therefore, imagine what a life
I have been leading. In the summer, and we had an Italian
one, I bore up very well, because we were often in the garden,
but since the return of winter, which always makes me ill, and
their added tiresomeness, I am quite overpowered. The
whole winter long I have a fever, which comes on every
evening, and prevents my sleeping the whole night; sometimes it leaves me for a fortnight, but then it begins again,
but in summer I am as strong and healthy as possible. The

approach of winter fills me with horror, because I know I have eight long months of suffering and sickness. The only amusement I have is Sunday evening, to see Miss F. and some others like her, and the only subject of conversation is to laugh at the Russians, or dress. My God, what a life! But complaint is useless, and therefore I shall not indulge in it. I have said, so as those I love live, I will bear all without a murmur. If ever I am independent, I will instantly retire to some solitude; I will see no one, not even you nor Mary, and there I will live until the horrible disgust I feel at all that is human be somewhat removed by quiet and retirement. My heart is too full of hatred to be fit for society in its present mood. I am very sorry for the death of little Charles. The chances for succession are now so equally balanced—the life of an old man and the life of *one* young child—that I confess I see less hope than ever of the will's taking effect. It is frightful for the despairing to have their hopes suspended thus upon a single hair. Pray do not forget to write to me when Trelawny is come. How glad I shall be to know he is in England, and yet how frightened for fear he should catch cold. I wish you would tell me how you occupy your days; at what hour you do this, and at what hour that. From 11 till 4 I teach my children, then we dine; at 5 we rise from the table. They have half an hour's dawdling, for play it cannot be called, as they are in the drawing-room, and then they learn two hours more. At 8 we drink tea, and then they go to bed, which is never over till 11, because all must have their hair curled, which takes up an enormous time.

Since I have written the first part of my letter I have thought over my affairs. I must go to Petersburgh, because it is quite another town from Moscow, and being so much more foreign in their manners and ways of thinking, I shall be less tormented. I have decided to go, therefore I wish you very much to endeavour to procure me letters of intro-duction. If Trelawny comes home, beg him to do so for me, because, as he will be much in fashion, some of the numerous dear female friends he will instantly have will do it for him.

If I could have a letter of recommendation, not a letter of introduction, to the English ambassador or his wife, I should be able to get over the difficulties which now beset my passage. Do think of this, Jane. My head is so completely giddy from worry and torment, that I am unable to think upon my own affairs; only this I know, that I am in a tottering situation. It is absolutely necessary that I should have letters of recommendation, and to people high in the world at Petersburgh, because it is very common in Russia for adventurers, such as opera dancers too old to dance any more, and milliners, and that class of women to come here. They are received with open arms by the Russians, who are very hospitable, and then naturally they betray themselves by their atrocious conduct, and are thrown off; and I have known since I have been here several lamentable instances of this, and I shall be classed with these people if I cannot procure letters to people whose countenance and protection must refute the possibility of such a supposition. I must confess to you that my pride never could stand this, for ·these adventurers are such detestable people that I have the utmost horror of them. What a miserable imposture is life, that such as follow philosophy, nature and truth, should be classed with the very refuse of mankind; that people who ought to be cited as models of virtue and self-sacrifice should be trampled under foot with the dregs of vice. It was not thus in the time of the Greeks; and this reflection makes me tired of life, for I might have been understood in the time of Socrates, but never shall be by the moderns. For this reason I do not wish to live, as I cannot be understood; in order, therefore, not to be despised, I must renounce all worldly concerns whatever. I have long done so, and therefore you will not wonder that I have long since given my parting look to life. Do not be surprised I am so dull; I am surrounded by difficulties which I am afraid I never shall get out of, and after so many years of trouble and anguish it is natural I should wish it were over. Do not, my dearest Jane, mention to my mother the harm her indiscretion has done, for though I shall frankly tell her of it, yet it would wound her if she were to know I had told you, and there is already so much pain in the world it is frightful to add ever so little to the stock. You can merely say I have asked for letters of introduction at Petersburgh.

From the time of her first arrival in England after Edward's death, Hogg had been Jane Williams' persistent, devoted, and long-suffering admirer. Not many months after receiving Clare's letter, she changed her name and her abode, and was thenceforward known as Mrs. Hogg. Mary's familiar intercourse with her might, in any case, have been somewhat checked by this event, but such a change would have been a small matter compared to the bitter discovery she was soon to make, that, while accepting her affection, Jane had never really cared for her; that her feeling had been of the most superficial sort. Once independent of Mary, and under other protection, she talked away for the benefit and amusement of other people,—talked of their past life, prating of her power over Shelley and his devotion to her, —of Mary's gloom during those sad first weeks at Lerici,—intimating that jealousy of herself was the cause. Stories which lost nothing in the telling, wherein Jane Williams figured as a good angel, while Mary Shelley was made to appear in an unfavourable or even an absurd light.

Mary had no suspicion, no foreboding of the mine that was preparing to explode under her feet. She sympathised in her friend's happiness, for she could not regard it but as happiness for one in Jane's circumstances to be able to accept the love and protection of a devoted man. She herself could not do it, but she often felt a wish that she were differently constituted. She knew it was impossible ; but no tinge of envy or bitterness coloured her words to Trelawny when she wrote to tell him of Jane's resolution.

. . . This is to be an eventful summer to us. Janey is writing to you and will tell her own tale best. The person to whom she unites herself is one of my oldest friends, the early friend of my own Shelley. It was he who chose to share the honour, as he generously termed it, of Shelley's expulsion from Oxford. (And yet he is unlike what you may conceive to be the ideal of the best friend of Shelley.) He is a man of talent, —of wit,—he has sensibility and even romance in his disposition, but his exterior is composed and, at a superficial glance, cold. He has loved Jane devotedly and ardently since she first arrived in England, almost five years ago. At first she was too faithfully attached to the memory of Edward, nor was he exactly the being to satisfy her imagination ; but his sincere and long-tried love has at last gained the day.

. . . Nor will I fear for her in the risk she must run when she confides her future happiness to another's constancy and good principles. He is a man of honour, he longs for home, for domestic life, and he well knows that none could make such so happy as Jane. He is liberal in his opinions, constant in his attachments, if she is happy with him now she will be always. . . . Of course after all that has passed it is our wish that all this shall be as little talked of as possible, the obscurity in which we have lived favours this. We shall remove hence during the summer, for of course we shall still continue near each other. I, as ever, must derive my only pleasure and solace from her society.

Before the summer of 1827 was over the cloud burst.

Mary's journal in June is less mournful than usual. Congenial society always had the power of cheering her and making her forget herself. And in her acquaintance with Thomas Moore she found a novelty which yet was akin to past enjoyment.

Journal, June 26 (1827).—I have just made acquaintance with Tom Moore. He reminds me delightfully of the past, and I like him much. There is something warm and genuine in his feelings and manner which is very attractive, and redeems him from the sin of worldliness with which he has been charged.

July 2.—Moore breakfasted with me on Sunday. We talked of past times,—of Shelley and Lord Byron. He was very agreeable, and I never felt myself so perfectly at my ease with any one. I do not know why this is; he seems to understand and to like me. This is a new and unexpected pleasure. I have been so long exiled from the style of society in which I spent the better part of my life; it is an evanescent pleasure, but I will enjoy it while I can.

July 11.—Moore has left town; his singing is something new and strange and beautiful. I have enjoyed his visits, and spent several happy hours in his society. That is much.

July 13.—My friend has proved false and treacherous! Miserable discovery. For four years I was devoted to her, and earned only ingratitude. Not for worlds would I attempt to transfer the deathly blackness of my meditations to these pages. Let no trace remain save the deep, bleeding, hidden wound of my lost heart of such a tale of horror and despair. Writing, study, quiet, such remedies I must seek. What deadly cold flows through my veins! My head weighed down; my limbs sink under me. I start at every sound as the messenger of fresh misery, and despair invests my soul with trembling horror.

October 9.—Quanto bene mi rammento sette anni fa, in questa medesima stagione i pensieri, I sentimenti del mio cuore! Allora cominciai Valperga—allora sola col mio Bene fui felice. Allora le nuvole furono spinte dal furioso vento davanti alla luna, nuvole magnifiche, che in forme grandiose e bianche parevano stabili quanto le montagne e sotto la tirannia del vento si mostravano piu fragili che un velo di seta minutissima, scendeva allor la pioggia, gli albori si spogliavano. Autunno bello fosti allora, ed ora bello terribile, malinconico ci sei, ed io, dove sono?

By those who hold their hearts safe at home in their own keeping, these little breezes are called "storms in tea-cups." The matter was of no importance to any one but Mary. The aspect of her outward life was unchanged by this heart-shipwreck over which the world's waves closed and left no sign.

CHAPTER XXI

July 1827–August 1830

MANY weary months passed away. Mary said nothing to the shallow-hearted woman who had so grievously injured her. Jane had been so dear to her, and was so inextricably bound up with a beloved past, that she shrank from disturbing the superficial friendship which she nevertheless knew to be hollow.

To one of Mary's temperament there was actual danger in living alone with such a sorrow, and it was a happy thing when, in August, an unforeseen distraction occurred to compel her thoughts into a new channel. She received from an unknown correspondent a letter, resulting in an acquaintance which, though it passed out of her life without leaving any permanent mark, was, at the time, not unfruitful of interest.

The letter was as follows—

FRANCES WRIGHT TO MRS. SHELLEY.

PARIS, 22d *August* 1827.

I shall preface this letter with no apology; the motive

which dictates it will furnish, as I trust, a sufficient introduction
both for it and its writer.   As the daughter of your father and
mother (known to me only by their works and opinions), as
the friend and companion of a man distinguished during life,
and preserved in the remembrance of the public as one
distinguished not by genius merely, but, as I imagine, by the
strength of his opinions and his fearlessness in their expression ;
—viewed only in these relations you would be to me an object
of interest and—permit the word, for I use it in no vulgar sense
—of curiosity.   But I have heard (vaguely indeed, for I have
not even the advantage of knowing one who claims your personal acquaintance, nor have I, in my active pursuits and
engagements in distant countries, had occasion to peruse
your works), yet I have heard, or read, or both, that which has
fostered the belief that you share at once the sentiments and
talents of those from whom you drew your being.   If you
possess the opinions of your father and the generous feelings
of your mother, I feel that I could travel far to see you.   It is
rare in this world, especially in our sex, to meet with those
opinions united with those feelings, and with the manners
and disposition calculated to command respect and conciliate
affection.   It is so rare, that to obtain the knowledge of such
might well authorise a more abrupt intrusion than one by
letter ; but, pledged as I am to the cause of what appears to
me moral truth and moral liberty, that I (should) neglect any
means for discovering a real friend of that cause, I were almost
failing to a duty.

In thus addressing my inquiries respecting you to yourself, it were perhaps fitting that I should enter into some
explanations respecting my own views and the objects which
have fixed my attention.   I conceive, however, the very
motive of this letter as herein explained, with the printed paper
I shall enclose with it, will supply a sufficient assurance of the
heterodoxy of my opinions and the nature of my exertions for
their support and furtherance.   It will be necessary to explain,
however, what will strike you but indistinctly in the deed of
Nashoba, that the object of the experiment has in view an

association based on those principles of moral liberty and
equality heretofore advocated by your father. That these
principles form its base and its cement, and that while we
endeavour to undermine the slavery of colour existing in the
North American Republic, we essay equally to destroy the
slavery of mind now reigning there as in other countries. With
one nation we find the aristocracy of colour, with another
that of rank, with all perhaps those of wealth, instruction,
and sex.

Our circle already comprises a few united co-operators,
whose choice of associates will be guided by their moral fitness
only ; saving that, for the protection and support of all, each
must be fitted to exercise some useful employment, or to supply
200 dollars per annum as an equivalent for their support. The
present generation will in all probability supply but a limited
number of individuals suited in opinion and disposition to such
a state of society ; but that that number, however limited, may
best find their happiness and best exercise their utility by unit-
ing their interests, their society, and their talents, I feel a conviction. In this conviction I have devoted my time and fortune
to laying the foundations of an establishment where affection
shall form the only marriage, kind feeling and kind action the
only religion, respect for the feelings and liberties of others to
the only restraint, and union of interest the bond of peace and
security. With the protection of the negro in view, whose
cruel sufferings and degradation had attracted my special
sympathy, it was necessary to seek the land of his bondage,
to study his condition and imagine a means for effecting his
liberation ; with the emancipation of the human mind in view,
from the shackles of moral and religious superstition, it was
necessary to seek a country where political institutions should
allow free scope for experiment ; and with a practice in view
in opposition to all the laws of public opinion, it was necessary
to seek the seclusion of a new country, and build up a city of
refuge in the wilderness itself. Youth, a good constitution,
and a fixed purpose enabled me to surmount the fatigues,
difficulties, and privations of the necessary journeys, and the

first opening of a settlement in the American forests.   Fifteen
months have placed the establishment in a fair way of progress,
in the hands of united and firm associates, comprising a family
of colour from New Orleans.   As might be expected, my
health gave way under the continued fatigues of mind and
body [incidental] to the first twelvemonth.   A brain fever,
followed by a variety of sufferings, seemed to point to a sea-
voyage as the only chance of recovery.   Accordingly I left
Nashoba in May last, was placed on board a steamboat on the
Mississippi for Orleans, then on board a vessel for Havre, and
landed in fifty days almost restored to health.   I am now in
an advanced state of convalescence, but still obliged to avoid
fatigue either bodily or mental.   The approaching marriage of
a dear friend also retains me in Paris, and as I shall return by
way of New Orleans to my forest home in the month of
November, or December, I do not expect to visit London.
The bearer of this letter, should he, as I trust, be able· to
deliver it, will be able to furnish any intelligence you may
desire respecting Nashoba and its inhabitants.   In the name
of Robert Dale Owen you will recognise one of the trustees,
and a son of Robert Owen of Lanark.

Whatever be the fate of this letter, I wish to convey to
Mary Wollstonecraft Godwin Shelley my respect and admiration of those from whom she holds those names, and my
fond desire to connect her with them in my esteem, and in
the knowledge of mutual sympathy to sign myself her friend,

FRANCES WRIGHT.

My address while in Europe—Aux soins du General Lafayette, Rue d'Anjou, and 7 St. Honoré, à Paris.

The bearer of this letter would seem to have
been Robert Dale Owen himself.   His name
must have recalled to Mary's mind the letter she
had received at Geneva, long, long ago, from poor
Fanny, describing and commenting on the schemes

for social regeneration of his father, Robert Owen.

Mary Shelley's feeling towards Frances Wright's schemes in 1827 may have been accurately expressed by Fanny Godwin's words in 1816.

. . . "The outline of his plan is this: 'That no human being shall work more than two or three hours every day; that they shall be all equal; that no one shall dress but after the plainest and simplest manner; that they be allowed to follow any religion, or no religion, as they please; and that their studies shall be Mechanics and Chemistry.' I hate and am sick at heart at the misery I see my fellow-beings suffering, but I own I should not like to live to see the extinction of all genius, talent, and elevated generous feeling in Great Britain, which I conceive to be the natural consequence of Mr. Owen's plan."

But any plan for human improvement, any unselfish effort to promote the common weal, commanded the sure sympathy of Shelley's widow and Mary Wollstonecraft's daughter, whether her judgment accorded perfectly or not with that of its promoters. She responded warmly to the letter of her correspondent, who wrote back in almost rapturous terms—

FRANCES WRIGHT TO MARY SHELLEY.

PARIS, 15*th September* 1827.

My Friend, my dear Friend—How sweet are the sentiments with which I write that sacred word—so often prostituted, so seldom bestowed with the glow of satisfaction and delight with which I now employ it! Most surely will I go to

England, most surely to Brighton, to wheresoever you may be.
The fond belief of my heart is realised, and more than realised.
You are the daughter of your mother. I opened your letter
with some trepidation, and perused it with more emotion than
now suits my shattered nerves. I have read it again and
again, and acknowledge it before I sleep. Most fully, most
deeply does my heart render back the sympathy yours gives.
It fills up the sad history you have sketched of blighted affections and ruined hopes. I too have suffered, and we must
have done so perhaps to feel for the suffering. We must have
loved and mourned, and felt the chill of disappointment, and
sighed over the moral blank of a heartless world ere we can
be moved to sympathy for calamity, or roused to attempt its
alleviation. The curiosity you express shall be most willingly
answered in (as I trust) our approaching meeting. You will
see then that I have greatly pitied and greatly dared, only
because I have greatly suffered and widely observed. I have
sometimes feared lest too early affliction and too frequent disappointment had blunted my sensibilities, when a *rencontre*
with some one of the rare beings dropt amid the dull mul-
titude, like oases in the desert, has refreshed my better
feelings, and reconciled me with others and with myself.
That the child of your parents should be one among these
sweet visitants is greatly soothing and greatly inspiring. But
have we only discovered each other to lament that we are not
united? I cannot, will not think it. When we meet,—and
meet we must, and I hope soon,—how eagerly, and yet tremb-
lingly, shall I inquire into all the circumstances likely to favour
an approach in our destinies. I am now on the eve of separation from a beloved friend, whom marriage is about to remove
to Germany, while I run back to my forests. And I must
return without a bosom intimate? Yes; our little circle has
mind, has heart, has right opinions, right feelings, co-operates
in an experiment having in view human happiness, yet I do
want one of my own sex to commune with, and sometimes to
lean upon in all the confidence of equality of friendship. You
see I am not so disinterested as you suppose. Delightful

indeed it is to aid the progress of human improvement, and sweet is the peace we derive from aiding the happiness of others. But still the heart craves something more ere it can say—I am satisfied.

I must tell, not write, of the hopes of Nashoba, and of all your sympathising heart wishes to hear. On the 28th instant I shall be in London, where I must pass some days with a friend about to sail for Madeira. Then, unless you should come to London, I will seek you at Brighton, Arundel, anywhere you may name. Let me find directions from you. I will not say, use no ceremony with me—none can ever enter between us. Our intercourse begins in the confidence, if not in the fulness of friendship. I have not seen you, and yet my heart loves you.

I cannot take Brighton in my way ; my sweet friend, Julia Garnett, detaining me here until the latest moment, which may admit of my reaching London on the 28th. I must not see you in passing. However short our meeting, it must have some repose in it. The feelings which draw me towards you have in them I know not what of respect, of pitying sympathy, of expectation, and of tenderness. They must steal some quiet undivided hours from the short space I have yet to pass in Europe. Tell me when they shall be, and where. I expect to sail for America with Mr. Owen and his family early in November, and may leave London to visit a maternal friend in the north of England towards the 20th of October. Direct to me to the care of Mr. Robert Bayley, 4 Basinghall Street, London.

Permit me the assurance of my respect and affection, and accord me the title, as I feel the sentiments, of a friend,

FRANCES WRIGHT.

Circumstances conspired to postpone the desired meeting for some weeks, but the following extract from another letter of Fanny Wright's shows how friendly was the correspondence.

Yes, I do "understand the happiness flowing from confidence and entire sympathy, independent of worldly circumstances." I know the latter compared to the former are nothing.

A delicate nursling of European luxury and aristocracy, I thought and felt for myself, and for martyrised humankind, and have preferred all hazards, all privations in the forests of the New World to the dear-bought comforts of miscalled civilisation. I have made the hard earth my bed, the saddle of my horse my pillow, and have staked my life and fortune on an experiment having in view moral liberty and human improvement. Many of course think me mad, and if to be mad mean to be one of a minority, I am so, and very mad indeed, for our minority is very small. Should that few succeed in mastering the first difficulties, weaker spirits, though often not less amiable, may carry forward the good work. But the fewer we are who now think alike, the more we are of value to each other. To know you, therefore, is a strong desire of my heart, and all things consistent with my engagements (which I may call duties, since they are connected with the work I have in hand) will I do to facilitate our meeting.

Soon after this Mary made Frances Wright's acquaintance, and heard from herself all the story of her stirring life. She was not of American, but of Scottish birth (Dundee), and had been very early left an orphan. Her father had been a man of great ability and culture, of advanced liberal opinions, and independent fortune. Fanny had been educated in England by a maternal aunt, and in 1818, when twenty-three years of age, had gone with her younger sister to the United States. Since that time her life had been as adventurous

as it was independent.   Enthusiastic, original,
and handsome, she found friends and adherents
wherever she went.   Two years she spent in the
States, where she found sympathy and stimulus
for her speculative energies, and free scope for her
untried powers.   She had written a tragedy,
forcible and effective, which was published at
Philadelphia and acted at New York.   After that
she had been three years in Paris, where she
enjoyed the friendship and sympathy of Lafayette
and other liberal leaders.   In 1824 she was once
more in America, fired with the idea of solving
the slavery question.   She purchased a tract of
land on the Nashoba river (Tennessee), and
settled negroes there, assuming, in her impetuosity,
that to convert slaves into freemen it was only
necessary to remove their fetters, and that they
would soon work out their liberty.   She found
out her error.   In Shelley's words, slightly varied,
" How should slaves produce anything but idleness, even as the seed produces the plant ?"   The
slaves, freed from the lash, remained slaves as
before, only they did very little work.   Fanny
Wright was disappointed ; but, as her letters
plainly show, her schemes went much farther
than negro emancipation ; she aimed at nothing
short of a complete social reconstruction, to be
illustrated on a small scale at the Nashoba settlement.

Overwork, exposure to the sun, and continuous excitement, told, at last, on her constitution. As she informed Mrs. Shelley in her first letter, she had broken down with brain fever, and, when convalescent, had been ordered to Europe.

In Mary Wollstonecraft's daughter she found a friend, hardly an adherent. Fundamentally, their principles were alike, but their natures were differently attuned. Neither mentally nor physically had Mary Shelley the temperament of a revolutionary innovator. She had plenty of moral courage, but she was too scrupulous, too reflective, and too tender. The cause of liberty was sacred to her, so long as it bore the fruit of justice, self-sacrifice, fidelity to duty. Fanny Wright worshipped liberty for its own sake, confident that every other good would follow it, with the generous, unpractical certainty of conviction that proceeds as much from a sanguine disposition as from a set of opinions. Experience and disappointment have little power over these temperaments, and so they never grow old—or prudent. It may well be that all the ideas, all the great changes, in which is summed up the history of progress, have originated with natures like these. They are the salt of the earth ; but man cannot live by salt alone, and their ideas are carried out for them in detail, and the actual everyday work of the world is unconsciously accomplished, by those who, having put their hand to the plough, do not look back, nor yet far forward.

Still, it was a remarkable meeting, that of these two women. Fanny Wright was a person who, once seen, was not easily forgotten. "She was like Minerva;" such is the recollection of Mrs. Shelley's son. Mrs. Trollope has described her personal appearance when, three years later, she was creating a great sensation by lecturing in the chief American cities—

> She came on the stage surrounded by a bodyguard of Quaker ladies in the full costume of their sect. . . . Her tall and majestic figure, the deep and almost solemn expression of her eyes, the simple contour of her finely-formed head, her garment of plain white muslin, which hung around her in folds that recalled the drapery of a Grecian statue,—all contributed to produce an effect unlike anything that I had ever seen before, or ever expect to see again.

On the other hand the following is Robert Dale Owen's sketch of Mary Shelley.

> . . . In person she was of middle height and graceful figure. Her face, though not regularly beautiful, was comely and spiritual, of winning expression, and with a look of inborn refinement as well as culture. It had a touch of sadness when at rest. She impressed me as a person of warm social feelings, dependent for happiness on living encouragement, needing a guiding and sustaining hand.

It is certain that Mary felt a warm interest in

her new friend. She made her acquainted with
Godwin, and lost no opportunity of seeing and
communing with her during her stay in England ;
nor did they part till Fanny Wright was actually
on board ship.

"Dear love," wrote Fanny, from Torbay, "how your figure
lives in my mind's eye as I saw you borne away from me till
I lost sight of your little back among the shipping !"

From Nashoba, a few months later, she addressed another letter to Mary, which, though
slightly out of place, is given here. There had,
apparently, been some passing discord between
her and the founder of the "New Harmony"
colony.[1]

FRANCES WRIGHT TO MRS. SHELLEY.

NASHOBA, 20*th March* 1828.

Very, very welcome was your letter of the 16th November,
which awaited my return from a little excursion down the
Mississippi, undertaken soon after my arrival. Bless your
sweet kind heart, my sweet Mary ! Your little enclosure,
together with a little billet brought me by Dale, and which
came to the address of Mr. Trollope's chambers just as he left
London, is all the news I have yet received of or from our
knight-errant. Once among Greeks and Turks, correspondence
must be pretty much out of the question, so unless he address
to you some more French compliments from Toulon, I shall

---

[1] Fanny Wright subsequently married a Frenchman, M. Phiquepal
Darusmont. Under the head of "Darusmont" a sketch of her life, by
Mr. R. Garnett, containing many highly interesting details of her career,
is to be found in the *Dictionary of National Biography*.

not look to hear of him for some months. Ay, truly, they are incomprehensible animals, these same *soi-disant* lords of this poor planet! Like their old progenitor, Father Adam, they walk about boasting of their wisdom, strength, and sovereignty, while they have not sense so much as to swallow an apple without the aid of an Eve to put it down their throats. I thank thee for thine attempt to cram caution and wisdom into the cranium of my wandering friend. Thy good offices may afford a chance for his bringing his head on his shoulders to these forests, which otherwise would certainly be left on the shores of the Euxine, on the top of Caucasus, or at the sources of the Nile.

I wrote thee hastily of my arrival and all our wellbeing in my last, and of Dale's *amende honorable*, and of Fanny's departure up the Western waters, nor have I now leisure for details too tedious for the pen, though so short to give by the tongue. Dale arrived, his sweet kind heart all unthawed, and truly when he left us for Harmony I think the very last thin flake of Scotch ice had melted from him. Camilla and Whitby leave me also in a few days for Harmony, from whence the latter will probably travel back with Dale, and Whitby go up the Ohio to engage a mechanic for the building of our houses. I hoped to have sent you, with this, the last communication of our little knot of trustees, in which we have stated the modification of our plan which we have found it advisable to adopt, with the reasons of the same. We have not been able to get it printed at Memphis, so Dale is to have it thrown off at Harmony, from whence you will receive it. The substance of it is, that we have reduced our co-operation to a simple association, each throwing in from our private funds 100 dollars per annum for the expenses of the table, including those of the cook, whom we hire from the Institution, she being one of the slaves gifted to it. All other expenses regard us individually, and need not amount to 100 dollars more. Also, each of us builds his house or room, the cost of which, simple furniture included, does not surpass 500 dollars. The property of the trust will stand thus free of all burden whatsoever, to be devoted to the foundation of a school, in which we would fain attempt a thorough co-operative education, looking only to the next generation to effect what we in vain attempted ourselves. You see that the change consists in demanding as a requisite for admission an independent income of 200 dollars, instead of receiving labour as an equivalent.

Yes, dear Mary, I do find the quiet of these forests and our ill-fenced cabins of rough logs more soothing to the spirit, and now no less suited to the body than the warm luxurious houses of European society. Yet that it would be so with you, or to any less broken in by enthusiastic devotion to human reform and mental liberty than our little knot of associates, I cannot judge. I now almost forget the extent of the change made in the last few years in my habits, yet more than in my views and feelings; but when I recall it, I sometimes doubt if many could imitate it without feeling the sacrifices almost equal to the gains; to me sacrifices are nothing. I have not felt them as such, and now forget that there were any made.

Farewell, dear Mary. Recall me affectionately and respectfully to the memory of your Father. You will wear me in your own, I know. Camilla sends her affectionate wishes.—Yours fondly, F. WRIGHT.

It was probably in connection with Fanny Wright's visit that Mrs. Shelley had, in October of 1827, contemplated the possibility of a flying trip to the Continent; an idea which alarmed her father (for his own sake) not a little, although she had taken care to assure him of her intended speedy return. He was in as bad a way, financially, and as dependent as ever, but proud of the fact that he kept up his good spirits through it all, and sorry for Mary that she could not say as much.

GODWIN TO MARY.

GOWER PLACE, *9th October* 1827.

DEAR MARY—We received your letter yesterday, and I sent you the *Examiner.*

Nothing on earth, as you may perceive, could have induced me to break silence respecting my circumstances, short of your letter of the 1st instant, announcing a trip to the Continent, without the least hint when you should return. It seems to me so contrary to the course of nature that a father should look for supplies to his daughter, that it is painful to me at any time to think of it.

You say that [as] you had announced some time ago that you must be in town in November, I should have inferred that that was irreversible. All I can answer is, that I did not so infer.

I called yesterday, agreeably to your suggestion, upon young Evans; but all I got from him was, that the thing was quite out of his way; to which he added (and I reproved him for it accordingly) that we had better go to the Jews. I called on Hodgetts on the 7th of September, and asked him to lend me £20 or £30. He said, "Would a month hence do? he could then furnish £20." Last Saturday he supped here, and brought me £10, adding that was all he could do. I have heard nothing either from Peacock or from your anonymous friend. I wrote to you, of course, at Brighton on Saturday (before supper-time), which letter I suppose you have received.

How differently you and I are organised. In my seventy-second year I am all cheerfulness, and never anticipate the evil day (with distressing feelings) till to do so is absolutely unavoidable. Would to God you were my daughter in all but my poverty! But I am afraid you are a Wollstonecraft. We are so curiously made that one atom put in the wrong place in our original structure will often make us unhappy for life. But my present cheerfulness is greatly owing to *Cromwell*, and the nature of my occupation, which gives me an object *omnium horarum*—a stream for ever running, and for ever new. Do you remember Denham's verses on the Thames at Cooper's Hill?—

> Oh ! could I flow like thee, and make thy stream
> My great example, as it is my theme !
> Though deep, yet clear, though gentle, yet not dull ;
> Strong, without rage ; without o'erflowing, full.

Though I cannot attain this in my *Commonwealth*, you, perhaps, may in your *Warbeck*.

May blessings shower on you as fast as the perpendicular rain at this moment falls by my window! prays your affectionate Father,   WILLIAM GODWIN.

During most of this autumn Mrs. Shelley and her boy were staying at Arundel, in Sussex, with, or in the near neighbourhood of her friends, the Miss Robinsons. There were several sisters, to one of whom, Julia, Mrs. Shelley was much attached.

While at Arundel another letter reached her from Trelawny, who was contemplating the possibility of a return to England.

TRELAWNY TO MRS. SHELLEY.

ZANTE, IONIAN ISLANDS, 24*th October* 1827.

DEAREST MARY—I received your letter dated July, and replied to both you and Hunt; but I was then at Cerigo, and as the communication of the islands is carried on by a succession of boats, letters are sometimes lost. I have now your letter from Arundel, 9th September. It gives me pleasure to hear your anxieties as to money matters are at an end; it is

one weighty misery off your heart.   You err most egregiously
if you think I am occupied with women or intrigues, or that
my time passes pleasantly.   The reverse of all this is the case ;
neither women nor amusements of any sort occupy my time,
and a sadder or more accursed kind of existence I never in all
my experience of life endured, or, I think, fell to the lot of
human being.   I have been detained here for these last ten
months by a villainous law-suit, which may yet endure some
months longer, and then I shall return to you as the same
unconnected, lone, and wandering vagabond you first knew
me.   I have suffered a continual succession of fevers during
the summer ; at present they have discontinued their attack ;
but they have, added to what I suffered in Greece, cut me
damnably, and I fancy now I must look like an old patriarch
who has outlived his generation.   I cannot tell whether to
congratulate Jane or not ; the foundation she has built on for
happiness implies neither stability nor permanent security ;
for a summer bower 'tis well enough to beguile away the
summer months, but for the winter of life I, for my part,
should like something more durable than a fabric made up of
vows and promises.   Nor can I say whether it would be wise
or beneficial to either should Clare consent to reside with you
in England ; in any other country it might be desirable, but
in England it is questionable.

The only motive which has deterred me from writing to
Jane and Clare is that I have been long sick and ill at ease,
daily anticipating my return to the Continent, and concocting
plans whereby I might meet you all, for one hour after long
absence is worth a thousand letters.   And as to my heart, it
is pretty much as you left it ; no new impressions have been
made on it or earlier affections erased.   As we advance in the
stage of life we look back with deeper recollections from where
we first started ; at least, I find it so.   Since the death of
Odysseus, for whom I had the sincerest friendship, I have felt
no private interest for any individual in this country.   The
Egyptian fleet, and part of the Turkish, amounting to some
hundred sail, including transports, have been totally destroyed

by the united squadron of England, France, and Russia in the harbour of Navarino; so we soon expect to see a portion of Greece wrested from the Turks, and something definitely arranged for the benefit of the Greeks.—Dearest Mary, I am ever your EDWARD TRELAWNY.

To Jane and Clare say all that is affectionate from me, and forget not Leigh Hunt and his Mary Ann. *I* would write them all, but I am sick at heart.

All these months the gnawing sorrow of her friend's faithlessness lay like an ambush at Mary's heart. In responding to Fanny Wright's overtures of friendship she had sought a distraction from the bitter thoughts and deep dejection which had been mainly instrumental in driving her from town. But in vain, like the hunted hare, she buried her head and hoped to be forgotten. Slanderous gossip advances like a prairie-fire, laying everything waste, and defying all attempts to stop or extinguish it. Jane Williams' stories were repeated, and, very likely, improved upon. They got known in a certain set. Mary Shelley might still have chosen not to hear or not to notice, had she been allowed. But who may ignore such things in peace? As the French dramatist says in *Nos Intimes,* "*Les amis sont toujours là.*" *Les amis* are there to enlighten you—if you are ignorant—as to your enemies in disguise, to save you from illusions, and to point out to you— should you forget it—the duty of upholding,

at any sacrifice, your own interests and your
own dignity.

Journal, February 12, 1828.—Moore is in town. By his
advice I disclosed my discoveries to Jane. How strangely
are we made! She is horror-struck and miserable at losing
my friendship; and yet how unpardonably she trifled with my
feelings, and made me all falsely a fable to others.

The visit of Moore has been an agreeable variety to my
monotonous life. I see few people—Lord Dillon, G. Paul,
the Robinsons, *voilà tout*.

Mrs. Shelley to Mrs. Hogg.

Since Monday I have been ceaselessly occupied by the
scene begun and interrupted, which filled me with a pain that
now thrills me as I revert to it. I then strove to speak, but
your tears overcame me, whilst the struggle gave me an appearance of coldness.

If I revert to my devotion to you, it is to prove that no
worldly motives could estrange me from the partner of my
miseries. Often, having you at Kentish Town, I have wept
from the overflow of affection; often thanked God who had
given you to me. Could any but yourself have destroyed such
engrossing and passionate love? And what are the consequences of the change?

When first I heard that you did not love me, every hope
of my life deserted me. The depression I sank under, and to
which I am now a prey, undermines my health. How many
hours this dreary winter I have paced my solitary room, driven
nearly to madness, and I could not expel from my mind the
memories of harrowing import that one after another intruded
themselves! It was not long ago that, eagerly desiring death,
though death should only be oblivion, I thought that how to
purchase oblivion of what was revealed to me last July, a tor-
tuous death would be a bed of roses.

Do not ask me, I beseech you, a detail of the revelations

made to me.   Some of those most painful you made to
several; others, of less import, but which tended more,
perhaps, than the more important to show that you loved
me not, were made only to two.

I could not write of these, far less speak of them.   If any
doubt remain on your mind as to what I know, write to Isabel,[1]
and she will inform you of the extent of her communication
to me.   I have been an altered being since then; long I
thought that almost a deathblow was given, so heavily and
unremittingly did the thought press on and sting me; but one
lives on through all to be a wreck.

Though I was conscious that, having spoken of me as you
did, you could not love me, I could not easily detach myself
from the atmosphere of light and beauty that ever surrounded
you.   Now I tried to keep you, feeling the while that I had lost
you; but you penetrated the change, and I owe it to you not
to disguise the cause.   What will become of us, my poor girl?

   .   .   .   .

This explains my estrangement.   While with you I was
solely occupied by endeavouring not to think or feel, for had
I done either I should not have been so calm as I daresay I
appeared. . . . Nothing but my Father could have drawn me
to town again; his claims only prevent me now from burying
myself in the country.   I have known no peace since July.
I never expect to know it again.   Is it not best, then, that
you forget the unhappy -   M. W. S.?

We hear no more of this painful episode.   It
did not put a stop to Jane's intercourse with Mary.
Friendship, in the old sense, could never be.   But,
to the end of Mary's life, her letters show the
tenderness, the half-maternal solicitude she ever
felt for the companion and sharer of her deepest
affliction.

[1] Miss Robinson.

Another distraction came to her now in the shape of an invitation to Paris, which she accepted, although she was feeling far from well, a fact which she attributed to depression of spirits, but which proved to have quite another cause.

Journal, April 11 (1828).—I depart for Paris, sick at heart, yet pining to see my friend (Julia Robinson).

A lady, an intimate friend of hers at this time, who, in a little book called *Traits of Character*, has given a very interesting (though, in some details, inaccurate) sketch of Mary Shelley, says that her visit to Paris was eagerly looked forward to by many. "Honour to the authoress and admiration for the woman awaited her." But, directly after her arrival, she was prostrated on a sick—it was feared, death-bed. Her journal, three months later, tells the sequel.

Journal, July 8, *Hastings.*—There was a reason for my depression : I was sickening of the small-pox. I was confined to my bed the moment I arrived in Paris. The nature of my disorder was concealed from me till my convalescence, and I am so easily duped. Health, buoyant and bright, succeeded to my illness. The Parisians were very amiable, and, a monster to look at as I was, I tried to be agreeable, to compensate to them.

The same authoress asserts that neither when she recovered nor ever after was she in appearance the Mary Shelley of the past. She was not scarred by the disease ("which in its natural form she had had in childhood"), but the pearly delicacy and transparency of her skin and the brightness and luxuriance of her soft hair were grievously dimmed.

She bore this trial to womanly vanity well and bravely, for she had that within which passeth show—high intellectual endowments, and, better still, a true, loving, faithful heart.

The external effects of her illness must, to a great degree, have disappeared in course of time, for those who never knew her till some twenty years later than this revert to their first impression of her in words almost identical with those used by Christy Baxter when, at ninety years of age, she described Mary Godwin at fifteen as "white, bright, and clear."

If, however, she had any womanly vanity at all, it must have been a trial to her that, just now, her old friend Trelawny should return for a few months to England. She did not see him till November, when Clare also arrived, on a flying visit to her native land. But, before their meeting, she had received some characteristic letters from Trelawny.

TRELAWNY TO MRS. SHELLEY.

SOUTHAMPTON, *8th July* 1828.

DEAR MARY—My moving about and having had much to do must be my excuse for not writing as often as I should do. That it is but an excuse I allow; the truth would be better, but who nowadays ever thinks of speaking truth? The true reason, then, is that I am getting old, and writing has become irksome. You cannot plead either, so write on, dear Mary.

I love you sincerely, no one better. Time has not quenched the fire of my nature ; my feelings and passions burn fierce as ever, and will till they have consumed me. I wear the burnished livery of the sun.

To whom am I a neighbour? and near whom? I dwell amongst tame and civilised human beings, with somewhat the same feelings as we may guess the lion feels when, torn from his native wilderness, he is tortured into domestic intercourse with what Shakespeare calls "forked animals," the most abhorrent to his nature.

You see by this how little my real nature is altered, but now to reply to yours. I cannot decidedly say or fix a period of our meeting. It shall be soon, if you stay there, at Hastings ; but I have business on hand I wish to conclude, and now that I can see you when I determine to do so, I, as you see, postpone the engagement because it is within my grasp. Such is the perverseness of human nature ! Nevertheless, I will write, and I pray you to do so likewise. You are my dear and long true friend, and as such I love you.—Yours, dear,

TRELAWNY.

I shall remain ten or twelve days here, so address Southampton ; it is enough.

TRELAWNY TO MRS. SHELLEY.

TREWITHEN, *September* 1828.

DEAR MARY—I really do not know why I am everlastingly boring you with letters. Perhaps it is to prevent you forgetting me ; or to prove to you that I do not forget you ; or I like it, which is a woman's reason. . . .

How is Jane (Hogg)? Do remember me kindly to her. I hope you are friends, and that I shall see her in town. I have no right to be discontented or fastidious when she is not. I trust she is contented with her lot; if she is, she has an advantage over most of us. Death and Time have made sad havoc amongst my old friends here ; they are never idle, and yet we go on as if they concerned us not, and thus dream our lives away till we wake no more, and then our bodies are thrown into a hole in the earth, like a dead dog's, that infects the atmosphere, and the void is filled up, and we are forgotten.

Can such things be, and overcome us like a summer cloud, without our special wonder? . . .

Trelawny's visit to England was of short duration. Before the end of the next February (1829) he was in Florence, overflowing with new plans, and, as usual, imparting them eagerly, certain of sympathy, to Mrs. Shelley. His renewed intercourse with her had led to no diminution of friendship. He may have found her even more attractive than when she was younger; more equable in spirits, more lenient in her judgments, her whole disposition mellowed and ripened in the stern school of adversity.

Their correspondence, which for two or three years was very frequent, opened, however, with a difference of opinion. Trelawny was ambitious of writing Shelley's biography, and wanted Mary to help him by giving him the facts for it.

TRELAWNY TO MRS. SHELLEY.

POSTE RESTANTE, FLORENCE, 11*th March* 1829.

DEAR MARY—I arrived here some sixteen or seventeen days back. I travelled in a very leisurely way; whilst on the road I used expedition, but I stayed at Lyons, Turin, Genoa, and Leghorn. I have taken up my quarters with Brown. I thought I should get a letter here from you or Clare, but was disappointed. The letter you addressed to Paris I received; tell Clare I was pained at her silence, yet though she neglects to write to me, I shall not follow her example, but will write her in a few days.

My principal object in writing to you now is to tell you that I am actually writing my own life. Brown and Landor are spurring me on, and are to review it sheet by sheet, as it is written ; moreover, I am commencing as a tribute of my great love for the memory of Shelley his life and moral character. Landor and Brown are in this to have a hand, therefore I am collecting every information regarding him. I always wished you to do this, Mary ; if you will not, as of the living I love him and you best, incompetent as I am, I must do my best to show him to the world as I found him. Do you approve of this ? Will you aid in it ? without which it cannot be done. Will you give documents ? Will you write anecdotes ? or—be explicit on this, dear—give me your opinion ; if you in the least dislike it, say so, and there is an end of it ; if on the contrary, set about doing it without loss of time. Both this and my life will be sent you to peruse and approve or alter before publication, and I need not say that you will have free scope to expunge all you disapprove of.

I shall say no more till I get your reply to this.

The winter here, if ten or twelve days somewhat cold can be called winter, has been clear, dry, and sunny ; ever since my arrival in Italy I have been sitting without fire, and with open windows. Come away, dear Mary, from the horrible climate you are in ; life is not endurable where you are.

Florence is very gay, and a weight was taken from my mind, and body too, in getting on this side of the Alps. Heaven and hell cannot be very much more dissimilar. . . .

You may suppose I have now writing enough without scrawling long letters, so pardon this short one, dear Mary, from your affectionate   E. J. TRELAWNY.

P.S.—Love to Clare.

MRS. SHELLEY TO TRELAWNY.

April 1829.

MY DEAR TRELAWNY—Your letter reminded me of my misdeeds of omission, and of not writing to you as I ought,

and it assured me of your kind thoughts in that happy land
where as angels in heaven you can afford pity to us Arctic
islanders. It is too bad, is it not, that when such a Paradise
does exist as fair Italy, one should be chained here, without
the infliction of such absolutely cold weather? I have never
suffered a more ungenial winter. Winter it is still; a cold east
wind has prevailed the last six weeks, making exercise in the
open air a positive punishment. This is truly English; half a
page about the weather, but here this subject has every importance; is it fine? you guess I am happy and enjoying myself;
is it as it always is? you know that one is fighting against a
domestic enemy which saps at the very foundations of pleasure.

I am glad that you are occupying yourself, and I hope
that your two friends will not cease urging you till you really
put to paper the strange wild adventures you recount so well.
With regard to the other subject, you may guess, my dear
Friend, that I have often thought, often done more than think
on the subject. There is nothing I shrink from more fearfully
than publicity. I have too much of it, and, what is worse, I
am forced by my hard situation to meet it in a thousand ways.
Could you write my husband's life without naming me, it
would be something; but even then I should be terrified at
the rousing the slumbering voice of the public;—each critique,
each mention of your work might drag me forward. Nor
indeed is it possible to write Shelley's life in that way. Many
men have his opinions,—none heartily and conscientiously act
on them as he did,—it is his act that marks him.

You know me, or you do not—in which case I will tell you
what I am—a silly goose, who, far from wishing to stand forward to assert myself in any way, now that I am alone in the
world, have but the time to wrap night and the obscurity of
insignificance around me. This is weakness, but I cannot
help it; to be in print, the subject of men's observations, of
the bitter hard world's commentaries, to be attacked or
defended, this ill becomes one who knows how little she
possesses worthy to attract attention, and whose chief merit—

if it be one—is a love of that privacy which no woman can emerge from without regret.

Shelley's life must be written. I hope one day to do it myself, but it must not be published now. There are too many concerned to speak against him; it is still too sore a subject. Your tribute of praise, in a way that cannot do harm, can be introduced into your own life. But remember, I pray for omission, for it is not that you will not be too kind, too eager to do me more than justice. But I only seek to be forgotten.

Clare has written to you she is about to return to Germany. She will, I suppose, explain to you the circumstances that make her return to the lady she was before with desirable. She will go to Carlsbad, and the baths will be of great service to her. Her health is improved, though very far from restored. For myself, I am as usual well in health and longing for summer, when I may enjoy the peace that alone is left me. I am another person under the genial influence of the sun; I can live unrepining with no other enjoyment but the country made bright and cheerful by its beams; till then I languish. Percy is quite well; he grows very fast and looks very healthy.

It gives me great pleasure to hear from you, dear friend, so write often. I have now answered your letter, though I can hardly call this one. So you may very soon expect another. How are your dogs? and where is Roberts? Have you given up all idea of shooting? I hear Medwin is a great man at Florence, so Pisa and economy are at an end. Adieu. —Yours, M. S.

The fiery " Pirate " was much disappointed at Mary's refusal to collaborate with him, and quite unable to understand her unwillingness to be the instrument of making the facts of her own and Shelley's life the subject of public discussion. His resentment soon passed away, but his first wrath was evidently expressed with characteristic vigour.

MARY SHELLEY TO TRELAWNY.

15th December 1829.

. . . Your last letter was not at all kind. You are angry
with me, but what do you ask, and what do I refuse? You
talk of writing Shelley's life, and ask me for materials.
Shelley's life, as far as the public have to do with it, consisted
of few events, and these are publicly known; the private
events were sad and tragical. How would you relate them?
As Hunt has, slurring over the real truth? Wherefore write
fiction? and the truth, any part of it, is hardly for the rude
cold world to handle. His merits are acknowledged, his
virtues;—to bring forward actions which, right or wrong (and
that would be a matter of dispute), were in their results
tremendous, would be to awaken calumnies and give his
enemies a voice.

.   .   .   .

As to giving Moore materials for Lord Byron's life, I thought
—I think—I did right. I think I have achieved a great good
by it. I wish it to be kept secret—decidedly I am averse to
its being published, for it would destroy me to be brought
forward in print. I commit myself on this point to your
generosity. I confided the fact to you as I would anything
I did, being my dearest friend, and had no idea that I was to
find in you a harsh censor and public denouncer. . . .

Did I uphold Medwin? I thought that I had always disliked him. I am sure I thought him a great annoyance, and he
was always borrowing crowns which he never meant to pay and
we could ill spare. He was Jane's friend more than any one's.

To be sure, we did not desire a duel, nor a horsewhipping,
and Lord Byron and Mrs. B. . . . worked hard to promote
peace.—Affectionately yours,   M. W. S.

During this year Mrs. Shelley was busily employed on her own novel, *Perkin Warbeck*, the
subject of which may have occurred to her in con-

nection with the historic associations of Arundel Castle. It is a work of great ingenuity and research, though hardly so spontaneous in conception as her earlier books. In spite of her retired life she had come to be looked on as a celebrity, and many distinguished literary people sought her acquaintance. Among these was Lord Dillon, conspicuous by his good looks, his conversational powers, his many rare qualities of head and heart, and his numerous oddities. Between him and Mrs. Shelley a strong mutual regard existed, and the following letter is of sufficient interest to be inserted here. The writer had desired Mary's opinion on the subject of one of his poems.

LORD DILLON TO MRS. SHELLEY.

DITCHLEY, 18*th March* 1829.

MY DEAR MRS. SHELLEY—I return you many thanks for your letter and your favourable opinion. It is singular that you should have hit upon the two parts that I almost think the best of all my poem. I fear that my delineations of women do not please you, or persons who think as you do. I have a classic feeling about your sex—that is to say, I prefer nature to what is called delicacy. . . . I must be excused, however; I have never loved or much liked women of refined sentiment, but those of strong and blunt feelings and passions. . . . Pray tell me candidly, for I believe you to be sincere, though at first I doubted it, for your manner is reserved, and that put me on my guard; but now I admit you to my full confidence, which I seldom give. Is not Eccelino considered as too free? Tell me then truly—I never quote whenever I write to a person. You may trust me. You might tell me

all the secrets in the world; they would never be breathed.
I shall see you in May, and then we may converse more
freely, but I own you look more sly than I think you are,
and therefore I never was so candid with you as I think I
ought to be. Have not people who did not know you taken
you for a cunning person? You have puzzled me very much.
Women always feel flattered when they are told they have
puzzled people. I will tell you what has puzzled me. Your
writings and your manner are not in accordance. I should
have thought of you—if I had only read you—that you were
a sort of my Sybil, outpouringly enthusiastic, rather indiscreet,
and even extravagant; but you are cool, quiet, and feminine
to the last degree—I mean in delicacy of manner and expression. Explain this to me. Shall I desire my brother to
call on you with respect to Mr. Peter in the Tower? He is
his friend, not mine. He is very clever, and I think you
would like him. Pray tell Miss G. to write to me.—Yours
most truly, DILLON.

Journal, October 8 (1829).—I was at Sir Thomas Lawrence's to-day whilst Moore was sitting, and passed a delightful
morning. We then went to the Charter House, and I saw his
son, a beautiful boy.

January 9 (1830).—Poor Lawrence is dead.

Having seen him so lately, the suddenness of this event
affects me deeply. His death opens all wounds. I see all
those I love die around me, while I lament.

January 22.—I have begun a new kind of life somewhat,
going a little into society and forming a variety of acquaintances. People like me, and flatter and follow me, and then
I am left alone again, poverty being a barrier I cannot pass.
Still I am often amused and sometimes interested.

March 23.—I gave a *soirée*, which succeeded very well.
Mrs. Hare is going, and I am very sorry. She likes me, and
she is gentle and good. Her husband is clever and her set
very agreeable, rendered so by the reunion of some of the
best people about town.

Mrs. Shelley now resided in Somerset Street, Portman Square. Her occasional " at homes," though of necessity simple in character, were not on that account the less frequented. Here might be met many of the most famous and most charming men and women of their day, and here Moore would thrill all hearts and bring tears to all eyes by his exquisitely pathetic singing of his own melodies.

The hostess herself, gentle and winning, was an object of more admiration than would ever be suspected from the simple, almost deprecatory tone of her scraps of journal. Among her MSS. are numerous anonymous poems addressed to her, some sentimental, others high-flown in compliment, though none, unfortunately, of sufficient literary merit to be, in themselves, worth preserving. But, whether they afforded her amusement or gratification, it is probable that she had to work too hard and too continuously to give more than a passing thought to such things. From the following letter of Clare's it may be inferred that *Perkin Warbeck*, which appeared in 1830, was, in a pecuniary sense, something of a disappointment, and that this was the more vexatious as Mary had lent Clare money during her visit to England, and would have been glad, now, to be repaid, not, however, on her own account, but that of Marshall, Godwin's former amanuensis and her kind friend

in her childhood, whom, it is evident, she was helping to support in his old age.

CLARE TO MRS. SHELLEY.

DRESDEN, 28*th March* 1830.

MY DEAR MARY—At last I take up the pen to write to you.
At least thus much can I affirm, that I take it up, but whether
I shall ever get to the end of my task and complete this letter
is beyond me to decide.   One of the causes of my long delay
has been the hope of being able to send you the money for
Marshall.   I was to have been paid in February, but as yet
have received neither money nor notice from Mrs. K. . . .   By
this I am led to think she does not intend to do so until
her return here in May.   I am vexed, for I have been reproach-
ing myself the whole winter with this debt.   Of this be sure,
the instant I am paid I will despatch what I owe you to London. . . .   Here I was interrupted, and for two days have
been unable to continue.   How delighted I was with the news
of Percy's health, as also with his letter, though I am afraid it
was written unwillingly and cost him a world of pains.   Poor
child ! he little thinks how much I am attached to him !   When
I first saw him I thought him cold, but afterwards he discovered
so much intellect in all his speeches, and so much originality in
his doings, that I willingly pardoned him for not being interested
in anything but himself.   In some weeks he will again be at
home for Easter.   But what is this to me, since I shall not
see him, nor perhaps even ever again.   It seems settled that my
destination is Vienna.   The negotiation with Mrs. K. . . . has
been broken off on my showing great unwillingness to go to
Italy ; that it may not be renewed I will not say.   She now
talks of going to Nice, to which place I have no objection in
the world to accompany her.   But nothing of this can be
settled till she comes, for as neither of us can speak frankly in
our letters, owing to their being subject to her husband's
inspection, we have as yet done nothing but mutually mis-
interpret the circumspect and circuitous phraseology in which

our real meaning was wrapped.   Nothing can equal the letters
she has written to me; they were detached pieces of agony.
How she lived at all after bringing such productions into the
world I cannot guess.   Instruments of torture are nothing to
them.   She favoured me with one every week, which was a
very clever contrivance on her part to keep us in an agitation
equal to the one she suffered at Moghiteff.   Thanks to her
and Natalie's perpetual indisposition, I have passed a tolerably
disagreeable winter.   At home I was employed in rubbings,
stretchings, putting on trusses, dressing ulcers, applying leeches,
and bandaging swollen glands.   Out-of-doors our recreations
were [all] baths, baths of bullock's blood, mud baths, steam
baths, soap baths, and electricity.   If I had served in a
hospital I should not have been more constantly employed
with sickness and its appendages.   I could understand this
order of things pretty well, and even perhaps from custom find
some beauty in their deformity if the sky were pitch black
and the stars red ; but when I see them so beautiful I cannot
help imagining that they were made to look down upon a life
more consonant with their own natures than the one I lead,
and I am filled with the most bitter dislike of it.   I ought to
confess, however, that it is a great mitigation of my disagreeable
life to live in Dresden ; such is the structure of existence here
that a thousand alleviations to misery are offered.   Here, as
in Italy, you cannot walk the streets without meeting with
some object which affords ready and agreeable occupation to
the mind.   I never yet was in a place where I met so much
to please and so little to shock me.   In vain I endeavour to
recollect anything I could wish otherwise ; not a fault presents
itself.   The more I become acquainted with the town and see its
smallness, the more I am struck with the uncommon resources
in literature *e le belle arti* it possesses.   With what regret
shall I leave it for Vienna.   Farewell, then, a long farewell to
Mount Olympus and its treasures of wisdom, science, poetry,
and skill ; the vales may be green and many rills trill through
them, and many flocks pasture there, but the inhabitants will
be as vile and miserable to me as were the shepherds of

Admetus to Apollo when he kept their company.   At any rate
Vienna is better than Russia.   I trust and hope when I am
there you will make some little effort to procure the newspapers
and reviews and new works ; this alone can soften the mortification I shall feel in being obliged to live in that city.   Already
I have lost the little I had gained in my English, and I can
only write with an effort that is painful to me ; it precludes
the possibility of my finding any pleasure in composition.   I
pause a hundred times and lean upon my hand to endeavour
to find words to express the idea that is in my mind.   It is a
vain endeavour ; the idea is there, but no words, and I leave
my task unfinished.   Another favour I have to ask you, which
is, if I should require your mediation to get a book published
at Paris, you will write to your friends there, and otherwise
interest yourself as warmly as you can about it.   Promise me
this, and give me an answer upon it as quick as you can.   I
have had many letters from Charles.   His affairs have taken
the most favourable turn at Vienna.   Everything is *couleur de
rose.*   More employment than he can accept seems likely to
be offered to him ; this is consolatory.   He talks with rapture
of his future plans, has taken a charming house, painted and
furnished a pretty room for me, and will send Antonia and the
babes to the lovely hills at some miles from the town so soon
as they arrive.

Mamma has written to me everything concerning Colburn ;
this is indeed a disappointment, and the more galling because
odiously unjust.   Let me hear if your plan of writing the
Memoirs of Josephine is likely to be put into execution.   This
perhaps would pay you better.   I tremble for the anxiety of
mind you suffer about Papa and your own pecuniary resources.

What says the world to Moore's *Lord Byron?*   I saw some
extracts in a review, and cannot express the pleasure I experienced in finding it was sad stuff.   It was the journal of the
Noble Lord, and I should say contained as fine a picture of
indigestion as one could expect to meet with in Dr. Paris,
Graham, or Johnson.   Of Trelawny I know little.   He wrote

to me, describing where he was living and what kind of life he was leading. I have not yet answered him, although I make a sacred promise every day not to let it go over my head without so doing. But there is a certain want of sympathy between us which makes writing to him extremely disagreeable to me. I admire, esteem, and love him; some excellent qualities he possesses in a degree that is unsurpassed, but then it is exactly in another direction from my centre and my impetus. He likes a turbid and troubled life, I a quiet one; he is full of fine feelings and has no principles, I am full of fine principles but never had a feeling; he receives all his impressions through his heart, I through my head. *Que voulez vous? Le moyen de se recontrer* when one is bound for the North Pole and the other for the South?

What a terrible description you give of your winter. Ours, though severe, was an exceedingly fine one. From the time I arrived here until now there has not been a day that was not perfectly dry and clear. Within this last week we have had a great deal of rain. I well understand how much your spirits must have been affected by three months' incessant foggy raw weather. In my mind nothing can compensate for a bad climate. How I wish I could draw you to Dresden. You would go into society and would see a quantity of things which, treated by your pen, would bring you in a good profit. Life is very cheap here, and in the summer you might take a course of Josephlitz or Carlsbad, which would set up your health and enable you to bear the winter of London with tolerable philosophy. Forgive me if I don't write descriptions. It is impossible, situated as I am. I have not one moment free from annoyance from morning till night. This state of things depresses my mind terribly. When I have a moment of leisure it is breathed in a prayer for death. You will not wonder, therefore, that I think the Miss Booths right in their manner of acting; what is the use of trifling or mincing the matter with so despotic a ruler as the Disposer of the Universe? The one who is left is much to be pitied, for now she must die by herself, and that I think is as disagreeable as to live by

oneself. In your next pray mention something about politics
and how the London University is getting on. The accounts
here of the distress in England are awful. Foreigners talk of
that country as they would of Torre del Greco or Torre dell'
Annunciata at the announcement of an eruption of Vesuvius.
I should think my mother must be delighted to be no more
plagued with us; it was really a great bother and no pleasure
for her. She writes me a delightful account of Papa's health
and spirits. Heaven grant it may continue. I am reading
Political Justice, and am filled with admiration at the vastness
of the plan, and the clearness and skill, nothing less than
immortal, with which it is executed.

Farewell! write to me about your novel and particularly
the opinion it creates in society. Pray write. The letters of
my acquaintances (friends I have none) are my only pleasure.
Natalie is pretty well; the knee is better, inasmuch as the
swelling is smaller, but the weakness is as great as ever. We
sit opposite to one another in perfect wretchedness; I because
I am obliged to entreat her all day to do what she does not
like, and she because she is entreated.   C. C.

My love to William.

During the next five years the "Author of
Frankenstein" wrote several short tales (some of
which were published in the *Keepsake*, an annual
periodical, the precursor of the *Book of Beauty*),
but no new novel. She was to have abundant
employment in furthering the work of another.

CHAPTER XXII

August 1830–October 1831

To all who know Trelawny's curious book, the
following correspondence, which tells the story of
its publication and preparation for the press, will
in itself be interesting. To readers of Mary
Shelley's life it has a strong additional interest as
illustrating, better than any second-hand narrative
can do, the unique kind of friendship subsisting
between her and Trelawny, and which, based on
genuine mutual regard and admiration, and a
common devotion to the memory of Shelley and of
a golden age which ended at his death, proved
stronger than all obstacles, and, in spite of
occasional eclipses through hasty words and mis-
understandings, in spite of wide differences in temperament, in habits, in opinions, and morals, yet
survived with a kind of dogged vitality for years.

Shelley said of *Epipsychidion* that it was "an
idealised history of his life and feelings." *The
Adventures of a Younger Son* is an idealised history of Trelawny's youth and exploits, and very

amusing it is, though rather gruesome in some of its details; a romance of adventures, of hair-breadth escapes by flood and field. As will be seen, the original MS. had to be somewhat toned down before it was presented to the public, but it is, as it stands, quite sufficiently forcible, as well as blood-curdling, for most readers.

The letters may now be left to tell their own tale.

TRELAWNY TO MRS. SHELLEY.

16th August 1830.

My dear Mary—That my letter may not be detained, I shall say nothing about Continental politics.

My principal motive in writing is to inform you that I have nearly completed the first portion of *my History*, enough for three ordinary volumes, which I wish published forthwith. The Johnsons, as I told you before, are totally ruined by an Indian bankruptcy; the smallness of my income prevents my supporting them. Mr. Johnson is gone to India to see if he can save aught from the ruin of his large fortune. In the meantime his wife is almost destitute; this spurs me on. Brown, who is experienced in these matters, declares I shall have no difficulty in getting a very considerable sum for the MS. now. I shall want some friend to dispose of it for me. My name is not to appear or to be disclosed to the bookseller or any other person. The publisher who may purchase it is to be articled down to publish the work without omitting or altering a single word, there being nothing actionable, though a great deal objectionable, inasmuch as it is tinctured with the prejudices and passions of the author's mind. However, there is nothing to prevent women reading it but its general want of merit. The opinion of the two or three who have read it is that it will be very successful, but I know how little value can be attached to such critics. I'll tell you what I think—that it is good, and might have been better; it is [filled] with events that, if not marred by my manner of narrating, must be interesting. I therefore plainly foresee it will be generally read or not at all. Who will undertake to, in the first place, dispose of it, and, in the second, watch its progress through the press? I care not who publishes it: the highest bidder shall have it. Murray would not like it, it is too violent; parsons and *Scots*, and, in short, also others are spoken of irreverently, if not pro- fanely. But when I have your reply I shall send the MS. to England, and your eyes will be the judge, so tell me precisely your movements.—Your attached   E. J. T.

Poste Restante, Florence.

When does Moore conclude his *Life of Byron*? If I knew his address I could give him a useful hint that would be of service to the fame of the Poet.

TRELAWNY TO MRS. SHELLEY.

FLORENCE, 28*th October* 1830.

DEAREST MARY—My friend Baring left Florence on the 25th to proceed directly to London, so that he will be there as soon as you can get this letter. He took charge of my MSS., and promised to leave them at Hookham's, Bond Street, addressed to you. I therefore pray you lose no time in inquiring about them; they are divided into chapters and volumes, copied out in a plain hand, and all ready to go to press. They have been corrected with the greatest care, and I do not think you will have any trouble with them on that score. All I want you to do is to read them attentively, and then show them to Murray and Colburn, or any other pub- lisher, and to hear if they will publish them and what they will give. You may say the author cannot at present be *named*, but that, when the work goes forth in the world, there are many who will recognise it. Besides the second series, which treats of Byron, Shelley, Greece, etc., will at once remove the veil, and the publisher who has the first shall have that. Yet at present I wish the first series to go forth strictly anonymous,

and therefore you must on no account trust the publisher with
my name. Surely there is matter enough in the book to make
it interesting, if only viewed in the light of a *romance*. You
will see that I have divided it into very short chapters, in the
style of Fielding, and that I have selected mottoes from the
only three poets who were the staunch advocates of liberty,
and my contemporaries. I have left eight or nine blanks in
the mottoes for you to fill up from the work of one of those
poets. Brown, who was very anxious about the fame of Keats,
has given many of his MSS. for the purpose. Now, if you
could find any from the MSS. of Shelley or Byron, they would
excite much interest, and their being strictly applicable is not
of much importance. If you cannot, why, fill them up from
the published works of Byron, Shelley, or Keats, but no others
are to be admitted. When you have read the work and heard
the opinion of the booksellers, write to me before you settle
anything; only remember I am very anxious that no alterations or omissions should be made, and that the mottoes,
whether long or short, double or treble, should not be curtailed. Will not Hogg assist you? I might get other people,
but there is no person I have such confidence in as you, and
the affair is one of confidence and trust, and are we not bound
and united together by ties stronger than those which earth
has to impose? Dearest friend, I am obliged hastily to conclude.—Yours affectionately, E. J. TRELAWNY.

George Baring, Esq., who takes my book, is the brother of
the banker; he has read it, and is in my confidence, and will
be very ready to see and confer with you and do anything.
He is an excellent person. I shall be very anxious till I hear
from you.

MRS. SHELLEY TO TRELAWNY.

33 SOMERSET STREET,
27th December 1830.

MY DEAR TRELAWNY—At present I can only satisfy your
impatience with the information that I have received your MS.

and read the greater part of it. Soon I hope to say more.
George Baring did not come to England, but after considerable delay forwarded it to me from Cologne.

I am delighted with your work; it is full of passion, energy,
and novelty; it concerns the sea, and that is a subject of the
greatest interest to me. I should imagine that it must command success.

But, my dear friend, allow me to persuade you to permit
certain omissions. In one of your letters to me you say that
"there is nothing in it that a woman could not read." You
are correct for the most part, and yet without the omission of
a few words here and there—the scene before you go to school
with the mate of your ship—and above all the scene of the
burning of the house, following your scene with your Scotch
enemy—I am sure that yours will be a book interdicted to
women. Certain words and phrases, pardoned in the days of
Fielding, are now justly interdicted, and any gross piece of ill
taste will make your booksellers draw back.

I have named all the objectionable passages, and I beseech
you to let me deal with them as I would with Lord Byron's
Don Juan, when I omitted all that hurt my taste. Without
this yielding on your part I shall experience great difficulty in
disposing of your work; besides that I, your partial friend,
strongly object to coarseness, now wholly out of date, and beg
you for my sake to make the omissions necessary for your obtaining feminine readers. Amidst so much that is beautiful and
imaginative and exalting, why leave spots which, believe me, are
blemishes? I hope soon to write to you again on the subject.

The burnings, the alarms, the absorbing politics of the day
render booksellers almost averse to publishing at all. God
knows how it will all end, but it looks as if the autocrats would
have the good sense to make the necessary sacrifices to a
starving people.

I heard from Clare to-day; she is well and still at Nice. I
suppose there is no hope of seeing you here. As for me, I of
course still continue a prisoner. Percy is quite well, and is
growing more and more like Shelley. Since it is necessary to

live, it is a great good to have this tie to life, but it is a weari-
some affair. I hope you are happy.——Yours, my dearest friend,
ever, MARY SHELLEY.

TRELAWNY TO MRS. SHELLEY.

FIRENZE, 19*th January* 1831.

MY DEAREST MARY—For, notwithstanding what you may
think of me, you every day become dearer to me. The men
I have linked myself to in my wild career through life have
almost all been prematurely cut off, and the only friends which
are left me are women, and they are strange beings. I have
lost them all by some means or other ; they are dead to me in
being married, or (for you are all slaves) separated by obstacles
which are insurmountable, and as Lord Chatham observes,
" Friendship is a weed of slow growth in aged bosoms." But
now to your letter. I to-day received yours of the 27th of
December ; you say you have received my MS. It has been
a painful and arduous undertaking narrating my life. I have
omitted a great deal, and avoided being a pander to the
public taste for the sake of novelty or effect. Landor, a man
of superior literary acquirements ; Kirkup, an artist of superior
taste ; Baring, a man of the world and very religious ; Mrs.
Baring, moral and squeamish ; Lady Burghersh, aristocratic
and proud as a queen ; and lastly, Charles Brown, a plain
downright Cockney critic, learned in the trade of authorship,
and has served his time as a literary scribe. All these male
and female critics have read and passed their opinions on my
narrative, and therefore you must excuse my apparent pre-
sumption in answering your objections to my book with an
appearance of presumptuous dictation. Your objections to the
coarseness of those scenes you have mentioned have been fore-
seen, and, without further preface or apology, I shall briefly
state my wishes on the subject. Let Hogg or Horace Smith
read it, and, without your *giving any* opinion, hear theirs ; then
let the booksellers, Colburn or others, see it, and then if it is
their general opinion that there are *words* which are better

omitted, why I must submit to their being omitted; but do not prompt them by prematurely giving your opinion. My life, though I have sent it you, as the dearest friend I have, is not written for the amusement of women; it is not a novel. If you begin clipping the wings of my true story, if you begin erasing words, you must then omit sentences, then chapters; it will be pruning an Indian jungle down to a clipped French garden. I shall be so appalled at my MS. in its printed form, that I shall have no heart to go on with it. Dear Mary, I love women, and you know it, but my life is not dedicated to them; it is to men I write, and my first three volumes are principally adapted to sailors. England is a nautical nation, and, if they like it, the book will amply repay the publisher, and I predict it will be popular with sailors, for it is true to its text. By the time you get this letter the time of publishing is come, and we are too far apart to continue corresponding on the subject. Let Hogg, Horace Smith, or any one you like, read the MS.; or the booksellers; if they absolutely object to any particular words or short passages, why let them be omitted by leaving blanks; but I should prefer a first edition as it now stands, and then a second as the bookseller thought best. In the same way that *Anastasius* was published, the suppression of the first edition of that work did not prevent its success. All men lament that *Don Juan* was not published as it was written, as under any form it would have been interdicted to women, and yet under any form they would have unavoidably read it.

Brown, who is learned in the bookselling trade, says I should get £200 per volume. Do not dispose of it under any circumstances for less than £500 the three volumes. Have you seen a book written by a man named Millingen? He has written an article on me, and I am answering it. My reply to it I shall send you. The *Literary Gazette*, which published the extract regarding me, I have replied to, and to them I send my reply; the book I have not seen. If they refuse, as the article I write is amusing, you will have no difficulty in getting it admitted in some of the London maga-

zines. It will be forwarded to you in a few days, so you see
I am now fairly coming forward in a new character. I have
laid down the sword for the pen. Brown has just called with
the article in question copied, and I send it together.

I have spoken to you about filling up the mottoes; the
title of my book I wish to be simply thus—*The Life of a Man*,
and not *The Discarded Son*, which looks too much like
romance or a common novel. . . .

Florence is very gay, and there are many pretty girls here,
and balls every night. Tell Mrs. Paul not to be angry at my
calling her and her sisters by their Christian names, for I am
very lawless, as you know, in that particular, and not very
particular on other things.

Brown talks of writing to you about the mottoes to my
book, as he is very anxious about those of his friend Keats.
Have you any MS. of Shelley's or Byron's to fill up the eight
or ten I left blank? Remember the short chapters are to be
adhered to in its printed form. I shall have no excitement to
go on writing till I see what I have already written in print.
By the bye, my next volumes will to general readers be far
more interesting, and published with my name, or at least
called Treloen, which is our original family name.

TRELAWNY TO MRS. SHELLEY.

POSTE RESTANTE, FIRENZE,
5th April 1831.

MY DEAR MARY—Since your letter, dated December 1830,
I have not had a single line from you, yet in that you promised
to write in a few days. Why is this? or have you written,
and has your letter miscarried, or have not my letters reached
you? I was anxious to have published the first part of my
life this year, and if it had succeeded in interesting general
readers, it would have induced me to have proceeded to its
completion, for I cannot doubt that if the first part, published
anonymously, and treating of people, countries, and things
little known, should suit the public palate, that the latter,

treating of people that everybody knows, and of things generally interesting, must be successful.   But till I see the effect
of the first part, I cannot possibly proceed to the second, and
time is fleeting, and I am lost in idleness.   I cannot write a
line, and thus six months, in which I had leisure to have
finished my narrative, are lost, and I am now deeply engaged
in a wild scheme which will lead me to the East, and it is
firmly my belief that when I again leave Europe it will be for
ever.   I have had too many hair-breadth escapes to hope that
fortune will bear me up.   My present Quixotic expedition is
to be in the region wherein is still standing the column erected
by Sardanapalus, and on it by him inscribed words to the
effect : *Il faut jouir des plaisirs de la vie ; tout le reste n'est
rien.*

At present I can only say, if nothing materially intervenes
to prevent me, that in the autumn of this year I shall bend my
steps towards the above-mentioned column, and try the effect
of it.

I am sick to death of the pleasureless life I lead here, and
I should rather the tinkling of the little bell, which I hear
summoning the dead to its last resting-place, was ringing for
my body than endure the petty vexations of what is called
civilised life, and see what I saw a few days back, the Austrian
tyrants trampling on their helot Italians ; but letters are not
safe.—Your affectionate friend,   E. J. T.

MRS. SHELLEY TO TRELAWNY.

SOMERSET STREET, 22*d March* 1831.

MY DEAR TRELAWNY—What can you think of me and of
my silence ?   I can guess by the contents of your letters and
your not having yet received answers.   Believe me that if I
am at all to blame in this it arises from an error in judgment,
not from want of zeal.   Every post-day I have waited for the
next, expecting to be able to communicate something defini-
tive, and now still I am waiting ; however, I trust that this
letter will contain some certain intelligence before I send it.

After all, I have done no more than send your manuscripts to Colburn, and I am still in expectation of his answer. In the first place, they insist on certain parts being expunged,—parts of which I alone had the courage to speak to you, but which had before been remarked upon as inadmissible. These, however (with trifling exceptions), occur only in the first volume. The task of deciding upon them may very properly be left to Horace Smith, if he will undertake it—we shall see. Meanwhile, Colburn has not made up his mind as to the price. He will not give £500. The terms he will offer I shall hope to send before I close this letter, so I will say no more except to excuse my having conceded so much time to his dilatoriness. In all I have done I may be wrong; I commonly act from my own judgment; but alas! I have great experience. I *believe* that, if I sent your work to Murray, he would return it in two months unread; simply saying that he does not print novels. Your end part would be a temptation, did not your intention to be severe on Moore make it improbable that he would like to engage in it; and he would keep me as long as Colburn in uncertainty; still this may be right to do, and I shall expect your further instructions by return of post. However, in one way you may help yourself. You know Lockhart. He reads and judges for Murray; write to him; your letter shall accompany the MS. to him. Still, this thing must not be done hastily, for if I take the MS. out of Colburn's hands, and, failing to dispose of it elsewhere, I come back to him, he will doubtless retreat from his original proposal. There are other booksellers in the world, doubtless, than these two, but, occupied as England is by political questions, and impoverished miserably, there are few who have enterprise at this juncture to offer a price. I quote examples. My father and myself would find it impossible to make any tolerable arrangement with any one except Colburn. He at least may be some guide as to what you may expect. Mr. Brown remembers the golden days of authors. When I first returned to England I found no difficulty in making agreements with publishers; they came to seek me; now money is scarce, and readers fewer than ever.

I leave the rest of this page blank. I shall fill it up before it goes on Friday.

Friday, 25th March.

At length, my dear friend, I have received the ulti- matum of these great people. They offer you £300, and another £100 on a second edition; as this was sent me in writing, and there is no time for further communication before post-hour, I cannot *officially* state the number of the edition. I should think 1000. I think that perhaps they may be brought to say £400 at once, or £300 at once and £200 on the second edition. There can be no time for par- leying, and therefore you must make up your mind whether after doing good battle, if necessary, I shall accept their terms. Believe *my experience* and that of those about me; you will not get a better offer from others, because money is not to be had, and Bulwer and other fashionable and selling authors are now obliged to content themselves with half of what they got before. If you decline this offer, I will, if you please, try Murray; he will keep me two months at least, and the worst is, if he won't do anything, Colburn will diminish his bargain, and we shall be in a greater mess than ever. I know that, as a woman, I am timid, and therefore a bad negotiator, except that I have perseverance and zeal, and, I repeat, experi- ence of things as they are. Mr. Brown knows what they were, but they are sadly changed. The omissions mentioned must be made, but I will watch over them, and the mottoes and all that shall be most carefully attended to, depend on me.

Do not be displeased, my dear friend, that I take advantage of this enormous sheet of paper to save postage, and ask you to tear off one half sheet, and to send it to Mrs. Hare. You talk of my visiting Italy. It is impossible for me to tell you how much I repine at my imprisonment here, but I dare not anticipate a change to take me there for a long time. England, its ungenial clime, its difficult society, and the annoyances to which I am subjected in it weigh on my spirits more than ever, for every step I take only shows me how impossible [it is], situated as I am, that I should be otherwise than wretched. My sanguine disposition and capacity to endure have borne me up hitherto, but I am sinking at last; but to quit so stupid a topic and to tell you news, did you hear that Medwin contrived to get himself gazetted for full pay in the Guards? I fancy that he employed his connection with the Shelleys, who are connected with the King through the Fitz Clarences. However, a week after he was gazetted as retiring. I suppose the officers cut him at mess; his poor wife and children! how I pity them! Jane is quite well, living in tranquillity. Hogg continues all that she can desire. . . .

She lives where she did; her children are well, and so is my Percy, who grows more like Shelley. I hear that your old favourite, Margaret Shelley, is prettier than ever; your Miss Burdett is married. I have been having lithographed your letter to me about Caroline. I wish to disperse about 100 copies among the many hapless fair who imagine themselves to have been the sole object of your tenderness. Clare is to have a first copy. Have you heard from poor dear Clare? She announced a little time ago that she was to visit Italy with the Kaisaroff to see you. I envied her, but I hear from her brother Charles that she has now quarrelled with Madame K., and that she will go to Vienna. God grant that her sufferings end soon. I begin to anticipate it, for I hear that Sir Tim is in a bad way. I shall hear more certain intelligence after Easter. Mrs. P. spends her Easter with Caroline, who lives in the neighbourhood, and will dine at Field Place. I have not seen Mrs. Aldridge since her marriage; she has scarcely been in town, but I shall see her this spring, when she comes up as she intends. You know, of course, that Elizabeth St. Aubyn is married, so you know that your ladies desert you sadly. If Clare and I were either to die or marry you would be left without a Dulcinea at all, with the exception of the sixscore new objects for idolatry you may have found among the pretty girls in Florence. Take courage, however; I am scarcely a Dulcinea, being your friend and not the Lady of your love, but such as I am, I do not think that I shall either die or marry this year, whatever may happen the next; as it is only spring you have some time before you.

We are all here on the *qui vive* about the Reform Bill; if it pass, and Tories and all expect it, well,—if not, Parliament is dissolved immediately, and they say that the new writs are in preparation. The Whigs triumphed gloriously in the boldness of their measure. England will be free if it is carried. I have had very bad accounts from Rome, but you are quiet as usual in Florence. I am scarcely wicked enough to desire that you should be driven home, nor do I expect it, and yet how glad I should be to see you. You never mention Zela. Adieu, my dear Trelawny.—I am always affectionately yours,

MARY W. SHELLEY.

Hunt has set up a little 2d. paper, the *Tatler*, which is succeeding; this keeps him above water. I have not seen him very lately. He lives a long way off. He is the same as ever, a person whom all must love and regret.

TRELAWNY TO MRS. SHELLEY.

POSTE RESTANTE, FIRENZE,
8th April 1831.

DEAR MARY—The day after I had despatched a scolding letter to you, I received your Titanic letter, and sent Mrs. Hare her fathom of it. . . .

Now, let's to business. I thank you for the trouble you have taken about the MS. Let Colburn have it, and try to get £400 down, for as to what may be promised on a second edition, I am told is mere humbug. When my work is completed I have no doubt the first part will be reprinted, but get what you can paid down at once; as to the rest, I have only to say that I consent to Horace Smith being the sole arbitrator of what is necessary to be omitted, but do not let him be prompted, and tell him only to omit what is *absolutely indispensable*. Say to him that it is a friend of Shelley's who asks him this favour, but do not let him or any other individual

know that I am the author.   If my name is known, and the
work can be brought home to me, the consequences will be
most disastrous.   I beseech you bear this in mind.   Let
all the mottoes appear in their respective chapters without any
omission, regardless of their number to each chapter, for they
are all good, and fill up the eight or ten I left blank from
Byron and Shelley; if from MS. so much the better.   The
changes in the opinions of all mankind on political and other
topics are favourable to such writers as I and the Poets of
Liberty whom I have selected.   We shall no longer be hooted
at; it is our turn to triumph now.   Would those glorious
spirits, to whose genius the present age owes so much, could
witness the triumphant success of these opinions.   I think I
see Shelley's fine eyes glisten, and faded cheek glow with fire
unearthly.   England, France, and Belgium free, the rest of
Europe must follow; the theories of tyrants all over the world
are shaken as by an earthquake; they may be propped up for
a time, but their fall is inevitable.   I am forgetting the main
business of my letter.   I hope, Mary, that you have not told
Colburn or any one else that I am the author of the book.
Remember that I must have the title simply *A Man's Life*,
and that I should like to have as many copies for my friends
as you can get from Colburn—ten, I hope—and that you will
continue to report progress, and tell me when it is come out.
You must have a copy, Horace Smith one, and Jane and Lady
Burghersh; she is to be heard of at Apsley House—Duke of
Wellington's—and then I have some friends here; you must
send me a parcel by sea.   If the time is unfavourable for
publication, from men's minds being engrossed with politics,
yet it is so far an advantage that my politics go with the times,
and not as they would have been some years back, obnoxious
and premature.   I decide on Colburn as publisher, not from
liberality of his terms, but his courage, and trusting that as
little as possible will be omitted; and, by the bye, I wish you
to keep copies, for I have none, of those parts which are
omitted.   Enough of this.   Of Clare I have seen nothing.
Do not you, dear Mary, abandon me by following the evil

examples of my other ladies. I should not wonder if fate, without our choice, united us; and who can control his fate? I blindly follow his decrees, dear Mary.—Your

E. J. T.

MRS. SHELLEY TO TRELAWNY.

SOMERSET STREET, 14*th June* 1831.

MY DEAR TRELAWNY—Your work is in progress at last, and is being printed with great rapidity. Horace Smith undertook the revision, and sent a very favourable report of it to the publishers; to me he says : " Having written to you a few days ago, I have only to annex a copy of my letter to Colburn and Bentley, whence you will gather my opinion of the MS.; it is a most powerful, but rather perilous work, which will be much praised and much abused by the liberal and bigoted. I have read it with great pleasure and think it admirable, in everything but the conclusion;" by this he means, as he says to Colburn and Bentley, "The conclusion is abrupt and disappointing, especially as previous allusions have been made to his later life which is not given. Probably it is meant to be continued, and if so it would be better to state it, for I have no doubt that his first part will create a sufficient sensation to ensure the sale of a second."

In his former letter to me H. S. says : " Any one who has proved himself the friend of yourself and of him whom we all deplore I consider to have strong claims on my regard, and I therefore willingly undertake the revision of the MS. Pray assure the author that I feel flattered by this little mark of his confidence in my judgment, and that it will always give me pleasure to render him these or any other services." And now, my dear Trelawny, I hope you will not be angry at the title given to your book; the responsibility of doing anything for any one so far away as you is painful, and I have had many qualms, but what could I do? The publishers strongly objected to the *History of a Man* as being no title at all, or rather one to lead astray. The one adopted is taken from the first words of your MS., where you declare yourself a younger son—words pregnant of meaning in this country, where to be the younger son of a man of property is to be virtually discarded,—and they will speak volumes to the English reader; it is called, therefore, *The Adventures of a Younger Son.* If you are angry with me for this I shall be sorry, but I knew not what to do.   Your MS. will be preserved for you; and remember, also, that it is pretty well known whom it is by. I suppose the persons who read the MS. in Italy have talked, and, as I told you, your mother speaks openly about it. Still it will not appear in print, in no newspaper accounts over which I have any control as emanating from the publisher. Let me know immediately how I am to dispose of the dozen copies I shall receive on your account.   One must go to H. Smith, another to me, and to whom else?   The rest I will send to you in Italy.

There is another thing that annoys me especially.   You will be paid in bills dating from the day of publication, now not far distant; three of various dates.   To what man of business of yours can I consign these? the first I should think I could get discounted at once, and send you the cash; but tell me what I am to do.   I know that all these hitches and draw-backs will make you vituperate womankind, and had I ever set myself up for a woman of business, or known how to manage my own affairs, I might be hurt; but you know my irremediable deficiencies on those subjects, and I represented them strongly to you before I undertook my task; and all I can say in addition is, that as far as I have seen, both have been obliged to make the same concessions, so be as forgiving and indulgent as you can.

We are full here of reform or revolution, whichever it is to be; I should think something approaching the latter, though the first may be included in the last.   Will you come over and sit for the new parliament? what are you doing?   Have you seen Clare? how is she?   She never writes except on special occasions, when she wants anything.   Tell her that Percy is quite well.

You tell me not to marry,—but I will,—any one who will

take me out of my present desolate and uncomfortable position. Any one,—and with all this do you think that I shall marry? Never,—neither you nor anybody else. Mary Shelley shall be written on my tomb,—and why? I cannot tell, except that it is so pretty a name that though I were to preach to myself for years, I never should have the heart to get rid of it.

Adieu, my dear friend. I shall be very anxious to hear from you; to hear that you are not angry about all the *contretemps* attendant on your publication, and to receive your further directions.—Yours very truly,   M. W. SHELLEY.

TRELAWNY TO MRS. SHELLEY.

POSTE RESTANTE, FIRENZE,
29th June 1831.

DEAR MARY—Your letter, dated 14th June, I have received, after a long interval, and your letter before that is dated 22d March. It would appear by your last that you must have written another letter between March and June, by allusions in this last respecting my Mother. If so, it has never reached me, so that if it contained anything which is necessary for me to know, I pray you let me have a transcript, so far as your memory will serve to give it me. I am altogether ignorant of what arrangements you have made with Colburn; and am only in possession of the facts contained in the second, to wit, that Horace Smith is revising the work for publication. I trust he will not be too liberal with the pruning-knife. When will the cant and humbug of these costermonger times be reformed? Nevertheless tell H. Smith that the author is fully sensible of his kindness and (for once, at least, in his life) with all his heart joins his voice to that of the world in paying tribute to the sterling ability of Mr. Horace Smith; and I remember Shelley and others speaking of him as one often essayed on the touchstone of proof, and never found wanting. Horace Smith's criticism on the *Life* is flattering, and as regards the perilous part—why I never have, and never shall, crouch to those I utterly despise, to wit, the bigoted. The Roman

Pontiff might as well have threatened me with excommunication when on board the *Grub*, if I failed to strike my top-sails, and lower my proud flag to the lubberly craft which bore his silly banner, bedaubed with mitres, crosses, and St. Peter's Keys.

I did not mean to call my book *The History of a Man*, but simply thus, *A Man's Life;* "Adventures" and "Younger Son" are commonplace, and I don't like it; but if it is to be so, why, I shall not waste words in idle complaints: would it were as I had written it. By the bye, you say justly the MS. ends abruptly; the truth is, as you know, it is only the first part of my life, and to conclude it will fill three more volumes: that it is to be concluded, I thought I had stated in a paragraph annexed to the last chapter of that which is now in the press, which should run thus—

"I am, or rather have, continued this history of my life, and it will prove I have not been a passive instrument of despotism, nor shall I be found consorting with those base, sycophantic, and mercenary wretches who crouch and crawl and fawn on kings, and priests, and lords, and all in authority under them. On my return to Europe, its tyrants had gathered together all their helots and gladiators to restore the cursed dynasty of the Bourbons, and thousands of slaves went forth to extinguish and exterminate liberty, truth, and justice. I went forth, too, my hand ever against them, and when tyranny had triumphed, I wandered an exile in the world and leagued myself with men worthy to be called so, for they, inspired by wisdom, uncoiled the frauds contained in lying legends, which had so long fatally deluded the majority of mankind. Alas! those apostles have not lived to see the tree they planted fructify; would they had tarried a little while to behold this new era of 1830-31, how they would have rejoiced to behold the leagued conspiracy of kings broken, and their bloodhound priests and nobles muzzled, their impious confederacy to enslave and rob the people paralysed by a blow that has shaken their usurpation to the base, and must inevitably be followed by their final overthrow. Yes, the sun of freedom is dawning on the pallid slaves of Europe," etc.

The conclusion of this diatribe I am certain you have, and if you have not the beginning, why put it in beginning with the words : " I have continued the history of my life."

If I thought there was a probability that I could get a seat in the reformed House of Commons, I would go to England, or if there was a probability of revolution. I was more delighted with your resolve not to change your name than with any other portion of your letter. Trelawny, too, is a good name, and sounds as well as Shelley ; it fills the mouth as well and will as soon raise a spirit. By the bye, when you send my books, send me also Mary Wollstonecraft's *Rights of Women*, and Godwin's new work on *Man*, and tell me what you are now writing. The Hares are at Lucca Baths. Never omit to tell me what you know of Caroline. Do you think there is any opening among the demagogues for me ? It is a bustling world at present, and likely so to continue. I must play a part. Write, Mary mine, speedily.

Is my book advertised ? If so, the motto from Byron should accompany it.

Clare only remained in Florence about ten days ; some sudden death of a relative of the family she resides with recalled them to Russia. I saw her three or four times. She was very miserable, and looked so pale, thin, and haggard. The people she lived with were bigots, and treated her very badly. I wished to serve her, but had no means. Poor lady, I pity her ; her life has been one of continued misery. I hope on Sir Timothy's death it will be bettered ; her spirits are broken, and she looks fifty ; I have not heard of her since her departure. Mrs. Hare once saw her, but she was so prejudiced against her, from stories she had heard against her from the Beauclercs, that she could hardly be induced to notice her. You are aware that I do not wish my book to appear as if written for publication, and therefore have avoided all allusions which might induce people to think otherwise. I wish all the mottoes to be inserted, as they are a selection of beautiful poetry, and many of them not published.

The bills, you say, Colburn and Bentley are to give you ;.

perhaps Horace Smith may further favour me by getting them
negotiated. I am too much indebted to him to act so scurvily
as not to treat him with entire confidence, so with the in-
junction of secrecy you may tell him my name. If he dislikes the affair of the bills, as I cannot employ any of my
people of business, why give the bills, or rather place them in
the hands of a man who keeps a glover's shop (I know him well).
His name is Moon, and his shop is corner one in Orange Street,
Bloomsbury Square. When I get your reply, I will, if necessary,
write to him on the subject. I pray you write me on receipt
of this. My child Zella is growing up very pretty, and with a
soul of fire. She is living with friends of mine near Lucca.

The only copies of the book I wish you to give away are to
Horace Smith, Mary Shelley, Lady Burghersh, No. 1 Hyde
Park Terrace, Oxford Road, and Jane Williams, to remind her
that she is not forgotten. Shelley's tomb and mine in Rome,
is, I am told, in a very dilapidated state. I will see to its repair. Send me out six copies by sea; one if you can sooner.
Address them to Henry Dunn, Leghorn.

E. J. Trelawny.

Trelawny to Mrs. Shelley.

Poste Restante, Firenze,
19th July 1831.

*   *   *   *   *   *   *

By the bye, Mary, if it is not too late, I should wish
the name of Zella to be spelt in the correct Arabic, thus,
Zellâ, in my book. I changed it in common with several
others of the names to prevent my own being too generally recognised; with regard to hers, if not too late, I should
now wish it to appear in its proper form, besides which, in
the chapter towards the conclusion, wherein I narrate an
account of a pestilence which was raging in the town of
Batavia, I wish the word Java fever to be erased, and cholera
morbus substituted. For we alone had the former malady on
board the schooner, having brought it into the Batavia Roads

with us, but on our arrival there we found the cholera raging with virulence, most of those attacked expiring in the interval of the setting and rising of the sun. Luis, our steward, I thought died from fever, as we had had it previously on board, but the medicals pronounced it or denounced it cholera. If the alteration can be made, it will be interesting, as in the history of the cholera I see published, they only traced the origin to 1816, when the fact is, it was in 1811 that I am speaking of, and no doubt it has existed for thousands of years before, but it is only of late, like the natives of Hindoostan, it has visited Europe. It is sent by Nemesis, a fitting retribution for the gold and spices we have robbed them of. The malediction of my Malayan friends has come to pass, for I have no doubt the Russian caravans which supply that empire with tea, silks, and spices introduced the cholera, or gave it into the bargain, or as *bona mano.* I wish you would write, for I am principally detained here by wishing to get a letter from you ere I go to some other place.—Yours, and truly, E. T.

MRS. SHELLEY TO TRELAWNY.

SOMERSET STREET, *26th July* 1831.

MY DEAR TRELAWNY—Your third volume is now printing, so I should imagine that it will very soon be published; everything shall be attended to as you wish. The letter to which I alluded in my former one was a tiny one enclosed to Clare, which perhaps you have received by this time. It mentioned the time of the agreement; £300 in bills of three, six, and eight months, dated from the day of publication, and £100 more on a second edition. The mention I made of your mother was, that she speaks openly in society of your forthcoming memoirs, so that I should imagine very little real secrecy will attend them. However, you will but gain reputation and admiration through them.

I hope you are going on, for your continuation will, I am sure, be ardently looked for. I am so sorry for the delay of all last winter, yet I did my best to conclude the affair; but

the state of the nation has so paralysed bookselling that publishers were very backward, though Colburn was in his heart
eager to get at your book. As to the price, I have taken pains
to ascertain; and you receive as much as is given to the best
novelists at this juncture, which may console your vanity if it
does not fill your pocket.

The Reform Bill will pass, and a considerable revolution in
the government of the country will, I imagine, be the consequence.

You have talents of a high order. You have powers; these,
with industry and discretion, would advance you in any career.
You ought not, indeed you ought not to throw away yourself
as you do. Still, I would not advise your return on the
speculation, because England is so sad a place that the mere
absence from it I consider a peculiar blessing.

My name will *never* be Trelawny. I am not so young as I
was when you first knew me, but I am as proud. I must have
the entire affection, devotion, and, above all, the solicitous
protection of any one who would win me. You belong to
womenkind in general, and Mary Shelley will *never* be yours.

I write in haste, but I will write soon again, more at length.
You shall have your copies the moment I receive them.
Believe me, with all gratitude and affection, yours,

M. W. SHELLEY.

Jane thanks you for the book promised. I am infinitely
chagrined at what you tell me concerning Clare. If the B.'s
spoke against her, that means Mrs. B. and her stories were
gathered from Lord Byron, who feared Clare and did not
spare her; and the stories he told were such as to excuse
the prejudice of any one.

THE SAME TO THE SAME.

SOMERSET STREET, *2d October* 1831.

MY DEAR TRELAWNY—I suppose that I have now some
certain intelligence to send you, though I fear that it will both

disappoint and annoy you. I am indeed ashamed that I have not been able to keep these people in better order, but I trusted to honesty, when I ought to have ensured it; however, thus it stands : your book is to be published in the course of the month, and then your bills are to be dated. As soon as I get them I will dispose of them as you direct, and you will receive notice on the subject without delay. I cannot procure for you a copy until then ; they pretend that it is not all printed. If I can get an opportunity I will send you one by private hand, at any rate I shall send them by sea without delay. I will write to Smith about negotiating your bills, and I have no doubt that I shall be able somehow or other to get you money on them. I will go myself to the City to pay Barr's correspondent as soon as I get the cash. Thus your *pretty dear* (how fascinating is flattery) will do her best, as soon as these tiresome people fulfil their engagements. In some degree they have the right on their side, as the day of publication is a usual time from which to date the bills, and that was the time which I acceded to ; but they talked of such hurry and speed that I expected that that day was nearer at hand than it now appears to be. November *is* the publishing month, and no new things are coming out now. In fact, the Reform Bill swallows up every other thought. You have heard of the Lords' majority against it, much longer than was expected, because it was not imagined that so many bishops would vote against Government. . . .

Do whenever you write send me news of Clare. She never writes herself, and we are all excessively anxious about her. I hope she is better. God knows when fate will do anything for us. I despair. Percy is well, I fancy that he will go to Harrow in the spring ; it is not yet finally arranged, but this is what I wish, and therefore I suppose it will be, as they have promised to increase my allowance for him, and leave me pretty nearly free, only with Eton prohibited ; but Harrow is now in high reputation under a new head-master. I am delighted to hear that Zella is in such good hands, it is so necessary in this world of woe that children should learn betimes to yield to necessity ; a girl allowed to run wild makes an unhappy woman.

Hunt has set up a penny daily paper, literary and theatrical ; it is succeeding very well, but his health is wretched, and when you consider that his sons, now young men, do not contribute a penny towards their own support, you may guess that the burthen on him is very heavy.   I see them very seldom, for they live a good way off, and when I go he is out, she busy, and I am entertained by the children, who do not edify me.   Jane has just moved into a house about half a mile further from town, on the same road ; they have furnished it themselves.   Dina improves, or rather she always was, and continues to be, a very nice child.

.   .   .   .

The *Adventures* did not reach a second edition in their original form ; the first edition failed, indeed, to repay its expenses ; but they were afterwards republished in *Colburn's Family Library*. The second part of Trelawny's Autobiography took the chatty and discursive form, so popular at the present day, of "Reminiscences."   It is universally known as *Recollections*[1] *of Shelley, Byron, and the Author*.

So long as Shelley and Byron survive as objects of interest in this world, so long must this fascinating book share their existence.   As originally published, it has not a dull page.   Lifelike as if written at the moment it all happened, it yet has the pictorial sense of proportion which can rarely exist till a writer stands at such a distance

[1] "Recollections" in the original ; "Records" in the later and, now, better known edition.

(of time) from the scenes he describes that he can estimate them, not only as they are, but in their relation to surrounding objects.   It would seem as if, for the conversations at least, Trelawny must sometimes have drawn on his imagination as well as his memory ; if so, it can only be replied that, by his success, he has triumphantly vindicated his artistic right to do so.   Terse, original, and characteristic, each speech paints its speaker in colours which we know and feel to be true.   Nothing seems set down for effect ; it is spontaneous, unstudied, everyday reality.   And if the history of Trelawny's own exploits in Greece somewhat recall the " tarasconnades " of his early adventures, it at least puts a thrilling finish to a book it was hard to conclude without falling into bathos. As a writer on Shelley, Trelawny surely stands alone.   Many authors have praised Shelley, others have condemned and decried him, others again have tried to pity and "excuse" him. No one has apprehended as happily as Trelawny the peculiar *timbre*, if it may be so described, of his nature, or has brought out so vividly, and with so few happy touches, his moral and social characteristics.   Saint or sinner, the Shelley of Trelawny is no lay figure, no statue even, no hero of romance ; it is *Shelley*, the man, the boy, the poet.   Trelawny assures us that Hogg's picture of Shelley as a youth is absolutely faithful.   But

Hogg's picture only shows us Shelley in his
" salad days," and even that we are never allowed
to contemplate without the companion-portrait of
the biographer, smiling with cynical amusement
while he yields his tribute of heartfelt, but
patronising praise.

The conclusions to which Hogg had come by
observation Trelawny arrived at by intuition.
Fiery and imaginative, his nature was by far the
more sympathetic of the two ; though it may be
that, in virtue of very unlikeness, Hogg would
have proved, in the long run, the fitter companion
for Shelley.

Between Trelawny and Mary there existed
the same kind of adjustable difference. His
descriptions of her have been largely drawn upon
in earlier chapters of the present work, and need
not be reverted to here. She had been seven
years dead when the *Recollections* were published.
Twenty years later, when Mary Shelley had been
twenty-seven years in her grave, there appeared
a second edition of the book. In those twenty
years, what change had come over the spirit of its
pages ? An undefinable difference, like that which
comes over the face of Nature when the wind
changes from west to east,—and yet not so undefinable either, for it had power to reverse some
very definite facts. Byron's feet, for instance,
which—as the result of an investigation after

death—were described, in 1858, as having, both,
been "clubbed and withered to the knee," "the
feet and legs of a sylvan satyr," are, in 1878,
pronounced to have been *faultless*, but for the
contraction of the back sinews (the "Tendon
Achilles"), which prevented his heels from resting
on the ground. "Unfortunately," to quote Mr.
Garnett's comment on this discrepancy, in his
article on *Shelley's Last Days*, "as in the natural
world the same agencies that are elevating one
portion of the earth's surface are at the same time
depressing another, so, in the microcosm of Mr.
Trelawny's memory and judgment, the embellish-
ment of Lord Byron's feet has been accompanied
by a corresponding deterioration of Mrs. Shelley's
heart and head."

Yes; the Mary Shelley with whom, in early
days, even Trelawny could find no fault, save
perhaps for a tendency to mournfulness in solitude
and an occasional fit of literary abstraction when
she might have been looking after the com-
missariat—who in later years was his trusty friend,
his sole correspondent, his literary editor, his man
of business—and withal his "pretty dear" "every
day dearer" to him, "Mary — my Mary" —
superior surely to the rest of her sex, with whom
at one time it seems plain enough that he would
have been nothing loth to enter into an alliance,
offensive and defensive, for life, would she but

have preferred the name of Trelawny to that of
Shelley,—this Mary whose voice had been silent
for seven and twenty years, and to whom he
himself had raised a monument of praise, rises
from her tomb as conventional and commonplace,
unsympathetic and jealous, narrow, orthodox, and
worldly.

Yet she had borne with his exactions and scold-
ings and humours for friendship's sake, and with full
faith in the loyalty and generosity of his heart. A
pure and delicate-minded woman, she had not been
scandalised by his lawless morals. She had had
the courage to withstand him when he was wrong,
working for him the while like a devoted slave.
Never was a more true and disinterested friendship than hers for him; and he, who knew her
better than most people did, was well aware of it.

Where then was the change? Alas! it was
in himself. In this revolving world, where "Time
that gave doth now his gift confound," and where
"nought may endure but mutability," the "flourish
set on youth" is soon transfixed.

Greek fevers and gunshot wounds told on the
"Pirate's" disposition as well as on his constitution.
The habits of mind he had cultivated and been
proud of,—combativeness, opposition to all authority as such—finally became his masters; he
could not even acquiesce in his own experience.
Age and the ravages of Time were to blame

for his morbid censoriousness; Time — that "feeds on the rarities of Nature's truth." These later recollections are but the distorted images of a blurred mirror. But, none the less, the tale is a sad one. We can but echo Trelawny's own words to Mary [1]—"Can such things be, and overcome us like a summer cloud, without our especial wonder?"

[1] Page 191.

CHAPTER XXIII

October 1831–October 1839

TRELAWNY'S book was only one among many things which claimed Mrs. Shelley's attention during these three years.

In 1830 Godwin published his *Thoughts on Man*. The relative positions of father and daughter had come to be reversed, and Mary now negotiated with the publishers for the sale of his work, as he had formerly done for her. Godwin himself set a high value, even for him, on this book, and anticipated for it a future and an influence which were not to be realised.

GODWIN TO MARY.

15th April 1830.

DEAR MARY—If you do me the favour to see Murray, I know not how far you can utter the following things ; or if you do, how far they will have any weight with his highness ; yet I cannot but wish you should have them in your mind.

The book I offer is a collection of ten new and interesting truths, illustrated in no unpopular style. They are the fruit of thirty years' meditation (it being so long since I wrote the *Enquirer*), in the full maturity of my understanding.

The book, therefore, will be very far from being merely one book more added to the number of books already existing in English literature. It must, as I conceive, when published make a deep impression, and cause the thinking part of the public to perceive—There are here laid before us ten interesting truths never before delivered.

Whether it is published during my life or after my death it is a light that cannot be extinguished—" the precious life-blood of a discerning spirit, embalmed and treasured up on purpose to a life beyond life."

In the following amusing letter Clare gives Mary a few commissions. She was to interest her literary acquaintance in Paris in the publication and success of a French poem by a friend of Clare's at Moscow, the greatest wish of whose heart was to appear in print. She was also to find a means of preventing the French translatress of Moore's *Life of Byron* from introducing Clare's name into her elucidatory footnotes. This was indeed all-important to Clare, as any revival of scandal about her might have robbed her of the means of subsistence, but it was also an extremely difficult and delicate task for Mary. But no one ever hesitated to make her of use. Her friends estimated her power by her goodwill, and her goodwill by their own need of her services; and they were generally right, for the will never failed, and the way was generally found.

CLARE TO MRS. SHELLEY.

NICE, 11*th December* 1830.

MY DEAR MARY—Your last letter, although so melancholy,.

gave me much pleasure, merely, therefore, because it came from you.

I intended to have written to all and each of you, but until now have not been able to put my resolution into execution. It must seem to you that I am strangely neglectful of my friends, or perhaps you think since I am so near Trelawny that I have been taking a lesson from him in the art of cultivating one's friendships; but neither of these is the case, my silence is quite on another principle than this.

I am not desperately in love, nor just risen from my bed at four in the afternoon in order to write my millionth love letter, nor am I indifferent to those whom time and the malice of fortune have yet spared to me, but simply I have been too busy.

Since I have been at Nice I have had to change lodgings four times; besides this, we were a long time without a maid, and received and paid innumerable visits. My whole day was spent in shifting my character. In the morning I arose a waiting-maid, and, having attended to the toilette of Natalie, sank into a house-maid, a laundry-maid, and, after noon, I fear me, a cook, having to look to the cleaning of the rooms, the getting up of linen, and the preparation of various pottages fit for the patient near me. At mid-day I turned into a governess, gave my lessons, and at four or five became a fine lady for the rest of the day, and paid visits or received them, for at Nice it is the custom, so soon as a stranger arrives, that everybody *comme il faut* in the place comes to call upon you; nor can you shut your doors against them even if you were dying, for as Nice is the resort of the sick, and as everybody either is sick or has been sick, nursing has become the common business.

So we went on day after day. We had *dejeuners dansants, soirées dansantes* (*diners dansants* are considered as *de trop* by order of the physicians), *bals parés, théatres, opéras, grands diners, petits soupers, concerts, visites de matin, promenades à âne, parties de campagne, réunions littéraires, grands cercles, promenades en bateau, coteries choisies, thunder-storms* from the

sea, and *political storms* from France; in short, if we had only
had an earthquake, or the shock of one, we should have run
through the whole series of modifications of which human
existence is susceptible.   *Voilà Paris, Voilà Paris,* as the song
says.

You may perhaps expect that the novelty of society should
have suggested to me remarks and observations as multifarious
as the forms under which I observed it.   Sorry I am to say
that either from its poverty, or from my own poverty of intellect, I have not gathered from it anything beyond the following
couple of conclusions, that people of the world, disguise themselves as they may, possess but two qualities, a great want of
understanding, and a vast pretension to sentiment.   From
this duplexity arises the duplicity with which they are so
often charged, and no wonder, for with hearts so heavy, and
heads so light, how is it possible to keep anything like a
straightforward course ?   In alleviation of this, I must confess
that wherever I went I carried about with me my own identity
(that unhappy identity which has cost me so dear, and of
which, with all my pains, I have never been able to lose a
particle), and contemplated the people I judge through the
medium of its rusty atoms.

I must speak to you of an affair that interests me deeply.
M. Gambs has informed me that he has sent to Paris a poem
of his in manuscript called *Möise.*   He gave it to the Prince
Nicolas Scherbatoff at Moscow, just upon his setting out for
Paris ; this is many months ago.   Whether the Prince gave
any promise to endeavour to get it published I do not know ;
but if he did, he is such a very indolent and selfish man
that his efforts would never get the thing done.   M. Gambs
has written to me to ask if you have any literary friends in
Paris who would be kind enough to interest themselves about
it.   The address of the Prince is as follows : Son Excellence
Le Prince Nicolas Scherbatoff, Rue St. Lazare, No. 17, à
Paris.   Can you not get some one to call upon him to ask
about the manuscript, and to propose it to some bookseller ?

This some one may enter into a direct correspondence with

M. Gambs by addressing him Chez M. Lenhold, Marchand de
Musique, à Moscow. I should be highly delighted if you
could settle things in this way, as I know my friend has nothing
more at heart than to appear in print, and that I should be
glad to be the means of communicating some pleasure to an
existence which I know is almost utterly without it, and of
showing my gratitude for the kindness and goodness he has
showered upon me ; nor, as far as my poor judgment goes, is
the work unworthy of inspiring interest, and of being saved
from oblivion. It pleased me much when it was read to
me ; but then it is true I was in a desert, and there a drop
of water will often seem to us more precious than the finest
jewel.

Another subject connected with Paris also presses itself
on my mind. In Moore's *Life of Lord Byron* only the most
distant allusion was made to Lady Caroline Lamb ; yet, in the
French translation, its performer, Madame Sophie Bellay (or
some such name) had the indelicacy to unveil the mystery in
a note, and to expose it in distinct and staring characters to
the public. This piece of impudence was harmless to Lady
Caroline, since her independence of others was assured beyond
a doubt ; but to any one whose bread depends upon the public
a printed exposure of their conduct will infallibly bring on
destitution, and reduce them to the necessity of weighing upon
their relations for support.

I know the subject is a disagreeable one, and that you do
not like disagreeable subjects. I know nothing of business or
whether there exists any means of averting this blow ; perhaps
a representation to the translator of the evils that would follow
would be sufficient ; but as I have no means of trying this, I
am reduced to suggest the subject to your attention, with the
firm hope that you will find some method of warding off the
threatened mischief.

What you tell me of the state of family resources has naturally depressed my spirits. Will the future never cease unrolling
new shapes of misery ? Stair above stair of wretchedness is
all we know ; the present, bad as it is, is always better than

what comes after. Of all the crowd of eager inquirers at the
Delphic shrine was there ever found one who thanked, or had
any reason to thank, the Pythia for what she disclosed to him?
For me, I have long abandoned hope and the future, and am
now diligently pursuing and retracing the past, going the back
way as it were to eternity in order to avoid the disappointments and perplexities of an unknown course. But I must
beg pardon for my cowardice and disagreeableness, and leave
it, or else I shall be recollected with as much reluctance as
the Pythia.

I wish I could give you any idea of the beauty of Nice.
So long as I can walk about beside the sounding sea, beneath
its ambient heaven, and gaze upon the far hills enshrined in
purple light, I catch such pleasure from their loveliness that I
am happy without happiness; but when I come home, then it
seems to me as if all the phantasmagoria of hell danced before
my eyes.

Mrs. K. has arrived and in no very amiable humour.
The only conversation I hear is, first, the numberless perfec-
tions of herself, husband, and child; this, as it is true, would
be well enough, but still upon repetition it tires; second, the
infinite superiority of Russia over all other countries, since it
is an established truth that liberty and civilisation are the most
dreadful of all evils. I, to avoid ill-temper, assent to all they
say; then in company, when opposed in their doctrines, they
drag me forward, and the tacit consent I have given, as an
argument in favour of their way of thinking, and I am at once
set down by everybody either as a fawning creature or an utter
fool. However, I am glad she has come, as the responsibility
of Natalie's health was too much. For heaven's sake excuse
me to dear Jane that I have not written. My first moment
shall be given to do so.

I think of England and my friends all day long. Entreat
everybody to write to me. Do pray do so yourself. My love
to my Mother and Papa, and William and everybody. How
happy was I that Percy was well.—In haste, ever yours,

                                C. CLAIRMONT.

Mrs. Shelley's mind was much occupied during 1831 by the serious question of sending her son to a public school. She wished to give him the best possible education, and she wished, too, to give it him in such a form as would place him at no disadvantage among other young men when he took his place in English society.

Shelley (she mentions in one of her letters) had expressed himself in favour of a public school, but Shelley's family had also to be consulted, and she seems to have had reason to hope they would help in the matter.

They quite concurred in her views for Percy, only putting a veto on Eton, where legends of his father's school-days might still be lingering about. Nothing was better than that she should send him to a public school—*if she could.* These last words were implied, not expressed. But a public school education in England is not to be given on a very limited income. Funds had to be found; and Mrs. Shelley made, through the lawyer, a direct request to Sir Timothy for assistance.

She received the following answer—

MR. WHITTON TO MRS. SHELLEY.

STONE HALL, *6th November* 1831

DEAR MADAM—I have been, from the time I received your last favour to the present, in correspondence with Sir Timothy Shelley as to your wishes of an advance upon the

£300 per annum he now makes to you, and I recommended him to consult his friend and solicitor, Mr. Steadman, of Horsham, thereon, and which he did.

You have not perhaps well put together and estimated on the great amount of the charges upon the estate by the late Mr. Shelley, and on the legacies given by his will; but looking at all these, and the very limited interest of the estate now vested in you, Sir Timothy has paused in his consideration thereof, and in the result has brought his mind, that, having regard to the other provisions he is bound to make for his other children, he ought not to increase the allowance to you, and upon that ground he declines so doing; and therefore feels the necessity of your making such arrangements as you may find necessary to make the £300 per annum answer the purposes for yourself and for your son, and he has this morning stated to me his fixed determination to abide thereby; and I lose not a moment, after I receive this communication from him, to make it known to you, and I trust and hope you will find it practicable to give him a good education out of the £300 a year.—I remain, Madam, your very obedient servant,   WM. WHITTON.

The seeming brutality of the concluding sentence must in fairness be ascribed to the writer and not to those he represented.

To Mrs. Shelley, knowing the impossibility of carrying out the public school plan on her own income, the wishes and hopes must have sounded a mockery. It had to be done, however, if it was the best thing for the boy. The money must be earned, and she worked on.

One day she received from her father a new kind of petition, which, showing the effect on him of advancing years, must have struck a pang to her heart. She was accustomed to his requests for money, but now he wrote to her for *an idea*.

GODWIN TO MRS. SHELLEY.

13th April 1832.

MY DEAR MARY—You desire me to write to you, if I have anything particular to say.

I write, then, to say that I am still in the same dismaying predicament in which I have been for weeks past—at a loss for materials to make up my third volume. This is by no means what I expected.

I knew, and I know, that incidents of hair-breadth escapes and adventures are innumerable, and that without having fixed on any one of them, I took for granted they would come when I called for them. Such is the mischievous effect, the anxious expectation, that is produced by past success.

I believe that when I came to push with all my force against the barriers that seemed to shut me in they would give way, and place all the treasures of invention before me.

Meanwhile, it unfortunately happens that I cannot lay my present disappointment to the charge of advancing age.

I find all my faculties and all my strength in full bloom about me. My disappointment has put that to a sharp trial. I thought that the severe stretch of my faculties would cause them to yield, and subside into feebleness and torpor. No such thing. Day after day, week after week, I apply to this one question, without remission and with discernment. But I cannot please myself. If I make the round of all my thoughts, and come home empty-handed, it would seem that in the flower and vigour of my youth I should have done the same.

Meanwhile, my situation is deplorable. I am not free to choose the thing I would do. I have written two volumes and a quarter, and have received five-sixths of the price of my work.

I am afraid you will think I am useless, by teasing you with

"conceptions only proper to myself." But it is not altogether
so. A bystander may see a point of game which a player
overlooks. Though I cannot furnish myself with satisfactory
incidents I have disciplined my mind into a tone that would
enable me to improve them, if offered to me.

My mind is like a train of gunpowder, and a single spark,
now happily communicated, might set the whole in motion
and activity.

Do not tease yourself about my calamity; but give it one
serious thought. Who knows what such a thought may
produce?—Your affectionate Father,   WILLIAM GODWIN.

In the spring of 1832 the cholera appeared in
London. Clare, at a distance, was torn to pieces
between real apprehension for the safety of her
friends, and distracting fears lest the disease
should select among them for its victim some one
on whose life depended the realisation of Shelley's
will. For Percy especially ·she was solicitous.
Mary must take him away at once, to the seaside
—anywhere : if money was an obstacle she, Clare,
was ready to help to defray the cost out of her
salary.

Mrs. Shelley did leave London, although, it
may safely be asserted, at no one's expense but
her own. She stayed for a month at Southend,
and afterwards for a longer time at Sandgate.

Besides contributing tales and occasionally
verses to the *Keepsake*, she was employed now
and during the next two or three years in preparing and writing the Italian and Spanish Lives of
Literary Men for Lardner's *Cabinet Cyclopædia*.

These included, among the Italians—Petrarch, Boccaccio, Bojardo, Macchiavelli, Metastasio, Goldoni, Alfieri, Ugo Foscolo, etc.; among the Spanish and Portuguese—Cervantes, Lope de Vega, Calderon, Camoens, and a host of others, besides notices of the Troubadours, the " Romances Moriscos," and the early poets of Portugal.

Clare, too, tried her hand at a story, to which she begged Mary to be a kind of godmother.

I have written a tale, which I think will do for the *Keepsake.* I shall send it home for your perusal. Will you correct it? Do write and let me know where I may send it, so as to be sure to find you. Will you be angry with me if I beg you to write the last scene of it? I am now so unwell I can't.

My only time for writing is after 10 at night; the rest of the tale was composed at that hour, after having been scolding and talking and giving lessons from 7 in the morning.

It was very near its end when I got so ill, I gave it up. If you cannot do anything with it you can at least make curl-papers of it, and that is always something. Do not mention it to anybody; should it be printed one can speak of it, and if you judge it not worthy, then it is no use mortifying my vanity.

The truth, is I should never think of writing, knowing well my incapacity for it, but I want to gain money. What would one not do for that, since it is the only key of freedom? One is even impudent enough to ask a great authoress to finish one's tale for one. I think, in your hands, it might get into the *Keepsake,* for it is about a Pole, and that is the topic of the day.

If it should get any money, half will naturally belong to

you.   Should you have the kindness to arrange it, Julia would
perhaps also be so kind as to copy it out for me, that the
alterations in your hand may not be seen.   I wish it to be
signed " Mont Obscur." . . .

Mary did what was asked of her.   Trelawny,
now in England again, had influence in some
literary quarters, and, at her request, willingly consented to exert it on Clare's behalf.

Meanwhile he requested her to receive his
eldest daughter on a visit of considerable length.

TRELAWNY TO MRS. SHELLEY.

17*th July* 1832.

MY DEAR MARY—I am awaiting an occasion of sending
—— to Italy, my friend, Lady D., undertaking the charge
of her.

It may be a month before she leaves England.   At the
end of this month Mrs. B. leaves London, and you will do
me a great service if you will permit my daughter to reside
with you till I can make the necessary arrangements for going
abroad; she has been reared in a rough school, like her
father.   I wish her to live and do as you do, and that you
will not put yourself to the slightest inconvenience on her
account.

As we are poor, the rich are our inheritance, and we are
justified on all and every occasion to rob and use them.

But we must be honest and just amongst ourselves, therefore —— must to the last fraction pay her own expenses, and
neither put you to expense nor inconvenience.   For the rest,
I should like —— to learn to lean upon herself alone—to see
the practical part of life : to learn housekeeping on trifling
means, and to benefit by her intercourse with a woman like
you ; but I am ill at compliments.

If you will permit —— to come to you, I will send or

bring her to you about the 25th of this month.   I should like
you and —— to know each other before she leaves England,
and thus I have selected you to take charge of her in preference to any other person ; but say if it chimes in with your
wishes.

Adieu, dear Mary.—Your attached friend,

EDWARD TRELAWNY.

By the bye, tell me where the Sandgate coach starts from,
its time of leaving London, and its time of arrival at Sandgate,
and where you are, and if they will give you another bedroom
in the house you are lodging in ; and if you have any intention of leaving Sandgate soon.

TRELAWNY TO MRS. SHELLEY.

27th July 1832.

MY DEAR MARY—You told me in your letter that it would
be more convenient for you to receive —— on the last of the
month, so I made my arrangements accordingly.   I now find
it will suit me better to come to you on Wednesday, so that
you may expect —— on the evening of that day by the coach
you mention.   I shall of course put up at the inn.

As to your style of lodging or living, —— is not such a
fool as to let that have any weight with her ; if you were in
a cobbler's stall she would be satisfied ; and as to the dulness
of the place, why, that must mainly depend on ourselves.
Brompton is not so very gay, and the reason of my removing —— to Italy is that Mrs. B. was about sending her to
reside with strangers at Lincoln ; besides —— is acting
entirely by her own free choice, and she gladly preferred
Sandgate to Lincoln.   At all events, come we shall ; and if
you, by barricading or otherwise, oppose our entrance, why
I shall do to you, not as I would have others do unto me,
but as I do unto others,—make an onslaught on your dwelling, carry your tenement by assault, and give the place up to
plunder.

So on Wednesday evening (at 5, by your account) you must be prepared to quietly yield up possession or take the consequences. So as you shall deport yourself, you will find me your friend or foe,   TRELAWNY.

Mary's guest stayed with her over a month. During this time she was saddened by the sudden death of her friendly acquaintance, Lord Dillon. She was anxious, too, about her father, whose equable spirits had failed him this year. No assistance seemed to avail much to ease his circumstances; he was not far from his eightieth year, and still his hopes were anchored in a yet-to-be-written novel.

"I feel myself able and willing to do everything, and to do it well," so he wrote, "and nobody disposed to give me the requisite encouragement. If I can agree with these tyrants" (his publishers) "for £300, £400, or £500 for a novel, and to be subsisted by them while I write it, I probably shall not starve for a twelvemonth to come . . . but this dancing attendance wears my spirits and destroys my tranquillity. 'Hands have I, but I handle not; I have feet, but I walk not; neither is there any breath in my nostrils.'

"Meanwhile my life wears away, and 'there is no work, nor device, nor knowledge, nor wisdom in the grave whither I go.' But, indeed, I am wrong in talking of that, for I write now, not for marble to be placed over my remains, but for bread to put into my mouth."

Mary tried in the summer to tempt him down to Sandgate for a change. But the weather was very cold, and he declined.

28th August 1832.

DEAR MARY—

> See, Winter comes, to rule the varied year,
> Sullen and sad, with all his rising train—
> Vapours, and clouds, and storms.

I am shivering over a little fire at the bottom of my grate, and have small inclination to tempt the sea-breezes and the waves; we must therefore defer our meeting till it comes within the walls of London.

. . . . . .

Au revoir ! To what am I reserved ? I know.not.

> The wide (no not) the unbounded prospect lies before me,
> But shadows, clouds, and darkness rest upon it.

A new shadow was now to fall upon the poor old man, in the death from cholera of his only son, Mary's half-brother, William. This son in his early youth had given some trouble and caused some anxiety, but his character, as he grew up, had become steadier and more settled. He was happily married, and seemed likely to be a source of real comfort and satisfaction to his parents in their old age. By profession he was a reporter, but he had his hereditary share of literary ability and of talent " turned for the relation of fictitious adventures," and left in MS. a novel called *Transfusion*, published by his father after his death, with the motto—

> Some noble spirits, judging by themselves,
> May yet conjecture what I might have been.

Although inevitably somewhat hardened against misfortune of the heart by his self-centred habits of mind and anxiety about money, Godwin was much saddened by this loss, and to Mrs. Godwin it was a very great and bitter grief indeed.

Clare saw at once in this the beginning of fresh troubles; the realisation of all the gloomy forebodings in which she had indulged. She wrote to Jane Hogg—

That nasty year, 1832, could not go over without imitating in some respects 1822, and bringing death and misfortune to us. From the time it came in till it went out I trembled, expecting at every moment to hear the most gloomy tidings.

William's death came, and fulfilled my anticipations; misfortune as it was, it was not such a heavy one to me as the loss of others might have been. I, however, was fond of him, because I did not view his faults in that desponding light which his other relations did. I have seen more of the world, and, comparing him with other young men, his frugality, his industry, his attachment to his wife, and his talents, raised him, in my opinion, considerably above the common par.

But in our family, if you cannot write an epic poem or novel that by its originality knocks all other novels on the head, you are a despicable creature, not worth acknowledging. What would they have done or said had their children been fond of dress, fond of cards, drunken, profligate, as most people's children are?

To Mary she wrote in a somewhat different tone, assuming that she, Clare, was the victim on whom all misfortune really fell, and wondering at Mary's incredible temerity in allowing her boy, that all-important heir-apparent, to face the perils of a public school.

And then, losing sight for a moment of her own

feverish anxiety, she gives a vivid sketch of Mrs. Mason's family.

MISS CLAIRMONT TO MRS. SHELLEY.

PISA, 26th October 1832.

MY DEAR MARY—Though your last letter was on so melancholy a subject, yet I am so destitute of all happiness that to receive it was one to me.

I have not yet got over the shock of William's death; from the moment I heard of it until now I have been in a complete state of annihilation. How long it will last I am sure I cannot tell; I hope not much longer, or perhaps I shall go mad.

A horrible and most inevitable future is the image that torments me, just as it did ten years ago, in this very city. But I won't torment you, who have a thousand enjoyments that veil it from you, and need not feel the blow till it comes. Our fates were always different; mine is to feel the shadow of coming misfortunes, and to sicken beneath it. There seems to have been great imprudence on William's part: my Mother says he went to Bartholomew Fair the day before he was taken ill; then he did not have medical assistance so soon as ill, which they say is of the highest importance in the cholera, so altogether I suppose his life was thrown away—a most lucky circumstance for himself, but God knows what it will be for the Godwins.

His death changed my plans. I had settled to go to Vienna, but as the cholera is still there, I no longer considered myself free to offer another of my Mother's children to be its victim. Mrs. Mason represented the imprudence of it, considering my weak health, the depressed state of my spirits for the last twelve years, the fatigue of the long journey, and the chilliness of the season of the year, which are all things that predispose excessively to the disease, and I yielded out of regard to my Mother. I thought she would prefer anything to my dying, or else at Vienna, Charles tells me, I could earn more than I am likely to earn here. For the same reason

Paris was abandoned. I beg you will tell her this, and hope she will think I have done well.

In the meantime I stay with Mrs. Mason, and have got an engagement as day governess with an English family, which will supply me with money for my own expenses, but nothing more. In the spring they wish to take me entirely, but the pay is not brilliant. When I know more about them I will tell you. Nothing can equal Mrs. Mason's kindness to me. Hers is the only house, except my Mother's, in which all my life I have always felt at home. With her, I am as her child ; from the merest trifle to the greatest object, she treats me as if her happiness depended on mine. Then she understands me so completely. I have no need to disguise my sentiments ; to barricade myself up in silence, as I do almost with every-body, for fear they should see what passes in my mind, and hate me for it, because it does not resemble what passes in theirs. This ought to be a great happiness to me, and would, did not her unhappiness and her precarious state of health darken it with the torture of fear. It is too bitter, after a long life passed in unbroken misery, to find a good only that you may lose it.

Laurette's marriage is to take place at the end of November. Mrs. Mason having tried every means to hinder it, and seeing that she cannot, is now impatient it should be over. Their present state is too painful. She cannot disguise her dislike of Galloni ; he having nearly killed her with his scenes, and Laurette cannot sympathise with her ; being on the point of marrying him, and feeling grateful for his excessive attach-ment, she wishes to think as well of him as she can. It is the first time the mother and daughter have ever divided in opinion, and galls both in a way that seems unreasonable to those who live in the world, and are accustomed to meet rebuffs in their dearest feelings at every moment. But our friends live in solitude, and have nursed themselves into a height of romance about everything. They both think their destinies annihilated, because the union of their minds has suffered this interruption. However, no violence mingles with

this sentiment and excites displeasure; on the contrary, I wish
it did, for it would be easier to heal than the tragic immutable
sorrow with which they take it.

While these two dissolve in quiet grief, Nerina, the Italian,
agitates herself on the question; she forgets all her own love
affairs, and all the sabre slashes and dagger stabs of her own
poor heart, to fall into fainting fits and convulsions every time
she sees Laurette and her mother fix their eyes mournfully
upon each other; then she talks and writes upon the subject
incessantly, even till 3 o'clock in the morning. She has a
band of young friends of both sexes, and with them, either by
word of mouth or by letter, she *sfogares* herself of her hatred
of Galloni, of the unparalleled cruelty of Laurette's fate, and
of the terrific grave that is yawning for her mother; her mind
is discursive, and she introduces into her lamentations observations upon the faulty manner in which she and her sister have
been educated, strictures upon the nature of love, objurgations
against the whole race of man, and eloquent appeals to the
female sex to prefer patriotism to matrimony.

All the life that is left in the house is now concentrated in
Nerina, and I am sure she cannot complain of a dearth of
sensations, for she takes good care to feel with everything
around her, for if the chair does but knock the table, she
shudders and quakes for both, and runs into her own study to
write it down in her journal. Into this small study she always
hurries me, and pours out her soul, and I am well pleased to
listen, for she is full of genius; when the tide has flowed so
long, it has spent itself, we generally pause, and then begin to
laugh at the ridiculous figures human beings cut in struggling
all their might and main against a destiny which forces millions
and millions of enormous planets on their way, and against
which all struggling is useless.

8th November.

My letter has been lying by all this time, I not having
time to write. I am afraid this winter I shall scarcely be
able to keep up a correspondence at all. I must be out at

9 in the morning, and am not home before 10 at night.
I inhabit at Mrs. Mason's a room without a fire, so that
when I get home there is no sitting in it without perishing
with cold.   I cannot sit with the Masons, because they have
a set of young men every night to see them, and I do not
wish to make their acquaintance.   I walk straight into my
own room on my return.   Writing either letters or articles
will be a matter of great difficulty.   The season is very cold
here.   My health always diminishes in proportion to the
cold.

I am very glad to hear that Percy likes Harrow, but I
shudder from head to foot when I think of your boldness in
sending him there.   I think in certain things you are the
most daring woman I ever knew.   There are few mothers who,
having suffered the misfortunes you have, and having such
advantages depending upon the life of an only son, would
venture to expose that life to the dangers of a public school.

As for me, it is not for nothing that my fate has been taken
out of my own hands and put into those of people who have
wantonly torn it into miserable shreds and remnants ; having
once endured to have my whole happiness sacrificed to the
gratification of some of their foolish whims, why I can endure
it again, and so my mind is made up and my resolution taken.
I confess, I could wish there were another world in which
people were to answer for what they do in this !   I wish this,
because without it I am afraid it will become a law that those
who inflict must always go on inflicting, and those who have
once suffered must always go on suffering.

I hope nothing will happen to Percy ; but the year, the
school itself that you have chosen, and the ashes [1] that lie near
it, and the hauntings of my own mind, all seem to announce
the approach of that consummation which I dread.

I am very glad you are delighted with Trelawny.   My
affections are entirely without jealousy ; the more those I
love love others, and are loved by them, the better pleased

---

[1] Allegra was buried at Harrow.

am I.   I am in a vile humour for writing a letter; you would
not wonder at it if you knew how I am plagued.   I can say
from experience that the wonderful variety there is of miseries
in this world is truly astonishing; if some Linnæus would
class them as he did flowers, the number of their kinds would
far surpass the boasted infinitude of the vegetable creation.
Not a day nor hour passes but introduces me to some new
pain, and each one contains within itself swarms of smaller
ones—animalculæ pains which float up and down in it, and
compose its existence and their own.   What Mademoiselle de
L'Espinasse was for love, I am for pain,—all my letters are on
the same subject, and yet I hope I do not repeat myself, for
truly, with such diversity of experience, I ought not.

Our friends here send their best love to you, and are
interested in your perilous destiny.   I have just received a
letter from my Mother, and in obedience to her representations
draw my breath as peacefully as I can till the month of
January.   Will you explain to me one phrase of her letter?
Talking of the chances of their getting money, she says:
"Then Miss Northcote is not expected to live over the
winter," and not a word beside.   Who in the world is Miss
Northcote? and what influence can her death have in bettering
their prospects?

Notwithstanding my writing such a beastly letter as this to
you, pray do write.   I work myself into the most dreadful
state of irritation when I am long without letters from some
of you.   Tell Jane I entreat her to write, and tell my Mother
that the bill of lading of the parcel for me is come, but Mrs.
Mason sent it off to Leghorn without my seeing it, and was
too ill herself to look at the date, so I know not when it was
shipped, but as Mr. Routh has the bill, I suppose I shall hear
when it has arrived and performed quarantine.

Thank Trelawny for me for his kindness about the article.
Pisa is very dull yet.   I am told there are seven or eight
English families arrived, but I have not seen them.

Farewell, my dear Mary.   Be well and happy, and excuse
my dulness.—Yours ever affectionately,   C. CLAIRMONT.

One term's experience was enough to convince Mrs. Shelley that she could only afford to continue her son's school education by leaving London herself and settling with him at Harrow for some years.

In January 1833 she wrote an account of her affairs to her old friend, Mrs. Gisborne—

Never was poor body so worried as I have been ever since I last wrote, I think; worries which plague and press on one, and keep one fretting. Money, of course, is the Alpha and Omega of my tale. Harrow proves so fearfully expensive that I have been sadly put to it to pay Percy's bill for one quarter (£60, *soltanto*), and, to achieve it, am hampered for the whole year. My only resource is to live at Harrow, for in every other respect I like the school, and would not take him from it. He will become a home boarder, and school expenses will be very light. I shall take a house, being promised many facilities for furnishing it by a kind friend.

To go and live at pretty Harrow, with my boy, who improves each day and is everything I could wish, is no bad prospect, but I have much to go through, and am so poor that I can hardly turn myself. It is hard on my poor dear Father, and I sometimes think it hard on myself to leave a knot of acquaintances I like; but that is a fiction, for half the times I am asked out I cannot go because of the expense, and I am suffering now for the times when I do go, and so incur debt.

No, Maria mine, God never intended me to do other than struggle through life, supported by such blessings as make existence more than tolerable, and yet surrounded by such difficulties as make fortitude a necessary virtue, and destroy all idea of great and good luck. I might have been much worse off, and I repeat this to myself ten thousand times a day to console myself for not being better.

My Father's novel is printed, and, I suppose, will come out soon. Poor dear fellow! It is hard work for him.

I am in all the tremor of fearing what I shall get for my novel, which is nearly finished. His and my comfort depend on it. I do not know whether you will like it. I cannot guess whether it will succeed. There is no writhing interest; nothing wonderful nor tragic—will it be dull? *Chi lo sa?* We shall see. I shall, of course, be very glad if it succeeds.

Percy went back to Harrow to-day. He likes his school much. Have I any other news for you? Trelawny is gone to America; he is about to cross to Charlestown directly there is a prospect of war—war in America. I am truly sorry. Brothers should not fight for the different and various portions of their inheritance. What is the use of republican principles and liberty if peace is not the offspring? War is the companion and friend of monarchy; if it be the same of freedom, the gain is not much to mankind between a sovereign and president.

.   .   .   .

Not long after taking up her residence at Harrow, which she did in April 1833, Mrs. Shelley was attacked by influenza, then prevailing in a virulent form. She did not wholly recover from its effects till after the Midsummer holidays, which she spent at Putney for change of air. She found the solitude of her new abode very trying. Her boy had, of course, his school pursuits and interests to occupy him, and, though her literary work served while it lasted to ward off depression, the constant mental strain was attended with an inevitable degree of reaction for which a little genial and sympathetic human intercourse would have been the best—indeed, the only—cure.

As for her father, now she had gone he missed her sadly.

GODWIN TO MRS. SHELLEY.

July 1833.

DEAR MARY—I shall certainly not come to you on Monday. It would do neither of us good. I am a good deal of a spoiled child. And were I not so, and could rouse myself, like Diogenes, to be independent of all outward comforts, you would treat me as if I could not, so that it would come to the same thing.

What a while it is since I saw you! The last time was the 10th of May,—towards two months,—we who used to see each other two or three times a week! But for the scale of miles at the bottom of the map, you might as well be at Timbuctoo or in the deserts of Arabia.

Oh, this vile Harrow! Your illness, for its commencement or duration, is owing to that place. At one time I was seriously alarmed for you.

And now that I hope you are better, with what tenaciousness does it cling to you! If I ever see you again I wonder whether I shall know you. I am much tormented by my place, by my book, and hardly suppose I shall ever be tranquil again.

I am disposed to adopt the song of Simeon, and to say, "Lord, now lettest thou thy servant depart in peace!" At seventy years of age, what is there worth living for? I have enjoyed existence, been active, strenuous, proud, but my eyes are dim, and my energies forsake me.—Your affectionate Father,   WILLIAM GODWIN.

The next letter is addressed to Trelawny, now in America.

MRS. SHELLEY TO TRELAWNY.

HARROW, 7*th May* 1834.

DEAR TRELAWNY—I confess I have been sadly remiss in not writing to you. I have written once, however, as you

have written once (but once) to me. I wrote in answer to
your letter. I am sorry you did not get it, as it contained a
great deal of gossip. It was misdirected by a mistake of
Jane's. . . . It was sent at the end of last September to New
York. I told you in it of the infidelity of several of your
womankind,— how Mrs. R. S. was flirting with Bulwer, to the
infinite jealousy of Mrs. Bulwer, and making themselves the
talk of the town. . . . Such and much tittle-tattle was in that
letter, all old news now. . . . The S.'s (Captain Robert and
wife, I mean) went to Paris and were ruined, and are returned
under a cloud to rusticate in the country in England.

Bulwer is making the amiable to his own wife, who is worth
in beauty all the Mrs. R. S.'s in the world. . . .

Jane has been a good deal indisposed, and has grown very
thin. Jeff had an appointment which took him away for
several months, and she pined and grew ill on his absence ; she
is now reviving under the beneficent influence of his presence.

I called on your mother a week or two ago ; she always
asks after you with *empressement*, and is very civil indeed
to me. She was looking well, but —— tells me, in her note
enclosing your letter, that she is ill of the same illness as she
had two years ago, but not so bad. I think she lives too well.

—— is expecting to be confined in a very few weeks, or
even days. She is very happy with B. . . . He is a thoroughly
good-natured and estimable man ; it is a pity he is not younger
and handsomer ; however, she is a good girl, and contented
with her lot ; we are very good friends. . . . I should like
much to see your friend, Lady Dorothea, but, though in
Europe, I am very far from her. I live on my hill, descending
to town now and then. I should go oftener if I were richer.
Percy continues quite well, and enjoys my living at Harrow,
which is more than I do, I am sorry to say, but there is
no help.

My Father is in good health. Mrs. Godwin has been very
ill lately, but is now better.

I thought Fanny Kemble was to marry and settle in

America: what a singular likeness you have discovered! I never saw her, except on the stage.

So much for news. They say it is a long lane that has no turning. I have travelled the same road for nearly twelve years; adversity, poverty, and loneliness being my companions. I suppose it will change at last, but I have nothing to tell of myself except that Percy is well, which is the beginning and end of my existence.

I am glad you are beginning to respect women's feelings. . . . You have heard of Sir H.'s death. Mrs. B. (who is great friends with S., now Sir William, an M.P.) says that it is believed that he has left all he could to the Catholic members of his family. Why not come over and marry Letitia, who in consequence will be rich? and, I daresay, still beautiful in your eyes, though thirty-four.

We have had a mild, fine winter, and the weather now is as warm, sunny, and cheering as an Italian May. We have thousands of birds and flowers innumerable, and the trees of spring in the fields.

Jane's children are well. The time will come, I suppose, when we may meet again more (richly) provided by fortune, but youth will have flown, and that in a woman is something. . . .

I have always felt certain that I should never again change my name, and that is a comfort, it is a pretty and a dear one. Adieu, write to me often, and I will behave better, and as soon as I have accumulated a little news, write again.—Ever yours,   M. W. S.

MRS. SHELLEY TO MRS. GISBORNE.

17th July 1834.

I am satisfied with my plan as regards him (Percy). I like the school, and the affection thus cultivated for me will, I trust, be the blessing of my life.

Still there are many drawbacks; this is a dull, inhospitable place. I came counting on the kindness of a friend who lived

here, but she died of the influenza, and I live in a silence and
loneliness not possible anywhere except in England, where
people are so *islanded* individually in habits; I often languish
for sympathy, and pine for social festivity.

Percy is much, but I think of you and Henry, and shrink
from binding up my life in a child who may hereafter divide
his fate from mine. But I have no resource; everything
earthly fails me but him; except on his account I live but to
suffer. Those I loved are false or dead; those I love, absent
and suffering; and I, absent and poor, can be of no use
to them. Of course, in this picture, I subtract the enjoyment of good health and usually good spirits,—these are
blessings; but when driven to think, I feel so desolate, so
unprotected, so oppressed and injured, that my heart is ready
to break with despair. I came here, as I said, in April
1833, and 9th June was attacked by the influenza, so as to be
confined to my bed; nor did I recover the effects for several
months.

In September, during Percy's holidays, I went to Putney,
and recovered youth and health; Julia Robinson was with
me, and we spent days in Richmond Park and on Putney
Heath, often walking twelve or fourteen miles, which I did
without any sense of fatigue. I sorely regretted returning
here. I am too poor to furnish. I have lodgings in the
town,—disagreeable ones,—yet often, in spite of care and
sorrow, I feel wholly compensated by my boy. . . . God help
me if anything was to happen to him—I should not survive
it a week. Besides his society I have also a good deal of
occupation.

I have finished a novel, which, if you meet with, read, as I
think there are parts which will please you. I am engaged
writing the lives of some of the Italian *literati* for Dr. Lardner's
Cyclopædia. I have written those of Petrarch, Boccaccio, etc.,
and am now engaged on Macchiavelli; this takes up my time,
and is a source of interest and pleasure.

My Father, I suppose you know, has a tiny, shabby place
under Government. The retrenchments of Parliament en-

danger and render us anxious. He is quite well, but old age takes from his enjoyments. Mrs. Godwin, after influenza, has been suffering from the tic-doloreux in her arm most dreadfully; they are trying all sorts of poisons on her with little effect. Their discomfort and low spirits will force me to spend Percy's holidays in town, to be near them. Jane and Jeff are well; he was sent last autumn and winter by Lord Brougham as one of the Corporation Commissioners; he was away for months, and Jane took the opportunity to fall desperately in love with him—she pined and grew ill, and wasted away for him. The children are quite well. Dina spent a week here lately; she is a sweet girl. Edward improves daily under the excellent care taken of his education. I leave Jane to inform you of their progress in Greek. Dina plays wonderfully well, and has shown great taste for drawing, but this last is not cultivated.

I did not go to the Abbey, nor the Opera, nor hear Grisi; I am shut out from all things—like you—by poverty and loneliness. Percy's pleasures are not mine; I have no other companion.

What effect Paganini would have had on you, I cannot tell; he threw me into hysterics. I delight in him more than I can express. His wild, ethereal figure, rapt look, and the sounds he draws from his violin are all superhuman—of human expression. It is interesting to see the astonishment and admiration of Spagnoletti and Nervi as they watch his evolutions.

Bulwer is a man of extraordinary and delightful talent. He went to Italy and Sicily last winter, and, I hear, disliked the inhabitants. Yet, notwithstanding, I am sure he will spread inexpressible and graceful interest over the *Last Days of Pompeii*, the subject of his new novel. Trelawny is in America, and not likely to return. Hunt lives at Chelsea, and thrives, I hear, by his London pursuit. I have not seen him for more than a year, for reasons I will not here detail—they concern his family, not him.

Clare is in a situation in Pisa, near Mrs. Mason. Laurette

and Nerina are married; the elder badly, to one who won
her at the dagger's point—a sad unintelligible story; Nerina,
to the best and most delightful Pistoiese, by name Bartolomeo
Cini—both to Italians. Laurette lives at Genoa, Nerina at
Livorno; the latter is only newly a bride, and happier than
words can express. My Italian maid, Maria, says to Clare,
Non vedrò ora mai la mia Padrona ed il mio Bimbo? her
Bimbo—as tall as I am and large in proportion—has good
health withal. . . .

Pray write one word of information concerning your health
before I attribute your silence to forgetfulness; but you must
not trifle now with the anxiety you have awakened. I will
write again soon. With kindest regards to your poor, good
husband, the fondest hopes that your health is improved, and
anxious expectation of a letter, believe me, ever affectionately
yours,   M. W. SHELLEY.

MRS. SHELLEY TO MRS. GISBORNE.

HARROW, 30*th October* 1834.

MY DEAREST MARIA—Thank you many times for your
kind dear letter. God grant that your constitution may yet bear
up a long time, and that you may continue impressed with
the idea of your happiness. To be loved is indeed necessary.
Sympathy and companionship are the only sweets to make the
nauseous draught of life go down; and I, who feel this, live
in a solitude such as, since the days of hermits in the desert,
no one was ever before condemned to! I see no one, speak
to no one—except perhaps for a chance half-hour in the course
of a fortnight. I never walk beyond my garden, because I
cannot walk alone. You will say I ought to force myself; so
I thought once, and tried, but it would not do. The sense of
desolation was too oppressive. I only find relief from the
sadness of my position by living a dreamy existence from
which realities are excluded; but going out disturbed this; I
wept; my heart beat with a sense of injury and wrong; I was
better shut up. Poverty prevents me from visiting town; I

am too far for visitors to reach me; I must bear to the end. Twelve years have I spent, the currents of life benumbed by poverty; life and hope are over for me, but I think of Percy!

Yet for the present something more is needed—something not so *unnatural* as my present life. Not that I often feel *ennui*—I am too much employed—but it hurts me, it destroys the spring of my mind, and makes me at once over-sensitive with my fellow-creatures, and yet their victim and their dupe. It takes all strength from my character, and makes me—who by nature am too much so—timid. I used to have one resource, a belief in my *good fortune;* this is exchanged after twelve years—one adversity, blotted and sprinkled with many adversities; a dark ground, with sad figures painted on it—to a belief in my ill fortune.

Percy is spared to me, because I am to live. He is a blessing; my heart acknowledges that perhaps he is as great an one as any human being possesses; and indeed, my dear friend, while I suffer, I do not repine while he remains. He is not all you say; he has no ambition, and his talents are not so transcendent as you appear to imagine; but he is a fine, spirited, clever boy, and I think promises good things; if hereafter I have reason to be proud of him, these melancholy days and weeks at Harrow will brighten in my imagination—and they are not melancholy. I am seldom so, but they are not right, and it will be a good thing if they terminate happily soon.

At the same time, I cannot in the least regret having come here : it was the only way I had of educating Percy at a public school, of which institution, at least here at Harrow, the more I see the more I like; besides that, it was Shelley's wish that his son should be brought up at one. It is, indeed, peculiarly suited to Percy; and whatever he may be, he will be twice as much as if he had been brought up in the narrow confinement of a private school.

The boys here have liberty to the verge of licence; yet of the latter, save the breaking of a few windows now and then, there is none. His life is not quite what it would be if he did not live with me, but the greater scope given to the cultivation of the affections is surely an advantage.

*   *   *   *   *   *   *

You heard of the dreadful fire at the Houses of Parliament. We saw it here from the commencement, raging like a volcano; it was dreadful to see, but, fortunately, I was not aware of the site. Papa lives close to the Speaker's, so you may imagine my alarm when the news reached me, fortunately without foundation, as the fire did not gain that part of the Speaker's house near them, so they were not even inconvenienced. The poor dear Speaker has lost dreadfully; what was not burnt is broken, soaked, and drenched—all their pretty things; and imagine the furniture and princely chambers—the house was a palace. For the sake of convenience to the Commons, they are to take up their abode in the ruins. With kindest wishes for you and S. G., ever dearest friend, your affectionate

MARY W. SHELLEY.

THE SAME TO THE SAME.

February 1835.

. . . I must tell you that I have had the offer of £600 for an edition of Shelley's works, with *Life and Notes*. I am afraid it cannot be arranged, yet at least, and the *Life* is out of the question; but in talking over it the question of letters comes up. You know how I shrink from all private detail for the public; but Shelley's letters are beautifully written, and everything private might be omitted.

Would you allow the publisher to treat with you for their being added to my edition? If I could arrange all as I wish, they might be an acquisition to the books, and being transacted through me, you could not see any inconvenience in receiving the price they would be worth to the bookseller. This is all *in aria* as yet, but I should like to know what you think about it. I write all this, yet am very anxious to hear from you; never mind postage, but do write.

Percy is reading the *Antigone;* he has begun mathematics.

Mrs. Cleveland[1] and Jane dined with me the other day. Mrs. Cleveland thought Percy wonderfully improved.

The volume of Lardner's *Cyclopædia*, with my *Lives*, was published on the first of this month; it is called *Lives of Eminent Literary Men*, vol. i. The lives of Dante and Ariosto are by Mr. Montgomery, the rest are mine.

Do write, my dearest Maria, and believe me ever and ever, affectionately yours, M. W. SHELLEY.

Lodore, Mrs. Shelley's fifth novel, came out in 1835. It differs from the others in being a novel of society, and has been stigmatised, rather unjustly, as weak and colourless, although at the time of its publication it had a great success. It is written in a style which is now out of date, and undoubtedly fails to fulfil the promise of power held out by *Frankenstein* and to some extent by *Valperga*, but it bears on every page the impress of the refinement and sensibility of the author, and has, moreover, a special interest of its own, due to the fact that some of the incidents are taken from actual occurrences in her early life, and some of the characters sketched from people she had known.

Thus, in the description of Clorinda, it is impossible not to recognise Emilia Viviani. The whole episode of Edward Villier's arrest and imprisonment for debt, and his young wife's anxieties, is an echo of her own experience at the time when Shelley was hiding from the bailiffs and

---

[1] Jane's mother.

meeting her by stealth in St. Paul's or Holborn.
Lodore himself has some affinity to Byron, and
possibly the account of his separation from his wife
and of their daughter's girlhood is a fanciful train
of thought suggested by Byron's domestic history.
Most of Mary's novels present the contrast of the
Shelleyan and Byronic types. In this instance
the latter was recognised by Clare, and drew from
her one of those bitter tirades against Byron,
which, natural enough in her at the outset, became
in the course of years quite morbidly venomous.
Not content with laying Allegra's death to his
charge, she, in her later letters, accuses him of
treacherously plotting and conspiring, out of hatred
to herself, to do away with the child, an allegation
unjust and false. In the present instance, however, she only entered an excited protest against
his continual reappearance as the hero of a novel.

Mrs. Hare admired *Lodore* amazingly ; so do I, or should
I, if it were not for that modification of the beastly character
of Lord Byron of which you have composed Lodore. I stick
to *Frankenstein*, merely because that vile spirit does not haunt
its pages as it does in all your other novels, now as Castruccio.
now as Raymond,[1] now as Lodore. Good God ! to think a
person of your genius, whose moral tact ought to be proportionately exalted, should think it a task befitting its powers
to gild and embellish and pass off as beautiful what was the
merest compound of vanity, folly, and every miserable weakness that ever met together in one human being ! As I do
not want to be severe on the poor man, because he is dead

---

[1] In *The Last Man.*

and cannot defend himself, I have only taken the lighter defects of his character, or else I might say that never was a nature more profoundly corrupted than his became, or was more radically vulgar than his was from the very outset. Never was there an individual less adapted, except perhaps Alcibiades, for being held up as anything but an object of commiseration, or as an example of how contemptible is even intellectual greatness when not joined with moral greatness. I shall be anxious to see if the hero of your new novel will be another beautified Byron. Thank heaven! you have not taken to drawing your women upon the same model. Cornelia I like the least of them; she is the most like him, because she is so heartlessly proud and selfish, but all the others are angels of light.

Euthanasia [1] is Shelley in female attire, and what a glorious being she is! No author, much less the ones—French, English, or German—of our day, can bring a woman that matches her. Shakespeare has not a specimen so perfect of what a woman ought to be; his, for amiability, deep feeling, wit, are as high as possible, but they want her commanding wisdom, her profound benevolence.

I am glad to hear you are writing again; I am always in a fright lest you should take it into your head to do what the warriors do after they have acquired great fame,—retire and rest upon your laurels. That would be very comfortable for you, but very vexing to me, who am always wanting to see women distinguishing themselves in literature, and who believe there has not been or ever will be one so calculated as yourself to raise our sex upon that point. If you would but know your own value and exert your powers you could give the men a most immense drubbing! You could write upon metaphysics, politics, jurisprudence, astronomy, mathematics—all those highest subjects which they taunt us with being incapable of treating, and surpass them; and what a consolation it would be, when they begin some of their prosy, lying, but

---

[1] The heroine of *Valperga.*

plausible attacks upon female inferiority, to stop their mouths in a moment with your name, and then to add, "and if women, whilst suffering the heaviest slavery, could out-do you, what would they not achieve were they free?

With this manifesto on the subject of women's genius in general and of Mary's in particular—perhaps just redeemed by its tinge of irony from the last degree of absurdity—it is curious to contrast Mrs. Shelley's own conclusions, drawn from weary personal experience, and expressed, towards the end of the following letter, in a mood which permitted her no illusions and few hopes.

MRS. SHELLEY TO MRS. GISBORNE.

HARROW, 11*th June* 1835.

MY DEAREST FRIEND—It is so inexpressibly warm that were not a frank lying before me ready for you, I do not think I should have courage to write. Do not be surprised, therefore, at stupidity and want of connection. I cannot collect my ideas, and this is a goodwill offering rather than a letter.

Still I am anxious to thank S. G. for the pleasure I have received from his tale of Italy—a tale all Italy, breathing of the land I love. The descriptions are beautiful, and he has shed a charm round the concentrated and undemonstrative person of his gentle heroine. I suppose she is the reality of the story; did you know her?

It is difficult, however, to judge how to procure for it the publication it deserves. I have no personal acquaintance with the editors of any of the annuals—I had with that of the *Keepsake*, but that is now in Mrs. Norton's hands, and she has not asked me to write, so I know nothing about it ; but there arises a stronger objection from the length of the story. As the merit lies in the beauty of the details, I do not see how it could be cut down to *one quarter* of its present length, which is as long as any tale printed in an annual. When I write for them, I am worried to death to make my things shorter and shorter, till I fancy people think ideas can be conveyed by intuition, and that it is a superstition to consider words necessary for their expression.

I was so very delighted to get your last letter, to be sure the "Wisest of Men" said no news was good news, but I am not apt to think so, and was uneasy. I hope this weather does not oppress you. What an odd climate! A week ago I had a fire, and now it is warmer than Italy; warmer at least in a box pervious to the sun than in the stone palaces where one can breathe freely. My Father is well. He had a cough in the winter, but after we had persuaded him to see a doctor it was easily got rid of. He writes to me himself, "I am now well, now nervous, now old, now young." One sign of age is, that his horror is so great of change of place that I cannot persuade him ever to visit me here. One would think that the sight of the fields would refresh him, but he likes his own nest better than all, though he greatly feels the annoyance of so seldom seeing me.

Indeed, my kind Maria, you made me smile when you asked me to be civil to the brother of your kind doctor. I thought I had explained my situation to you. You must consider me as one buried alive. I hardly ever go to town; less often I see any one here. My kind and dear young friends, the Misses Robinson, are at Brussels. I am cut off from my kind. What I suffer! What I have suffered! I, to whom sympathy, companionship, the interchange of thought is more necessary than the air I breathe, I will not say. Tears are in my eyes when I think of days, weeks, months, even years spent alone—eternally alone. It does me great harm, but no more of so odious a subject. Let me speak rather of my Percy; to see him bright and good is an unspeakable blessing; but no child can be a companion. He is very fond of me, and would be wretched if he saw me unhappy; but he is with his boys all day long, and I am alone, so I can weep unseen. He gets on very well, and is a fine boy, very stout; this hot weather, though he exposes himself to the sun, instead of making him languid, heightens the colour in his cheeks and brightens his eyes. He is always gay and in good humour, which is a great blessing.

You talk about my poetry and about the encouragement I am to find from Jane and my Father. When they read all the fine things you said they thought it right to attack me about it, but I answered them simply, "She exaggerates; you read the best thing I ever wrote in the *Keepsake* and thought nothing of it." I do not know whether you remember the verses I mean. I will copy it in another part; it was written for music. Poor dear Lord Dillon spoke of it as you do of the rest; but "one swallow does not make a summer." I can never write verses except under the influence of strong senti-ment, and seldom even then. As to a tragedy, Shelley used to urge me, which produced his own. When I returned first to England and saw Kean, I was in a fit of enthusiasm, and wished much to write for the stage, but my Father very earnestly dissuaded me. I think that he was in the wrong. I think myself that I could have written a good tragedy, but not now. My good friend, every feeling I have is blighted, I have no ambition, no care for fame. Loneliness has made a wreck of me. I was always a dependent thing, wanting fosterage and support. I am left to myself, crushed by fortune, and I am nothing.

You speak of woman's intellect. We can scarcely do more than judge by ourselves. I know that, however clever I may be, there is in me a vacillation, a weakness, a want of eagle-winged resolution that appertains to my intellect as well as to my moral character, and renders me what I am, one of broken purposes, failing thoughts, and a heart all wounds. My mother had more energy of character, still she had not sufficient fire of imagination. In short, my belief is, whether there be sex in souls or not, that the sex of our material mechanism makes us quite different creatures, better, though weaker, but wanting in the higher grades of intellect.

I am almost sorry to send you this letter, it is so querulous and sad; yet, if I write with any effusion, the truth will creep out, and my life since you left has been so stained by sorrow and disappointments. I have been so barbarously handled both by fortune and my fellow-creatures, that I am no longer the same as when you knew me. I have no hope. In a few years, when I get over my present feelings and live wholly in Percy, I shall be happier. I have devoted myself to him as no mother ever did, and idolise him; and the reward will come when I can forget a thousand memories and griefs that are as yet alive and burning, and I have nothing to do but brood.

Percy is gone two miles off to bathe; he can swim, and I am obliged to leave the rest to fate. It is no use coddling, yet it costs me many pangs; but he is singularly trustworthy and careful. Do write, and believe me ever your truly attached friend,
                                                M. W. S.

A DIRGE

I

This morn thy gallant bark, love,
    Sailed on a stormy sea;
'Tis noon, and tempests dark, love,
Have wrecked it on the lee.
Ah woe! ah woe! ah woe!
    By spirits of the deep
He's cradled on the billow
    To his unwaking sleep.

II

Thou liest upon the shore, love,
    Beside the knelling surge,
But sea-nymphs ever more, love,
Shall sadly chant thy dirge.

Oh come! oh come! oh come!
　　Ye spirits of the deep;
While near his seaweed pillow
　　My lonely watch I keep.

III

From far across the sea, love,
　　I hear a wild lament,
By Echo's voice for thee, love,
　　From ocean's caverns sent.
Oh list! oh list! oh list!
　　Ye spirits of the deep,
Loud sounds their wail of sorrow,
　　While I for ever weep.

P.S.—Do you not guess why neither these nor those I sent you could please those you mention? Papa loves not the memory of Shelley, because he feels that he injured him; and Jane—do you not understand enough of her to be convinced of the thoughts that make it distasteful to her that I should feel, and above all be thought by others to feel, and to have a right to feel? Oh! the human heart! It is a strange puzzle.

The weary, baffled tone of this letter was partly due to a low state of health, which resulted in a severe attack of illness. During her boy's Midsummer holidays she went to Dover in search of strength, and, while there, received a letter from Trelawny, who had returned from America, as vivacious and irrepressible as ever.

TRELAWNY TO MRS. SHELLEY.

BEDFORD HOTEL, BRIGHTON,
12th September 1835.

MARY, DEAR—Six days I rest, and do all that I have to do on the seventh, because it is forbidden. If they would make it felony to obey the Commandments (without benefit of clergy), don't you think the pleasures of breaking the law would make me keep them?

*   *   *   *   *   *   *

I cannot surmise *one* of the "thousand reasons" which you say are to prevent my seeing you. On the contrary, your being "chained to your rock" enables me to play the vulture at discretion. It is well for you, therefore, that I am "the most prudent of men." What a host of virtues I am gifted with! When I am dead, lady mine, build a temple over me and make pilgrimages. Talking of tombs, let it be agreed between you and me that whichever *first* has *five hundred pounds* at his disposal shall dedicate it to the placing a fitting monument over the ashes of Shelley.

We will go to Rome together. The time, too, cannot be far distant, considering all things. Remember me to Percy. I shall direct this to Jane's, not that I think you are there. Adieu, Mary!—Your   E. Trelawny.

During the latter part of Mary's residence in London she had seen a great deal of Mrs. Norton, who was much attracted by her and very fond of her society, finding in her a most sympathetic friend and confidant at the time of those domestic troubles, culminating in the separation from her children, which afterwards obtained a melancholy publicity. Mrs. Shelley never became wholly intimate with her brilliant contemporary. Reserve, and a certain pride of poverty, forbade it, but she greatly admired her, and they constantly corresponded.

1835.

. . . "I do not wonder," Mary wrote to Trelawny, "at your not being able to deny yourself the pleasure of Mrs.

Norton's society. I never saw a woman I thought so fascinating. Had I been a man I should certainly have fallen in love with her ; as a woman, ten years ago, I should have been spellbound, and, had she taken the trouble, she might have wound me round her finger. Ten years ago I was so ready to give myself away, and being afraid of men, I was apt to get *tousymousy* for women ; experience and suffering have altered all that. I am more wrapt up in myself, my own feelings, disasters, and prospects for Percy. I am now proof, as Hamlet says, both against man and woman.

" There is something in the pretty way in which Mrs. Norton's witticisms glide, as it were, from her lips, that is very charming ; and then her colour, which is so variable, the eloquent blood which ebbs and flows, mounting, as she speaks, to her neck and temples, and then receding as fast ; it reminds me of the frequent quotation of 'eloquent blood,' and gives a peculiar attraction to her conversation—not to speak of fine eyes and open brow.

" Now do not in your usual silly way show her what I say. She is, despite all her talents and sweetness, a London lady. She would quiz me—not, perhaps, to you—well do I know the London *ton*—but to every one else—in her prettiest manner."

The day after this she was writing again to Mrs. Gisborne.

13th October 1835.

Of myself, my dearest Maria, I can give but a bad account. Solitude, many cares, and many deep sorrows brought on this summer an illness, from which I am only now recovering. I can never forget, nor cease to be grateful to Jane for her excessive kindness to me, when I needed it most, confined, as I was, to my sofa, unable to move. I went to Dover during Percy's holidays, and change of air and bathing made me so much better that I thought myself well, but on my return here I had a relapse, from which now this last week I am, I trust, fast recovering. Bark and port wine seem the chief means of my getting well. But in the midst of all this I had to write to meet my expenses. I have published a second volume of Italian Lives in Lardner's *Encyclopædia.* All in that volume, except Galileo and Tasso, are mine. The last is chief, I allow, and I grieve that it had been engaged to Mr. M. before I began to write. I am now about to write a volume of Spanish and Portuguese Lives. This is an arduous task, from my own ignorance, and the difficulty of getting books and information. The booksellers want me to write another novel, *Lodore* having succeeded so well, but I have not as yet strength for such an undertaking.

Then there is no Spanish circulating library. I cannot, while here, read in the Museum if I would, and I would not if I could. I do not like finding myself a stray bird alone among men, even if I knew them.[1] One hears how happy people will be to lend me their books, but when it comes to the point it is very difficult to get at them. However, as I am rather persevering, I hope to conquer these obstacles after all. Percy grows; he is taller than I am, and very stout. If he does not turn out an honour to his parents, it will be through no deficiency in virtue or in talents, but from a dislike of mingling with his fellow-creatures, except the two or three friends he cannot do without. He may be the happier for it; he has a good understanding, and great integrity of character. Adieu, my dear friend.—Ever affectionately yours,

MARY W. SHELLEY.

In April 1836 poor old Godwin died, and with him passed away a large part of Mary's life. Of those in whose existence her own was summed up only her son now remained, and even he was

---

[1] Things have changed at the British Museum, not a little, since these words were written.

not more dependent on her than her father had
been. Godwin had been to his daughter one of
those lifelong cares which, when they disappear,
leave a blank that nothing seems to fill, too often
because the survivor has borne the burden so
long as to exhaust the power and energy indispensable to recovery. But she had also been
attached to him all her life with an "excessive
and romantic attachment," only overcome in one
instance by a stronger devotion still—a defection
she never could and never did repent of, but for
which her whole subsequent life had been passed
in attempting to make up. If she confided any
of her feelings to her diary, no fragment has
survived.

She busied herself in trying to obtain from
Government some assistance — an annuity if
possible—for Mrs. Godwin. It was very seldom
in her life that Mary asked anybody for anything,
and the present exception was made in favour of
one whom she did not love, and who had never
been a good friend to her. But had Mrs. Godwin
been her own mother instead of a disagreeable,
jealous, old stepmother, she could not have made
greater exertions in her behalf. Mrs. Norton was
ready and willing to help by bringing influence to
bear in powerful quarters, and gave Mary some
shrewd advice as to the wording of her letter to
Lord Melbourne. She wrote—

. . . Press *not* on the politics of Mr. Godwin (for God knows how much gratitude for that ever survives), but on his *celebrity*, the widow's *age* and *ill health*, and (if your proud little spirit will bear it) on your own *toils;* for, after all, the truth is that you, being generous, will, rather than see the old creature starve, work your brains and your pen ; and you have your son and delicate health to hinder you from having *means* to help her.

As to petitioning, no one dislikes begging more than I do, especially when one begs for what seems mere justice; but I have long observed that though people will resist *claims* (however just), they like to do *favours.* Therefore, when *I* beg, I am a crawling lizard, a humble toad, a brown snake in cold weather, or any other simile most feebly *rampante* — the reverse of *rampant*, which would be the natural attitude for petitioning,—but which must never be assumed except in the poodle style, standing with one's paws bent to catch the bits of bread on one's nose.

Forgive my jesting ; upon my honour I feel sincerely anxious for your anxiety, and sad enough on my own affairs, but Irish blood *will* dance. My meaning is, that if one asks *at all*, one should rather think of the person written to than one's own feelings. He is an indolent man—talk of your literary labours; a kind man—speak of her age and infirmities; a patron of all *genius*—talk of your father's *and your own ;* a prudent man—speak of the likelihood of the pension being a short grant (as you have done); lastly, he is a *great* man—take it all as a personal favour. As to not apologising for the intrusion, we ought always to kneel down and beg pardon for daring to remind people we are not so well off as they are.

What was asked was that Godwin's small salary, or a part of it, should be continued to Mrs. Godwin for her life. As the nominal office Godwin had held was abolished at his death, this could not be; but Lord Melbourne pledged himself to do what he could to obtain assistance for the widow in some form or other, so it is probable that Mary effected her purpose.

TRELAWNY TO MRS. SHELLEY.

HASTINGS, 25*th September* 1836.

MARY, DEAR—Your letter was exceedingly welcome; it was honoured accordingly. You divine truly; I am leading a vegetable sort of a life. They say the place is pretty, the air is good, the sea is fine. I would willingly exchange a pretty place for a pretty girl. The air is keen and shrewish, and as to the sea, I am satisfied with a bath of less dimensions. Notwithstanding the want of sun, and the abundance of cold winds, I lave my sides daily in the brine, and thus I am gradually cooling down to the temperature—of the things round about me—so that the thinnest skinned feminine may handle me without fear of consequences. Possibly you may think that I am like the torpid snake that the forester warmed by his hearth. No, I am not. I am steeling myself with Plato and Platonics; so now farewell to love and womankind. "Othello's occupation's gone."

*   *   *   *   *   *   *

From an allusion in one of Mrs. Norton's letters to Mary, it appears likely that what follows refers to Fanny Kemble (Mrs. Butler).

You say, "Had I seen those eyes you saw the other day." Yes, the darts shot from those eyes are still rankling in my body; yet it is a pleasing pain. The wound of the scorpion is healed by applying the scorpion to the wound. Is she not a glorious being? Have you ever seen such a presence? Is she not dazzling? There is enchantment in all her ways. Talk of the divine power of music, why, she is all melody, and

poetry, and beauty, and harmony.   How envious and malig-
nant must the English be not to do her homage universal.
They never had, or will have again, such a woman as that.   I
would rather be her slave than king of such an island of
Calibans.   You have a soul, and sense, and a deep feeling for
your sex, and revere such "cunning patterns of excelling
nature," therefore—besides, I owe it you—I will transcribe
what she says of you : "I was nervous, it was my first visit
to any one, and there is a gentle frankness in her manner, and
a vague remembrance of the thought and feeling in her books
which prevents my being as with a 'visiting acquaintance.'"

*　　*　　*　　*　　*　　*　　*

Zella is doing wondrous well, and chance has placed her
with a womankind that even I (setting beauty aside) am satisfied with.   By the bye, I wish most earnestly you could get
me some good *morality* in the shape of Italian and French.
It is indispensable to the keeping alive her remembrance of
those languages, and not a book is to be had here, nor do
I know exactly how to get them by any other means, so pray
think of it.

*　　*　　*　　*　　*　　*　　*

I am inundated with letters from America, and am answering them by Mrs. Jameson ; she sailing immediately is a very
heavy loss to me.   She is the friendliest-hearted woman in the
world.   I would rather lose anything than her. . . .

I don't think I shall stay here much longer ; it is a bad
holding ground ; my cable is chafing.   I shall drift somewhere
or other.   It is well for Mamma Percy has so much of her
temperate blood.   When us three meet, we shall be able to
ice the wine by placing it between us ; that will be nice, as the
girls say.

A glance from Mrs. Nesbitt has shaken my firm nerves a
little.   There is a mystery—a deep well of feeling in those
star-like eyes of hers.   It is strange that actresses are the only
true and natural people ; they only act in the proper season
and place, whilst all the rest seem eternally playing a part, and
like dilettanti acting, damn'd absurdly.   J. Trelawny.

From Brighton, at New Year, Mrs. Shelley sent Trelawny a cheery greeting.

BRIGHTON, *3d January* 1837.

MY DEAR TRELAWNY—This day will please you; it is a thaw; what snow we had! Hundreds of people have been employed to remove it during the last week; at first they cut down deep several feet as if it had been clay, and piled it up in glittering pyramids and masses; then they began to cart it on to the beach; it was a new sort of Augean stable, a never-ending labour. Yesterday, when I was out, it was only got rid of in a very few and very circumscribed spots. Nature is more of a Hercules; she puts out a little finger in the shape of gentle thaw, and it recedes and disappears.

* * * * * * *

Percy arrived yesterday, having rather whetted than satisfied his appetite by going seven times to the play. He plays like Apollo on the flageolet, and like Apollo is self-taught. Jane thinks him a miracle! it is very odd. He got a frock-coat at Mettes, and, if you had not disappointed us with your handkerchief, he would have been complete; he is a good deal grown, though not tall enough to satisfy me; however, there is time yet. He is quite a child still, full of theatres and balloons and music, yet I think there is a gentleness about him which shows the advent of the reign of petticoats—how I dread it!

* * * * * * *

Poor Jane writes dismally. She is so weak that she has frequent fainting fits; she went to a physician, who ordered her to wean the child, and now she takes three glasses of wine a day, and every other strengthening medicament, but she is very feeble, and has a cough and tendency to inflammation on the chest. I implored her to come down here to change the air, and Jeff gave leave, and would have given the money; but fear lest his dinner should be overdone while she was away, and lest the children should get a finger scratched, makes her resolve not to come; what bad bogie is this? If she got stronger how much better they would be in consequence! I think her in a critical state, but she will not allow of a remedy.

* * * * * * *

Poor dear little Zella. I hope she is well and happy. . . . Thank you for your offer about money. I have plenty at present, and hope to do well hereafter. You are very thoughtful, which is a great virtue. I have not heard from your mother or Charlotte since you left; a day or two afterwards I saw Betsy Freeman; she was to go to her place the next day. I paid her for her work; she looked so radiantly happy that you would have thought she was going to be married rather than to a place of hardship. I never saw any one look so happy. I told her to let me know how she got on, and to apply to me if she wanted assistance. . . . I am glad you are amused at your brother's. I really imagined that Fanny Butler had been the attraction, till, sending to the Gloucester, I found you were gone by the Southampton coach, and then I suspected another magnet—till I find that you are in all peace, or rather war, at Sherfield House—much better so.

I am better a great deal; quite well, I believe I ought to call myself, only I feel a little odd at times. I have seen nothing of the S.'s. I have met with scarce an acquaintance here, which is odd; but then I do not look for them. I am too lazy. I hope this letter will catch you before you leave your present perch.—Believe me always, yours truly,

M. W. SHELLEY.

Will this be a happy New Year? Tell me; the last I can't say much for, but I always fear worse to come. Nobody's mare is dead,—if this frost does not kill,—my own (such as it will be) is far enough off still.

The next letter is dated only three weeks later. What happened in that short time to account for its complete change of tone does not appear, except that from one allusion it may be inferred that Mrs. Shelley was overtaken by unexpected money difficulties at a moment when she had fancied herself tolerably at ease on that score. Nothing more likely, for in the matter of helping others she never learnt prudence or the art of self-defence.[1] Probably, however, there was a deeper cause for her sombre mood. She was being pressed on all sides to write the biography of her father. The task would have been well suited to her powers; she looked on it, moreover, in the light of a duty which she wished and intended to perform. Fragments and sketches of hers for this book have been published, and are among the best specimens of her writing. But circumstances—scruples—similar to those which had hindered her from writing Shelley's life stood between her and the present fulfilment of the task. There were few people to whom she could bring herself to explain her reasons, and those few need not have required, still less insisted on any such explanation. But Trelawny, hot and vehement, could and would not see why Mary did not rush into the field at once, to immortalise the man whose system of philosophy, more than any other writer's, had moulded Shelley's. He never spared words, and he prob-

---

[1] In a letter of Clare's, before this time, referring to the marriage of one of the Miss Robinsons, she remarks, "I am quite glad to think that for the future you may only have Percy and yourself to maintain."

ably taxed her with cowardice or indolence, time-serving and " worldliness."

Shaken by her father's loss, and saddened by that of her friends, Mr. and Mrs. Gisborne, who had died within a short time of each other shortly before this, exhausted by work, her feelings warped by solitude, struggle, and disappointment, this challenge to explain her conduct evoked the most mournful of all her letters, as explicit as any one could wish ; true in its bitterness, and most bitter in its truth.

MRS. SHELLEY TO TRELAWNY.

BRIGHTON, *Thursday*, 27*th January* 1837.

DEAR TRELAWNY—I am very glad to hear that you are amused and happy ; fate seems to have turned her sunny side to you, and I hope you will long enjoy yourself. I know of but one pleasure in the world — sympathy with another, or others, rather ; leaving out of the question the affections, the society of agreeable, gifted, congenial-minded beings is the only pleasure worth having in the world. My fate has debarred me from this enjoyment, but you seem in the midst of it.

With regard to my Father's life I certainly could not answer it to my conscience to give it up. I shall therefore do it, but I must wait. This year I have to fight my poor Percy's battle, to try and get him sent to College without further dilapidation of his ruined prospects, and he has now to enter life at College. That this should be undertaken at a moment when a cry was raised against his mother, and that not on the question of *politics* but *religion*, would mar all. I must see him fairly launched before I commit myself to the fury of the waves.

A sense of duty towards my Father, whose passion was

posthumous fame, makes me ready, as far as I am concerned, to meet the misery that must be mine if I become an object of scurrility and attack; for the rest, for my own private satisfaction, all I ask is obscurity. What can I care for the parties that divide the world, or the opinions that possess it? What has my life been? What is it? Since I lost Shelley I have been alone, and worse. I had my Father's fate for many a year pressing me to the earth; I had Percy's education and welfare to guard over, and in all this I had no one friendly hand stretched out to support me. Shut out from even the possibility of making such an impression as my personal merits might occasion, without a human being to aid or encourage, or even to advise me, I toiled on my weary solitary way. The only persons who deigned to share those melancholy hours, and to afford me the balm of affection, were those dear girls[1] whom you chose so long to abuse. Do you think that I have not felt, that I do not feel all this? If I have been able to stand up against the breakers which have dashed against my stranded, wrecked bark, it has been by a sort of passive, dogged resistance, which has broken my heart, while it a little supported my spirit. My happiness, my health, my fortunes, all are wrecked. Percy alone remains to me, and to do him good is the sole aim of my life. One thing I will add; if I have ever found kindness, it has not been from liberals; to disengage myself from them was the first act of my freedom. The consequence was that I gained peace and civil usage, which they denied me; more I do not ask; of fate I only ask a grave. I know not what my future life is, and shudder, but it must be borne, and for Percy's sake I must battle on.

If you wish for a copy of my novel[2] you shall have one, but I did not order it to be sent to you, because, being a rover, all luggage burthens. I have told them to send it to your mother, at which you will scoff, but it was the only way I had to show my sense of her kindness. You may pick and choose those from whom you deign to receive kindness; you

---

[1] The Miss Robinsons.   [2] *Lodore*.

are a man at a feast, champagne and comfits your diet, and you naturally scoff at me and my dry crust in a corner. Often have you scoffed and sneered at all the aliment of kindness or society that fate has afforded me. I have been silent, for the hungry cannot be dainty, but it is useless to tell a pampered man this. Remember in all this, except in one or two instances, my complaint is not against *persons*, but *fate.* Fate has been my enemy throughout. I have no wish to increase her animosity or her power by exposing [myself] more than I possibly can to her venomous attacks.

You have sent me no address, so I direct this to your Mother; give her and Charlotte my love, and tell them I think I shall be in town at the beginning of next month; my time in this house is up on the 3d, and I ought to be in town with Percy to take him to Sir Tim's solicitors, and so begin my attack. I should advise you, by the bye, not to read my novel; you will not like it. I cannot *teach;* I can only paint—such as my paintings are,—and you will not approve of much of what I deem natural feeling, because it is not founded on the new light.

I had a long letter from Mrs. N[orton]. I admire her excessively, and I *think* I could love her infinitely, but I shall not be asked nor tried, and shall take very good care not to press myself. I know what her relations think.

If you are still so rich, and can lend me £20 till my quarter, I shall be glad. I do not know that I absolutely [need] it here now, but may run short at last, so, if not inconvenient, will you send it next week?

I shall soon be in town, I suppose; *where,* I do not yet know. I dread my return, for I shall have a thousand worries.

Despite unfavourable weather, quiet and ease have much restored my health, but mental annoyance will soon make me as ill as ever. Only writing this letter makes me feel half dead. Still, to be thus at peace is an expensive luxury, and I must forego it for other duties, which I have been allowed to forget for a time, but my holiday is past.

Happy is Fanny Butler if she can shed tears and not be destroyed by them; this luxury is denied me. I am obliged to guard against low spirits as my worst disease, and I do guard, and usually I am not in low spirits. Why then do you awaken me to thought and suffering by forcing me to explain the motives of my conduct? Could you not trust that I thought anxiously, decided carefully, and from disinterested motives, not to save myself, but my child, from evil. Pray let the stream flow quietly by, as glittering on the surface as it may, and do not awaken the deep waters which are full of briny bitterness. I never wish any one to dive into the secret depths; be content, if I can render the surface safe sailing, that I do not annoy you with clouds and tempests, but turn the silvery side outward, as I ought, for God knows I would not render any living creature so miserable as I could easily be; and I would also guard myself from the sense of woe which I tie hard about, and sink low, low, out of sight and fathom line.

Adieu. Excuse all this; it is your own fault; speak of yourself. Never speak of me, and you will never again be annoyed with so much stupidity.—Yours truly, M. S.

The painful mood of this letter was not destined to find present relief. From her father's death in 1836 till the year 1840 was to be perhaps the hardest, dreariest, and most laborious time she had ever known. No chance had she now to distract her mind or avoid the most painful themes. Her very occupation was to tie her down to these. She was preparing her edition of Shelley's works, with notes. The prohibition as to bringing his name before the public seems to have been withdrawn or at any rate slackened; it had probably become evident, even to those least disposed to see, that the undesirable publicity, if not given by the right

person, would inevitably be given by the wrong
one.   Much may also have been due to the
fact that Mr. Whitton, Sir Timothy's solicitor,
was dead, and had been replaced by another
gentleman who, unlike his predecessor, used his
influence to promote milder counsels and a
better mutual understanding than had prevailed
hitherto.

This task was accepted by Mary as the most
sacred of duties, but it is probable that if circumstances had permitted her to fulfil it in the years
which immediately followed Shelley's death she
would have suffered from it less than now.   It
might not have been so well done, she might have
written at too great length, or have indulged in
too much expression of personal feeling ; and in the
case of omissions from his writings, the decision
might have been even harder to make.   Still it
would have cost her less.   Her heart, occupied by
one subject, would have found a kind of relief in
the necessity for dwelling on it.   But seventeen
years had elapsed, and she was forty-two, and very
tired.   Seventeen years of struggle, labour, and
loneliness ; even the mournful satisfaction of retrospect poisoned and distorted by Jane Williams'
duplicity.   She could no longer dwell on the
thought of that affection which had consoled her
in her supreme misfortune.

Mary had had many and bitter troubles and

losses, but nothing entered into her soul so deeply as the defection of this friend. Alienation is worse than bereavement. Other sorrows had left her desolate ; this one left her different.

Hence the fact that an undertaking which would once have been a painful pleasure was too often a veritable martyrdom. Who does not remember Hans Andersen's little princess, in his story of the *White Swans*, who freed her eleven brothers from the evil enchantment which held them transformed, by spinning shirts of stinging-nettles ? Such nettle-shirts had Mary now to weave and spin, to exorcise the evil spirits which had power of misrepresenting and defaming Shelley's memory, and to save Percy for ever from their sinister spells.

Her health was weak, her heart was sore, her life was lonely, and, in spite of her undaunted efforts, she was still so badly off that she was, as the last letter shows, reduced to accepting Trelawny's offer of a loan of money. Nor was it only her work that she had on her mind ; she was also very anxious about her son's future. He had, at this time, an idea of entering the Diplomatic Service, and his mother overcame her diffidence so far as to try and procure an opening for him— no easy thing to find. Among the people she consulted and asked was Lytton Bulwer ; his answer was not encouraging.

SIR E. L. BULWER TO MRS. SHELLEY.

HERTFORD STREET, 17*th March* 1839.

MY DEAR MRS. SHELLEY—Many thanks for your kind congratulations. I am delighted to find you like *Richelieu.*

With regard to your son, with his high prospects, the diplomacy may do very well; but of all professions it is the most difficult to rise in. The first steps are long and tedious. An Attaché at a small Court is an exile without pay, and very little opening to talent. However, for young men of fortune and expectations it fills up some years agreeably enough, what with flirting, dressing, dancing, and perhaps, if one has good luck, a harmless duel or two!

To be serious, it is better than being idle, and one certainly learns languages, knowledge of the world, and good manners. Perhaps I may send my son, some seventeen years hence, if my brother is then a minister, into that career. But it will depend on his prospects. Are you sure that you can get an attachéship? It requires a good deal of interest, and there are plenty of candidates among young men of rank, and, I fear, claims more pressing and urging than the memory of genius. I could not procure that place for a most intimate friend of mine a little time ago. I will take my chance some evening, but I fear not Thursday; in fact, I am so occupied just at present that till after Easter I have scarcely a moment to myself, and at Easter I must go to Lincoln.—Yours ever,

E. L. BULWER.

Mrs. Norton interested herself in the matter. She could not effect much, but she was sympathetic and kind.

"You have your troubles," she wrote, "struggling for one who, I trust, will hereafter repay you for every weary hour and years of self-denial, and I shall be glad to hear from you now and then how all goes on with you and him, so do not forget me when you have a spare half hour, and if ever I have any good news to send, do not doubt my then writing by the first post, for I think my happiest moments now are when, in the strange mixture of helplessness and power which has made the warp and woof of my destiny, I can accidentally serve some one who has had more of the world's buffets than its good fortune."

Some scraps of journal belonging to 1839 afford a little insight into Mrs. Shelley's difficulties while editing her husband's MSS.

Journal, February 12 (1839).—I almost think that my present occupation will end in a fit of illness. I am editing Shelley's Poems, and writing notes for them. I desire to do Shelley honour in the notes to the best of my knowledge and ability ; for the rest, they are or are not well written ; it little matters to me which. Would that I had more literary vanity, or vanity of any kind ; I were happier. As it is, I am torn to pieces by memory. Would that all were mute in the grave !

I *much* disliked the leaving out any of *Queen Mab.* I dislike it still more than I can express, and I even wish I had resisted to the last ; but when I was told that certain portions would injure the copyright of all the volumes to the publisher, I yielded. I had consulted Hunt, Hogg, and Peacock ; they all said I had a right to do as I liked, and offered no one objection. Trelawny sent back the volume to Moxon in a rage at seeing parts left out. . . .

Hogg has written me an insulting letter because I left out the dedication to Harriet. . . .

Little does Jefferson, how little does any one, know me ! When Clarke's edition of *Queen Mab* came to us at the Baths of Pisa, Shelley expressed great pleasure that these verses were omitted. This recollection caused me to do the same. It was to do him honour. What could it be to me? There are other verses I should well like to obliterate for ever, but they will be printed ; and any to her could in no way tend to my discomfort, or gratify one ungenerous feeling. They shall be restored, though I do not feel easy as to the good I do Shelley. I may have been mistaken. Jefferson might mistake me and be angry; that were nothing. He has done far more, and done his best to give another poke to the poisonous dagger which has long rankled in my heart. I cannot forgive any man that insults any woman. She cannot call him out,—she disdains words of retort; she must endure, but it is never to be forgiven; not, " indeed, cherished as matter of enmity '— that I never feel,—but of caution to shield oneself from the like again.

In so arduous a task, others might ask for encouragement and kindness from their friends,—I know mine better. I am unstable, sometimes melancholy, and have been called on some occasions imperious; but I never did an ungenerous act in my life. I sympathise warmly with others, and have wasted my heart in their love and service.

All this together is making me feel very ill, and my holiday at Woodlay only did me good while it lasted.

March. . . . Illness did ensue. What an illness! driving me to the verge of insanity. Often I felt the cord would snap, and I should no longer be able to rule my thoughts; with fearful struggles, miserable relapses, after long repose I became somewhat better.

October 5, 1839.—Twice in my life I have believed myself to be dying, and my soul being alive, though the bodily functions were faint and perishing, I had opportunity to look Death in the face, and I did not fear it—far from it. My feelings, especially in the first and most perilous instance, was, I go to no new creation. I enter under no new laws. The God that made this beautiful world (and I was then at Lerici, surrounded by the most beautiful manifestation of the visible creation) made that into which I go; as there is beauty and love here, such is there, and I feel as if my spirit would when it left my frame be received and sustained by a beneficent and gentle Power.

I had no fear, rather, though I had no active wish but a

passive satisfaction in death.   Whether the nature of my illness —debility from loss of blood, without pain—caused this tranquillity of soul, I cannot tell ; but so it was, and it had this blessed effect, that I have never since anticipated death with terror, and even if a violent death (which is the most repugnant to human nature) menaced me, I think I could, after the first shock, turn to the memory of that hour, and renew its emotion of perfect resignation.

The darkest moment is that which precedes the dawn.   These unhappy years were like the series of " clearing showers" which often concludes a stormy day.   The clouds were lifting, and though Mary Shelley could never be other than what sorrow and endurance had made her, the remaining years of her life were to bring alleviations to her lot,—slanting rays of afternoon sunshine, powerless, indeed, to warm into life the tender buds of morning, but which illumined the landscape and lightened her path, and shed over her a mild radiance which she reflected back on others, affording to them the brightness she herself could know no more, and diffusing around her that sensation of peace which she was to know now, perhaps, for the first time.

CHAPTER XXIV

OCTOBER 1839–FEBRUARY 1851

MRS. SHELLEY's annotated edition of Shelley's works was completed by the appearance, in 1840, of the collected prose writings; along with which was republished the *Journal of a Six Weeks' Tour* (a joint composition) and her own two letters from Geneva, reprinted in the present work.

Mary's correspondence with Carlyle on the subject of a motto for her book was the occasion of the following note—

5 CHEYNE ROW, CHELSEA,
3d December 1839.

DEAR MRS. SHELLEY—There does some indistinct remembrance of a sentence like the one you mention hover in my head; but I cannot anywhere lay hand on it. Indeed, I rather think it was to this effect: "Treat men as what they should be, and you help to make them so." Further, is it not rather one of Wilhelm's kind speeches than of the Uncle's or the Fair Saint's? James Fraser shall this day send you a copy of the work; you, with your own clear eyes, shall look for yourself.

I have no horse now; the mud forced me to send it into the country till dry weather came again. Layton House is so much the farther off. *Tant pis pour moi.*—Yours always truly,   T. CARLYLE.

The words ultimately prefixed to the collection are the following, from Carlyle—

That thou, O my Brother, impart to me truly how it stands with thee in that inner heart of thine; what lively images of things past thy memory has painted there; what hopes, what thoughts, affections, knowledge, do now dwell there. For this and no other object that I can see was the gift of hearing and speech bestowed on us two.

The proceeds of this work were such as to set her for some time at comparative ease on the score of money; the Godwin quicksand was no longer there to engulf them.

Journal, June 1, 1840 (Brighton).—I must mark this evening, tired as I am, for it is one among few—soothing and balmy. Long oppressed by care, disappointment, and ill health, which all combined to depress and irritate me, I felt almost to have lost the spring of happy reverie. On such a night it returns—the calm sea, the soft breeze, the silver bow new bent in the western heaven—Nature in her sweetest mood, raised one's thoughts to God and imparted peace.

Indeed I have many, many blessings, and ought to be grateful, as I am, though the poison lurks among them; for it is my strange fate that all my friends are sufferers—ill health or adversity bears heavily on them, and I can do little good, and lately ill health and extreme depression have even marred the little I could do. If I could restore health, administer balm to the wounded heart, and banish care from those I love, I were in myself happy, while I am loved, and Percy continues the blessing that he is. Still, who on such a night must not feel the weight of sorrow lessened? For myself, I repose in gentle and grateful reverie, and hope for others. I am content for myself. Years have—how much!—cooled the ardent and swift spirit that at such hours bore me freely along. Yet, though I no longer soar, I repose. Though I no longer deem all things attainable, I enjoy what is ; and while I feel that whatever I have lost of youth and hope, I have acquired the enduring affection of a noble heart, and Percy shows such excellent dispositions that I feel that I am much the gainer in life.

Fate does indeed visit some too heavily—poor R. for instance, God restore him! God and good angels guard us ! surely this world, stored outwardly with shapes and influences of beauty and good, is peopled in its intellectual life by myriads of loving spirits that mould our thoughts to good, influence beneficially the course of events, and minister to the destiny of man. Whether the beloved dead make a portion of this company I dare not guess, but that such exist I feel—far off, when we are worldly, evil, selfish ; drawing near and imparting joy and sympathy when we rise to noble thoughts and disinterested action. Such surely gather round one on such an evening, and make part of that atmosphere of love, so hushed, so soft, on which the soul reposes and is blest.

These serene lines were written by Mrs. Shelley within a few days of leaving England on the first of those tours described by her in the series of letters published as *Rambles in Germany and Italy.* It had been arranged that her son and two college friends, both of whom, like him, were studying for their degree, should go abroad for the Long Vacation, and that Mrs. Shelley should form one of the reading party. Paris was to be the general rendezvous. Mrs. Shelley, who was staying at Brighton, intended travelling *via* Dieppe, but her health was so far from strong that she shrank from the long crossing, and started from Dover instead. She was now accompanied by a lady's-maid, a circumstance which relieved her from some of the fatigue incidental to a journey. They travelled by diligence; a new experience to her, as, in her former wanderings with Shelley, they had had their own carriage (save indeed on the first tour of all, when they set off to walk through France with a donkey); and in more recent years she had travelled, in England, by the newly-introduced railroads—

"To which, whatever their faults may be, I feel eternally grateful," she says; adding afterwards, "a pleasant day it will be when there is one from Calais to Paris."

So recent a time, and yet how remote it seems! Mary had never been a good traveller, but she found now, to her surprise and satisfaction, that in spite of her nervous suffering she was better able than formerly to stand the fatigue of a journey. She had painful sensations, but

the fatigue I endured seemed to take away weariness instead of occasioning it. I felt light of limb and in good spirits. On the shores of France I shook the dust of accumulated cares from off me: I forgot disappointment and banished sorrow: weariness of body replaced beneficially weariness of soul—so much heavier, so much harder to bear.

Change, in short, did her more good than travelling did her harm.

"I feel a good deal of the gipsy coming upon me," she wrote a few days later, "now that I am leaving Paris. I bid adieu to all acquaintances, and set out to wander in new lands, surrounded by companions fresh to the world, unacquainted with its sorrows, and who enjoy with zest every passing amusement. I myself, apt to be too serious, but easily awakened to sympathy, forget the past and the future, and am ready to be amused by all I see as much or even more than they."

From Paris they journeyed to Metz and Trèves, down the Moselle and the Rhine, by Schaffhausen and Zurich, over the Splugen Pass to Cadenabbia on the Lake of Como. Here they established themselves for two months. Mrs. Shelley occupied herself in the study of Italian literature, while the young men were busy with their Cambridge work. Her son's friends were devoted to her, and no wonder. Indeed, her amiability and sweetness, her enjoyment of travelling, her wide culture and great store of knowledge, her acuteness of observation, and the keen interest she took in all she saw, must have made her a most fascinating companion. On leaving Como they visited Milan, and, on their way home, passing through Genoa, Mary looked again on the Villa Diodati, and the little Maison Chapuis nestling below, where she had begun to write *Frankenstein.* All unaltered; but in her, what a change! Shelley, Byron, the blue-eyed William, where were they? Where was Fanny, whose long letters had kept them informed of English affairs? Mary herself, and Clare, were they the same people as the two girls, one fair, one dark, who had excited so much idle and impertinent speculation in the tourists from whose curiosity Byron had fled?

But where are the snows of yester-year?

In autumn Mrs. Shelley and her son returned to England; but the next year they again went abroad, and this time for a longer sojourn.

They were now better off than they had ever been, for, after Percy had attained his majority and taken his degree, his grandfather made him an allowance of £400 a year; a free gift, not subject to the condition of repayment. This welcome relief from care came not a day too soon. Mrs. Shelley's strength was much shaken, her attacks of nervous illness were more frequent, and, had she had to resume her life of unvaried toil, the results might have been serious.

It is probably to this event that Mrs. Norton refers in the following note of congratulation—

MRS. NORTON TO MRS. SHELLEY.

DEAR MRS. SHELLEY—I cannot tell you how sincerely glad I was to get a note so cheerful, and cheerful on such good grounds as your last. I hope it is the *dawn*, that your day of struggling is over, and nothing to come but gradually increasing comfort. With tolerable prudence, and abroad, I should hope Percy would find his allowance quite sufficient, and I think it will be a relief that may lift your mind and do your health good to see him properly provided for.

I am too ill to leave the sofa or I should (by rights) be at Lord Palmerston's this evening, but, when I see any one likely

to support the very modest request made to Lord P., I will
speak about it to them ; I have little doubt that, since they
are not asked for a paid attachéship, you will succeed.

   . . . In three weeks I am to set up the magnificence of a
:" one 'orse chay" myself, and then Fulham and the various
streets of London where friends and foes live will become
attainable ; at present I have never stirred over the threshold
since I came up from Brighton.—Ever yours very truly,

Car. Norton.

They began their second tour by a residence
at Kissingen, where Mrs. Shelley had been ad-
vised to take the waters for her health. The
" Cur" over (by which she benefited a good deal),
they proceeded to Gotha, Weimar, Leipzig, Berlin,
and Dresden—all perfectly new ground to Mary.
Dresden and its treasures of art were a delight
to her, only marred by the overwhelming heat
of the summer.

Through Saxon Switzerland they travelled to
Prague, and Mary was roused to enthusiasm by
the intense romantic interest of the Bohemian
capital, as she was afterwards by the magnificent
scenery of the approach to Linz (of which she
gives in her letters a vivid description), and of
Salzburg and the Salzkammergut.

Through the Tyrol, over the Brenner Pass, by
the Lake of Garda, they came to Verona, and
finally to Venice—another place fraught to Mary
with associations unspeakable.

Many a scene which I have since visited and admired has
faded in my mind, as a painting in a diorama melts away, and

another struggles into the changing canvass; but this road was as distinct in my mind as if traversed yesterday. I will not here dwell on the sad circumstances that clouded my first visit to Venice. Death hovered over the scene. Gathered into myself, with my "mind's eye" I saw those before me long departed, and I was agitated again by emotions, by passions—and those the deepest a woman's heart can harbour —a dread to see her child even at that instant expire, which then occupied me. It is a strange, but, to any person who has suffered, a familiar circumstance, that those who are enduring mental or corporeal agony are strangely alive to immediate external objects, and their imagination even exercises its wild power over them. . . . I have experienced it; and the particular shape of a room, the progress of shadows on a wall, the peculiar flickering of trees, the exact succession of objects on a journey, have been indelibly engraved in my memory, as marked in and associated with hours and minutes when the nerves were strung to their utmost tension by endurance of pain, or the far severer infliction of mental anguish. Thus the banks of the Brenta presented to me a moving scene; not a palace, not a tree of which I did not recognise, as marked and recorded, at a moment when life and death hung upon our speedy arrival at Venice.

And at Fusina, as then, I now beheld the domes and towers of the Queen of Ocean arise from the waves with a majesty unrivalled upon earth.

They spent the winter at Florence, and by April were in Rome. This indeed was the Holy Land of Mary Shelley's pilgrimage. There was the spot where William lay; there the tomb which held the heart of Shelley. Mary may well have felt as if standing by her own graveside. Was not her heart of hearts buried with them? And there, too, was the empty grave where now

Trelawny lies ; the touching witness to that undying devotion of his to Shelley's memory which
Mary never forgot.

None of this is touched upon—it could not be
—in the published letters.   The Eternal City
itself filled her with such emotions and interests
as not even she had ever felt before.   It is
curious to compare some of these with her earlier
letters from abroad, and to notice how, while her
power of observation was undiminished, the intellectual faculties of thought and comparison had developed and widened, while her interest was as keen
as in her younger days, nay keener, for her attention
now, poor thing, was comparatively undivided.

Scenery, art, historical associations, the political
and social state of the countries she visited, and
the characteristics of the people, nothing was lost
on her, and on all she saw she brought to bear
the ripened faculties of a reflective and most
appreciative mind.   Some of her remarks on
Italian politics are almost prophetic in their clear-
sighted sagacity.[1]   That after all she had suffered

[1] Such as the following, taken from the Preface: We have lately
been accustomed to look on Italy as a discontented province of Austria,
forgetful that her supremacy dates only from the downfall of Napoleon.
From the invasion of Charles VIII till 1815 Italy has been a battlefield,
where the Spaniard, the French, and the German have fought for mastery;
and we are blind indeed if we do not see that such will occur again, at
least among the two last.   Supposing a war to arise between them, one of
the first acts of aggression on the part of France would be to try to drive
the Germans from Italy.   Even if peace continue, it is felt that the papal
power is tottering to its fall,—it is only supported because the French will
not allow Austria to extend her dominions, and the Austrian is eager to

she should have retained such keen powers of enjoyment as she did may well excite wonder. Perhaps this enjoyment culminated at Sorrento, where she and her son positively revelled in the luxuriant beauty and witchery of a perfect southern summer.

Her impressions of these two tours were published in the form of letters, and entitled *Rambles in Germany and Italy*, and were dedicated to Samuel Rogers in 1844.

He thus acknowledged the copy of the work she sent him—

> St. James's Place,
> *30th July* 1844.
>
> What can I say to you in return for the honour you have done me—an honour so undeserved ! If some feelings make us eloquent, it is not so with others, and I can only thank you from the bottom of my heart, and assure you how highly I shall value and how carefully I shall preserve the two precious volumes on every account—for your sake and for their own. —Ever yours most sincerely,   S. Rogers.

In the spring of 1844 it became evident that Sir Timothy Shelley's life was drawing to a close.

prevent any change that may afford pretence for the French to interfere. Did the present Pope act with any degree of prudence, his power, thus propped, might last some time longer; but as it is, who can say how soon, for the sake of peace in the rest of Italy, it may not be necessary to curtail his territories.

The French feel this, and begin to dream of dominion across the Alps; the occupation of Ancona was a feeler put out; it gained no positive object except to check Austria; for the rest its best effect was to reiterate the lesson they have often taught, that no faith should be given to their promises of liberation.

In anticipation of what was soon to happen,
Mary, always mindful of her promise to Leigh
Hunt, wrote to him as follows—

PUTNEY, 20*th April* 1844.

MY DEAR HUNT—The tidings from Field Place seem to
say that ere long there will be a change; if nothing untoward
happens to us till then, it will be for the better. Twenty
years ago, in memory of what Shelley's intentions were, I said
that you should be considered one of the legatees to the amount
of £2000. I need scarcely mention that when Shelley talked
of leaving you this sum he contemplated reducing other
legacies, and that one among them is (by a mistake of the
solicitor) just double what he intended it to be.

Twenty years have, of course, much changed my position.
Twenty years ago it was supposed that Sir Timothy would not
live five years. Meanwhile a large debt has accumulated, for
I must pay back all on which Percy and I have subsisted, as
well as what I borrowed for Percy's going to college. In fact,
I scarcely know how our affairs will be. Moreover, Percy
shares now my right; that promise was made without his
concurrence, and he must concur to render it of avail. Nor
do I like to ask him to do so till our affairs are so settled
that we know what we shall have—whether Shelley's uncle
may not go to law; in short, till we see our way before us.

It is both my and Percy's great wish to feel that you are
no longer so burdened by care and necessity; in that he is as
desirous as I can be; but the form and the degree in which
we can do this must at first be uncertain. From the time of
Sir Timothy's death I shall give directions to my banker to
honour your quarterly cheques for £30 a quarter; and I
shall take steps to secure this to you, and to Marianne if she
should survive you.

Percy has read this letter, and approves. I know your
real delicacy about money matters, and that you will at once
be ready to enter into my views; and feel assured that if any

present debt should press, if we have any command of money, we will take care to free you from it.

With love to Marianne, affectionately yours,

MARY SHELLEY.

Sir Timothy died in this year, and Mary's son succeeded to the baronetcy and estates. The fortune he inherited was much encumbered, as, besides paying Shelley's numerous legacies and the portions of several members of the family, he had also to refund, with interest, all the money advanced to his mother for their maintenance for the last twenty-one years, amounting now to a large sum, which he met by means of a mortgage effected on the estates. But all was done at last. Clare was freed from the necessity for toil and servitude; she was, indeed, well off, as she inherited altogether £12,000. Hers is the legacy to which Mrs. Shelley alludes as being, by a mistake, double what had been intended. When Shelley made his will, he bequeathed to her £6000. Not long before the end of his life he added a codicil, to the effect that *these* £6000 should be invested for her benefit, intending in this way (it is supposed) to secure to her the interest of this sum, and to protect her against recklessness on her own part or needy rapacity on the part of others. Through the omission in the lawyer's draft of the word "these" this codicil was construed into a second bequest of £6000,

which she received.   The Hunts, by Shelley's
bounty and the generosity of his wife and son,
were made comparatively easy in their circumstances.   Byron had declined to be numbered
among Shelley's legatees ; not so Mr. Hogg,
whose letter on the occasion is too characteristic
to omit.

Hogg to Mrs. Shelley.

Dear Mary—I have just had an interview with Mr.
Gregson.   He spoke of your affairs cheerfully, and thinks
that, with prudence and economy, you and your baronet-boy
will do well ; and such, I trust and earnestly hope, will be the
result of this long turmoil of worldly perplexity.

Mr. Gregson paid me the noble tribute of the most generous
and kind and munificent affection of our incomparable friend.
He not only paid the legacy, but very obligingly offered me
some interest ; for which offer, and for such prompt payment,
I return my best thanks to yourself and to Percy.

I was glad to hear from Mr. Gregson, for the honour of
poesy, that Lord Byron had declined to receive his legacy.
How much I wish that my scanty fortunes would justify the
like refusal on my part !

I daresay you wish that you were a good deal richer—that
this had happened and not that—and that a great deal, which
was quite impossible, had been done, and so on !   I should
be sorry to believe that you were quite contented ; such a
state of mind, so preposterous and unnatural, especially in any
person whose circumstances were affluent, would surely portend
some great calamity.

I hope that I may venture to look forward to the time
when the Baronet will inhabit Field Place in a style not unworthy of his name.   My desire grows daily in the strength
to keep up *families*, for it is only from these that Shelleys and
Byrons proceed.

THOMAS JEFFERSON HOGG,
AS HE SAT PLAYING AT CHESS AT BOSCOMBE.
FROM A SKETCH BY R. EASTON.

To face Page 305 (Vol. ii.)

If low people sometimes effect a little in some particular line, they always show that they are poor, creeping creatures in the main and in general.

However this may be, and whatever you or yours may take of Shelley property, "either by heirship or conquest," as they say in Scotland, I hope that you may not be included in the unbroken entail of gout, which takes so largely from the comforts, and adds so greatly to the irritability natural to yours, dear Mary, very faithfully,   T. J. HOGG.

For many and good reasons there could be little real sympathy between Hogg and Mary Shelley. In lieu of it she willingly accepted his genuine enthusiasm for Shelley, and she was a better friend to him than he was to her. The veiled impertinence of his tone to her must have severely tried her patience, if not her endurance. Indeed, the mocking style of his ironical eulogies of her talents, and her fidelity to the memory of her husband are more offensive to those who know what she was than any ill-humoured tirade of Trelawny's.

The high esteem in which Mrs. Shelley was held by the eminent literary men who were her contemporaries is pleasantly attested in a number of letters and notes addressed to her by T. Moore, Samuel Rogers, Carlyle, Bulwer, Prosper Meri-mée, and others; letters for the most part of no great importance except in so far as they show the familiar and friendly terms existing between the writers and Mrs. Shelley. One, however, from

Walter Savage Landor, deserves insertion here for its intrinsic interest—

DEAR MRS. SHELLEY—It would be very ungrateful in me to delay for a single post an answer to your very kind letter. If only three or four like yourself (supposing there are that number in one generation) are gratified by my writings, I am quite content. Hardly do I know whether in the whole course of fifty years I have been so fortunate. For one of my earliest resolutions in life was never to read what was written about me, favourable or unfavourable; and another was, to keep as clear as possible of all literary men, well knowing their jealousies and animosities, and so little did I seek celebrity, or even renown, that on making a present of my Gebir and afterwards of my later poems to the bookseller, I insisted that they should not even be advertised. Whatever I have written since I have placed at the disposal and discretion of some friend. Are not you a little too enthusiastic in believing that writers can be much improved by studying my writings? I mean in their style. The style is a part of the mind, just as feathers are part of the bird. The style of Addison is admired—it is very lax and incorrect. But in his manner there is the shyness of the Loves; there is the graceful shyness of a beautiful girl not quite grown up! People feel the cool current of delight, and never look for its source. However, he wrote the Vision of Mirza, and no prose man in any age of the world had written anything so delightful. Alas! so far from being able to teach men how to write, it will be twenty years before I teach them how to spell. They will write simile, foreign, sovereign, therefore, impel, compel, rebel, etc. I wish they would turn back to Hooker, not for theology—the thorns of theology are good only to heat the oven for the reception of wholesome food. But Hooker and Jonson and Milton spelt many words better than we do. We need not wear their coats, but we may take the gold buttons off them and put them on smoother stuff.—Believe me, dear Mrs. Shelley, very truly yours,   W. S. LANDOR.

Of individuals as of nations, it may be true that those are happiest who have no history. The later years of Mrs. Shelley, which offer no event of public interest, were tranquil and comparatively happy. She brought out no new work after 1844.[1] It had been her intention, now that the prohibition which constituted the chief obstacle was removed, to undertake the long-projected *Life of Shelley*. It seemed the more desirable as there was· no lack of attempts at biography. Chief among these was the series of articles entitled "Shelley Papers," contributed by Mr. Hogg to the *New Monthly* magazine during 1832. They were afterwards incorporated with that so-called *Life of Shelley* which deals only with Shelley's first youth, and which, though it consists of one halfpennyworth of Shelley to an intolerable deal of Hogg, is yet a classic, and one of the most amusing classics in the world; so amusing, indeed, that, for its sake, we might address the author somewhat as Sterne is said to have apostrophised Mrs. Cibber, after hearing her sing a pathetic air of Handel, "Man, for this be all thy sins forgiven thee!" The second chapter of the book includes some fragments of biography by Mary, a facsimile of one of which, in her handwriting, is given here.

Medwin's *Life of Shelley*, inaccurate and false

[1] She had published her last novel, *Falkner*, in 1837.

in facts, distasteful in style and manner, had caused
Mrs. Shelley serious annoyance.   The author,
who wrote for money chiefly, actually offered to
suppress the book *for a consideration;* a proposal
which Mrs. Shelley treated with the silent contempt it deserved.   These were, however, strong
arguments in favour of her undertaking the book
herself.   She summoned up her resolution and
began to collect her materials.

But it was not to be.   Her powers and her
health were unequal to the task.   The parallel
between her and the Princess of the nettle-shirts
was to be carried out to the bitter end, for the
last nettle-shirt lacked a sleeve, and the youngest
brother always retained one swan's wing instead
of an arm.   The last service Mary could have
rendered to Shelley was never to be completed,
and so the exact details of certain passages of
Shelley's life must remain for ever, to some
extent, matters of speculation.   No one but Mary
could have supplied the true history, and, as she
herself had said, in the introductory note to her
edition of his poems, it was not yet time to do
that.   Too many were living who might have
been wounded or injured ; nay, there still are too
many to admit of a biographer's speaking with
perfect frankness.   But, although she might have
furnished to some circumstances a key which is
now for ever lost, it is equally true that there was

much to be said, which hardly could, and most
certainly never would have been told by her. Of
his earliest youth and his life with Harriet she
could, herself, know nothing but by hearsay. But
the chief difficulty lay in the fact that too much
of her own history was interwoven with his.
How could she, now, or at any time, have placed
herself, as an observer, so far outside the subject
of her story as to speak of her married life with
Shelley, of its influence on the development of
his character and genius, of the effect of that
development, and of her constant association
with it on herself? Yet any life of him which
left this out of account would have been most in-
complete. More than that, no biography of such
a man as Shelley can be completely successful
which is written under great restrictions and
difficulties. To paint a life-like picture of a
nature like his requires a genius akin to his,
aglow with the fervour of confident enthusiasm.

It was, then, as well that Mary never wrote
the book. The invaluable notes which she did
write to Shelley's poems have done for him all
that it was in her power to accomplish, and all
that is necessary. They put the reader in
possession of the knowledge it concerns him
to have; that of the scenes or the circumstances which inspired or suggested the poems
themselves.

In 1847 she became acquainted with the lady
to whom her son was afterwards married, and
who was to be to Mrs. Shelley a kind of daughter
and sister in one.   No one, except her son, is
living who knew Mary so well and loved her so
enthusiastically.   A mutual friend had urged them
to become acquainted, assuring them both "they
ought to know each other, they would suit so
perfectly."   Some people think that this course is
one which tends oftener to postpone than to
promote the desired intimacy.   In the present
case it was justified by the result.   Mrs. Shelley
called.   Her future daughter-in-law, on entering
the room, beheld something utterly unlike what
she had imagined or expected in the famous Mrs.
Shelley,—a fair, lovely, almost girlish-looking
being, "as slight as a reed," with beautiful clear
eyes, who put out her hand as she rose, saying
half timidly, "I'm Mary Shelley."   From that
moment—we have her word for it—the future
wife of Sir Percy had lost her heart to his mother!
Their intercourse was frequent, and soon became
necessary to both.   The younger lady had had
much experience of sorrow, and this drew the
bond all the closer.

Not for some time after this meeting did Sir
Percy appear on the scene.   His engagement
followed at no distant date, and after his marriage
he, with his wife and his mother, who never

during her life was to be parted from them, again went abroad.

The cup of such happiness as in this world was possible to Mary Shelley seemed now to be full, but the time was to be short during which she could taste it. She only lived three years longer, years chequered by very great anxiety (on account of illness), yet to those who now look back on them they seem as if lived under a charm. To live with Mary Shelley was indeed like entertaining an angel. Perfect unselfishness, *selflessness* indeed, characterised her at all times.

One illustration of this is afforded by her repression of the terror she felt when she saw Shelley's passion for the sea asserting itself in his son. Her own nerves had been shaken and her life darkened by a catastrophe, but not for this would she let it overshadow the lives of others. Not even when her son, with a friend, went off to Norway in a little yacht, and she was dependent for news of them on a three weeks' post, would she ever let him know the mortal anxiety she endured, but after his marriage she told it to her daughter-in-law, saying, "Now he will never wish to go to sea."

But of herself she never seemed to think at all; she lived in and for others. Her gifts and attainments, far from being obtruded, were kept out of sight; modest almost to excess as she was,

she yet knew the secret of putting others at their
ease.   She was ready with sympathy and help
and gentle counsel for all who needed them, and
to the friends of her son she was such a friend as
they will never forget.

The thought of Shelley, the idea of his presence, never seemed to leave her mind for a
moment.   She would constantly refer to what he
might think, or do, or approve of, almost as if he
had been in the next room.   Of his history, or
her own, she never spoke, nor did she ever refer
to other people connected with their early life,
unless there was something good to be said of
them.   Of those who had behaved ill to her, no
word—on the subject of their behaviour—passed
her lips.   Her daughter-in-law had so little idea
of what her associations were with Clare, that on
one occasion when Miss Clairmont was coming to
stay at Field Place, and Lady Shelley, who did
not like her, expressed a half-formed intention of
being absent during her visit and leaving Mrs.
Shelley to entertain her, she was completely taken
aback by the exclamation which escaped Mary's
lips, "Don't go, dear! don't leave me alone with
her! she has been the bane of my life ever since
I was three years old!"

No more was ever said, but this was enough,
even to those who did not know all, to reveal a
long history of endurance.

Clare came, and more than once, to stay at Field Place, but her excitability and eccentricity had so much increased as, at times, to be little if at all under her own control, and after one unmistakable proof of this, it was deemed (by those who cared for Mrs. Shelley) desirable that she should go and return no more.

She died at Florence in 1878.

Mary Shelley's strength was ebbing, her nervous ailments increased, and the result was a loss of power in one side. Life at Field Place had had to be abandoned on grounds of health (not her own), and Sir Percy Shelley had purchased Boscombe Manor for their country home, anticipating great pleasure from his mother's enjoyment of the beautiful spot and fine climate. But she became worse, and never could be moved from her house in Chester Square till she was taken to her last resting-place. She died on the 21st of February 1851.

She died, "and her place among those who knew her intimately has never been filled up. She walked beside them, like a spirit of good, to comfort and benefit, to lighten the darkness of life, to cheer it with her sympathy and love."

These, her own words about Shelley, may with equal fitness be applied to her.

Her grave is in Bournemouth Churchyard,

where, some time after, her father and mother were laid by her side.

As an author Mary Shelley did not accomplish all that was expected of her. Her letters from abroad, both during her earlier and later tours, the descriptive fragments intended for her father's biography, and above all her notes on Shelley's works, are indeed valuable and enduring contributions to literature. But it was in imaginative work that she had aspired to excel, and in which both Shelley and Godwin had urged her to persevere, confident that she could achieve a brilliant success. None of her novels, however, except *Frankenstein*, can be said to have survived the generation for which they were written. Only in that work has she left an abiding mark on literature. Yet her powers were very great, her culture very extensive, her ambition very high.

The friend whose description of her has been quoted in an earlier chapter tries to account for this. She says—

I think a partial solution for the circumscribed fame of Mrs. Shelley as a writer may be traced to her own shrinking and sensitive retiringness of nature. If, as Thackeray, perhaps justly, observes, "Persons, to succeed largely in this world, must assert themselves," most assuredly Mary Shelley never tried that path to distinction. . . .

I never knew, in my life, either man or woman whose

whole character was so entirely in harmony: no jarring dis-
cords—no incongruous, anomalous, antagonistic opposites met
to disturb the perfect unity, and to counteract one day the
impressions of the former. Gentleness was ever and always
her distinguishing characteristic. Many years' friendship never
showed me a deviation from it. But with this softness there
was neither irresolution nor feebleness. . . .

Many have fancied and accused her of being cold and apa-
thetic. She was no such thing. She had warm, strong affections: as daughter, wife, and mother she was exemplary and
devoted. Besides this, she was a faithful, unswerving friend.

. . . .

She was not a mirthful—scarcely could be called a cheerful person; and at times was subject to deep and profound
fits of despondency, when she would shut herself up, and be
quite inaccessible to all. Her undeviating love of truth was
ever acted on—never swerved from. Her worst enemy could
never charge her with falsification—even equivocation. Truth
—truth—truth—was the governing principle in all the words
she uttered, the thoughts and judgments she expressed. Hence
she was most intolerant to deceit and falsehood, in any shape
or guise, and those who attempted to practise it on her
aroused as much bitter indignation as her nature was capable
of. . . .

It is too often the case that authors talk too much of their
writings, and all thereunto belonging. Mrs. Shelley was the
extremest reverse of this. In fact, she was almost morbidly
averse to the least allusion to herself as an authoress. To call
on her and find her table covered with all the accessories and
unmistakable traces of *book-making*, such as copy, proofs for
correction, etc., made her nearly as nervous and unself-
possessed as if she had been detected in the commission of
some offence against the conventionalities of society, or the
code of morality. . . .

I really think she deemed it unwomanly to print and publish; and had it not been for the hard cash which, like so
many of her craft, she so often stood in need of, I do not

think she would ever have come before the world as an authoress. . . .

Like all raised in supremacy above their fellows, either mentally or physically, Mrs. Shelley had her enemies and detractors. But none ever dared to impugn the correctness of her conduct. From the hour of her early widowhood to the period of her death, she might have married advantageously several times. But she often said, " I know not what temptation could make me change the name of Shelley."

But the true cause lay deeper still, and may afford a clue to more puzzles than this one. What Mary Godwin might have become had she remained Mary Godwin for six or eight years longer it is impossible now to do more than guess at. But the free growth of her own original nature was checked and a new bent given to it by her early union with Shelley. Two original geniuses can rarely develop side by side, certainly not in marriage, least of all in a happy marriage. Two minds may, indeed, work consentaneously, but one, however unconsciously, will take the lead ; should the other preserve its complete independence, angles must of necessity develop, and the first fitness of things disappear. And in a marriage of enthusiastic devotion and mutual admiration, the younger or the weaker mind, however candid, will shirk or stop short of conclusions which, it instinctively feels, may lead to collision. On the other hand, strong and pronounced views or peculiarities on the part of one may tend to elicit

their exact opposite on the part of the other ; both
results being equally remote from real independence of thought. However it may be, either in
marriage or in any intellectual partnership, it is a
general truth that from the moment one mind is
penetrated by the influence of another, its own
native power over other minds has gone, and for
ever. And Mary parted with this power at sixteen, before she knew what it was to have it.
When she left her father's house with Shelley she
was but a child, a thing of promise, everything
about her yet to be decided. Shelley himself was
a half-formed creature, but of infinite possibilities
and extraordinary powers, and Mary's development had not only to keep pace with his, but to
keep in time and tune with his. Sterne said of
Lady Elizabeth Hastings that "to have loved
her was a liberal education." To love Shelley
adequately and worthily was that and more—it
was a vocation, a career,—enough for a life-time
and an exceptional one.

Every reader of the present biography must see
too that in Mary Shelley's case physical causes
had much to do with the limit of her intellectual
achievements. Between seventeen and twenty-
five she had drawn too largely on the reserve
funds of life. Weak health and illness, a roving
unsettled life, the birth and rearing, and then the
loss, of children ; great joys and great griefs, all

crowded into a few young years, and coinciding
with study and brain-work and the constant call on
her nervous energy necessitated by companionship
with Shelley, these exhausted her ; and when he
who was the beginning and end of her existence
disappeared, " and the light of her life as if gone
out,"[1] she was left,—left what those eight years had
made her, to begin again from the beginning all
alone.   And nobly she began, manfully she
struggled, and wonderfully, considering all things,
did she succeed.   No one, however, has more
than a certain, limited, amount of vitality to
express in his or her life ; the vital force may
take one form or another, but cannot be used twice
over.   The best of Mary's power spent itself in
active life, in ministering to another being, during
those eight years with Shelley.   What she gained
from him, and it was much, was paid back to him
a hundredfold.   When he was gone, and those
calls for outward activity were over, there lay
before her the life of literary labour and thought
for which nature and training had pre-eminently
fitted her.   But she could not call back the freshness of her powers nor the wholeness of her heart.
She did not fully know, or realise, then, the
amount of life-capital she had run through.   She
did realise it at a later time, and the very interesting entry in her journal, dated October 21, 1838,

[1] Carlyle's epitaph on his wife.

is a kind of profession of faith ; a summary of her
views of life ; the result of her reflections and of
her experience—

Journal, October 21.—I have been so often abused by
pretended friends for my lukewarmness in "the good cause,"
that I disdain to answer them.   I shall put down here a few
thoughts on this subject.   I am much of a self-examiner.
Vanity is not my fault, I think ; if it is, it is uncomfortable
vanity, for I have none that teaches me to be satisfied with
myself; far otherwise—and, if I use the word disdain, it is
that I think my qualities (such as they are) not appreciated from
unworthy causes.   In the first place, with regard to "the good
cause "—the cause of the advancement of freedom and knowledge, of the rights of women, etc.—I am not a person of
opinions.   I have said elsewhere that human beings differ
greatly in this.   Some have a passion for reforming the world,
others do not cling to particular opinions.   That my parents
and Shelley were of the former class makes me respect it.   I
respect such when joined to real disinterestedness, toleration, and a clear understanding.   My accusers, after such
as these, appear to me mere drivellers.   For myself, I
earnestly desire the good and enlightenment of my fellow-
creatures, and see all, in the present course, tending to the
same, and rejoice ; but I am not for violent extremes, which
only bring on an injurious reaction.   I have never written a
word in disfavour of liberalism : that I have not supported
it openly in writing arises from the following causes, as far as
I know—

That I have not argumentative powers : I see things pretty
clearly, but cannot demonstrate them.   Besides, I feel the
counter-arguments too strongly.   I do not feel that I could say
aught to support the cause efficiently ; besides that, on some
topics (especially with regard to my own sex) I am far from
making up my mind.   I believe we are sent here to educate
ourselves, and that self-denial, and disappointment, and self-
control are a part of our education ; that it is not by taking

away all restraining law that our improvement is to be achieved ;
and, though many things need great amendment, I can by no
means go so far as my friends would have me.   When I feel
that I can say what will benefit my fellow-creatures, I will speak;
not before.   Then, I recoil from the vulgar abuse of the inimi-
cal press.   I do more than recoil : proud and sensitive, I act on
the defensive—an inglorious position.   To hang back, as I do,
brings a penalty.   I was nursed and fed with a love of glory.
To be something great and good was the precept given me by
my Father ; Shelley reiterated it.   Alone and poor, I could
only be something by joining a party ; and there was much in
me—the woman's love of looking up, and being guided, and
being willing to do anything if any one supported and brought
me forward—which would have made me a good partisan.   But
Shelley died and I was alone.   My Father, from age and
domestic circumstances, could not *me faire valoir.*   My total
friendlessness, my horror of pushing, and inability to put
myself forward unless led, cherished and supported—all this
has sunk me in a state of loneliness no other human being
ever before, I believe, endured—except Robinson Crusoe.
How many tears and spasms of anguish this solitude has cost
me, lies buried in my memory.

If I had raved and ranted about what I did not understand,
had I adopted a set of opinions, and propagated them with enthusiasm ; had I been careless of attack, and eager for noto-
riety ; then the party to which I belonged had gathered round
me, and I had not been alone.

It has been the fashion with these same friends to accuse
me of worldliness.   There, indeed, in my own heart and conscience, I take a high ground.   I may distrust my own judgment too much—be too indolent and too timid ; but in conduct I am above merited blame.

I like society ; I believe all persons who have any talent
(who are in good health) do.   The soil that gives forth
nothing may lie ever fallow ; but that which produces—however humble its product—needs cultivation, change of harvest,
refreshing dews, and ripening sun.   Books do much ; but the

living intercourse is the vital heat. Debarred from that, how have I pined and died!

My early friends chose the position of enemies. When I first discovered that a trusted friend had acted falsely by me, I was nearly destroyed. My health was shaken. I remember thinking, with a burst of agonising tears, that I should prefer a bed of torture to the unutterable anguish a friend's falsehood engendered. There is no resentment; but the world can never be to me what it was before. Trust and confidence, and the heart's sincere devotion are gone.

I sought at that time to make acquaintances—to divert my mind from this anguish. I got entangled in various ways through my ready sympathy and too eager heart; but I never crouched to society—never sought it unworthily. If I have never written to vindicate the rights of women, I have ever befriended women when oppressed. At every risk I have befriended and supported victims to the social system; but I make no boast, for in truth it is simple justice I perform; and so I am still reviled for being worldly.

God grant a happier and a better day is near! Percy—my all-in-all—will, I trust, by his excellent understanding, his clear, bright, sincere spirit and affectionate heart, repay me for sad long years of desolation. His career may lead me into the thick of life or only gild a quiet home. I am content with either, and, as I grow older, I grow more fearless for myself— I become firmer in my opinions. The experienced, the suffering, the thoughtful, may at last speak unrebuked. If it be the will of God that I live, I may ally my name yet to "the Good Cause," though I do not expect to please my accusers.

Thus have I put down my thoughts. I may have deceived myself; I may be in the wrong; I try to examine myself; and such as I have written appears to me the exact truth.

Enough of this! The great work of life goes on. Death draws near. To be better after death than in life is one's hope and endeavour—to be so through self-schooling. If I write the above, it is that those who love me may hereafter know that I am not all to blame, nor merit the heavy accusations cast on me for not putting myself forward.   I cannot do that; it is against my nature.   As well cast me from a precipice and rail at me for not flying.

The true success of Mary Shelley's life was not, therefore, the intellectual triumph of which, during her youth, she had loved to dream, and which at one time seemed to be actually within her grasp, but the moral success of beauty of character.   To those people—a daily increasing number in this tired world—who erect the natural grace of animal spirits to the rank of the highest virtue, this success may appear hardly worth the name.   Yet it was a very real victory.   Her nature was not without faults or tendencies which, if undisciplined, might have developed into faults, but every year she lived seemed to mellow and ripen her finer qualities, while blemishes or weaknesses were suppressed or overcome, and finally disappeared altogether.

As to her theological views, about which the most contradictory opinions have been expressed, it can but be said that nothing in Mrs. Shelley's writings gives other people the right to formulate for her any dogmatic opinions at all.   Brought up in a purely rationalistic creed, her education had of course, no tinge of what is known as " personal religion," and it must be repeated here that none of her acts and views were founded, or should be judged as if they were founded on Biblical commands or prohibitions. That the temper of her mind, so to speak, was eminently religious there can be no doubt ; that she believed in God and a future state there are many allusions to show.[1] Perhaps no one, having lived with the so-called atheist, Shelley, could have accepted the idea of the limitation, or the extinction of intelligence and goodness. Her liberality of mind, however, was rewarded by abuse from some of her acquaintance, because her toleration was extended even to the orthodox.

Her moral opinions, had they ever been formulated, which they never were, would have approximated closely to those of Mary Wollstonecraft, limited, however, by an inability, like her father's, *not* to see both sides of a question, and also by the severest and most elevated standard of moral purity, of personal faith and loyalty. To be judged by such a standard she would have regarded as a woman's highest privilege. To claim as a "woman's right" any licence, any lowering of the standard of duty in these matters, would have been to her incomprehensible and impossible. But, with all this, she discriminated. Her standard was not that of the conventional world.

At every risk, as she says, she befriended

[1] "My belief is," she says in the preface to her edition of Shelley's prose works, "that spiritual improvement in this life prepares the way to a higher existence."

those whom she considered "victims to the social system." It was a difficult course; for, while her acquaintance of the "advanced" type accused her of cowardice and worldliness for not asserting herself as a champion of universal liberty, there were more who were ready to decry her for her friendly relations with Countess Guiccioli, Lady Mountcashel, and others not named here; to say nothing of Clare, to whom much of her happiness had been sacrificed. She refrained from pronouncing judgment, but reserved her liberty of action, and in all doubtful cases gave others the benefit of the doubt, and this without respect of persons. She would not excommunicate a humble individual for what was passed over in a man or woman of genius; nor condemn a woman for what, in a man, might be excused, or might even add to his social reputation. Least of all would she secure her own position by shunning those whose case had once been hers, and who in their after life had been less fortunate than she. Pure herself, she could be charitable, and she could be just.

The influence of such a wife on Shelley's more vehement, visionary temperament can hardly be over-estimated. Their moods did not always suit or coincide; each, at times, made the other suffer. It could not be otherwise with two natures so young, so strong, and so individual. But, if forbearance may have been sometimes called for on the one hand, and on the other a charity which is kind and thinks no evil, it was only a part of that discipline from which the married life of geniuses is not exempt, and which tests the temper and quality of the metal it tries ; an ordeal from which two noble natures come forth the purer and the stronger.

The indirect, unconscious power of elevation of character is great, and not even a Shelley but must be the better for association with it, not even he but must be the nobler, "yea, three times less unworthy" through the love of such a woman as Mary. He would not have been all he was without her sustaining and refining influence ; without the constant sense that in loving him she loved his ideals also. We owe him, in part, to her.

Love—the love of Love—was Shelley's life and creed. This, in Mary's creed, was interpreted as love of Shelley. By all the rest she strove to do her duty, but, when the end came, that survived as the one great fact of her life—a fact she might have uttered in words like his—

> And where is Truth? On tombs ; for such to thee
> Has been my heart ; and thy dead memory
> Has lain from (girlhood), many a changeful year,
> Unchangingly preserved, and buried there.

J. D. & Co.   *Printed by* R. & R. CLARK, *Edinburgh.*

In 2 vols. Crown 8vo, with 2 Portraits, 24s.

JOHN FRANCIS AND THE 'ATHENÆUM.'

A LITERARY CHRONICLE OF HALF A CENTURY.

By JOHN C. FRANCIS.

OPINIONS OF THE PRESS.

'The career of John Francis, publisher of the *Athenæum*, was worth telling for the zeal with which, for more than thirty years, he pursued the definite purpose of obtaining the abolition of the paper duty. . . . With equal ardour did Mr. Francis labour for half a century in publishing the weekly issue of the *Athenæum;* and these two volumes, which describe its progress from its birth in January, 1828, to the full perfection of its powers in 1882, are a fitting record of the literary history of that period.'—*Academy.*

'Anybody who wants a complete summary of what the world has been thinking and doing since Silk Buckingham, with Dr. Stebbing and Charles Knight and Sterling and Maurice as his staff, started the *Athenæum* in 1828, will find plenty to satisfy him in *John Francis, a Literary Chronicle of Half a Century.* . . . Mr. Francis's autobiography is not the least valuable part of this valuable record.'—*Graphic.*

'As a record of the literature of fifty years, and in a less complete degree of the progress of science and art, and as a memento of many notable characters in various fields of intellectual culture, these volumes are of considerable value.'—*Morning Post.*

'The volumes abound with curious and interesting statements, and in bringing before the public the most notable features of a distinguished journal from its infancy almost to the present hour, Mr. Francis deserves the thanks of all readers interested in literature.'—*Spectator.*

'No memoir of Mr. Francis would be complete without a corresponding history of the journal with which his name will for ever be identified. . . . The extraordinary variety of subjects and persons referred to, embracing as they do every event in literature, and referring to every person of distinction in science or letters, is a record of such magnitude that we can only indicate its outlines. To the literary historian the volumes will be of incalculable service.'—*Bookseller.*

'This literary chronicle of half a century must at once, or in course of a short time, take a place as a permanent work of reference.'—*Publishers' Circular.*

'Some valuable and interesting matter has been collected chronologically regarding the literary history of the last fifty years.'—*Murray's Magazine.*

'We have put before us a valuable collection of materials for the future history of the Victorian era of English literature.'—*Standard.*

'John Francis was a faithful servant, and also an earnest worker for the good of his fellow-creatures. Sunday schools, charitable societies, and mechanics' institutes found in him a patient and steady helper, and no one laboured more persistently and unselfishly to procure the abolition of the pernicious taxes on knowledge.'—*Daily Chronicle.*

'Such a life interests us, and carries with it a fruitful moral. . . . The history of the *Athenæum* also well deserved to be told.'—*Daily News.*

JOHN FRANCIS AND THE 'ATHENÆUM.'

Continued from over leaf.

'A worthy monument of the development of literature during the last fifty years. . . . The volumes contain not a little specially interesting to Scotsmen.'—*Scotsman.*

'Rich in literary and social interest, and afford a comprehensive survey of the intellectual progress of the nation.'—*Leeds Mercury.*

'It is in characters so sterling and admirable as this that the real strength of a nation lies. . . . The public will find in the book reading which, if light and easy, is also full of interest and suggestion. . . . We suspect that writers for the daily and weekly papers will find out that it is convenient to keep these volumes of handy size, and each having its own index, extending the one to 20, the other to 30 pages, at their elbow for reference.'—*Liverpool Mercury.*

'The book is, in fact, as it is described, a literary chronicle of the period with which it deals, and a chronicle put together with as much skill as taste and discrimination. The information given about notable people of the past is always interesting and often piquant, while it rarely fails to throw some new light on the individuality of the person to whom it refers.'—*Liverpool Daily Post.*

'Our survey has been unavoidably confined almost exclusively to the first volume; indeed, anything like an adequate account of the book is impossible, for it may be described as a history in notes of the literature of the period with which it deals. We confess that we have been able to find very few pages altogether barren of interest, and by far the larger portion of the book will be found irresistibly attractive by all who care anything for the history of literature in our own time.'—*Manchester Examiner.*

'It was a happy thought in this age of jubilees to associate with a literary chronicle of the last fifty years a biographical sketch of the life of John Francis. . . . As we glance through the contents there is scarcely a page which does not induce us to stop and read about the men and events that are summoned again before us.'—*Western Daily Mercury.*

'A mine of information on subjects connected with literature for the last fifty years.'—*Echo.*

'The volumes are full of interest. . . . The indexes of these two volumes show at a glance that a feast of memorabilia, of gossip, of reminiscence, is in store for the reader.'—*Nonconformist.*

'The thought of compiling these volumes was a happy one, and it has been ably carried out by Mr. John C. Francis, the son of the veteran publisher.'—*Literary World.*

'The entire work affords a comprehensive view of the intellectual life of the period it covers, which will be found extremely helpful by students of English literature.'—*Christian World.*

'No other fifty years of English literature contain so much to interest an English reader.'—*Freeman.*

'To literary men the two volumes will have much interest; they contain the raw material of history, and many of the gems which make it sparkle.'—*Sword and Trowel.*

RICHARD BENTLEY & SON, NEW BURLINGTON STREET,

Publishers in Ordinary to Her Majesty the Queen.